Three Early Novels

The Man Who Japed
Dr Futurity
Vulcan's Hammer

PHILIP K. DICK

The right of Philip K. Dick to be identified as the author
of this work has been asserted by him in accordance with
the Copyright, Designs and Patents Act 1988

This edition first published in Great Britain in 2013
by Gollancz
An imprint of the Orion Publishing Group
Orion House, 5 Upper St Martin's Lane,
London WC2H 9EA
An Hachette UK Company

1 3 5 7 9 10 8 6 4 2

A CIP catalogue record for this book
is available from the British Library

ISBN 978 0 575 13305 1

Typeset at The Spartan Press Ltd,
Lymington, Hants

Printed and bound by CPI Group (UK) Ltd,
Croydon, CR0 4YY

The Orion Publishing Group's policy is to use papers that
are natural, renewable and recyclable products and made
from wood grown in sustainable forests. The logging and
manufacturing processes are expected to conform to the
environmental regulations of the country of origin.

www.orionbooks.co.uk
www.gollancz.co.uk

THREE EARLY NOVELS

Also by Philip K. Dick

CONTENTS

THE MAN WHO JAPED

Cast of Characters

Allen Purcell
His attempt at humor was no laughing matter.

Dr Malparto
Was he using science to pierce Purcell's mind – or to crack it?

Prof. Sugermann
Living amid the radioactive rubble, his individualism remained uncontaminated.

Mrs Birmingham
In the name of Moral Reclaiming she raked up dirt!

Myron Mavis
He had spent more than just eight years as Director of Propaganda – he had spent himself.

Janet Purcell
If they took away her apartment, they'd take away her lease on life.

Sue Frost
She bought Purcell's ideas, but she couldn't buy him as a man.

1

At seven a.m., Allen Purcell, the forward-looking young president of the newest and most creative of the Research Agencies, lost a bedroom. But he gained a kitchen. The process was automatic, controlled by an iron-oxide-impregnated tape sealed in the wall. Allen had no authority over it, but the transfiguration was agreeable to him; he was already awake and ready to rise.

Squinting and yawning and now on his feet, he fumbled for the manual knob that released the stove. As usual the stove was stuck half in the wall and half out into the room. But all that was needed was a firm push. Allen pushed, and, with a wheeze, the stove emerged.

He was king of his domain: this one-room apartment within sight of the – blessed – Morec spire. The apartment was hard won. It had been his heritage, deeded to him by his family; the lease had been defended for over forty years. Its thin plasterboard walls formed a box of priceless worth; it was an empty space valued beyond money.

The stove, properly unfolded, became also sink and table and food cupboard. Two chairs hinged out from its underside, and beneath the stored supplies were dishes. Most of the room was consumed, but sufficient space remained in which to dress.

His wife Janet, with difficulty, had gotten into her slip. Now, frowning, she held an armload of skirt and looked around her in bewilderment. The central heating had not penetrated to their apartment as yet, and Janet shivered. In the cold autumn mornings she awoke with fright; she had been his wife three years but she had never adjusted to the shifts of the room.

3

'What's the matter?' he asked, shedding his pajamas. The air, to him, was invigorating; he took a deep breath.

'I'm going to reset the tape. Maybe for eleven.' She resumed dressing, a slow process with much wasted motion.

'The oven door,' he said, opening the oven for her. 'Lay your things there, like always.'

Nodding, she did so. The Agency had to be opened promptly at eight, which meant getting up early enough to make the half-hour walk along the clogged lanes. Even now sounds of activity filtered up from the ground level, and from other apartments. In the hall, scuffling footsteps were audible; the line was forming at the community bathroom.

'You go ahead,' he said to Janet, wanting her dressed and ready for the day. As she started off, he added: 'Don't forget your towel.'

Obediently, she collected her satchel of cosmetics, her soap and toothbrush and towel and personal articles, and left. Neighbors assembled in the hall greeted her.

'Morning, Mrs Purcell.'

Janet's sleepy voice: 'Morning, Mrs O'Neill.' And then the door closed.

While his wife was gone, Allen shook two corto-thiamin capsules from the medicine well. Janet owned all sorts of pills and sprays; in her early teens she had picked up undulant fever, one of the plagues revived by the attempt to create natural farms on the colony planets. The corto-thiamin was for his hangover. Last night he had drunk three glasses of wine, and on an empty stomach.

Entering the Hokkaido area had been a calculated risk. He had worked late at the Agency, until ten o'clock. Tired, but still restless, he had locked up and then rolled out a small Agency ship, a one-man sliver used to deliver rush orders to T-M. In the ship he had scooted out of Newer York, flown aimlessly, and finally turned East to visit Gates and Sugermann. But he hadn't stayed long; by eleven he was on his way back. And it had been necessary. Research was involved.

His Agency was totally outclassed by the giant four that made up the industry. Allen Purcell, Inc. had no financial latitude and

4

no backlog of ideas. Its packets were put together from day to day. His staff – artists, historian, moral consultant, dictionist, dramatist – tried to anticipate future trends rather than working from patterns that had been successful in the past. This was an advantage, as well as a defect. The big four were hidebound; they constructed a standard packet perfected over the years, basically the time-tested formula used by Major Streiter himself in the days before the revolution. Moral Reclamation, in those days, had consisted of wandering troops of actors and lecturers delivering messages, and the major had been a genius media. The basic formula was, of course, adequate, but new blood was needed. The major himself had been new blood; originally a powerful figure in the Afrikaans Empire – the re-created Transvaal State – he had revitalized the moral forces lying dormant in his own age.

'Your turn,' Janet said, returning. 'I left the soap and towel, so go right in.' As he started from the room she bent to get out the breakfast dishes.

Breakfast took the usual eleven minutes. Allen ate with customary directness; the corto-thiamin had eliminated his queasiness. Across from him Janet pushed her half-finished food away and began combing her hair. The window – with a touch of the switch – doubled as a mirror: another of the ingenious space-savers developed by the Committee's Housing Authority.

'You didn't get in until late,' Janet said presently. 'Last night, I mean.' She glanced up. 'Did you?'

Her question surprised him, because he had never known her to probe. Lost in the haze of her own uncertainties, Janet was incapable of venom. But, he realized, she was not probing. She was apprehensive. Probably she had lain awake wondering if he were all right, lain with her eyes open staring at the ceiling until eleven-forty, at which time he had made his appearance. As he had undressed, she had said nothing; she had kissed him as he slid in beside her, and then she had gone to sleep.

'Did you go to Hokkaido?' she wondered.

'For awhile. Sugermann gives me ideas . . . I find his talk stimulating. Remember the packet we did on Goethe? The business about lens-grinding? I never heard of that until Sugermann mentioned it. The optics angle made a good Morec – Goethe saw his real job. Prisms before poetry.'

'But—' She gestured, a familiar nervous motion of her hands. 'Sugermann's an egghead.'

'Nobody saw me.' He was reasonably certain of that; by ten o'clock Sunday night most people were in bed. Three glasses of wine with Sugermann, a half hour listening to Tom Gates play Chicago jazz on the phonograph, and that was all. He had done it a number of times before, and without untoward difficulty.

Bending down, he picked up the pair of oxfords he had worn. They were mud-spattered. And across each were great drops of dried red paint.

'That's from the art department,' Janet said. She had, in the first year of the Agency, acted as his receptionist and file clerk, and she knew the office layout. 'What were you doing with red paint?'

He didn't answer. He was still examining the shoes.

'And the mud,' Janet said. 'And look.' Reaching down, she plucked a bit of grass dried to the sole of one shoe. 'Where did you find grass at Hokkaido? Nothing grows in those ruins . . . it's contaminated, isn't it?'

'Yes,' he admitted. It certainly was. The island had been saturated during the war, bombed and bathed and doctored and infested with every possible kind of toxic and lethal substance. Moral Reclamation was useless, let alone gross physical rebuilding. Hokkaido was as sterile and dead as it had been in 1972, the final year of the war.

'It's domestic grass,' Janet said, feeling it. 'I can tell.' She had lived most of her life on colony planets. 'The texture's smooth. It wasn't imported . . . it grows here on Earth.'

With irritation he asked: 'Where on Earth?'

'The Park,' Janet said. 'That's the only place grass grows. The rest is all apartments and offices. You must have been there last night.'

Outside the window of the apartment the – blessed – Morec spire gleamed in the morning sun. Below it was the Park. The Park and spire comprised the hub of Morec, its *omphalos*. There, among the lawns and flowers and bushes, was the statue of Major

6

Streiter. It was the official statue, cast during his lifetime. The statue had been there one hundred and twenty-four years.

'I walked through the Park,' he admitted. He had stopped eating; his 'eggs' were cooling on his plate.

'But the paint,' Janet said. In her voice was the vague, troubled fear with which she met every crisis, the helpless sense of foreboding that always seemed to paralyse her ability to act. 'You didn't do anything wrong, did you?' She was, obviously, thinking of the lease.

Rubbing his forehead, Allen got to his feet. 'It's seven-thirty. I'll have to start to work.'

Janet also rose. 'But you didn't finish eating.' He always finished eating. 'You're not sick, are you?'

'Me,' he said. 'Sick?' He laughed, kissed her on the mouth, and then found his coat. 'When was I last sick?'

'Never,' she murmured, troubled and watching him. 'There's never anything the matter with you.'

At the base of the housing unit, businessmen were clustered at the block warden's table. The routine check was in progress, and Allen joined the group. The morning smelled of ozone, and its clean scent helped clear his head. And it restored his fundamental optimism.

The Parent Citizens Committee maintained a female functionary for each housing unit, and Mrs Birmingham was typical: plump, florid, in her middle fifties, she wore a flowered and ornate dress and wrote out her reports with a powerfully authoritative fountain pen. It was a respected position, and Mrs Birmingham had held the post for years.

'Good morning, Mr Purcell.' She beamed as his turn arrived.

'Hello, Mrs Birmingham.' He tipped his hat, since block wardens set great store by the little civilities. 'Looks like a nice day, assuming it doesn't cloud up.'

'Rain for the crops,' Mrs Birmingham said, which was a joke. Virtually all foods and manufactured items were brought in by autofac rocket; the limited domestic supply served only as a standard of judgment, a kind of recalled ideal. The woman made

7

a note on her long yellow pad. 'I . . . haven't seen your lovely wife yet, today.'

Allen always alibied for his wife's tardiness. 'Janet's getting ready for the Book Club meeting. Special day: she's been promoted to treasurer.'

'I'm so glad,' Mrs Birmingham said. 'She's such a sweet girl. A bit shy, though. She should mix more with people.'

'That's certainly true,' he agreed. 'She was brought up in the wide open spaces. Betelgeuse 4. Rocks and goats.'

He had expected that to end the interview – his own conduct was rarely in question – but suddenly Mrs Birmingham became rigid and business-like. 'You were out late last night, Mr Purcell. Did you have a good time?'

Lord, he cursed. A juvenile must have spotted him. 'Not very.' He wondered how much it had seen. If it tagged him early in the trip it might have followed the whole way.

'You visited Hokkaido,' Mrs Birmingham stated.

'Research,' he said, assuming the posture of defence. 'For the Agency.' This was the very dialectic of the moral society, and, in a perverse way, he enjoyed it. He was facing a bureaucrat who operated by rote, whereas *he* struck through the layers of habit and hit directly. This was the success of his Agency, and it was the success of his personal life. 'Telemedia's needs take precedence over personal feeling, Mrs Birmingham. You certainly understand that.'

His confidence did the trick, and Mrs Birmingham's saccharine smile returned. Making a scratch with her pen she asked: 'Will we see you at the block meeting next Wednesday? That's just the day after tomorrow.'

'Certainly,' Allen said. Over the decades he had learned to endure the interminable interchange, the stuffy presence of his neighbors packed together in one room. And the whirr of the juveniles as they surrendered their tapes to the Committee representatives. 'But I'm afraid I won't have much to contribute.' He was too busy with his ideas and plans to care who lapsed and in what way. 'I've been up to my neck in work.'

'Perhaps,' Mrs Birmingham said, in a partly bantering, partly

8

haughty thought-for-this-week voice, 'there might be a few criticisms of *you*.'

'Of me?' He winced with shock, and felt ill.

'It seems to me that when I was glancing over the reports, I noticed your name. Perhaps not. I could be mistaken. Goodness.' She laughed lightly. 'If so it's certainly the first time in years. But none of us is perfect; we're all mortal.'

'Hokkaido?' he demanded. *Or afterward.* The paint, the grass. There it was in a rush: the wet grass sparkling and slithering under him as he coasted dizzily downhill. The swaying staffs of trees. Above, as he lay gaping on his back, the dark-swept sky; clouds were figments of matter against the blackness. And he, lying stretched out, arms out, swallowing stars.

'Or afterward?' he demanded, but Mrs Birmingham had turned to the next man in line.

2

The lobby of the Mogentlock Building was active and stirring with noise, a constant coming-and-going of busy people as Allen approached the elevator. Because of Mrs Birmingham he was late. The elevator politely waited.

'Good morning, Mr Purcell.' The elevator's taped voice greeted him, and then the doors shut. 'Second floor Bevis and Company Import–Export. Third floor American Music Federation. Fourth floor Allen Purcell, Inc. Research Agency.' The elevator halted and opened its door.

In the outer reception lounge, Fred Luddy, his assistant, wandered about in a tantrum of discomfort.

'Morning,' Allen murmured vaguely, taking off his coat.

'Allen, *she's here*.' Luddy's face flushed scarlet. 'She got here before I did; I came up and there she was, sitting.'

'Who? Janet?' He had a mental image of a Committee representative driving her from the apartment and canceling the lease. Mrs Birmingham, with smiles, closing in on Janet as she sat absently combing her hair.

9

'Not Mrs Purcell,' Luddy said. He lowered his voice to a rasp. 'It's Sue Frost.'

Allen involuntarily craned his neck, but the inner door was closed. If Sue Frost was really sitting in there, it marked the first time a Committee Secretary had paid a call on him.

'I'll be darned,' he said.

Luddy yelped. 'She wants to see you!'

The Committee functioned through a series of departmental secretaries directly responsible to Ida Pease Hoyt, the linear descendant of Major Streiter. Sue Frost was the administrator of Telemedia, which was the official government trust controlling mass communications. He had never dealt with Mrs Frost, or even met her; he worked with the acting Director of T-M, a weary-voiced, bald-headed individual named Myron Mavis. It was Mavis who bought packets.

'What's she want?' Allen asked. Presumably, she had learned that Mavis was taking the Agency's output, and that the Agency was relatively new. With a sinking dread he anticipated one of the Committee's gloomy, protracted investigations. 'Better have Doris block my incoming calls.' Doris was one of his secretaries. 'You take over until Mrs Frost and I are through talking.'

Luddy followed after him in a dance of prayer. 'Good luck, Allen. I'll hold the fort for you. If you want the books—'

'Yes, I'll call you.' He opened the office door, and there was Sue Frost.

She was tall, and she was rather large-boned and muscular. Her suit was a simple hard weave, dark gray in color. She wore a flower in her hair, and she was altogether a strikingly handsome woman. At a guess, she was in her middle fifties. There was little or no softness to her, nothing of the fleshy and over-dressed motherliness that he saw in so many Committee women. Her legs were long, and, as she rose to her feet, her right hand lifted to welcome him in a forthright – almost masculine – handshake.

'Hello, Mr Purcell,' she said. Her voice was not overly expressive. 'I hope you don't mind my showing up this way, unannounced.'

'Not at all,' he murmured. 'Please sit down.'

She reseated herself, crossed her legs, contemplated him. Her eyes, he noticed, were an almost colorless straw. A strong kind of substance, and highly polished.

'Cigarette?' He extended his case, and she accepted a cigarette with a nod of thanks. He took one also, feeling like a gauche young man in the company of an older and more experienced woman.

He couldn't help thinking that Sue Frost was the type of urbane career woman ultimately not proposed to by the hero of Blake-Moffet's packets. There was an unsympathetic firmness about her. She was decidedly not the girl from next door.

'Undoubtedly,' Sue Frost began, 'you recognize this.' She unraveled the winding of a manila folder and displayed a sheaf of script. On the cover of the sheaf was his Agency's stamp; she had one of his packets, and she evidently had been reading it.

'Yes,' he admitted. 'That's one of ours.'

Sue Frost leafed through the packet, then laid it down on Allen's desk. 'Myron accepted this last month. Then he had qualms and he sent it along the line to me. I had a chance to go over it this weekend.'

Now the packet was turned so that Allen could catch the title. It was a high-quality piece he had personally participated in; as it stood it could have gone over any of T-M's media.

'Qualms,' Allen said. 'How do you mean?' He had a deep, cold sensation, as if he were involved in some eerie religious ritual. 'If the packet won't go, then turn it back to us. We'll create a credit; we've done it before.'

'The packet is beautifully handled,' Mrs Frost said, smoking. 'No, Myron certainly didn't want it back. Our theme concerns this man's attempt to grow an apple tree on a colony planet. But the tree dies. The Morec of it is—' She again picked up the packet. 'I'm not certain what the Morec is. Shouldn't he have tried to grow it?'

'Not there,' Allen said.

'You mean it belonged on Earth?'

'I mean he should have been working for the good of society, not off somewhere nourishing a private enterprise. He saw the colony as an end in itself. But they're means. *This* is the center.'

'*Omphalos*,' she agreed. 'The navel of the universe. And the tree—'

11

'The tree symbolizes an Earth product that withers when it's transplanted. His spiritual side died.'

'But he couldn't have grown it here. There's no room. It's all city.'

'Symbolically,' he explained. 'He should have put down his roots here.'

Sue Frost was silent for a moment, and he sat smoking uneasily, crossing and uncrossing his legs, feeling his tension grow, not diminish. Nearby, in another office, the switchboard buzzed. Doris' typewriter clacked.

'You see,' Sue Frost said, 'this conflicts with a fundamental. The Committee has put billions of dollars and years of work into outplanet agriculture. We've done everything possible to seed domestic plants in the colonies. They're supposed to supply us with our food. People realize it's a heartbreaking task, with endless disappointments . . . and you're saying that the outplanet orchards will fail.'

Allen started to speak and then changed his mind. He felt absolutely defeated. Mrs Frost was gazing at him searchingly, expecting him to defend himself in the usual fashion.

'Here's a note,' she said. 'You can read it. Myron's note on this, when it came to me.'

The note was in pencil and went:

'Sue—
The same outfit again. Top-drawer, but too coy.
You decide.

M.'

'What's he mean?' Allen said, now angered.

'He means the Morec doesn't come across.' She leaned toward him. 'Your agency has been in this only three years. You started out very well. What do you currently gross?'

'I'd have to see the books.' He got to his feet. 'May I get Luddy in here? I'd like him to see Myron's note.'

'Certainly,' Mrs Frost said.

Fred Luddy entered the office stiff-legged with apprehension. 'Thanks,' he muttered, as Allen gave him the packet. He read the note, but his eyes showed no spark of consciousness. He seemed tuned to invisible vibrations; the meaning reached him through the tension of the air, rather than the pencilled words.

'Well,' he said finally, in a daze. 'You can't win them all.'

'We'll take this packet back, naturally.' Allen began to strip the note from it, but Mrs Frost said:

'Is that your only response? I told you we want it; I made that clear. But we can't take it in the shape it's in. I think you should know that it was my decision to give your Agency the go-ahead. There was some dispute, and I was brought in from the first.' From the manila folder she took a second packet, a familiar one. 'Remember this? May, 2112. We argued for hours. Myron liked this, and I liked it. Nobody else did. Now Myron has cold feet.' She tossed the packet, the first the Agency had ever done, onto the desk.

After an interval Allen said: 'Myron's getting tired.'

'Very.' She nodded agreeably.

Hunched over, Fred Luddy said: 'Maybe we've been going at it too fast.' He cleared his throat, cracked his knuckles and glanced at the ceiling. Drops of warm sweat sparkled in his hair and along his smoothly-shaved jowls. 'We kind of got – excited.'

Speaking to Mrs Frost, Allen said: 'My position is simple. In that packet, we made the Morec that Earth is the center. That's the real fundamental, and I believe it. If I didn't believe it I couldn't have developed the packet. I'll withdraw the packet but I won't change it. I'm not going to preach morality without practicing it.'

Quakily, in a spasm of agonized back-pedalling, Luddy muttered: 'It's not a moral question, Al. It's a question of clarity. The Morec of that packet doesn't come across.' His voice had a ragged, guilty edge; Luddy knew what he was doing and he was ashamed. 'I – see Mrs Frost's point. Yes, I do. It looks as if we're scuttling the agricultural program, and naturally we don't mean that. Isn't that so, Al?'

'You're fired,' Allen said.

They both stared at him. Neither of them grasped that he was serious, that he had really done it.

'Go tell Doris to make out your check.' Allen took the packet from the desk and held onto it. 'I'm sorry, Mrs Frost, but I'm the only person qualified to speak for the Agency. We'll credit you for this packet and submit another. All right?'

She stubbed out her cigarette, rising, at the same time, to her feet. 'It's your decision.'

'Thanks,' he said, and felt a release of tension. Mrs Frost understood his stand, and approved. And that was crucial.

'I'm sorry,' Luddy muttered, ashen. 'That was a mistake on my part. The packet is fine. Perfectly sound as it now exists.' Plucking at Allen's sleeve, he drew him off in the corner. 'I admit I made a mistake.' His voice sank to a jumpy whisper. 'Let's discuss this further. I was simply trying to develop one possible viewpoint among many. You want me to express myself; I mean, it seems senseless to penalize me for working in the best interests of the Agency, as I see it.'

'I meant what I said,' Allen said.

'You did?' Luddy laughed. 'Naturally you meant it. You're the boss.' He was shaking. 'You really weren't kidding?'

Collecting her coat, Mrs Frost moved toward the door. 'I'd like to look over your Agency while I'm here. Do you mind?'

'Not at all,' Allen said. 'I'd be glad to show it to you. I'm quite proud of it.' He opened the door for her, and the two of them walked out into the hall. Luddy remained in the office, a sick, erratic look on his face.

'I don't care for him,' Mrs Frost said. 'I think you're better off without him.'

'That wasn't any fun,' Allen said. But he was feeling better.

3

In the hall outside Myron Mavis' office, the Telemedia workers were winding up their day. The T-M building formed a connected hollow square. The open area in the center was used for outdoor sets. Nothing was in process now, because it was five-thirty and everybody was leaving.

From a pay phone, Allen Purcell called his wife. 'I'll be late for dinner,' he said.

'Are – you all right?'

'I'm fine,' he said. 'But you go ahead and eat. Big doings, big crisis at the Agency. I'll catch something down here.' He added, 'I'm at Telemedia.'

'For very long?' Janet asked anxiously.

'Maybe for a long, long time,' he said, and hung up.

As he rejoined Sue Frost, she said to him, 'How long did Luddy work for you?'

'Since I opened the Agency.' The realization was sobering: three years. Presently he added: 'That's the only person I've ever let go.'

At the back of the office, Myron Mavis was turning over duplicates of the day's output to a bonded messenger of the Committee. The duplicates would be put on permanent file; in case of an investigation the material was there to examine.

To the formal young messenger, Mrs Frost said: 'Don't leave. I'm going back; you can go with me.'

The young man retired discreetly with his armload of metal drums. His uniform was the drab khaki of the Cohorts of Major Streiter, a select body composed of male descendants of the founder of Morec.

'A cousin,' Mrs Frost said. 'A very distant cousin-in-law on my father's side.' She nodded toward the young man, whose face was as expressionless as sand. 'Ralf Hadler. I like to keep him around.' She raised her voice. 'Ralf, go find the Getabout. It's parked somewhere in back.'

The Cohorts, either singly or in bunches, made Allen uncomfortable; they were humorless, as devout as machines, and, for their small number, they seemed to be everywhere. His fantasy was that the Cohorts were always in motion; in the course of one day, like a foraging ant, a member of the Cohorts roamed hundreds of miles.

'You'll come along,' Mrs Frost said to Mavis.

'Naturally,' Mavis murmured. He began clearing his desk of unfinished work. Mavis was an ulcer-mongerer, a high-strung worrier with rumpled shirt and baggy, unpressed tweeds, who flew into fragments when things got over his head. Allen recalled tangled interviews that had ended with Mavis in despair and his staff scurrying. If Mavis was going to be along, the next few hours would be hectic.

'We'll meet you at the Getabout,' Mrs Frost said to him. 'Finish up here, first. We'll wait.'

As she and Allen walked down the hall, Allen observed: 'This is a big place.' The idea of an organ – even a government organ – occupying an entire building struck him as grandiose. And much of it was underground. Telemedia, like cleanliness, was next to God; after T-M came the secretaries and the Committee itself.

'It's big,' Mrs Frost agreed, striding along the hall and holding her manila folder against her chest with both hands. 'But I don't know.'

'You don't know what?'

Cryptically, she said: 'Maybe it should be smaller. Remember what became of the giant reptiles.'

'You mean curtail its activities?' He tried to picture the vacuum that would be created. 'And what instead?'

'Sometimes I toy with the idea of slicing T-M into a number of units, interacting, but separately run. I'm not sure one person can or should take responsibility for the whole.'

'Well,' Allen said, thinking of Mavis, 'I suppose it cuts into his life-expectancy.'

'Myron has been Director of T-M for eight years. He's forty-two and he looks eighty. He's got only half a stomach. Someday I expect to phone and discover he's holed up at the Health Resort, doing business from there. Or from Other World, as they call that sanitarium of theirs.'

'That's a long way off,' Allen said. 'Either place.'

They had come to the door leading out, and Mrs Frost halted. 'You've been in a position to watch T-M. What do you think of it? Be honest with me. Would you call it efficient?'

'The part I see is efficient.'

'What about the output? It buys your packets and it frames them for a medium. What's your reaction to the end result? Is the Morec garbled along the line? Do you feel your ideas survive projection?'

Allen tried to recall when he had last sat through a T-M concoction. His Agency monitored as a matter of routine, collecting its own duplicates of the items based on its packets. 'Last week,' he said, 'I watched a television show.'

The woman's gray eyebrows lifted mockingly. 'Half hour? Or entire hour?'

'The program was an hour but we saw only a portion of it. At a friend's apartment. Janet and I were over playing Juggle, and we were taking a break.'

'You don't mean you don't own a television set.'

'The people downstairs are domino for my block. They tumble the rest of us. Apparently the packets are getting over.'

They walked outside and got into the parked Getabout. Allen calculated that this zone, in terms of leasing, was in the lowest possible range: between 1 and 14. It was not crowded.

'Do you approve of the domino method?' Mrs Frost asked as they waited for Mavis.

'It's certainly economical.'

'But you have reservations.'

'The domino method operates on the assumption that people believe what their group believes, no more and no less. One unique individual would foul it up. One man who originated his own idea, instead of getting it from his block domino.'

Mrs Frost said: 'How interesting. An idea out of nothing.'

'Out of the individual human mind,' Allen said, aware that he wasn't being polite, but feeling, at the same time, that Mrs Frost respected him and really wanted to hear what he had to offer. 'A rare situation,' he admitted. 'But it could occur.'

There was a stir outside the car. Myron Mavis, a bulging brief-case under his arm, and the Cohort of Major Streiter, his young face stern and his messenger parcel chained to his belt, had arrived.

'I forgot about you,' Mrs Frost said to her cousin, as the two men got in. The Getabout was small, and there was barely room for all of them. Hadler was to drive. He started up the motor – powered by pile-driven steam – and the car moved cautiously along the lane. Along the route to the Committee building, they passed only three other Getabouts.

'Mr Purcell has a criticism of the domino method,' Mrs Frost said to Myron Mavis.

Mavis grunted unintelligibly, then blinked bloodshot eyes and roused himself. 'Uhuh,' he muttered. 'Fine.' He began pawing through a pocketful of papers. 'Let's go back to five-minute spots. Hit 'em, hit 'em.'

Behind the tiller, young Hadler sat very straight and rigid, his chin out-jutting. He gripped the tiller as a person walked across the lane ahead. The Getabout had reached a speed of twenty miles an hour, and all four of them were uneasy.

'We should either fly,' Mavis grated, 'or walk. Not this halfway business. All we need now is a couple of bottles of beer, and we're back in the old days.'

'Mr Purcell believes in the unique individual,' Mrs Frost said.

Mavis favored Allen with a glance. 'The Resort has that on its mind, too. An obsession, day and night.'

'I always assumed that was window dressing,' Mrs Frost said. 'To lure people into going over.'

'People go over because they're noose,' Mavis declared. *Noose* was a derisive term contracted from *neuro-psychiatric*. Allen disliked it. It had a blind, savage quality that made him think of the old hate terms, *nigger* and *kike*. 'They're weak, they're misfits, they can't take it. They haven't got the moral fiber to stick it out here; like babies, they want pleasure. They want candy and bottled pop. Comic books from mama Health Resort.'

On his face was an expression of great bitterness. The bitterness was like a solvent that had eaten through the wasted folds of flesh, exposing the bone. Allen had never seen Mavis so weary and discouraged.

'Well,' Mrs Frost said, also noticing, 'we don't want them anyway. It's better they should go over.'

'I sometimes wonder what they do with all those people,' Allen said. Nobody had accurate figures on the number of renegades who had fled to the Resort; because of the onus, the relatives preferred to state that the missing individual had gone to the colonies. Colonists were, after all, only failures; a noose was a voluntary expatriate who had declared himself an enemy of moral civilization.

'I've heard,' Mrs Frost said conversationally, 'that incoming supplicants are set to work in vast slave-labor camps. Or was that the Communists who did that?'

'Both,' Allen said. 'And with the revenue, the Resort is building a vast empire in outer space to dominate the universe. Huge robot armies, too. Women supplicants are—' He concluded briefly: 'Ill-used.'

At the tiller of the Getabout, Ralf Hadler said suddenly: 'Mrs Frost, there's a car behind us trying to pass. What'll I do?'

'Let it pass.' They all looked around. A Getabout, like their own, but with the sticker of the Pure Food and Drug League, was nosing its way to their left side. Hadler had gone white at this unforeseen dilemma, and their Getabout was veering witlessly.

'Pull over and stop,' Allen told him.

'Speed up,' Mavis said, turning in his seat and peering defiantly through the rear window. 'They don't own this lane.'

The Pure Food and Drug League Getabout continued to advance on them, equally uncertain of itself. As Hadler dribbled toward the right, it abruptly seized what seemed to be its chance and shot forward. Hadler then let his tiller slide between his hands, and two fenders scraped shatteringly.

Mavis, trembling, crept from their stopped Getabout. Mrs Frost followed him, and Allen and young Hadler got out on the other side. The Pure Food and Drug League car idled its motor, and the driver – alone inside – gaped out at them. He was a middle-aged gentleman, obviously at the end of a long day at the office.

'Maybe we could go back,' Mrs Frost said, holding her manila folder aimlessly. Mavis, reduced to impotence, wandered around the two Getabouts and poked here and there with his toe. Hadler stood like iron, betraying no feeling.

The fenders had combined, and one car would have to be jacked up. Allen inspected the damage, noted the angle at which the two metals had met, and then gave up. 'They have tow trucks,' he said to Mrs Frost. 'Have Ralf call the Transportation Pool.' He looked around him; they were not far from the Committee Building. 'We can walk from here.'

Without protest, Mrs Frost started off, and he followed.

'What about me?' Mavis demanded, hurrying a few steps.

'You can stay with the car,' Mrs Frost said. Hadler had already strode toward a building and phone booth; Mavis was alone with the gentleman from the Pure Food and Drug League. 'Tell the police what happened.'

A cop, on foot, was walking over. Not far behind him came a juvenile, attracted by the convocation of people.

'This is embarrassing,' Mrs Frost said presently, as the two of them walked toward the Committee Building.

'I suppose Ralf will go up before his block warden.' The picture of Mrs Birmingham entered his mind, the coyly sweet malevolence of the creature situated behind her table, dealing out trouble.

Mrs Frost said: 'The Cohorts have their own inquiry setup.' As they reached the front entrance of the building, she said thoughtfully: 'Mavis is completely burned out. He can't cope with any situation. He makes no decisions. Hasn't for months.'

Allen didn't comment. It wasn't his place.

'Maybe it's just as well,' Mrs Frost said. 'Leaving him back there. I'd rather see Mrs Hoyt without him trailing along.'

This was the first he had heard that they were meeting with Ida Pease Hoyt. Halting, he said: 'Maybe you should explain what you're going to do.'

'I believe you know what I'm going to do,' she said, continuing on.

And he did.

4

Allen Purcell returned home to his one-room apartment at the hour of nine-thirty p.m. Janet met him at the door.

'Did you eat?' she asked. 'You didn't.'

'No,' he admitted, entering the room.

'I'll fix you something.' She set back the wall tape and restored the kitchen, which had departed at eight. In a few minutes, 'Alaskan salmon' was baking in the oven, and the near-authentic odor drifted through the room. Janet put on an apron and began setting the table.

Throwing himself down on a chair, Allen opened the evening

paper. But he was too tired to read; he changed his mind and pushed the paper away. The meeting with Ida Pease Hoyt and Sue Frost had lasted three hours. It had been gruelling.

'Do you want to tell me what happened?' Janet asked.

'Later.' He fooled with a sugar cube at the table. 'How was the Book Club? Sir Walter Scott written anything good lately?'

'Not a thing,' she said shortly, responding to the tone of his voice.

'You believe Charles Dickens is here to stay?'

She turned from the stove. 'Something happened and I want to know what it is.'

Her concern made him relent. 'The Agency was *not* exposed as a vice den.'

'You said on the phone you went to T-M. And you said something terrible happened at the Agency.'

'I fired Fred Luddy, if you call that terrible. When'll the "salmon" be ready?'

'Soon. Five minutes.'

Allen said: 'Ida Pease Hoyt offered me Mavis' job. Director of Telemedia. Sue Frost did all the talking.'

For a moment Janet stood at the stove and then she began to cry.

'Why the heck are you crying?' Allen demanded.

Between sobs she choked: 'I don't know. I'm scared.'

He went on fooling with the sugar cube. Now it had broken in half, so he flattened the halves to grains. 'It wasn't much of a surprise. The post is always filled from the Agencies, and Mavis has been washed up for months. Eight years is a long time to be responsible for everybody's morality.'

'Yes, you – said – he should retire.' She blew her nose and rubbed her eyes. 'Last year you told me that.'

'Trouble is, he really wants to do the job.'

'Does he know?'

'Sue Frost told him. He finished up the meeting. The four of us sat around drinking coffee and settling it.'

'Then it *is* settled?'

Thinking of the look on Mavis' face when he left the meeting, Allen said: 'No. Not completely. Mavis resigned; his paper is in, and Sue's statement has gone out. The routine protocol. Years of devoted service, faithful adherence to the Principles of Moral Reclamation. I talked to him briefly in the hall afterward.' Actually, he had walked a quarter mile with Mavis, from the Committee Building to Mavis' apartment. 'He's got a piece of planet in the Sirius System. They're great on cattle. According to Mavis, you can't distinguish the taste and texture from the domestic herds.'

Janet said: 'What's undecided?'

'Maybe I won't take it.'

'Why not?'

'I want to be alive eight years from now. I don't want to be retiring to some God-forsaken rustic backwater ten light years away.'

Pushing her handkerchief into her breast pocket, Janet bent to turn off the oven. 'Once, when we were setting up the Agency, we talked about this. We were very frank.'

'What did we decide?' He remembered what they had decided. They decided to decide when the time came, because it might very well never come. And anyhow Janet was too busy worrying about the imminent collapse of the Agency. 'This is all so useless. We're acting as if the job is some sort of plum. It's not a plum and it never was. Nobody ever pretended it was. Why did Mavis take it? Because it seemed like the moral thing to do.'

'Public service,' Janet said faintly.

'The moral responsibility to serve. To take on the burden on civic life. The highest form of self-sacrifice, the *omphalos* of this whole—' He broke off.

'Rat race,' Janet said. 'Well, there'll be a little more money. Or does it pay less? I guess that isn't important.'

Allen said: 'My family has climbed a long way. I've done some climbing, too. This is what it's for; this is the goal. I'd like a buck for every packet I've done on the subject.' The packet Sue Frost had returned, in fact. The parable about the tree that died.

The tree had died in isolation, and perhaps the Morec of the packet was confused and obscure. But to him it came over clearly enough: a man was primarily responsible to his fellows, and it was with his fellows that he made his life.

'There're two men,' he said. 'Squatting in the ruins, off in Hokkaido. That place is contaminated. Everything's dead, there. They have one future; they're waiting for it. Gates and Sugermann would rather be dead than come back here. If they came back here they'd have to become social beings; they'd have to sacrifice some part of their ineffable selves. And that is certainly an awful thing.'

'That's not the only reason why they're out there,' Janet said, in a voice so low that he could barely hear her. 'I guess you've forgotten. I've been there, too. You took me with you, one time. When we were first married. I wanted to see.'

He remembered. But it didn't seem important. 'Probably it's a protest of some sort. They have some point they want to make, camping there in the ruins.'

'They're giving up their lives.'

'That doesn't take any effort. And somebody can always save them with quick-freeze.'

'But in dying they make an important point. Don't you think so? Maybe not.' She reflected. 'Myron Mavis made a point, too. Not a very different point. And you must see something in what Gates and Sugermann are doing; you keep going out there again and again. You were there last night.'

He nodded. 'I was.'

'What did Mrs Birmingham say?'

Without particular emotion he answered: 'A juvenile saw me, and I'm down for Wednesday's block meeting.'

'Because you went there? They never reported it before.'

'Maybe they never saw me before.'

'Do you know about afterward? Did the juvenile see that?'

'Let's hope not,' he said.

'It's in the paper.'

He snatched up the paper. It was in the paper, and it was on page one. The headlines were large.

STREITER STATUE DESECRATED
VANDALS IN PARK
INVESTIGATION UNDER WAY

'That was you,' Janet said tonelessly.

23

'It was,' he agreed. He read the headlines again. 'It really was me. And it took an hour to do. I left the paint can on a bench. They probably found it.'

'That's mentioned in the article. They noticed the statue this morning around six a.m., and they found the paint can at six-thirty.'

'What else did they find?'

'Read it,' Janet said.

Spreading the paper out flat on the table, he read it.

STREITER STATUE DESECRATED
VANDALS IN PARK
INVESTIGATION UNDER WAY

Newer York, Oct. 8 (T-M). Police are investigating the deliberate mutilation of the official statue of Major Jules Streiter, the founder of Moral Reclamation and the guiding leader of the revolution of 1985. Located in the Park of the Spire, the monument, a life-size statue of bronzed plastic, was struck from the original mold created by the founder's friend and life-long companion, Pietro Buetello, in March of the year 1990. The mutilation, described by police as deliberate and systematic, apparently took place during the night. The Park of the Spire is never closed to the public, since it represents the moral and spiritual center of Newer York.

'The paper was downstairs when I got home,' Janet said. 'As always. With the mail. I read it while I was eating dinner.'

'It's easy to see why you're upset.'

'Because of that? I'm not upset because of that. All they can do is unlease us, fine us, send you to prison for a year.'

'And bar our families from Earth.'

Janet shrugged. 'We'd live. They'd live. I've been thinking about it; I've had three hours and a half here alone in the apartment. At first I was—' She pondered. 'Well, it was hard to believe. But this morning we both knew something had happened; there was the mud and grass on your shoes, and the red paint. And nobody saw you?'

'A juvenile saw something.'

24

'Not that. They'd have picked you up. It must have seen something else.'

Allen said: 'I wonder how long it'll be.'

'Why should they find out? They'll think it's some person who lost his lease, somebody who's been forced back to the colonies. Or a noose.'

'I hate that word.'

'A supplicant, then. But why you? Not a man going to the top, a man who spent this afternoon with Sue Frost and Ida Pease Hoyt. It wouldn't make sense.'

'No,' he admitted. 'It doesn't.' Truthfully he added: 'Even to me.'

Janet walked over to the table. 'I wondered about that. You're not sure why you did it, are you?'

'I haven't an idea in the world.'

'What was in your mind?'

'A very clear desire,' he said. 'A fixed, overwhelming, and totally clear desire to get that statue once and for all. It took half a gallon of red paint, and some skillful use of a power-driven saw. The saw's back in the Agency shop, minus a blade. I busted the blade. I haven't sawed in years.'

'Do you remember precisely what you did?'

'No,' he answered.

'It isn't in the paper. They're vague about it. So whatever it was—' She smiled listlessly down at him. 'You did a good job.'

Later, when the baked 'Alaskan salmon' was nothing but a few bones on an empty dinner platter, Allen leaned back and lit a cigarette. At the stove Janet carefully washed pots and pans in the sink attachment. The apartment was peaceful.

'You'd think,' Allen said, 'this was like any other evening.'

'We might as well go on with what we were doing,' Janet said.

On the table by the couch was a pile of metal wheels and gears. Janet had been assembling an electric clock. Diagrams and instructions from an Edufacture kit were heaped with the parts. Instructional pastimes: Edufacture for the individual, Juggle for social gatherings. To keep idle hands occupied.

'How's the clock coming?' he asked.

25

'Almost done. After that comes a shaving wand for you. Mrs Duffy across the hall made one for her husband. I watched her. It isn't hard.'

Pointing to the stove Allen said: 'My family built that. Back in 2096, when I was eleven. I remember how silly it seemed; stoves were on sale, built by autofac at a third of the cost. Then my father and brother explained the Morec. I never forgot it.'

Janet said: 'I enjoy building things; it's fun.'

He went on smoking his cigarette, thinking how bizarre it was that he could be here when less than twenty-four hours ago, he had japed the statue.

'I japed it,' he said aloud.

'You—'

'A term we use in packet assembly. When a theme is harped on too much you get parody. When we make fun of a stale theme we say we've japed it.'

'Yes,' she agreed. 'I know. I've heard you parody some of Blake-Moffet's stuff.'

'The part that bothers me,' Allen said, 'is this. On Sunday night I japed the statue of Major Streiter. And on Monday morning Mrs Sue Frost came to the Agency. By six o'clock I was listening to Ida Pease Hoyt offer me the directorship of Tele-media.'

'How could there be a relationship?'

'It would have to be complex.' He finished his cigarette. 'So roundabout that everybody and everything in the universe would have to be brought in. But I feel it's there. Some deep, underlying causal connection, not chance. Not coincidence.'

'Tell me how you – japed it.'

'Can't. Don't remember.' He got to his feet. 'Don't you wait up. I'm going downtown to look at it; they probably haven't had time to start repairs.'

Janet said instantly: 'Please don't go out.'

'Very necessary,' he said, looking around for his coat. The closet had absorbed it, and he pulled the closet back into the room. 'There's a dim picture in my mind, nothing firm. All things considered, I really should have it clear. Maybe then I can decide about T-M.'

Without a word Janet passed by him and out into the hall. She was on her way to the bathroom, and he knew why. With her went a collection of bottles: she was going to swallow enough sedatives to last her the balance of the night.

'Take it easy,' he warned.

There was no answer from the closed bathroom door. Allen hung around a moment, and then left.

5

The Park was in shadows, and icy-dark. Here and there small groups of people had collected like pools of nocturnal rain water. Nobody spoke. They seemed to be waiting, hoping in some vague way for something to happen.

The statue had been erected immediately before the spire, on its own platform, in the center of a gravel ring. Benches surrounded the statue so that persons could feed the pigeons and doze and talk while contemplating its grandeur. The rest of the Park was sloping fields of wet grass, a few opaque humps of shrubs and trees, and, at one end, a gardener's shed.

Allen reached the center of the Park and halted. At first he was confused; nothing familiar was visible. Then he realized what had happened. The police had boarded the statue up. Here was a square wooden frame, a gigantic box. So he wasn't going to see it after all. He wasn't going to find out what he had done.

Presently, as he stood dully staring, he became aware that somebody was beside him. A seedy, spindly-armed citizen in a long, soiled overcoat, was also staring at the box.

For a long time neither man spoke. Finally the citizen hawked and spat into the grass. 'Sure can't see worth a d—n.'

Allen nodded.

'They put that up on purpose,' the thin citizen said. 'So you can't see. You know why?'

'Why?' Allen said.

The thin citizen leaned at him. 'Anarchists got to it. Mutilated it terribly. The police caught some of them; some they didn't

27

catch. The ringleader, they didn't catch him. But they will. And you know what they'll find?'

'What?' Allen said.

'They'll find he's paid by the Resort. And this is just the first.'

'Of what?'

'Within the next week,' the thin citizen revealed, 'public buildings are going to be bombed. The Committee building, T-M. And then they put the radioactive particles in the drinking water. You'll see. It already tastes wrong. The police know, but their hands are tied.'

Next to the thin citizen a short, fat, red-haired man smoking a cigar spoke irritably up. 'It was kids, that's all. A bunch of crazy kids with nothing else to do.'

The thin citizen laughed harshly. 'That's what they want you to think. Sure, a harmless prank. I'll tell you something: *the people that did this mean to overthrow Morec.* They won't rest until every scrap of morality and decency has been trampled into the ground. They want to see fornication and neon signs and dope come back. They want to see waste and rapacity rule sovereign, and vainglorious man writhe in the sinkpit of his own greed.'

'It was kids,' the short fat man repeated. 'Doesn't mean anything.'

'The wrath of Almighty God will roll up the heavens like a scroll,' the thin citizen was telling him, as Allen walked off. 'The atheists and fornicators will lie bloody in the streets, and the evil will be burned from men's hearts by the sacred fire.'

By herself, hands in the pockets of her coat, a girl watched Allen as he walked aimlessly along the path. He approached her, hesitated, and then said: 'What happened?'

The girl was dark-haired, deep-chested, with smooth, tanned skin that glowed faintly in the half-light of the Park. When she spoke her voice was controlled and without uncertainty. 'This morning they found the statue to be quite different. Didn't you read about it? There was an account in the newspaper.'

'I read about it,' he said. The girl was up on a rise of grass, and he joined her.

There, in the shadows below them, were the remnants of the statue, damaged in a cunning way. The image of bronzed plastic had been caught unguarded; in the night it had been asleep. Standing here now he could take an objective view; he could detach himself from the event and see it as an outsider, as a person – like these persons – coming by accident, and wondering.

Across the gravel were large ugly drops of red. It was the enamel from the art department of his Agency. But he could suppose the apocalyptic quality of it; he could imagine what these people imagined.

The trail of red was blood, the statue's blood. Up from the wet, loose-packed soil of the Park had crept its enemy; the enemy had taken hold and bitten through its carotid artery. The statue had bled all over its own legs and feet; it had gushed red slimy blood and died.

He, standing with the girl, knew it was dead. He could feel the emptiness behind the wooden box; the blood had run out leaving a hollow container. It seemed now as if the statue had tried to defend itself. But it had lost, and no quick-freeze would save it. The statue was dead forever.

'How long have you been here?' the girl asked.

'Just a couple of minutes,' he said.

'I was here this morning. I saw it on my way to work.'

Then he realized, she had seen it before the box was erected. 'What did they do to it?' he asked, earnestly eager to find out. 'Could you tell?'

The girl said: 'Don't be scared.'

'I'm not scared.' He was puzzled.

'You are. But it's all right.' She laughed. 'Now they'll have to take it down. They can't repair it.'

'You're glad,' he said, awed.

The girl's eyes filled with light, a rocking amusement. 'We should celebrate. Have ourselves a ball.' Then her eyes faded. 'If he can get away with it, whoever he was, whoever did it. Let's get out of here – okay? Come on.'

She led him across the grass to the sidewalk and the lane beyond. Hands in her pockets, she walked rapidly along, and he followed. The night air was chilly and sharp, and, gradually, it cleared from his mind the mystical dream-like presence of the Park.

'I'm glad to get out of there,' he murmured finally.

With an uneasy toss of her head the girl said: 'It's easy to go in there, hard to get out.'

'You felt it?'

'Of course. It wasn't so bad this morning, when I walked by. The sun was shining; it was daylight. But tonight—' She shivered. 'I was there an hour before you came and woke me up. Just standing, looking at it. In a trance.'

'What got me,' he said, 'were those drops. They looked like blood.'

'Just paint,' she answered matter-of-factly. Reaching into her coat she brought out a folded newspaper. 'Want to read? A common fast-drying enamel, used by a lot of offices. Nothing mysterious about it.'

'They haven't caught anybody,' he said, still feeling some of the unnatural detachment. But it was departing.

'Surprising how easily a person can do this and get away. Why not? Nobody guards the Park; nobody actually saw him.'

'What's your theory?'

'Well,' she said, kicking a bit of rock ahead of her. 'Somebody was bitter about losing his lease. Or somebody was expressing a subconscious resentment of Morec. Fighting back against the burden the system imposes.'

'Exactly what was done to the statue?'

'The paper didn't print the details. It's probably safer to play a thing like this down. You've seen the statue; you're familiar with the Buetello conception of Streiter. The traditional militant stance: one hand extended, one leg forward as if he were going into battle. Head up nobly. Deeply thoughtful expression.'

'Looking into the future,' Allen murmured.

'That's right.' The girl slowed down, spun on her heel and peered at the dark pavement. 'The criminal, or japer, or whatever he is, painted the statue red. You know that; you saw the drops. He sloshed it with stripes, painted the hair red, too. And—' She smiled brightly. 'Well, frankly, he severed the head, somehow. With a power cutting tool, evidently. Removed the head and placed it in the outstretched hand.'

'I see,' Allen said, listening intently.

'Then,' the girl continued, in a quiet monotone, 'the individual applied a high-temperature pack to the forward leg – the right leg. The statue is a poured thermoplastic. When the leg became flexible, the culprit reshaped its position. Major Streiter now appears to be holding his head in his hand, ready to kick it far into the park. Quite original, and *quite* embarrassing.'

After an interval Allen said: 'Under the circumstances you can't blame them for nailing a box around it.'

'They had to. But a number of people saw it before they put the box up. The first thing they did was get the Cohorts of Major Streiter over; they must have thought something else was going to happen. When I went by, there were all those sullen-looking young men in their brown uniforms, a ring of them around the statue. But you could see anyhow. Then, sometime during the day, they put up the box.' She added: 'You see, people laughed. Even the Cohorts. They couldn't help it. They snickered, and then it got away from them. I was so sorry for those young men . . . they hated to laugh so.'

Now the two of them had reached a lighted intersection. The girl halted. On her face was an expression of concern. She gazed up at him intently, studying him, her eyes large.

'You're in a terrible state,' she said. 'And it's my fault.'

'No,' he answered. 'My own fault.'

Her hand pressed against his arm. 'What's wrong?'

With irony he said: 'Job worries.'

'Oh.' She nodded. But she still held onto his arm with her tight fingers. 'Well, do you have a wife?'

'A very sweet one.'

'Does she help you?'

'She worries even more than I. Right now she's home taking pills. She has a fabulous collection.'

The girl said: 'Do you want help?'

'I do,' he answered, and was not surprised at his own candor. 'Very much.'

'That's what I thought.' The girl began to walk on, and he went along. She seemed to be weighing various possibilities.

'These days,' she said, 'it's hard to get help. You're not supposed to *want* help. I can give you an address. If I do, will you use it?'

'That's impossible to say.'

'Will you *try* to use it?'

'I've never asked for help in my life,' Allen said. 'I can't say what I'd do.'

'Here it is,' the girl said. She handed him a slip of folded paper. 'Put it away in your wallet. Don't look at it – just put it away until you want to use it. Then get it out.'

He put it away, and she watched fixedly.

'All right,' she said, satisfied. 'Good night.'

'You're leaving?' He wasn't surprised; it seemed perfectly natural.

'I'll see you again. I've seen you before.' She dwindled in the darkness of the side lane. 'Good night, Mr Purcell. Take care of yourself.'

Sometime later, after the girl was completely gone, he realized that she had been standing there in the Park waiting for him. Waiting, because she knew he would show up.

6

The next day Allen had still not given Mrs Frost an answer. The directorship of T-M was empty, with Mavis out and nobody in. The huge trust rolled along on momentum; and, he supposed, minor bureaucrats along the line continued to stamp forms and fill out papers. The monster lived, but not as it should.

Wondering how long he had to decide he phoned the Committee building and asked for Mrs Frost.

'Yes, sir,' a recorded voice answered. 'Secretary Frost is in conference. You may state a thirty-second message which will be transcribed for her attention. Thank you. Zeeeeeeeeeeeee!'

'Mrs Frost,' Allen said, 'there are a number of considerations involved, as I mentioned to you yesterday. Heading an Agency gives me a certain independence. You pointed out that my only customer is Telemedia, so that for all practical purposes I'm working for Telemedia. You also pointed out that as Director of Telemedia I would have more, not less, independence.'

He paused, wondering how to go on.

'On the other hand,' he said, and then the thirty seconds was up. He waited as the mechanism at the other end repeated its rigamarole, and then continued. 'My Agency, after all, was built up by my own hands. I'm free to alter it. I have complete control. T-M, on the other hand, is impersonal. Nobody can really dictate to it. T-M is like a glacier.'

That sounded terrible to him, but once on the tape it couldn't be unspoken. He finished up:

'Mrs Frost, I'm afraid I'll have to have time to think it over. I'm sorry, because I realize this puts you in an unpleasant position. But I'm afraid the delay is unavoidable. I'll try to have my answer within a week, and please don't think I'm stalling. I'm sincerely floundering. This is Allen Purcell.'

Ringing off, he sat back and brooded.

Here, in his office, the statue of Major Streiter seemed distant and unconvincing. He had one problem only: the job problem. Either he stayed with his Agency or he went upstairs to T-M. Put that way his dilemma sounded simple. He got out a coin and rolled it across the surface of his desk. If necessary he could leave the decision to chance.

The door opened and Doris, his secretary, entered. 'Good morning,' she said brightly. 'Fred Luddy wants a letter of recommendation from you. We made out his check. Two weeks, plus what was owed.' She seated herself across from him, pad and pencil ready. 'Do you want to dictate a letter?'

'That's hard to say.' He wanted to, because he liked Luddy and he hoped to see him get a halfway decent job. But at the same time he felt silly writing a letter of recommendation for a man he had fired as disloyal and dishonest, Morely speaking. 'Maybe I'll have to think about that, too.'

Doris arose. 'I'll tell him you're too busy. You'll have to see about it later.'

Relieved, he let her go with that story. No decision seemed possible right now, on any topic. Small or large, his problems revolved on an olympian level; they couldn't be hauled down to earth.

At least the police hadn't traced him. He was reasonably sure that Mrs Birmingham's juvenile lacked information on the Park episode. Tomorrow, at nine a.m., he'd find out. But he wasn't worried. The idea of police barging in to arrest and deport him was absurd. His real worry was the job – and himself.

He had told the girl he needed help, and he did. Not because he had japed the statue, but because he had japed it without understanding why. Odd that the brain could function on its own, without acquainting him with its purposes, its reasons. But the brain was an organ, like the spleen, heart, kidneys. And they went about their private activities. So why not the brain? Reasoned out that way, the bizarre quality evaporated.

But he still had to find out what was happening.

Reaching into his wallet he got out the slip of paper. On it, in a woman's neat hand, were four words.

Health Resort
Gretchen Malparto.

So the girl's name was Gretchen. And, as he had inferred, she was roaming around in the night soliciting for the Mental Health Resort, in violation of law.

The Health Resort, the last refuge for deserters and misfits, had reached out and put its hand on his shoulder.

He felt weak. He felt very morbid and shaky, as if he were running a fever: a low current of somewhat moist energy that could not be shaken off.

'Mr Purcell,' Doris' voice came through the open door. 'There's a return call in for you. The phone is taking it right now.'

'OK, Doris,' he said. With effort he roused himself from his thoughts and reached to snap on the phone. The tape obligingly skipped back and restarted itself, spewing the recorded call.

'Ten-o-five. Click. Zeeeeeeeeeeeeee! Mr Purcell.' Now a smooth, urbane female voice appeared. With further pessimism he recognized it. 'This is Mrs Sue Frost, answering your call of earlier this morning. I'm sorry I was not in when you called, Mr Purcell.' A pause. 'I am fully sympathetic with your situation. I can easily understand the position you're in.' Another pause, this one somewhat longer. 'Of course, Mr Purcell, you surely must realize that the offer of the directorship was predicated on the assumption that you were available for the job.'

The mechanism jumped to its next thirty-second segment.

'Ten-o-six. Click. Zeeeeeeeeeeeee! To go on.' Mrs Frost cleared her throat. 'It strikes us that a week is rather a long time, in view of the difficult status of Telemedia. There is no acting Director, since, as you're aware, Mr Mavis has already resigned. We hesitate to request a postponement of that resignation, but perhaps it will be necessary. Our suggestion is that you take until Saturday at the latest to decide. Understand, we're fully sympathetic with your situation, and we don't wish to rush you. But Telemedia is a vital trust, and it would be in the public interest that your decision come as quickly as possible. I'll expect to hear from you, then.'

Click, the mechanism went. The rest of the tape was blank.

From the tone of Mrs Frost's message Allen inferred that he had got an official statement of the Committee's position. He could imagine the tape being played back at an inquiry. It was for the record, and then some. Four point five days, he thought. Four point five days to decide what he was and what he ought to be.

Picking up the phone, he started to dial, then changed his mind. Calling from the Agency was too risky. Instead, he left the office.

'Going out again, Mr Purcell?' Doris asked, at her own desk.

'I'll be back shortly. Going over to the commissary for some supplies.' He tapped his coat pocket. 'Things Janet asked me to pick up.'

As soon as he was out of the Mogentlock Building he stepped into a public phone booth. Staring vacantly, he dialed.

'Mental Health Resort,' a bureaucratic, but friendly voice answered in his ear.

'Is there a Gretchen Malparto there?'

Time passed. 'Miss Malparto has left the Resort temporarily. Would you like to speak to Doctor Malparto?'

Obscurely nettled, Allen said: 'Her husband?'

'Doctor Malparto is Miss Malparto's brother. Who is calling, please?'

'I want an appointment,' Allen said. 'Business problems.'

'Yes, sir.' The rustle of papers. 'Your name, sir?'

He hesitated and then invented. 'I'll be in under the name Coates.'

'Yes, sir, Mr Coates.' There was no further questioning on that point. 'Would tomorrow at nine a.m. be satisfactory?'

He started to agree, and then remembered the block meeting. 'Better make it Thursday.'

'Thursday at nine,' the girl said briskly. 'With Doctor Malparto. Thank you very much for calling.'

Feeling a little better, Allen returned to the Agency.

7

In the highly moral society of 2114 A.D., the weekly block meetings operated on the stagger system. Wardens from surrounding housing units were able to sit at each, forming a board of which the indigenous warden was chairman. Since Mrs Birmingham was the warden in the Purcells' block, she, of the assembled middle-aged ladies, occupied the raised seat. Her compatriots, in flowered silk dresses, filled chairs on each side of her across the platform.

'I hate this room,' Janet said, pausing at the door.

Allen did, too. Down here on the first level of the housing unit, in this one large chamber, all the local Leagues, Committees, Clubs, Boards, Associations, and Orders met. The room smelled of stale sunlight, dust, and the infinite layers of paperwork that had piled up over the years. Here, official nosing and snooping originated. In this room a man's business was everybody's business. Centuries of Christian confessional culminated when the block assembled to explore its members' souls.

As always, there were more people than space. Many had to stand, and they filled the corners and aisles. The air conditioning system moaned and reshuffled the cloud of smoke. Allen was always puzzled by the smoke, since nobody seemed to have a cigarette and smoking was forbidden. But there it was. Perhaps it, like the shadow of purifying fire, was an accumulation from the past.

His attention fixed itself on the pack of juveniles. They were here, the earwig-like sleuths. Each juvenile was a foot and a half long. The species scuttled close to the ground – or up vertical surfaces – at ferocious speed, and they noticed everything. These juveniles were inactive. The wardens had unlocked the metal hulls and dug out the report tapes. The juveniles remained inert during the meeting, and then they were put back into service.

There was something sinister in these metal informers, but there was also something heartening. The juveniles did not accuse; they only reported what they heard and saw. They couldn't color their information and they couldn't make it up. Since the victim was indicted mechanically he was safe from hysterical hearsay, from malice and paranoia. But there could be no question of guilt; the evidence was already in. The issue to be settled here was merely the severity of moral lapse. The victim couldn't protest that he had been unjustly accused; all he could protest was his bad luck at having been overheard.

On the platform Mrs Birmingham held the agenda and looked to see if everybody had arrived. Failure to arrive was in itself a lapse. Apparently he and Janet completed the group; Mrs Birmingham signalled, and the meeting began.

'I guess we don't get to sit,' Janet murmured, as the door closed after them. Her face was pinched with anxiety; for her the weekly block meeting was a catastrophe which she met with hopelessness and despair. Each week she anticipated denouncement and downfall, but it never came. Years had gone by, and she had still not officially erred. But that only convinced her that doom was saving itself up for one grand spree.

'When they call me,' Allen said softly, 'you keep your mouth shut. Don't get in on either side. The less said the better chance I have.'

She glared at him with suffering. 'They'll tear you apart. Look at them.' She swept in the whole room. 'They're just waiting to get at somebody.'

'Most of them are bored and wish they were out.' As a matter of fact, several men were reading their morning newspapers. 'So take it easy. If nobody leaps to defend me it'll die down and maybe I'll get off with a verbal reprimand.' Assuming, of course, that nothing was in about the statue.

'We will first undertake the case of Miss J.E.,' Mrs Birmingham stated. Miss J.E. was Julie Ebberley, and everybody in the room knew her. Julie had been up time and again, but somehow she managed to hang onto the lease willed her by her family. Scared and wide-eyed, she now mounted the defendant's stage, a young blonde-haired girl with long legs and an intriguing bosom. Today she wore a modest print dress and low-heeled slippers. Her hair was tied back in a girlish knot.

'Miss J.E.,' Mrs Birmingham declared, 'did willingly and knowingly on the night of October 6, 2114, engage with a man in a vile enterprise.'

In most cases a 'vile enterprise' was sex. Allen half-closed his eyes and prepared to endure the session. A shuffling murmur ran through the room; the newspapers were put aside. Apathy dwindled. To Allen this was the offensive part: the leering need to hear a confession down to the last detail – a need which masqueraded as righteousness.

The first question came instantly. 'Was this the same man as the other times?'

Miss J.E. colored. 'Y-yes,' she admitted.

'Weren't you warned? Hadn't you been told in this very room to get yourself home at a decent hour and act like a good girl?'

In all probability this was now a different questioner. The voice was synthetic, issuing from a wall speaker. To preserve the aura of justice, questions were piped through a common channel, broken down and reassembled without characteristic timbre. The result was an impersonal accuser, who, when a sympathetic questioner appeared, became suddenly and a little oddly a defender.

'Let's hear what this "vile enterprise" was,' Allen said, and, as always, was revolted to hear his voice boom out dead and characterless. 'This may be a furor about nothing.'

On the platform Mrs Birmingham peered distastefully down,

seeking to identify the questioner. Then she read from the summary. 'Miss J.E. did willingly in the bathtub of the community bathroom of her housing unit – this unit – copulate.'

'I'd call that something,' the voice said, and then the dogs were loose. The accusations fell thick and fast, a blur of lascivious racket.

Beside Allen his wife huddled against him. He could feel her dread and he put his arm around her. In awhile the voice would be tearing at him.

At nine-fifteen the faction vaguely defending Miss J.E. seemed to have gained an edge. After a conference the council of block wardens released the girl with an oral reprimand, and she slipped gratefully from the room. Mrs Birmingham again arose with the agenda.

With relief Allen heard his own initials. He walked forward, listening to the charges, glad to get it over with. The juvenile – thank God – had reported about as expected.

'Mr A.P.,' Mrs Birmingham declared, 'did on the night of October 7, 2114, at 11:30 p.m., arrive home in a drunken state and did fall on the front steps of the housing unit and in so doing utter a morally objectionable word.'

Allen climbed the stage, and the session began.

There was always the danger that somewhere in the room a citizen waited with a deeply-buried quirk, a deposit of hate nourished and hoarded for just such an occasion as this. During the years that he had leased in this housing unit Allen might easily have slighted some nameless soul; the human mind being what it was, he might have set off a tireless vengeance by stepping ahead in line, failing to nod, treading on foot, or the like.

But as he looked around he saw no special emotion. Nobody glowered demonically, and nobody, except for his stricken wife, even appeared interested.

Considering the shallowness of the charge he had good reason to feel optimistic. All in all, he was well off. Realizing this, he faced his composite accuser cheerfully.

'Mr Purcell,' it said, 'you haven't been up before us in quite a spell.' It corrected: 'Mr A.P., I meant.'

39

'Not for several years,' he answered.

'How much had you had to drink?'

'Three glasses of wine.'

'And you were drunk on that?' The voice answered itself: 'That's the indictment.' It haggled, and then a clear question emerged. 'Where did you get drunk?'

Not wishing to volunteer material, Allen kept his answer brief. 'At Hokkaido.' Mrs Birmingham was aware of that, so evidently it didn't matter.

'What were you doing there?' the voice asked, and then it said: 'That's not relevant. That has nothing to do with it. Stick to the facts. What he did before he was drunk doesn't matter.'

To Allen it sounded like Janet. He let it battle on.

'Of course it matters. The importance of the act depends on the motives behind it. Did he mean to get drunk? Nobody *means* to get drunk. I'm sure I wouldn't know.'

Allen said: 'It was on an empty stomach, and I'm not used to liquor in any form.'

'What about the word he used? Yes, what about it? Well, we don't even know what it was. I think we're just as well off. Why, are you convinced he's the sort of man who would use words "like that"? All I mean is that knowing the particular word doesn't affect the situation.'

'And I was tired,' Allen added. Years of work with media had taught him the shortest routes to the Morec mind. 'Although it was Sunday I had spent the day at the office. I suppose I did more than was good for my health, but I like to have my desk clear on Monday.'

'A regular little gentleman,' the voice said. It retorted at once: 'With manners enough to keep personalities out of this. Bravo,' it said. 'That's telling him. Probably her.' And then, from the chaos of minds, a sharp sentiment took shape. As nearly as Allen could tell, it was one person. 'This is a mockery. Mr Purcell is one of our most distinguished members. As most of us know, Mr Purcell's Agency supplies a good deal of the material used by Telemedia. Are we supposed to believe that a man involved in the main-tenance of society's ethical standards is, himself, morally defect-ive? What does that say about our society in general? This a paradox is. It is just such high-minded men, devoted to public service, who set by their own examples our standards of conduct.'

Surprised, Allen peered across the room at his wife. Janet seemed bewildered. And the choice of words was not characteristic of her. Evidently it was somebody else.

'Mr Purcell's family leased here several decades,' the voice continued. 'Mr Purcell was born here. During his lifetime many persons have come and gone. Few of us have maintained a lease as long as he has. How many of us were here in this room before Mr Purcell? Think that over. The purpose of these sessions is not the humbling of the mighty. Mr Purcell isn't up there so we can deride and ridicule him. Some of us seem to imagine the more respectable a person is the more reason to attack him. When we attack Mr Purcell we attack our better selves. And there's no percentage in that.'

Allen felt embarrassed.

'These meetings,' the voice went on, 'operate on the idea that a man is morally responsible to his community. That's a good idea. But his community is also morally responsible to him. If it's going to ask him to come up and confess his sins, it's got to give him something in return. It's got to give him its respect and support. It should realize that having a citizen like Mr Purcell up here is a privilege. Mr Purcell's life is devoted to our welfare and the improvement of our society. If he wants to drink three glasses of wine once in his life and say one morally objectionable word, I think he should be allowed to. It's OK by me.'

There was silence. The roomful of people was cowed by piety. Nobody dared speak.

On the stage, Allen sat wishing somebody would attack. His embarrassment had become shame. The eulogizer was making a mistake; he didn't have the full picture.

'Wait a minute,' Allen protested. 'Let's get one thing straight. What I did was wrong. I haven't got any more right to get drunk and blaspheme than anybody else.'

The voice said: 'Let's pass on to the next case. There doesn't seem to be anything here.'

On the platform the middle-aged ladies conferred, and presently composed their verdict. Mrs Birmingham arose.

'The block-neighbors of Mr A.P. take this opportunity to reprimand him for his conduct of the night of October 7, but feel that in view of his excellent prior record no disciplinary action is indicated. You may step down, Mr A.P.'

Allen stepped down and rejoined his wife. Janet squeezed against him, wildly happy. 'Bless him, whoever he was.'

'I don't deserve it,' Allen said, disturbed.

'You do. Of course you do.' Her eyes shone recklessly. 'You're a wonderful person.'

Not far off, at one of the tables, was a mild little elderly fellow with thinning gray hair and a formal, set smile. Mr Wales glanced at Allen, then turned immediately away.

'That's the guy,' Allen decided. 'Wales.'

'Are you sure?'

The next accused was up on the stage, and Mrs Birmingham began reading the indictment. 'Mrs R.M. did knowingly and willingly on the afternoon of October 9, 2114, in a public place and in the presence of both men and women, take the name of the Lord in vain.'

The voice said: 'What a waste of time.' And the controversy was on.

After the meeting Allen approached Wales. The man had lingered outside the door, as if expecting him. Allen had noticed him in the hall a few times, but he didn't recall ever having said more than good morning to him.

'That was you,' Allen said.

They shook hands. 'I'm glad I could help you out, Mr Purcell.' Wales' voice was drab, perfectly ordinary. 'I saw you speak up for that girl. You always look out for the people up there. I said, if he ever gets up I'll do the same for him. We all like and respect you, Mr Purcell.'

'Thanks,' Allen said awkwardly.

As he and Janet walked back upstairs, Janet said: 'What's the matter?' She was in a delirium at having escaped from the meeting. 'Why do you look so glum?'

'I feel glum,' he said.

Doctor Malparto said: 'Good morning, Mr Coates. Please take off your coat and sit down. I want you to be comfortable.'

And then he felt strange and ill, because the man facing him was not 'Mr Coates' but Allen Purcell. Hurriedly getting to his feet Malparto excused himself and went out into the corridor. He was shaking with excitement. Behind him, Purcell looked vaguely puzzled, a tall, good-looking, rather overly-serious man in his late twenties, wearing a heavy overcoat. Here he was, the man Malparto had been expecting. But he hadn't expected him so soon.

With his key he unlocked his file and brought out Purcell's dossier. He glanced over the contents as he returned to his office. The report was as cryptic as before. Here was his prized-gram, and the irriducible syndrome remained. Malparto sighed with delight.

'I beg your pardon, Mr Purcell,' he said, closing the door after him. 'Sorry to keep you waiting.'

His patient frowned and said: 'Let's keep it "Coates." Or has that old wheeze about professional confidence gone by the boards?'

'Mr Coates, then.' Malparto reseated himself and put on his glasses. 'Mr Coates, I'll be frank. I've been expecting you. Your encephalogram came into my hands a week or so ago, and I had a Dickson report drawn on it. The profile is unique. I'm very much interested in you, and it's a matter of deep personal satisfaction to be permitted to handle your—' He coughed. 'Problem.' He had started to say *case*.

In the comfortable leather-covered chair, Mr Coates shifted restlessly. He lit a cigarette, scowled, rubbed at the crease of his trousers. 'I need help. It's one of the drawbacks of Morec that nobody gets help; they get cast out as defective.'

Malparto nodded in agreement.

'Also,' Mr Coates said, 'your sister came after me.'

To Malparto this was discouraging. Not only had Gretchen meddled, but she had meddled wisely. Mr Coates would have appeared eventually, but Gretchen had sawed the interval in half. He wondered what she had got out of it.

'Didn't you know that?' Mr Coates asked.

He decided to be honest. 'No, I didn't. But it's of no consequence.' He rattled through the report. 'Mr Coates, I'd like you to tell me in your own words what you feel your problem is.'

'Job problems.'

'In particular?'

Mr Coates chewed his lip. 'Director of T-M. It was offered to me this Monday.'

'You're currently operating an independent Research Agency?' Malparto consulted his notes. 'When do you have to decide?'

'By the day after tomorrow.'

'Very interesting.'

'Isn't it?' Mr Coates said.

'That doesn't give you long. Do you feel you can decide?'

'No.'

'Why not?'

His patient hesitated.

'Are you worried that a juvenile might be hiding in my closet?' Malparto smiled reassuringly. 'This is the only spot in our blessed civilization where juveniles are forbidden.'

'So I've heard.'

'A fluke of history. It seems that Major Streiter's wife had a predilection for psychoanalysts. A Fifth Avenue Jungian cured her partially-paralysed right arm. You know her type.'

Mr Coates nodded.

'So,' Malparto said, 'when the Committee Government was set up and the land was nationalized, we were permitted to keep our deeds. We – that is, the Psych Front left over from the war. Streiter was a canny person. Unusual ability. He saw the necessity—'

Mr Coates said: 'Sunday night somebody pulled a switch in my head. So I japed the statue of Major Streiter. That's why I can't accept the T-M directorship.'

'Ah,' Malparto said, and his eyes fastened on the -gram with its irreducible core. He had a sensation of hanging head downward

44

over an ocean; his lungs seemed filled with dancing foam. Carefully he removed his glasses and polished them with his handkerchief.

Beyond his office window lay the city, flat except for the Morec spire set dead-center. The city radiated in concentric zones, careful lines and swirls that intersected in an orderly manner. Across the planet, Doctor Malparto thought. Like the hide of a vast mammal half-submerged in mud. Half-buried in the drying clay of a stern and puritanical morality.

'You were born here,' he said. In his hands was the information, the history of his patient; he leafed through the pages.

'We all were,' Mr Coates said.

'You met your wife in the colonies. What were you doing on Bet-4?'

His patient said: 'Supervising a packet. I was consultant to the old Wing-Miller Agency. I wanted a packet rooted in the experience of the agricultural colonists.'

'You liked it there?'

'In a way. It was like the frontier. I remember a white-washed board farmhouse. That was her family's . . . her father's.' He was quiet a moment. 'He and I used to argue. He edited a small-town newspaper. All night – arguing and drinking coffee.'

'Did—' Malparto consulted the dossier. 'Did Janet participate?'

'Not much. She listened. I think she was afraid of her father. Maybe a little afraid of me.'

'You were twenty-five?'

'Yes,' Mr Coates said. 'Janet was twenty-two.'

Malparto, reading the information, said: 'Your own father was dead. Your mother was alive, still, was she not?'

'She died in 2111,' Mr Coates said. 'Not much later.'

Malparto put on his video and audio tape transports. 'May I keep a record of what we say?'

His patient pondered. 'You might as well. You've got me anyhow.'

'In my power? Like a wizard? Hardly. I've got your problem; by telling me you've transferred it to me.'

Mr Coates seemed to relax. 'Thanks,' he said.

45

'Consciously,' Malparto said, 'you don't know why you japed the statue; the motive is buried down deep. In all probability the statue episode forms part of a larger event – stretching, perhaps, over years. We'll never be able to understand it alone; its meaning lies in the circumstances preceding it.'

His patient grimaced. 'You're the wizard.'

'I wish you wouldn't think of me like that.' He was offended by what he identified as a lay stereotype; the man-in-the-street had come to regard the Resort analysts with a mixture of awe and dread, as if the Resort were a sort of temple and the analysts priests. As if there was some religious mumbo-jumbo involved; whereas, of course, it was all strictly scientific, in the best psycho-analytic tradition.

'Remember, Mr Coates,' he said, 'I can only help you if you wish to be helped.'

'How much is this going to cost?'

'An examination will be made of your income. You'll be charged according to your ability to pay.' This was characteristic of Morec training, this old Protestant frugality. Nothing must be wasted. A hard bargain must always be driven.

The Dutch Reformed Church, alive even in this troubled heretic . . . the power of that iron revolution that had crumbled the Age of Waste, put an end to 'sin and corruption,' and with it, leisure and peace of mind – the ability simply to sit down and take things easy. How must it have been? he wondered. In the days when idleness was permitted. The golden age, in a sense: but a curious mixture, too, an odd fusion of the liberty of the Renaissance plus the strictures of the Reformation. Both had been there; the two elements struggling in each individual. And, at last, final victory for the Dutch hellfire-preachers . . .

Mr Coates said: 'Let's see some of those drugs you people use. And those light and high-frequency gadgetry.'

'In due time.'

'Good Lord, I have to tell Mrs Frost by Saturday!'

Malparto said: 'Let's be realistic. No fundamental change can be worked in forty-eight hours. We ran out of miracles several centuries ago. This will be a long, arduous process with many setbacks.'

46

Mr Coates stirred fitfully.

'You tell me the japery is central,' Malparto said. 'So let's start there. What were you doing just prior to your entrance into the Park?'

'I visited a couple of friends.'

Malparto caught something in his patient's voice, and he said: 'Where? Here in Newer York?'

'In Hokkaido.'

'Does anybody live there?' He was amazed.

'A few people. They don't live long.'

'Have you ever been there before?'

'Now and then. I get ideas for packets.'

'And before that. What were you doing?'

'I worked at the Agency most of the day. Then I got – bored.'

'You went from the Agency directly to Hokkaido?'

His patient started to nod. And then he stopped, and a dark, intricate expression crossed his face. 'No. I walked around for awhile. I forgot about that. I remember visiting—' He paused for a long time. 'A commissary. To get some 3.2 beer. But why would I want beer? I don't particularly like beer.'

'Did anything happen?'

Mr Coates stared at him. 'I can't remember.'

Malparto made a notation.

'I left the Agency. And then a haze closes over the whole d—n thing. At least half an hour is cut out.'

Rising to his feet Malparto pressed a key on his desk intercom. 'Would you ask two therapists to step in here, please? And I'm not to be disturbed until further notice. Cancel my next appointment. When my sister comes in I'd like to see her. Yes, let her by. Thanks.' He closed the key.

Mr Coates, agitated, said: 'What now?'

'Now you get your wish.' Unlocking the supply closet he began wheeling out equipment. 'The drugs and gadgetry. So we can dig down and find out what happened between the time you left the Agency and the time you reached Hokkaido.'

9

The silence depressed him. He was alone in the Mogentlock Building, working in the center of a vast tomb. Outside, the sky was cloudy and overcast. At eight-thirty he gave up.

Eight-thirty. Not ten.

Closing his desk he left the Agency and went out onto the dark sidewalk. Nobody was in sight. The lanes were deserted; on Sunday evening there was no flood of commuters. He saw only the shapes of housing units, closed-up commissaries, the hostile sky.

His historical research had acquainted him with the vanished phenomenon of the neon sign. Now he would have wished for a few to break the monotony. The garish, blaring racket of commercials, ads, blinking signs – it had disappeared. Swept aside like a bundle of faded circus posters: to be pulped by history for the printing of textbooks.

Ahead, as he walked sightlessly along the lane, was a cluster of lights. The cluster drew him, and presently he found himself at an autofac receiving station.

The lights formed a hollow ring rising a few hundred feet. Within the circle an autofac ship was lowering itself, a tubby cylinder pitted and corroded by its trip. There were no humans aboard, and there were none at its point of origin. Nor was the receiving equipment manual. When the robot controls had landed the ship, other self-regulating machines would unload it, check the shipment, cart the boxes into the commissary, and store them. Only with the clerk and the customer did the human element come into it.

At the moment a small band of sidewalk superintendents was gathered around the station, following operations. As usual, the bulk of watchers were teenagers. Hands in their pockets, the boys gazed up raptly. Time passed and none of them stirred. None of them spoke. Nobody came and nobody went.

'Big,' one boy finally observed. He was tall, with dull red hair, pebbled skin. 'The ship.'

'Yes,' Allen agreed, also looking up. 'I wonder where it's from,' he said awkwardly. As far as he was concerned the industrial process was like the movement of planets: it functioned automatically and that was as it should be.

'It's from Bellatrix 7,' the boy stated, and two of his mute companions nodded. 'Tungsten products. They been unloading light-globes all day. Bellatrix's only a slave system. None of them habitable.'

'Nuts to Bellatrix,' a companion spoke up.

Allen was puzzled. 'Why?'

'Because you can't live there.'

'What do you care?'

The boys regarded him with contempt. 'Because we're going,' one of them croaked finally.

'Where?'

Contempt turned to disgust; the group of boys edged away from him. '*Out.* Where it's open. Where something's going on.'

The red-headed boy told him: 'On Sirius 9 they grow walnuts. Almost like here. You can't taste the difference. A whole planet of walnut trees. And on Sirius 8 they grow oranges. Only, the oranges died.'

'Mealy bug blight,' a companion said gloomily. 'Got all the oranges.'

The red-headed boy said: 'I'm personally going to Orionus. There they breed a real pig you can't tell from the original. I defy you to tell the difference; I defy you.'

'But that's away from center,' Allen said. 'Be realistic – it's taken your families decades to lease this close.'

'— —,' one of the boys said bitterly, and then they had melted away, leaving Allen to ponder an obvious fact.

Morec wasn't natural. As a way of life it had to be learned. That was the fact, and the unhappiness of the boys was there to remind him.

The commissary, to which the autofac receiving station belonged, was still open. He stepped through the entrance, reaching, as he did so, for his wallet.

'Sure,' the invisible clerk said, as the buy card was punched out. 'But only the 3.2 stuff. You really want to drink that?' The

49

window displaying the beer bottles glowed along the wall of items. 'It's made from hay.'

Once, a thousand years ago, he had punched the slot for 3.2 beer and got a fifth of scotch. God knew where it came from. Perhaps it had survived the war, had been discovered by a robot storekeeper and automatically placed in the single official rack. It had never happened again, but he continued to punch the slot, hoping in a wan, childish way. Evidently it was one of the implausible foul-ups that occurred even in the perfect society.

'Refund,' he requested, setting the unopened bottle on the counter. 'I've changed my mind.'

'I told you,' the clerk said, and restored Allen's buy card. Allen stood for a moment, empty-handed, his mind flat with futility. Then he walked outside again.

A moment later he was climbing the ramp to the tiny roof-top field used by the Agency for rush flights. The sliver was parked there, locked up in its shed.

'And that's all?' Malparto asked. He clicked off the overhanging trellis of wires and lenses that had been focussed on his patient. 'Nothing else happened between the time you left your office and the time you started for Hokkaido?'

'Nothing else.' Mr Coates lay prone on the table, his arms at his sides. Above him the two technicians examined their meters.

'That was the incident you couldn't remember?'

'Yes, the boys at the autofac station.'

'You were despondent?'

'I was,' Mr Coates agreed. His voice lacked emotion; under the blanket of drugs his personality had receded to diffusion.

'Why?'

'Because it was unfair.'

Malparto saw no point involved; the incident meant nothing to him. He had expected a sensational revelation of murder or copulation or excitement or all three together.

'Let's go on,' he said reluctantly. 'The Hokkaido episode itself.' Then he lingered. 'The incident with the boys. You genuinely feel it was crucial?'

'Yes,' Mr Coates said.

Malparto shrugged, and signalled to his technicians to restart the trellis of paraphernalia.

Darkness lay all around. The sliver dropped toward the island below, guiding itself, speaking to itself mechanically. He rested his head against the seat and closed his eyes. The *whoosh* of descent lessened, and, on the signal board, a blue light blinked.

There was no field to locate; all Hokkaido was a field. He tripped the landing release, and the ship coasted of its own accord across the surface of ash. Eventually the pattern of Sugermann's transmitter was intercepted and the ship changed its course. The pattern led it in and brought it down. With a faint bump and a few rattles the ship eased to a stop. Now the only sound was the hum of batteries recharging.

Allen opened the door and stepped haltingly out. The ash sank under his feet; it was like standing on mush. The ash was complicated, a mixture of organic and inorganic compounds. A fusion of people and their possessions into a common gray-black blur. During the postwar years the ash had made good mortar.

To his right was an insignificant glow. He walked toward it, and ultimately it became Tom Gates waving a flashlight.

'Morec to you,' Gates said. He was a bony, pop-eyed shrimp with uncombed hair and a nose bent like a macaw's.

'How're things?' Allen asked, as he plodded after the gaunt shape toward the neck of the underground shelter. Built during the war, the shelter was still intact. Gates and Sugermann had reinforced and improved it, Gates pounding nails and Sugermann overseeing.

'I was expecting Sugie. It's almost dawn on this side; he's been out all night buying supplies.' Gates giggled, a nervous high-pitched twitter. 'Trading big. We got a good hand, these days. Plenty of stuff people want; don't kid yourself.'

The stairs brought them down to the shelter's main room. It was a litter of books, furniture, paintings, cans and boxes and jars of food, carpets and bric-a-brac and just plain junk. The phonograph was blaring a Chicago version of 'I Can't Get Started.' Gates turned it down, grinning.

'Make yourself at home.' He tossed a box of crackers to Allen, and then a wedge of cheddar cheese. 'Not hot – perfectly safe. Man, we've been digging, digging. Under all this ash, way down. Gates and Sugermann, archeologists for hire.'

Remnants of the old. Tons of usable, partly usable, and ruined debris, objects of priceless worth, trinkets, indiscriminate trash. Allen seated himself on a carton of glassware. Vases and cups and tumblers and cut crystal.

'Pack rats,' he said, examining a chipped bowl designed by some long-dead craftsman of the twentieth century. On the bowl was a design: a faun and hunter. 'Not bad.'

'Sell it to you,' Gates offered. 'Five bucks.'

'Too much.'

'Three bucks, then. We've got to move this stuff. Fast turnover, assure profit.' Gates giggled happily. 'What do you want? Bottle of Beringer's chablis? One thousand dollars. Copy of the *Decameron*? Two thousand dollars. Electric waffle iron?' He computed. 'Depends on if you want the kind that becomes a sandwich grill. That's more.'

'Nothing for me,' Allen murmured. Before him was a huge pile of moldering newspapers, magazines, books, tied with brown cord. *Saturday Evening Post*, the top one read.

'Six years of the *Post*,' Gates said. 'From 1947 to 1952. Lovely condition. Say, fifteen bills.' He pawed into an opened stack beside the *Posts*, ripping and shredding violently. 'Here's a sweet item. *Yale Review*. One of those "little" magazines. Got stuff on Truman Capote, James Jones.' His eyes sparkled slyly. 'Plenty of sex.'

Allen examined a faded, water-logged book. It was cheaply bound, a bulging pulp with stained pages.

THE INDEFATIGABLE VIRGIN
Jack Woodsby

Opening at random he came across an absorbing paragraph.

'. . . Her breasts were like two cones of white marble bulging within the torn covering of her thin silk dress. As he pulled her against him he could feel the hot panting need of her wonderful body. Her eyes were half-shut and she was moaning faintly. "Please," she gasped, trying feebly to push him away. Her dress slipped entirely aside, revealing the pulsing fullness of her taut, firm flesh . . .'

'Good grief,' Allen said.

'Fine book,' Gates remarked, squatting down beside him. 'Lots more. Here.' He dug out another and pushed it at Allen. 'Read.'

I, THE KILLER

The author's name was blurred by time and decay. Opening the tattered paper-covered book, Allen read:

'. . . Again I shot her in the groin. Guts and blood spilled out, soaking through her torn skirt. The floor under my shoes was slippery with her gore. I accidentally crushed one of her mangled breasts under my heel, but what the hell, she was dead . . .'

Bending down, Allen pulled out a fat, mildewed, gray-bound book and opened it.

'. . . Stephen Dedalus watched through the webbed window the lapidary's fingers prove a time-dulled chain. Dust webbed the window and the showtrays. Dust darkened the toiling fingers with their vulture nails . . .'

'That's a hot one,' Gates said, peering over his shoulder. 'Go on, look through it. At the end especially.'

'Why is this here?' Allen asked.

Gates clapped his hands together and writhed. 'Man, that's *the* one. That's the spiciest of them all. You know how much I get for a copy of that? Ten thousand dollars!' He tried to grab the book, but Allen hung onto it.

'. . . Dust slept on dull coils of bronze and silver, lozenges of cinnabar, on rubies, leprous and wine-dark stones . . .'

53

Allen put down the book. 'That's not bad.' It gave him a queer feeling, and he reread the passage carefully.

There was a scraping at the stairs and Sugermann entered. 'What's not bad?' He saw the book and nodded. 'James Joyce. Excellent writer. *Ulysses* brings us a good deal, these days. More than Joyce himself ever got.' He tossed down his armload. 'Tom, there's a shipload up on the surface. Don't let me forget. We can get it down later.' He, a heavy-set, round-faced man, with a stubble of bluish beard, began peeling off his wool overcoat.

Examining the copy of *Ulysses*, Allen said: 'Why is this book with the others? It's entirely different.'

'Has the same words,' Sugermann said. He lit a cigarette and stuck it in a carved, ornate ivory holder. 'How are you these days, Mr Purcell? How's the Agency?'

'Fine,' he said. The book bothered him. 'But this—'

'This book is still pornography,' Sugermann said: 'Joyce, Hemingway. Degenerate trash. The Major's first Book Committee listed *Ulysses* on the hex-sheet back in 1988. Here.' Laboriously, he scooped up a handful of books; first one and then another was tossed into Allen's lap. 'A bunch more of them. Novels of the twentieth century. All gone, now. Banned. Burned. Destroyed.'

'But what was the purpose of these books? Why are they lumped with the junk? They weren't once, were they?'

Sugermann was amused, and Gates cackled and slapped his knee.

'What kind of Morec did they teach?' Allen demanded.

'They didn't,' Sugermann said. 'These particular novels even taught *un*Morec.'

'You've read these?' Allen scanned the volume of *Ulysses*. His interest and bewilderment grew. 'Why? What did you find?'

Sugermann considered. 'These, as discriminated from the others, are real books.'

'What's that mean?'

'Hard to say. They're about something.' A smile spread across Sugermann's face. 'I'm an egghead, Purcell. I'd tell you these books are literature. So better not ask me.'

'These guys,' Gates explained, breathing into Allen's face,

'wrote it all down, the way it was back in the Age of Waste.' He hammered a book with his fist. 'This tells. Everything's here.'

'But these ought to be preserved,' Allen said. 'They shouldn't be tossed in with the trash. We need them as historical records.'

'Certainly,' Sugermann said. 'So we'll know what life was like, then.'

'They're valuable.'

'Very valuable.'

Angrily, Allen said: 'They tell the truth!'

Sugermann bellowed with laughter. He got out a pocket handkerchief and wiped his eyes. 'That's so, Purcell. They tell the truth, the one and only absolute truth.' Suddenly he stopped laughing. 'Tom, give him the Joyce book. As a present from you and me.'

Gates was appalled. 'But *Ulysses* is worth a hundred bills!'

'Give it to him.' Sugermann sank into a growling, acrid stupor. 'He should have it.'

Allen said: 'I can't take it; it's worth too much.' And, he realized, he couldn't pay for it. He didn't have ten thousand dollars. And, he also realized, he wanted the book.

Sugermann glared at him for a long, disconcerting time. 'Morec,' he muttered at last. 'No gift-giving. OK, Allen. I'm sorry.' He roused himself and went into the next room. 'How about a glass of sherry?'

'That's good stuff,' Gates said. 'From Spain. The real thing.'

Re-emerging with the half-empty bottle, Sugermann found three glasses and filled them. 'Drink up, Purcell. To Goodness, Truth, and—' He considered. 'Morality.'

They drank.

Malparto made a final note and then signalled his technicians. The office lights came on as the trellis was wheeled away.

On the table the patient blinked, stirred, moved feebly.

'And then you came back?' Malparto asked.

'Yes,' Mr Coates said. 'I drank three glasses of sherry and then I flew back to Newer York.'

'And nothing else happened?'

Mr Coates, with an effort, sat up. 'I came back, parked the

sliver, got the tools and bucket of red paint, and japed the statue. I left the empty paint can on a bench and walked home.'

The first session was over and Malparto had learned absolutely nothing. Nothing had happened to his patient either before or at Hokkaido; he had met some boys, tried to buy a fifth of Scotch, had seen a book. That was all. It was senseless.

'Have you ever been Psi-tested?' Malparto asked.

'No.' His patient squinted with pain. 'Those drugs of yours gave me a headache.'

'I have a few routine tests I'd like to give you. Perhaps next time; it's a trifle late, today.' He had decided to cease the recall-therapy. There was no value in bringing to the surface past incidents and forgotten experiences. From now on he would work with the mind of Mr Coates, not with its contents.

'Learn anything?' Mr Coates asked, rising stiffly to his feet.

'A few things. One question. I'm curious to know the effect of this japery. In your opinion—'

'It gets me into trouble.'

'I don't mean on you. I mean on the Morec Society.'

Mr Coates considered. 'None. Except that it gives the police something to do. And the newspapers have something to print.'

'How about the people who see the japed statue?'

'Nobody sees it; they've got it boarded up.' Mr Coates rubbed his jaw. 'Your sister saw it. And some of the Cohorts saw it; they were rounded up to guard it.'

Malparto made a note of that.

'Gretchen said that some of the Cohorts laughed. It was japed in an odd way; I suppose you've heard.'

'I've heard,' Malparto said. Later, he could get the facts from his sister. 'So they laughed. Interesting.'

'Why?'

'Well, the Cohorts are the storm-troopers of the Morec Society. They go out and do the dirty work. They're the teeth, the vigilantes. And they don't usually laugh.'

At the office door Mr Coates had paused. 'I don't see the point.'

Doctor Malparto was thinking: *precognition*. The ability to

56

anticipate the future. 'I'll see you Monday,' he said, getting out his appointment book. 'At nine. Will that be satisfactory?'

Mr Coates said that it was satisfactory, and then he set off glumly for work.

10

As he entered his office at the Agency, Doris appeared and said: 'Mr Purcell, something has happened. Harry Priar wants to tell you.' Priar, who headed the Agency's art department, was his pro-tem assistant, taking Fred Luddy's place.

Priar materialized, looking somber. 'It's about Luddy.'

'Isn't he gone?' Allen said, removing his coat. Malparto's drugs still affected him; his head ached and he felt dulled.

'He's gone,' Priar said. 'Gone to Blake-Moffet. We got a tip from T-M this morning, before you showed up.'

Allen groaned.

'He knows everything we've got on tap,' Priar continued. 'All the new packets, all the current ideas. That means Blake-Moffet has them.'

'Make an inventory,' Allen said. 'See what he took.' He settled drearily down at his desk. 'Let me know as soon as you're finished.'

A whole day was consumed by inventory-taking. At five the information was in and on his desk.

'Picked us clean,' Priar said. He admiringly shook his head. 'Must have spent hours. Of course we can attach the material, try to get it back through the claims court.'

'Blake-Moffet will fight for years,' Allen said, fooling with the long yellow pad. 'By the time we get the packets back they'll be obsolete. We'll have to dream up new ones. Better ones.'

'This is really tough,' Priar said. 'Nothing like this ever happened before. We've had Blake-Moffet pirate stuff; we've lost stuff; we've been beaten to ideas. But we never had anybody at top level go over bag and baggage.'

'We never fired anybody before,' Allen reminded him. He was thinking how much Luddy resented the firing. 'They can do us

57

real harm. And with Luddy there they probably will. Grudge stuff. We've never run into that before. The personal element. Bitter, to-the-death tangling.'

After Priar left, Allen got up and paced around his office. Tomorrow was Friday, his last full day to decide about the directorship of T-M. The statue problem would still be with him the rest of the week; as Malparto said, therapy would drag on indefinitely.

Either he went into T-M as he was now or he declined the job. On Saturday he would still be the same elusive personality, with the same switches to be pulled from deep within.

It was depressing to consider how little practical help the Health Resort had given him. Doctor Malparto was off in the clouds, thinking in terms of a lifetime of test-giving, reaction-measuring. And meanwhile the practical situation floundered. He had to make a decision, and without Malparto's help. Without, in effect, anybody's help. He was back where he started before Gretchen gave him the folded slip.

Picking up the phone he called his apartment.

'Hello,' Janet's voice came, laden with dread.

'This is the Mortuary League,' Allen said. 'It is my duty to inform you that your husband was sucked into the manifold of an autofac ship and never heard from again.' He examined his watch. 'At precisely five-fifteen.'

A terrible hushed silence, and then Janet said: 'But that's *now*.'

'If you listen,' Allen said, 'you can hear him breathing. He's not gone yet, but he's pretty far down.'

Janet said: 'You inhuman monster.'

'What I want to find out,' Allen said, 'is what are we doing this evening?'

'I'm taking Lena's kids to the history museum.' Lena was his wife's married sister. 'You're not doing anything.'

'I'll tag along,' he decided. 'I want to discuss something with you.'

'Discuss what?' she asked instantly.

'Same old thing.' The history museum would make as good a place as any; so many people passed through that no juvenile

58

would single them out. 'I'll be home around six. What's for dinner?'

'How about "steak"?'

'Fine,' he said, and hung up.

After dinner they walked over to Lena's and picked up the two kids. Ned was eight and Pat was seven, and they scurried excitedly along the twilight lane and up the steps of the museum. Allen and his wife came more slowly, hand in hand, saying little. For once the evening was pleasant. The sky was cloud-scattered but mild, and many people were out to enjoy themselves in the few ways open to them.

'Museums,' Allen said. 'And art exhibits. And concerts. And lectures. And discussions of public affairs.' He thought of Gates' phonograph playing 'I Can't Get Started,' the taste of sherry, and, beyond everything else, the litter of the twentieth century that had focalized in the water-soaked copy of *Ulysses*. 'And there's always Juggle.'

Clinging wistfully to him, Janet said: 'Sometimes I wish I was a kid again. Look at them go.' The children had vanished inside the museum. To them the exhibits were still interesting; they hadn't wearied of the intricate tableaux.

'Someday,' Allen said, 'I'd like to take you where you can relax.' He wondered where that would be. Certainly no place in the Morec scheme. Perhaps on some remote colony planet, when they had grown old and been discarded. 'Your childhood days again. Where you can take off your shoes and wriggle your toes.' As he had first found her: a shy, thin, very pretty girl, living with her nonleased family on bucolic Betelgeuse 4.

'Could we sometime take a trip?' Janet asked. 'Anywhere – maybe to a place where there's open country and streams and—' She broke off. 'And grass.'

The hub of the museum was its twentieth century exhibit. An entire white-stucco house had been painstakingly reconstructed, with sidewalk and lawn, garage and parked Ford. The house was complete with furniture, robot mannikins, hot food on the table, scented water in the tile bathtub. It walked, talked, sang and glowed. The exhibit revolved in such a way that every part of the

59

interior was visible. Visitors lined up at the circular railing and watched as Life in the Age of Waste rotated by.

Over the house was an illuminated sign:

HOW THEY LIVED

'Can I press the button?' Ned yammered, racing up to Allen. 'Let me press it; nobody's pressed it. It's time to press it.'

'Sure,' Allen said. 'Go ahead. Before somebody beats you to it.'

Ned scampered back, squeezed to the railing where Pat waited, and jabbed the button. The spectators gazed benignly at the lush house and furnishings, knowing what was coming. They were watching, for awhile, at least, the last of the house. They drank in the opulence: the stocks of canned food, the great freezer and stove and sink and washer and drier, the car that seemed made of diamonds and emeralds.

Over the exhibit the sign winked out. An ugly cloud of smoke rolled up, obscuring the house. Its lights dimmed, turned dull red, and dried up. The exhibit trembled, and, to the spectators, a rumble came, the lazy tremor of a subterranean wind.

When the smoke departed, the house was gone. All that remained of the exhibit was an expanse of broken bones. A few steel supports jutted, and bricks and sections of stucco lay strewn everywhere.

In the ruins of the cellar the surviving mannikins huddled over their pitiful possessions: a tank of decontaminated water, a dog they were stewing, a radio, medicines. Only three mannikins had survived, and they were haggard and ill. Their clothing was in shreds and their skins were seared with radiation burns.

Over this hemisphere of the exhibit the sign concluded:

AND DIED

'Gee,' Ned said, returning. 'How do they do that?'

'Simple,' Allen said. 'The house isn't really in there, on that stage. It's an image projected from above. They merely substitute the alternate image. When you press the button it starts the cycle.'

'Can I press it again?' Ned begged. 'Please, I want to press it again; I want to blow the house up again.'

As they wandered on, Allen said to his wife: 'I wanted you to enjoy dinner. Have you?'

She clutched his arm. 'Tell me.'

'The whirlwind is coming back to be reaped. And it's an angry whirlwind. Luddy took off with everything he could lay his hands on, right to Blake-Moffet. He's probably vice president, with what he brought.'

She nodded forlornly. 'Oh.'

'In a way, we're ruined. We have no backlog; all we are is a bunch of clever ideas. And Luddy took them . . . roughly, us for the next year. That's how far ahead we had it. But that isn't the real problem. As an official of Blake-Moffet he'll be in a position to get back at me. And he will. Let's face it; I showed Luddy up for a sycophant. And that isn't fun.'

'What are you going to do?'

'Defend myself, naturally. Luddy was a hard worker, competent, with a good sense of organization. But he wasn't original. He could take somebody else's idea – my idea – and milk a great deal from it. He used to build up whole packets from the smallest grain. But I have him on the creativity. So I can still run rings around Blake-Moffet, assuming I'm in the field a year from now.'

'You sound almost – cheerful.'

'Why not?' He shrugged. 'It merely makes a bad situation worse. Blake-Moffet have always been the inertial stone dragging us into the grave. Every time they project a boy-gets-good-girl packet they blow the breath of age on us. We have to struggle out from under the dust before we can move.' He pointed. 'Like that house.'

The opulent twentieth century house, with its Ford and Bendix washer, had reappeared. The cycle had returned to its source.

'How they lived,' Allen quoted. 'And died. That could be us. We're living now, but that doesn't mean anything.'

'What happened at the Resort?'

'Nothing. I saw the Analyst; I recalled; I got up and left. Next Monday I go back.'

'Can they help you?'

'Sure, given time.'

Janet asked: 'What are you going to do?'

'Take the job. Go to work as Director of Telemedia.'

'I see.' Then she asked: 'Why?'

'Several reasons. First, because I can do a good job.'

'What about the statue?'

'The statue isn't going away. Someday I'll find out why I japed it, but not by Saturday morning. Meanwhile, I'll have to live. And make decisions. By the way . . . the salary's about what I'm making now.'

'If you're at T-M can Luddy hurt you more?'

'He can hurt the Agency more, because I'll be gone.' He reflected. 'Maybe I'll dismember it. I'll wait and see; it depends on how I do at T-M. In six months I may want to go back.'

'What about you?'

Truthfully, he said: 'He can hurt me more, too. I'll be fair game for everybody. Look at Mavis. Four giants in the field, and all of them trying to get into T-M. And I'll have one giant with a gnat stinging it.'

'I suppose,' Janet said, 'that's another of the several reasons. You want to tangle with Luddy head-on.'

'I want to meet him, yes. And I wouldn't mind hitting up against Blake-Moffet from that position. They're moribund; they're calcified. As Director of Telemedia I'll do my best to put them out of business.'

'They probably expect that.'

'Of course they do. One of their packets is enough for a year; I told Mrs Frost that. As a competitor of Blake-Moffet I could run alongside them for years, hitting them now and then, getting hit in return. But as Director of T-M we'll have a grandiose showdown. Once I'm in, there's no other way.'

Janet studied an exhibit of extinct flowers: poppies and lilies and gladioli and roses. 'When are you going to tell Mrs Frost?'

'I'll go over to her office tomorrow. She'll probably be expecting me . . . it's the last working day. Apparently she agrees with me on Blake-Moffet; this should please her. But that's another thing only time will tell.'

*

The next morning he rented a little Getabout from a dealer and drove from his housing unit to the Committee building

Myron Mavis, he reflected, would be giving up his within-walking-distance apartment. Protocol required that a man lease close to his job; in the next week or so it behooved him to ask for Mavis' setup. As Director of T-M he would need to live the role. There was slight latitude, and he was already resigned to the strictures. It was the price paid for public service in the higher brackets.

As soon as he entered the Committee building, the front secretary passed him through. There was no waiting, and within five minutes he was being ushered into Mrs Frost's private office.

She rose graciously. 'Mr Purcell. How nice.'

'You're looking well.' They shook hands. 'Is this a good time to talk to you?'

'Excellent,' Mrs Frost said, smiling. Today she wore a trim brown suit of some crisp fabric, unknown to him. 'Sit down.'

'Thank you.' He seated himself facing her. 'I see no point in waiting until the last moment.'

'You've decided?'

Allen said: 'I'll accept the job. And I apologize for stringing it out.'

Waving her hand, Mrs Frost dismissed his apology. 'You should have time.' And then her face glowed in a swift, beaming warmth of delight. 'I'm so glad.'

Touched, he said: 'So am I.' And he really meant it.

'When will you be ready to start?' She laughed and held up her hands. 'Look at me; I'm as nervous as you.'

'I want to start as soon as possible.' He consulted with himself; it would take at least a week to wind up affairs at the Agency. 'What about a week from Monday?'

She was disappointed, but she suppressed it. 'Yes, you should have that much time for the transfer. And – perhaps we can get together socially. For dinner some evening. And for Juggle. I'm quite a demon; I play every chance I get. And I'd like very much to meet your wife.'

'Fine,' Allen said, sharing her enthusiasm. 'We'll arrange that.'

11

The dream, large and gray, hanging like the tatters of a web, gathered itself around him and hugged him greedily. He screamed, but instead of sounds there drifted out of him stars. The stars rose until they reached the panoply of web, and there they stuck fast, and were extinguished.

He screamed again, and this time the force of his voice rolled him downhill. Crashing through dripping vines he came to rest in a muddy trough, a furrow half-clogged with water. The water, brackish, stung his nostrils, choking him. He gasped, floundered, crept against roots.

It was a moist jungle of growing things in which he lay. The steaming hulks of plants pressed and shoved for water. They drank noisily, grew and expanded, split with a showering burst of particles. Around him the jungle altered through centuries of life. Moonlight, strained through bulging leaves, drizzled gummy and yellow around him, as thick as syrup.

And, in the midst of the creeping plant-pulp, was an artificial structure.

Toward it he struggled, reaching. The structure was flat, thin, with a brittle hardness. It was opaque. It was made of boards.

Joy submerged him as he touched its side. He screamed, and this time the sound carried his body upward. He floated, drifted, clutched at the wood surface. His nails scrabbled, and splinters pierced his flesh. With a metal wheel he sawed through the wood and stripped it away, husk-like, dropping it and stamping on it. The wood broke loudly, echoing in the dream-silence.

Behind the wood was stone.

Gazing at the stone he felt awe. It had endured; it had not been carried away or destroyed. The stone loomed as he remembered it. No change had occurred, and that was very good. He felt the emotion all through him.

He reached out, and, bracing himself, plucked from the stone a round part of itself. Weighed down, he staggered off, and plunged head-first into the oozing warmth of plant-pulp.

For a time he lay gasping, his face pressed against slime. Once, an insect walked across his cheek. Far off, something stirred mournfully. At last, with great effort, he roused himself and began searching. The round stone lay half-buried in silt, at the edge of water. He found the metal wheel and cut away the groping roots. Then, bracing his knees, he lifted the stone and dragged it away, across a grassy hill so vast that it faded into infinity.

At the end of the hill he dropped the stone crashing into a little parked Getabout. Nobody saw him. It was almost dawn. The sky, streaked with yellow, would soon be drained, would soon become a hazy gray through which the sun could beat.

Getting into the front seat, he started up the steam pressure and drove carefully up the lane. The lane stretched out ahead of him, faintly damp, faintly luminous. On both sides housing units were jutting lumps of coal: oddly hardened organic substances. No light showed within them and nothing stirred.

When he reached his own housing unit he parked the car – making no sound – and began lugging the stone up the rear ramp. It took a long time, and he was trembling and perspiring when he reached his own floor. And still nobody saw him. He unlocked his door and dragged the stone inside.

Unhinged with relief, he sank down on the edge of the bed. It was over: he had done it. In her bed his wife stirred fretfully, sighed, turned over on her face. Janet did not wake up; nobody woke up. The city, the society, slept.

Presently he removed his clothes and climbed into bed. He fell asleep almost at once, his mind and body free of all tension, every trouble.

Dreamless, like an amoeba, he, too, slept.

12

Sunlight streamed through the bedroom, warm and pleasant. Beside Allen in the bed lay his wife, also warm and pleasant. Her hair had tumbled against his face and now he turned to kiss her.

'Uh,' Janet murmured, blinking.

'It's morning. Time to get up.' But he, himself, remained inert.

He felt lazy. Contentment spread through him; instead of getting up he put his arm around Janet and hugged her.

'Did the – tape go off?' she asked drowsily.

'This is Saturday. We're in charge, today.' Caressing Janet's shoulder he said: 'The pulsing fullness of firm flesh.'

'Thank you,' she murmured, yawning and stretching. Then she became serious. 'Allen, were you sick last night?' Sitting up quickly, she said: 'Around three o'clock you got out of bed and went to the bathroom. You were gone a long time.'

'How long?' He had no memory of it.

'I fell asleep. So I can't say. But a long time.'

In any case he felt fine, now. 'You're thinking of earlier this week. You've got everything confused.'

'No, it was last night. Early this morning.' Wide-awake, she slid from the bed and onto her feet. 'You didn't go out, did you?'

He thought about it. There was some vague phantasmagoria in his mind, a confusion of dreamlike events. The taste of brackish water, the wet presence of plants. 'I was on a distant jungle planet,' he decided. 'With torrid jungle priestesses whose breasts were like two cones of white marble.' He tried to recall how the passage had read. 'Bulging within the flimsy covering of her dress. Peeking through. Panting with hot need.'

Exasperated, she caught hold of his arm and tugged. 'Get up. I'm ashamed of you. You – adolescent.'

Allen got to his feet and began searching for his towel. His arms, he discovered, were stiff. He flexed and unflexed his muscles, rubbed his wrists, inspected a scratch.

'Did you cut yourself?' Janet asked, alarmed.

He had. And, he noticed, the suit he had left on a hanger the night before now lay in a chaotic tumble on the floor. Lifting it up he spread it out on the bed and smoothed it. The suit was muddy and one trouser leg was torn.

Outside in the hall, doors opened and tenants wandered out to form the bathroom line. Sleepy voices muttered.

'Shall I go first?' Janet asked.

Still examining his suit he nodded. 'Go ahead.'

'Thank you.' She opened the closet and reached for a slip and dress. 'You're always so sweet to let me—' Her voice trailed off.

66

'What is it?'

'*Allen!*'

He bounded to the closet and lifted her aside.

On the floor of the closet was a bronzed thermoplastic head. The head stared nobly past him at a fixed point beyond. The head was huge, larger than life, a great solemn Dutch gargoyle head resting between pairs of shoes and the laundry bag. It was the head of Major Streiter.

'Oh God,' Janet whispered, her hands to her face.

'Take it easy.' He had never heard her blaspheme, and it added the final stamp of menace and collapse. 'Go make sure the door's locked.'

'It is.' She returned. 'That's part of the statue, isn't it?' Her voice shrilled. 'Last night – *you went and got it.* That's where you were.'

The jungle hadn't been a dream. He had stumbled through the dark, deserted Park, falling among the flowers and grass. Getting up and going on until he came to the boarded-up statue.

'How – did you get it home?' she asked.

'In the Getabout.' The same Getabout, ironically, that he had rented to visit Sue Frost.

'What'll we do?' Janet said monotonously, her face stricken, caved in by the calamity. 'Allen, what'll happen?'

'You get dressed and go wash.' He began stripping off his pajamas. 'And don't speak to anybody. Not one d—n word.'

She gave a muffled yip, then turned, caught up her robe and towel, and left. Alone, Allen selected an undamaged suit and dressed. By the time he was tying his necktie he had remembered the night's sequence pretty much intact.

'Then it's going to go on,' Janet said, returning.

'Lock the door.'

'You're still doing it.' Her voice was thick, suppressed. In the bathroom she had swallowed a handful of sedatives and anti-anxiety pills. 'It's not over.'

'No,' he admitted. 'Apparently it's not.'

'What comes next?'

'Don't ask me. I'm as mystified as you.'

'You'll have to get rid of it.' She came toward him accusingly. 'You can't leave it around like part of a – corpse.'

'It's safe enough.' Presumably no one had seen him. Or, as before, he would already have been arrested.

'And you took that job. You're this way, doing insane things like this, and you accepted that job. You weren't drunk last night, were you?'

'No.'

'So that isn't it. What is it, then?'

'Ask Doctor Malparto.' He went to the phone and picked up the receiver. 'Or maybe I will. If he's there.' He dialed.

'Mental Health Resort,' the friendly, bureaucratic voice answered.

'Is Doctor Malparto there today? This is a patient of his.'

'Doctor Malparto will be in at eight. Shall I have him call you? Who is calling, please?'

'This is Mr – Coates,' Allen said. 'Tell Doctor Malparto I'd like an emergency appointment. Tell him I'll be in at eight. I'll wait there until he can see me.'

In his office at the Mental Health Resort, Doctor Malparto said with agitation: 'What do you suppose happened?'

'Let him in and ask him.' Gretchen stood by the window drinking a cup of coffee. 'Don't keep him out there in the lounge; he's pacing like an animal. You're both so—'

'I don't have all my testing apparatus. Some of it's loaned to Heely's staff.'

'He probably set fire to the Committee building.'

'Don't be funny!'

'Maybe he did. Ask him; I'm curious.'

'That night you bumped into him at the statue.' He eyed his sister hostilely. 'Did you know he had japed the statue?'

'I knew somebody had. No, I didn't know – what's the name you give him here?' She snatched up the dossier and leafed through it. 'I was unaware that *Mr Coates* was the japer. I went because I was interested. Nothing like that ever happened before.'

'Boring world, isn't it?' Malparto strode down the corridor to

68

the lounge and opened the door. 'Mr Coates, you may come in now.'

Mr Coates followed him rapidly. His face was strained and set, and he glared straight ahead. 'I'm glad you could see me.'

'You told the receptionist that it's urgent.' Malparto ushered him into his office. 'This is my sister, Gretchen. But you've already met.'

'Hello,' Gretchen said, sipping her coffee. 'What have you done this time?'

Malparto saw his patient flinch.

'Sit down,' Malparto said, showing him to a chair. Mr Coates went obediently, and Malparto seated himself facing him. Gretchen remained at the window with her coffee cup. She obviously intended to stay.

'Coffee?' she asked, to Malparto's annoyance. 'Black and hot. Real coffee, too. From vacuum tins, an old US Army supply depot. Here.' She filled a cup and passed it to Mr Coates, who accepted it. 'Almost the last.'

'Very good,' Mr Coates murmured.

'Now,' Malparto said, 'I don't as a rule hold sessions this early. But in view of your extreme—'

'I stole the statue's head,' Mr Coates interrupted. 'Last night, about three a.m.'

Extraordinary, Malparto thought.

'I took it home, hid it in the closet. This morning Janet found it. And I called you.'

'Do you –' Malparto hesitated, 'have any plans for it?'

'None that I'm aware of.'

Gretchen said: 'I wonder what the market value would be.'

'To help you,' Malparto said, glancing irritably at his sister, 'I must first gather information about your mind; I must learn its potentialities. Therefore I ask you to submit to a series of tests, the purpose of which is to determine your various psychic capacities.'

His patient looked dubious. 'Is that necessary?'

'The cause of your complex may lie outside the ordinary human range. It's my personal belief that you contain a unique psychological element.' He dimmed the office lights. 'You're familiar with the ESP deck?'

Mr Coates made a faint motion.

'I'm going to examine five cards,' Malparto said. 'You will not see their faces, only the backs. As I study them one by one I want you to tell me what each is. Are you ready to start?'

Mr Coates made an even fainter motion.

'Good.' Malparto drew a star card. He concentrated. 'Do you receive an impression?'

Mr Coates said: 'Circle.'

That was wrong, and Malparto went onto the next. 'What is this one?'

'Square.'

The telepathy test was a failure, and Malparto indicated so on his check-sheet. 'Now,' he stated, 'we'll try a different test. This will not involve the reading of my mind.' He shuffled the deck and laid five cards face-down on the desk. 'Study their backs and tell me each one in order.'

His patient got one out of the five.

'We'll leave the deck for a moment.' Malparto brought out the dice-rolling cage and set it into motion. 'Observe these dice. They fall in a random pattern. I want you to concentrate on a particular showing: seven, or five, anything that can come up.'

His patient concentrated on the dice for fifteen minutes. At the end of that time Malparto compared the showing with the statistical tables. No significant change could be observed.

'Back to the cards,' Malparto said, gathering up the deck. 'We'll give you a test for precognition. In this test I'll ask you what card I'm *about* to select.' He laid the deck down and waited.

'Circle,' Mr Coates said listlessly.

Malparto handed his sister the check-sheet, and he kept the precog test going for almost an hour. At the end of that time his patient was surly and exhausted, and the results were inconclusive.

'The cards don't lie,' Gretchen quoted, handing back the sheet.

'What do you mean by that?'

'I mean go on to the next test.'

'Mr Coates,' Malparto said, 'do you feel able to continue?'

His patient blearily raised his head. 'Is this getting us anywhere?'

'I think it is. It's clear that you don't possess any of the usual extra-sensory talents. It's my hunch that you're a Psi-plus. Your talent is of a less common nature.'

'EEP,' Gretchen said tartly. '*Extra* extra-sensory perception.'

'The first of this series,' Malparto said, ignoring her, 'will involve the projection of your will on another human.' He unfolded his blackboard and chalk stick. 'As I stand here, you concentrate on forcing me to write certain numbers. It should be your will superimposed over mine.'

Time passed. Finally, feeling a few vague tendrils of psychic will, Malparto wrote: 3–6–9.

'Wrong,' Mr Coates murmured. 'I was thinking 7,842.'

'Now,' Malparto said, setting out a small gray stone, 'I want you to duplicate this inorganic matter. Try to summon a replica immediately tangent to it.'

That test was a failure, too. Disappointed, Malparto put the stone away.

'Now levitation. Mr Coates, I want you to close your eyes and attempt – psychically – to lift yourself from the floor.'

Mr Coates attempted, without result.

'Next,' Malparto said, 'I want you to place your open palm against the wall behind you. Push, and at the same time, concentrate on passing your hand *between* the molecules of the wall.'

The hand failed to pass between the molecules.

'This time,' Malparto said gamely, 'we'll attempt to measure your ability to communicate with lower life forms.' A lizard, in a box, was brought out. 'Stand with your head near the lid. See if you can tune into the lizard's mental pattern.'

There was no result.

'Maybe the lizard has no mental pattern,' Mr Coates said.

'Nonsense.' Malparto's annoyance was growing wildly. He brought forth a hair resting in a dish of water. 'See if you can animate the hair. Try to transform it into a worm.'

Mr Coates failed.

'Were you really trying?' Gretchen asked.

Mr Coates smiled. 'Very hard.'

'I should think that would be easy enough,' she said. 'There's not much difference between a hair and a worm. On a cloudy day—'

'Now,' Malparto broke in, 'we'll test your ability to heal.' He had noticed the scratch on Allen's wrist. 'Direct your psychic powers toward that damaged tissue. Try to restore it to health.'

The scratch remained.

'Too bad,' Gretchen said. 'That would be a useful one.'

Malparto, overcome by abandon, brought out a water wand and asked his patient to divine. A bowl of water was skillfully hidden, and Mr Coates lumbered about the office. The wand did not dip.

'Bad wood,' Gretchen said.

Depressed, Malparto examined the list of remaining tests.

Ability to contact spirits of the dead

Capacity to transmute lead into gold

Ability to assume alternate forms

Ability to create rain of vermin and/or filth

Power to kill or damage at a distance

'I have a feeling,' he said finally, 'that due to fatigue you're growing subconsciously uncooperative. Therefore it's my decision that we defer the balance of the tests to some other time.'

Gretchen asked Mr Coates: 'Can you kindle fire? Can you slay seven with one blow? Can your father lick my father?'

'I can steal,' the patient said.

'That's not much. Anything else?'

He reflected. 'Afraid that's all.' Getting to his feet he said to Malparto: 'I assume the Monday appointment is void.'

'You're leaving?'

'Well,' he said, 'there's no point sticking around here.' He reached for the doorknob. 'We haven't got anywhere.'

'And you won't be coming back?'

At the door he paused. 'Probably not,' he decided. At the moment all he wanted to do was go home. 'If I change my mind I'll call you.' He started to pull the door shut.

That was when all the lights went out around him.

13

Rumble rumble.

The bus lifted from the stop and continued across roof tops. Houses sparkled beneath, in planned patterns, separated by lawns. A swimming pool lay like a blue eye. But, he noticed, the pool far below was not perfectly round. At one end the tiles formed a patio. He saw tables, beach umbrellas. Tiny shapes were people reclining at leisure.

'Four,' the bus said metallically.

A woman rose and found the rear door. The bus lowered to the stop, the door slithered aside, the woman stepped down.

'Watch your step,' the bus said. 'Exit by the rear.' It ascended, and again houses sparkled beneath.

Next to Allen the large gentleman mopped his forehead. 'Warm day.'

'Yes,' Allen agreed. To himself he said: *Say nothing. Do nothing. Don't even move.*

'You hold this a minute, young fellow? Like to tie my shoes.' The large gentleman passed his armload of bundles across. 'Go shopping, you have to lug it home. That's the gimmick.'

'Five,' the bus said. Nobody got up, so the bus continued. Below, a shopping section was visible: clump of bright stores.

'They say shop near home,' the large gentleman said, 'but you can save money if you go downtown. Sales, you know. They buy in quantity.' Out of a long paper bag he lifted a jacket. 'Nice, eh? Real cow.' He showed Allen a can of wax. 'Got to keep it moist or it cracks. Rain's bad for it. Another gimmick. But you can't have everything.'

'Exit by the rear,' the bus said. 'No smoking. Step to the back, please.' More houses passed beneath.

'You feel all right?' the large gentleman asked. 'Seems to me you look like you might have a touch of sunstroke. A lot of people, they go out in the sun on a hot day like this. Don't know any better.' He chuckled. 'Feel cold? Nauseated?'

'Yes,' Allen said.

'Probably been running around playing Quart. You a pretty

good quartist?' He sized Allen up. 'Good shoulders, arms. Young fellow like you probably be right-wing. Eh?'

'Not yet,' Allen said. He looked through the window of the bus and then down through the transparent floor at the city. Into his mind came the thought that he didn't even know where to get off. He didn't know where he was going or why or where he was now.

He was not in the Health Resort. That was the sole fact, and he took hold of it and made it the hub of his new universe. He made it the reference point and he began to creep cautiously from there.

This was not the Morec society, because there were no swimming pools and wide lawns and separate houses and glass-bottomed busses in the Morec society. There were no people basking in the sun in the middle of the day. There was no game called *Quart*. And this was not a vast historical exhibit such as the twentieth century house in the museum, because he could see the date on the magazine being read across the aisle, and it was the right month and year.

'Can I ask you something?' he said to the large gentleman.

'Surely.' The large gentleman beamed.

'What's the name of this town?'

The large gentleman's face changed color. 'Why, this is Chicago.'

'Six,' the bus said. Two young women got up, and the bus lowered to let them off. 'Exit at the rear. No smoking, please.'

Allen got up, squeezed to the aisle, and followed the women from the bus.

The air smelled fresh, full of the nearness of trees. He took a deep breath, walked a few steps, halted. The bus had let him off in a residential section; only houses were visible, set along wide, tree-lined streets. Children were playing, and, on the lawn of one house, a girl was sun-bathing. Her body was quite tan and her breasts were highly upraised. And her nipples were a pretty pastel pink.

If anything proved his separation from the Morec society it was the naked young lady stretched out on the grass. He had never seen anything like it. In spite of himself he walked that way.

'What are you looking at?' the girl asked, her head on her folded arms, face-up in the deep green lawn.

'I'm lost.' It was the first thing that entered his mind.

'This is Holly Street and the cross street is Glen. Where do you want to be?'

'I want to be home,' he said.

'Where's that?'

'I don't know.'

'Look at your ident card. In your wallet.'

He reached into his coat and brought out his wallet. The card was there, a strip of plastic with words and numbers punched into it.

2319 Pepper Lane

That was his address, and above it was his name. He read that, too.

Coates, John B.

'I slipped over,' he said.

'Over what?' She raised her head.

Bending down he showed her the ident card. 'Look, it says John Coates. But my name's Allen Purcell; I picked the name Coates at random.' He ran his thumb across the raised plastic, feeling it.

The girl sat up and tucked her bare, deeply-tanned legs under her. Her breasts, even as she sat, remained up-tilted. Her nipples projected prettily. 'Very interesting,' she said.

'Now I'm Mr Coates.'

'Then what happened to Allen Purcell?' She smoothed her hair back and smiled up.

'He must be back there,' Mr Coates said. 'But I'm Allen Purcell,' Allen said. 'It doesn't make sense.'

Sliding to her feet the girl put a hand on his shoulder and guided him to the sidewalk. 'On the corner is a cab-box. Ask the cab to take you home. Pepper Lane is about two miles from here. Do you want me to call it for you?'

'No,' he said. 'I can do it.'

He set off along the pavement, looking for the cab-box. Never having seen one, he walked past it.

75

'There,' the girl called, hands cupped to her mouth.

Nodding, he pulled the switch. A moment later the cab dropped to the pavement beside him and said: 'Where to, sir?'

The trip took only a minute. The cab landed; he pushed coins into its slot; and then he was standing before a house.

His house.

The house was big, imposing, dominating a ridge of cedars and peppers. Sprinklers hurled water across the sloping lawns on both sides of the brick path. In the rear was a garden of dahlias and wisteria, a tumbling patch of deep red and purple.

On the front porch was a baby. An agile sitter perched on the railing nearby, its lens monitoring. The baby noticed Mr Coates; smiling, it reached up its arm and burbled.

The front door – solid hard wood, with brass inlay – was wide open. From within the house drifted the sounds of music: a jazzy dance band.

He entered.

The living room was deserted. He examined the rug, the fireplace, the piano, and he recognized it from his research. Reaching, he plinked a few notes. Then he wandered into the dining room. A large mahogany table filled the center. On the table was a vase of iris. Along two walls was a line of mounted plates, glazed and ornate; he inspected them and then passed on, into a hall. Broad stairs led up: he gazed up, saw a landing and open doors, then turned toward the kitchen.

The kitchen overwhelmed him. It was long, gleaming-white, and it contained every kind of appliance he had heard of and some he had not. On the immense stove a meal was cooking, and he peered into a pot, sniffing. Lamb, he decided.

While he was sniffing there was a noise behind him. The back door opened and a woman entered, breathless and flushed.

'*Darling!*' she exclaimed, hurrying to him. 'When did you get home?'

She was dark, with tumbles of hair bouncing against her shoulders. Her eyes were huge and intense. She wore shorts and a halter and sandals.

She was Gretchen Malparto.

*

The clock on the mantel read four-thirty. Gretchen had drawn the drapes, and the living room was in shadow. Now she paced about, smoking, gesturing jerkily. She had changed to a print skirt and peasant blouse. The baby, whom Gretchen called 'Donna,' was upstairs in her crib, asleep.

'Something's wrong,' Gretchen repeated. 'I wish you'd tell me what it is. Damn it, do I have to beg?' Turning, she faced him defiantly. 'Johnny, this isn't like you.'

He lay on the couch, stretched out, a gin sling in one hand. Above him the ceiling was a mild green, and he contemplated it until Gretchen's voice shattered at him.

'Johnny, for Christ's sake!'

He roused himself. 'I'm right here. I'm not standing outdoors.'

'Tell me what happened.' She came over and settled on the arm of the couch. 'Is it because of what happened Wednesday?'

'What happened Wednesday?' He was, in a detached way, interested.

'At Frank's party. When you found me upstairs with—' She looked away. 'I forget his name. The tall, blond-haired one. You seemed mad; you were a little this way. Is that it? I thought we agreed not to interfere with each other. Or do you want it to work just one way?'

He asked: 'How long have we been married?'

'This is a lecture, I suppose.' She sighed. 'Go ahead. Then it's my turn.'

'Just answer my question.'

'I forget.'

Meditating, he said: 'I thought wives always knew.'

'Oh, come off it.' She pulled away and stalked over to the phonograph. 'Let's eat. I'll have it serve us. Or do you want to go out for dinner? Maybe you'll feel better where there's people – instead of cooped up here.'

He didn't feel cooped up. From where he lay he could see most of the downstairs of the house. Room after room . . . like living in an office building. Renting a whole floor; two floors. And in the back of the house, in the garden, was a three-room guest cottage.

In fact, he felt nothing at all. The gin sling had anesthetized him.

'Care to buy a head?' he asked her.

'I don't understand.'

'A stone head. Bronzed thermoplastic, to be absolutely accurate. Responds to cutting tools. Doesn't that ring a bell? You thought the job was quite original.'

'Rave away.'

He said: 'A year? Two years? Approximately.'

'We were married in April 2110. So it must be four years.'

'That's a good long time,' he said. 'Mrs Coates.'

'Yes, Mr Coates.'

'And this house?' He liked the house.

'This house,' Gretchen said fiercely, 'belonged to your mother. And I'm sick of hearing about it. I wish we had never moved here; I wish we had sold the goddamn thing. We could have got a good price two years ago; now real estate's down.'

'It'll go up. It always does.'

Glaring at him, Gretchen strode across the living room to the hall. 'I'll be upstairs, changing for dinner. Tell it to serve.'

'Serve,' he said.

With a snort of exasperation, Gretchen left. He heard the click of her heels on the stairs and then that, too, faded.

The house was lovely: it was spacious, luxuriously furnished, solidly built, and modern. It would last a century. The garden was full of flowers and the freezer was full of food. Like heaven, he thought. Like a vision of the after-reward, for all the years of public service. For all the sacrifice and struggle, bickerings and Mrs Birmingham. The ordeal of the block meetings. The tension and sternness of the Morec society.

A part of him reached out to this, and he knew what that part was named. John Coates was now in his own world, and it was the antithesis of Morec.

Close to his ear, a voice said: 'There remains some island of ego.'

A second voice, a woman's, said: 'But submerged.'

'Totally withdrawn,' the man said. 'The shock of failure. When the Psi-testing collapsed. He was at the edge of the Resort, starting back out. And he couldn't.'

The woman asked: 'Isn't there a better solution?'

'He needed one at that instant. He couldn't return to Morec, and he had found no help at the Resort. For that I'm partly to blame; I wasted time on the testing.'

'You thought it would help.' The woman seemed to be moving nearer. 'Can he hear us?'

'I doubt it. There's no way to tell. The catalepsy is complete, so he can't signal.'

'How long will it last?'

'Hard to say. Days, weeks, maybe the balance of his life.' Malparto's voice seemed to recede, and he strained to catch it. 'Maybe we should inform his wife.'

'Can you tell anything about his inner world?' Gretchen, too, was dimming. 'What kind of fantasy is he lost in?'

'An escape.' The voice vanished, then momentarily returned. 'Time will tell.' It was gone.

Struggling from the couch, Mr John Coates shouted: 'Did you hear them? *Did you?*'

At the top of the stairs Gretchen appeared, hairbrush in one hand, stockings over her arm. 'What's the matter?'

He appealed in despair. 'It was you and your brother. Couldn't you hear them? This is a—' He broke off.

'A what?' She came calmly downstairs. 'What are you talking about?'

A pool had formed where his drink glass had fallen; he bent down to sop it up. 'I have news for you,' he said. 'This isn't real. I'm sick; this is a psychotic retreat.'

'I'm surprised at you,' she said. 'Really, I am. You sound like a college sophomore. Solipsism – skepticism. Bishop Berkeley, all that ultimate-reality stuff.'

As his fingers touched the drink glass, the wall behind it vanished.

Still stooping, he saw out into the world beyond. He saw the street, other houses. He was afraid to lift his head. The mantel and fireplace, the rug and deep chairs . . . even the lamp and bric-a-brac, all were gone. Only a void. Emptiness.

'There it is,' Gretchen said. 'Right by your hand.'

He saw no glass now; it had vanished with the room. In spite of himself, he turned his head. There was nothing behind him. Gretchen was gone, too. He was standing alone in emptiness. Only the next house, a long way off, remained. Along the street a car moved, followed by a second. At a neighboring house a curtain was drawn. Darkness was descending everywhere.

'Gretchen,' he said.

There was no response. Only silence.

14

He closed his eyes and willed. He imagined the room: he pictured Gretchen, the coffee table, the package of cigarettes, the lighter beside it. He pictured the ashtray, the drapes, the couch and phonograph.

When he opened his eyes the room was back. But Gretchen was gone. He was alone in the house.

The shades were all down, and he had a deep intuition of lateness. As if, he thought, time had passed. A clock on the mantel read eight-thirty. Had four whole hours gone by? Four hours . . .

'Gretchen?' he said, experimentally. He went to the stairs and started up. Still no sign of her. The house was warm, the air pleasant and fresh. Somewhere an automatic heating unit functioned.

A room to his right was her bedroom. He glanced in.

The small ivory clock on the dressing table did not read eight-thirty. It read a quarter to five. Gretchen had over-looked it. She had not set it forward with the one downstairs.

Instantly he was running back downstairs, two steps at a time.

The voices had reached him as he lay on the couch. Kneeling, he pressed his hands under the fabric, across the arms and back, under the cushions. Finally he dragged the couch away from the wall.

The first speaker was mounted within a coil of backspring. A second and then a third were concealed under the rug; they were as flat as paper. He estimated that at least a dozen speakers had been mounted throughout the room.

Since Gretchen had been upstairs the control unit was undoubtedly there. Again he climbed the stairs and entered her bedroom.

At first he failed to recognize it. The control lay in plain sight, on the woman's dressing table, with the jars and tubes and packages of cosmetics. The hairbrush. He picked it up and rotated the plastic handle.

From downstairs boomed a man's voice. 'There remains some island of ego.'

Gretchen's voice answered. 'But submerged.'

'Totally withdrawn,' Malparto continued. 'The shock—'

Allen snapped the handle back, and the voices departed. The tape transport, mounted somewhere in the walls of the house, had halted in the middle of its cycle.

Downstairs again, he searched for the means by which Gretchen had dissolved the house. When he found it, he was chagrined. The unit was built into the fireplace, in open view, one of the many comfort-making gadgets. He pressed the stud and the room around him with its furnishings and rich textures seeped away. The outside world remained: houses, the street, the sky. A glimmer of stars.

The device was a mere romantic gadget. For long, dull evenings. Gretchen was an active girl.

In a closet, under a heap of blankets, he found a newspaper used as a shelf-liner; it was empirical proof. The newspaper was the Vega *Sentinel*. He was not in a fantasy world; he was on the fourth planet of the Vega System.

He was on Other World, the permanent refuge maintained by the Mental Health Resort. Maintained for persons who had come – not for therapy – but for sanctuary.

Finding the phone, he dialed zero.

'Number, please,' the operator said, the faint, tinny, and terribly reassuring voice.

'Give me one of the space ports,' he said. 'Any one that has inter-system service.'

A series of clicks, buzzes, and then he was connected with the ticket office. A methodical male voice on the other end of the wire said,

'Yes, sir. What can I do for you?'

'What's the fare to Earth?' He wondered, in a stricken way, just how long he had been here. A week? A month?'

'One way, first class. Nine hundred thirty dollars. Plus twenty percent luxury tax.' The voice was without emotion.

He had no such money. 'What's the next system in order?'

'Sirius.'

'How much is that?' He didn't have over fifty dollars in his wallet. And this planet was under the jurisdiction of the Health Resort: it had acquired it with its deed.

'One way, first class. Tax included . . . comes to seven hundred and forty-two dollars.'

He calculated. 'What's it cost to phone Earth?'

The ticket agent said, 'You'll have to ask the phone company, mister. That's not our business.'

When he had gotten the operator again, Allen said, 'I'd like to place a call to Earth.'

'Yes, sir.' She did not seem surprised. 'What number, sir?'

He gave Telemedia's number, and then the number on the phone he was using. It was as simple as that.

After several minutes of buzzing, the operator said, 'I'm sorry, sir. Your party does not answer.'

'What time is it there?'

A moment and then: 'In that time zone it is three a.m., sir.'

In a husky voice he said, 'Look, I've been kidnapped. I have to get out of here – back to Earth.'

'I suggest you call one of the inter-system transport fields, sir,' the operator said.

'All I've got is fifty bucks!'

'I'm sorry, sir. I can connect you with one of the fields if you wish.'

He hung up.

There was no point staying in the house, but he lingered long enough to type out a note – a note with a vengeance. He left the note in the middle of the coffee table, where Gretchen would be sure to see it.

Dear Mrs Coates,

    You remember Molly. Damned if I didn't run into her at the Brass Poker. Says she's pregnant, but you know how that kind are. Think I better stay with her until we can get her a you-know-what. Expensive, but it's the price you pay.

He signed it *Johnny* and then left the house.

Other World had plenty of roving taxis, and within five minutes he was in the downtown business district with its lights and flow of people.

At the space port a full-size ship stood upright on its tail. He guessed, with almost frenzied despair, that it was in the process of leaving for the next system. A line of supply trucks dashed back and forth; the ship was already in the final stages of loading.

Paying off the taxi, he tramped across the gravel parking lot of the field, down the street until he arrived at a syndrome of life: a restaurant doing an active business, full of patrons and noise and chatter. Feeling like a fool he buttoned his coat up around him and strode through the doorway to the cashier.

'Put up your hands, lady,' he said, jutting out his pocket. 'Before I put a McAllister heat beam through your head.'

The girl gasped, raised her hands, opened her mouth and gave a terrified bleat. Patrons at nearby tables glanced up in disbelief.

'OK,' Allen said, in a normally-loud voice. 'Now let's have the money. Push it across the counter before I blow out your brains with my McAllister heat beam.'

'Oh dear,' the girl said.

From behind him two Other World police wearing helmets and crisp blue uniforms appeared and grabbed his arms. The girl flopped out of sight and Allen's hand was yanked from his pocket.

'A noose,' one cop said. 'A super-noose. It's troublemakers like this ruin a clean neighborhood.'

'Let go of me,' Allen said. 'Before I blow off your heads with my McAllister heat beam.'

'Buddy,' one of the cops said, as they dragged him from the restaurant, 'this cancels the Resort's obligations to succor you. You've shown your unreliability by committing a felony.'

'I'll blow all of you to bits,' Allen said, as they bundled him into the police car. 'This heat beam talks.'

'Get his ident.' A cop snatched Allen's wallet. 'John B. Coates. 2319 Pepper Lane. Well, Mr Coates, you've had your chance. Now you're on your way back to Morec. How does that sound?'

'You won't live to send me back,' Allen said. The car was sprinting toward the field, and the big ship was still there. 'I'll get you. You'll see.'

The car, flying a foot above the gravel, turned onto the field and made directly for the ship. The siren came on; field attendants stopped work and watched.

'Tell them to hold it,' one of the cops said. He got out a microphone and contacted the field's tower. 'Another super-noose. Open up the fleebee.'

In a matter of seconds the car had come alongside the ship, the doors had united, and Allen was in the hands of the ship's sheriff.

'Welcome back to Morec,' a run-down fellow super-noose muttered, as Allen was deposited beside him in the restricted area.

'Thanks,' Allen said, with relief. 'It's good to be back.' Now he was wondering if he would reach Earth by Sunday. On Monday morning his job at Telemedia started. Had he lost too much time?

Whoosh, the floor went. The ship was rising.

15

The trip began Wednesday night, and by Sunday night he was back on Earth. The notation was arbitrary, of course, but the interval was real. Tired, sweaty, Allen emerged from the ship and back into the Morec society.

The field was not far from the Spire and his housing unit, but he balked at the idea of walking. It seemed unnecessarily strict; the supplicants in Other World showed no sign of degeneracy because they rode busses. Going into a phone booth at the field he called Janet.

'Oh!' she gasped. 'They released you? You're – all right?'

He asked: 'What did Malparto tell you?'

'They said you had gone to Other World for treatment. They said you might be there several weeks.'

Now it made even more sense. In several weeks he would have lost his directorship and his status in the Morec world. After that it wouldn't matter if he discovered the hoax or not; without a lease, without a job, he would fairly well have to remain on Vega 4.

'Did he say anything about you joining me?'

There was a hasty flutter from the phone. 'Y-yes, he did. He said you'd adjust to Other World, but if you couldn't adjust to this, then—'

'I didn't adjust to Other World. Just a lot of people lounging around sun-bathing. Is that Getabout still there? The one I rented?'

Janet, it developed, had returned the Getabout to the rental outfit. The charge was steep, and the Health Resort had already begun to tap his salary. Somehow that seemed to complete the outrage: the Resort, in the guise of helping him, had kidnapped him, and then billed him for services rendered.

'I'll get another.' He started to hang up, then asked: 'Has Mrs Frost been around?'

'She phoned several times.'

That sounded ominous. 'What'd you tell her? That my mind gave out and I fled to the Resort?'

'I said you were winding up your affairs and couldn't be disturbed.' Janet breathed huskily into the phone, deafening him. 'Allen, I'm so glad you're back. I was so worried.'

'How many pills did you swallow?'

'Well, quite a few. I – couldn't sleep.'

He hung up, dug out another quarter, and dialed Sue Frost's personal number. After a time she answered . . . the familiar calm, dignified voice.

'This is Allen,' he said. 'Allen Purcell. I just wanted to check with you. Things coming along all right at your end?'

'Mr Purcell,' she said harshly, 'be at my apartment in ten minutes. This is an order!'

Click.

He stared at the dead phone. Then he left the phone booth and started walking.

The Frost apartment directly overlooked the Spire, as did the apartments of all Committee Secretaries. Allen took a reassuring breath and then climbed the stairs. A clean shirt, a bath, and a long rest would have helped, but there was no time for luxuries. And he could, of course, pass his appearance off as the effects of a week or so spent closing down business; he had been slaving night and day at the Agency, trying to get all the loose ends to come out. With that in mind he rang Mrs Frost's doorbell.

'Come in.' She stood aside and he entered. In the single room sat Myron Mavis looking weary, and Ida Pease Hoyt looking grim and formal.

'Hello,' Allen said, with a strong sense of doom.

'Now,' Mrs Frost said, coming around in front of him. 'Where have you been? You weren't at your Agency; we checked there a number of times. We even sent a bonded representative to sit in with your staff. A Mr Priar is operating Allen Purcell, Inc. during your absence.'

Allen wondered if he should lie or tell the truth. He decided to lie. The Morec society couldn't bear the truth; it would punish him and keep on going. And somebody else would be named Director of T-M, a creature of Blake-Moffet.

'Harry Priar is acting administrator,' he said. 'As Myron here is acting Director of T-M until I take over. Are you trying to say I've been on salary the last week?' That certainly wasn't so. 'The understanding was clear enough: I go to work next Monday, tomorrow. This past week has been my own. T-M has no more claim over me this past week than it had last year.'

'The point—' Mrs Frost began, and then the doorbell sounded. 'Excuse me. This should be them now.'

When the door opened Tony Blake from Blake-Moffet entered. Behind him was Fred Luddy, a briefcase under his arm. 'Good evening, Sue,' Tony Blake said agreeably. He was a portly, well-dressed man in his late fifties, with snow-white hair and rimless glasses. 'Evening, Myron. This is an honor, Mrs Hoyt. Evening, Allen. Glad to see you back.'

Luddy said nothing. They all seated themselves, facing one another, swapping tension and hauteur. Allen was acutely aware of his baggy suit and unstarched shirt; by the minute he looked less like an overworked businessman and more like a college radical from the Age of Waste.

'To continue,' Mrs Frost said. 'Mr Purcell, you were not at your Agency as your wife told us. At first we were puzzled, because we believed there was going to be mutual confidence between us. It seemed odd that a situation of this sort, with you dropping mysteriously out of sight, and these vague evasions and denials by your—'

'Now look here,' Allen said. 'You're not addressing a metazoon and a mammal; you're addressing a human being who's a citizen of the Morec society. Either you speak to me civilly or I leave now. I'm tired and I'd like to get some sleep. I'll leave it up to you.'

Curtly, Mrs Hoyt said: 'He's quite right, Sue. Stop playing boss, and for heaven's sake get that righteous look off your face. Leave that to God.'

'Perhaps you don't have confidence in me,' Mrs Frost answered, turning. 'Should we settle that first?'

Sprawled out in his chair, Myron Mavis snickered. 'Yes, I'd like this one better. Do settle it first, Sue.'

Mrs Frost became flustered. 'Really, this whole thing is getting out of hand. Why don't I fix coffee?' She arose. 'And there's a little brandy, if nobody feels it's contrary to public interest.'

'We're sinking,' Mavis said, grinning across at Allen. 'Glub, glub. Under the waves of sin.'

The tension ebbed and both Blake and Luddy began shuffling, conferring, murmuring. Luddy put on his horn-rimmed glasses and two serious heads were bent over the contents of his briefcase. Mrs Frost went to the hotplate and put on the coffee-maker. Still seated, Mrs Hoyt regarded a spot on the floor and spoke to no one. As always, she wore heavy furs, dark stockings, and low-heeled shoes. Allen had a great deal of respect for her; he knew her for an adroit manipulator.

'You're related to Major Streiter,' he said. 'Isn't that what I've heard?'

Mrs Hoyt favored him with a look. 'Yes, Mr Purcell. The Major was a progenitor on my father's side.'

'Terrible about the statue,' Blake put in. 'Imagine an outbreak like that. It defies description.'

Allen had forgotten about the statue. And the head. It was still in the closet, unless Janet had done something with it. No wonder she had gulped down bottles of pills: the head had been there with her, all during the week.

'They'll catch him,' Luddy said, with vigor. 'Or them. Personally it's my conviction that an organized gang is involved.'

'There's something almost satanic in it,' Sue Frost said. 'Stealing the head, that way. Coming back a few days later and – right in front of the police – stealing it and taking it heaven knows where. I wonder if it'll ever turn up.' She located cups and saucers.

When the coffee had been served, the discussion took up where it had left off. But moderation prevailed. Cooler heads were at work.

'Certainly there's no reason to quarrel,' Mrs Frost said. 'I suppose I was upset. Honestly, Allen, look at the spot you put us in. Last Sunday – a week ago – I picked up the phone and called your apartment. I wanted to catch you with your wife so we could decide on our Juggle evening.'

'I'm sorry,' Allen murmured, scrutinizing the wall and mentally twiddling his thumbs. In some ways this was the worst part, the rhetoric of apology.

'Would you like to tell us what happened?' Mrs Frost continued. Her savoir-faire had returned, and she smiled with her usual grace and charm. 'Consider this a friendly inquiry. We're all your friends, even Mr Luddy.'

'What's the Blake-Moffet team doing here?' he asked. 'I can't see how this concerns them. Maybe I'm being overly blunt, but this seems to be a matter between you and me and Mrs Hoyt.'

A pained exchange of glances informed him that there was more to it. As if the presence of Blake and Luddy hadn't said that already.

'Come on, Sue,' Mrs Hoyt rumbled in her gravelly voice.

'When we couldn't get in touch with you,' Mrs Frost went on, 'we had a conference and we decided to sit on it. After all, you're a grown man. But then Mr Blake called us. T-M has done a great deal of business with Blake-Moffet over the years, and we all know one another. Mr Blake showed us some disturbing material, and we—'

'What material?' Allen demanded. 'Let's have a look at it.'

Blake answered. 'It's here, Purcell. Don't get upset; all in due time.' He tossed some papers over, and Allen caught them. While he examined them Mrs Frost said:

'I'd like to ask you, Allen. As a personal friend. Never mind those papers; I'll tell you what it is. You haven't separated from your wife, have you? You haven't had a quarrel you'd rather keep quiet, something that's come up between you that means a more or less permanent altercation?'

'Is that what this is about?' He felt as if he had been dipped in sheer cold. It was one of those eternal blind alleys that Morec worriers got themselves into. Divorce, scandal, sex, other women – the whole confused gamut of marital difficulty.

'Naturally,' Mrs Hoyt said, 'it would be incumbent on you to refuse the directorship under such circumstances. A man in such a high position of trust – well, you're familiar with the rest.'

The papers in his hands danced in a jumble of words, phrases, dates and locations. He gave up and tossed them aside. 'And Blake's got documentation on this?' They were after him, but they had got themselves onto a false lead. Luckily for him. 'Let's hear it.'

Blake cleared his throat and said: 'Two weeks ago you worked alone at your Agency. At eight-thirty you locked up and left. You walked at random, entered a commissary, then returned to the Agency and took a ship.'

'What then?' He wondered how far they had gone.

'Then you eluded pursuit. We, ah, weren't equipped to follow.'

'I went to Hokkaido. Ask my block warden. I drank three glasses of wine, came home, fell on the front steps. It's all a matter of record; I was brought up and exonerated.'

'So.' Blake nodded. 'Well, then. It's our contention that you met a woman; that you had met her before; that you have willingly and knowingly committed adultery with this woman.'

'Thus collapses the juvenile system,' Allen said bitterly. 'Here ends empirical evidence. Back comes witch-burning. Hysterics and innuendo.'

'You left your Agency,' Blake continued, 'on Tuesday of that week, to make a phone call from a public booth. It was a call you couldn't make in your office, for fear of being overheard.'

'To this girl?' They were ingenious, at least. And they probably believed it. 'What's the girl's name?'

'Grace Maldini,' Blake said. 'About twenty-four years old, standing five-foot-five, weighing about one twenty-five. Dark hair, dark skin, presumably of Italian extraction.'

It was Gretchen, of course. Now he was really perplexed.

'On Thursday morning you were two hours late to work. You walked off and were lost along the commute lanes. You deliberately chose routes through the thickest traffic.'

'Conjecture,' Allen said. But it had been true; he was on his way to the Health Resort. Grace Maldini? What on earth was that about?

'On Saturday morning of that week,' Blake continued, 'you did the same thing. You shook off anybody who might have been following you and met this girl at an unknown point. You did not return to your apartment that day. That night, a week ago yesterday, you boarded an inter-S ship in the company of the girl, who registered herself as Miss Grace Maldini. You registered under the name John Coates. When the ship reached Centaurus, you and the girl transferred to a second ship, and again you shook monitoring. You did not return to Earth during the entire week. It was within that period that your wife described you as "completing work at your Agency." This evening, about thirty minutes ago, you stepped off an inter-S ship, dressed as you are now, entered a phone booth, and then came here.'

They were all looking at him, waiting with interest. This was an ultimate block meeting: avid curiosity, the need to hear every lurid detail. And, with that, the solemn Morec of duty.

At least he knew how he had been gotten from Earth to Other World. Malparto's therapeutic drugs had kept him docile, while Gretchen thought up names and made the arrangements. Four days in her company: the first emergence of John Coates.

'Produce the girl,' Allen said.

Nobody spoke.

'Where is she?' They could look forever for Grace Maldini.

And without her it was so much hearsay. 'Let's see her. Where does she live? What's her lease? Where does she work? Where is she right now?'

Blake produced a photograph, and Allen examined it. A blurred print: he and Gretchen seated side by side in large chairs. Gretchen was reading a magazine and he was asleep. Taken on the ship, no doubt, from the other end of the lounge.

'Incredible,' he mocked. 'There I am, and a woman's sitting next to me.'

Myron Mavis took the picture, studied it, and sneered. 'Not worth a cent. Not worth the merest particle of a rusty Mexican cent. Take it back.'

Mrs Hoyt said thoughtfully: 'Myron's right. This isn't proof of anything.'

'Why did you assume the name Coates?' Luddy spoke up. 'If you're so innocent—'

'Prove that, too,' Mavis said. 'This is ridiculous. I'm going home; I'm tired, and Purcell looks tired. Tomorrow is Monday and you know what that means for all of us.'

Mrs Frost arose, folded her arms, and said to Allen: 'We all agree it isn't remotely possible to call this material *proof*. But it's disturbing. Evidently you did make these phone calls; you did go somewhere out of the ordinary; you have been gone the last week. What you tell me I'll believe. So will Mrs Hoyt.'

Mrs Hoyt inclined her head.

'Have you left your wife?' Mrs Frost asked. 'One simple question. Yes or no.'

'No,' he said, and it was really, actually true. There was no lie involved. He looked her straight in the eye. 'No adultery, no affair, no secret love. I went to Hokkaido and got material. I phoned a male friend.' Some friend. 'I visited the same friend. This last week has been an unfortunate involvement in circumstances beyond my control, growing out of my retiring from my Agency and accepting the directorship. My motives and actions have been in the public interest, and my conscience is totally clear.'

Mrs Hoyt said: 'Let the boy go. So he can take a bath and get some sleep.'

Her hand out, Sue Frost approached Allen. 'I'm sorry. I am. You know that.'

They shook, and Allen said: 'Tomorrow morning, at eight?'

'Fine.' She smiled sheepishly. 'But we had to check. A charge of this sort – you understand.'

He did. Turning to Blake and Luddy, who were stuffing their material back in its briefcase, Allen said: 'Packet number 355-B. Faithful husband the victim of old women living in the housing unit who cook up a kettle of filth and then get it tossed in their faces.'

Hurriedly, glancing down, Blake murmured good nights and departed. Luddy followed after him. Allen wondered how long the false lead would keep him alive.

16

His new office at Telemedia had been cleaned, swept, repainted, and his desk had been moved from the Agency as a gesture of continuity. By ten o'clock Monday morning, Allen had got the feel of things. He had sat in the big swivel chair, used the pencil sharpener, stood before the one-way viewing wall covertly surveying his building-sized staff.

While he was stabilizing himself, Myron Mavis, looking as if he hadn't gone to bed, appeared to wish him luck.

'Not a bad layout,' Mavis said. 'Gets plenty of sunlight, good air. Very healthy; look at me.'

'I hope you're not selling your hoofs for glue,' Allen said, feeling humble.

'Not for awhile. Come on.' Mavis guided him out of the office. 'I'll introduce you to the staff.'

They squeezed past bundles of congratulatory 'flowers' along the corridor. The reek of crypto-flora assailed them, and Allen halted to examine cards. 'Like a hot house,' he said. 'Here's one from Mrs Hoyt.'

There was a bundle from Sue Frost, from Harry Priar, and from Janet. There were gaudy bundles from the four giant Agencies, including Blake-Moffet. All bore formal greetings. Their representatives would be in shortly. And there were unmarked bundles with no cards. He wondered who had sent them. Persons in the housing unit; perhaps little Mr Wales who had stuck up for him during the block meeting. Others, from anonymous individuals who wished him luck. There was a single bunch, very small, which he picked up; some sort of blue growth.

'Those are real,' Mavis said. 'Smell them. Bluebells, I think they were called. Somebody must have dredged them up from the past.'

Probably Gates and Sugermann. And one of the anonymous bundles could represent the Mental Health Resort. In the back of his mind was the conviction that Malparto would be seeking to recover his investment.

The staff quit work and lined up for his inspection. He shook hands, made random inquiries, spoke sage comments, greeted personnel he remembered. It was almost noon by the time he and Mavis had made the circuit of the building.

'That was kind of a bad scrape, last night,' Mavis said, as they returned to the office. 'Blake-Moffet has been after the directorship for years. It must hurt like h—l to see you in.'

Allen opened the file he had brought and rummaged for a packet. 'Remember this?' He passed it to Mavis. 'Everything started with this.'

'Oh yes.' Mavis nodded. 'The tree that died. The anti-colonization Morec.'

'You know better than that,' Allen said.

Mavis looked bland. 'Symbol of spiritual starvation, then. Severed from the folk-soul. You're going to put that through? The new Renaissance in propaganda. What Dante did for the afterworld, you're going to do for this.'

'This particular packet,' Allen said, 'is long overdue. It should have come out months ago. I suppose I could start out cautiously, process only what's already been bought. Interfere with the staff as little as possible. Let them go the way they've been going – the low-risk approach.' He opened the packet. 'But.'

'Not but.' Mavis leaned close, put the side of his hand to his lips, and whispered hoarsely: 'The watchword is *Excelsior*.'

He shook hands with Allen, wished him luck, hung lonelily around the building for an hour or so, and then was gone.

Watching Mavis shuffle off, Allen was conscious of his own burden. But the sense of weight made him cheerful.

'Seven with one blow,' he said.

'Yes, Mr Purcell,' a battery of intercoms responded, as secretaries came to life.

'My father can lick your father,' Allen said. 'I'm just testing the equipment. You can go back to sleep, or whatever it is you're doing.'

Removing his coat he settled himself at his desk and began dividing up the packet. There was still nothing in it he cared to alter, so he marked it 'satisfactory' and tossed it in the basket. The basket whisked it off, and somewhere down the long chain of command, the packet was received and put into process.

He picked up the phone and called his wife.

'Where are you?' she said, as if she was afraid to believe it. 'Are you . . .'

'I'm there,' he said.

'H-how's the job?'

'Power unlimited.'

She seemed to relax. 'You want to celebrate tonight?'

The idea sounded good. 'Sure. This is our big triumph; we should enjoy it.' He tried to think what would be appropriate. 'I could bring home a quart of ice cream.'

Janet said: 'I'd feel better if you told me what happened last night with Mrs Frost.'

There was no point in giving her grounds for her anxiety. 'You worry too much. It came out all right, and that's what matters. This morning I put through the tree packet. Remember that? Now they can't bury it in dust. I'm going to transfer my best men from the Agency, men like Harry Priar. I'll trim down the staff here until I have something manageable.'

'You won't make the projections too hard to understand, will you? I mean, don't put together things over people's heads.'

'Nobody can say what's "over people's heads," ' Allen said. 'The aged-in-the-stalk formula material is on its way out, and all sorts of new stuff is coming in. We'll try a little of everything.'

94

Wistfully, Janet said: 'Remember how much fun it was when we started? Forming the Agency, hitting T-M with our new ideas, our new kind of packets.'

He remembered. 'Just keep thinking about that. I'll see you tonight. Everything's coming out fine, so don't worry.' He added goodbye, and then hung up.

'Mr Purcell,' his desk intercom said, 'there are a number of people waiting to see you.'

'OK, Doris,' he said.

'Vivian, Mr Purcell.' What sounded like a giggle. 'Shall I send the first one in?'

'Send him, her, or it in,' Allen said. He folded his hands in front of him and scrutinized the door.

The first person was a woman, and she was Gretchen Malparto.

17

Gretchen wore a tight blue suit, carried a beaded purse, was pale and drawn, dark-eyed with tension. She smelled of fresh flowers and looked beautiful and expensive. Closing the door, she said:

'I got your note.'

'The baby was a boy. Six pounds.' The office seemed filled with tiny drifting particles; he rested his palms against the desk and closed his eyes. When he opened his eyes the particles were gone but Gretchen was still there; she had seated herself, crossed her legs, and was fingering the edge of her skirt.

'When did you arrive back here?' she asked.

'Sunday night.'

'I got in this morning.' Her eyebrows wavered and across her face flitted a blind, crumpled pain. 'You certainly walked right out.'

'Well,' he said, 'I figured out where I was.'

'Was it so bad?'

Allen said: 'I can call people in here and have you tossed out. I can have you barred; I can have all kinds of things done to you. I can even have you arrested and prosecuted for a felony, you and

95

your brother and that demented outfit you run. But that puts an end to me. Even Vivian walking in to take dictation is the end, with you sitting there.'

'Who's Vivian?'

'One of my new secretaries. She comes along with the job.'

Color had returned to Gretchen's features. 'You're exaggerating.'

Allen went over and examined the door. It had a lock, so he locked it. He then went to the intercom, pressed the button, and said: 'I don't want to be disturbed.'

'Yes, Mr Purcell,' Vivian's voice sounded.

Picking up the phone, Allen called his Agency. Harry Priar answered. 'Harry,' Allen said, 'get over here to T-M in something, a sliver or a Getabout. Park as close as you can and then come upstairs to my office.'

'What's going on?'

'When you're here, phone me from my secretary's desk. Don't use the intercom.' He hung up, bent over, and ripped the intercom loose. 'These things are natural taps,' he explained to Gretchen.

'You're really serious.'

'Bet you I am.' He folded his arms, leaned against the side of the desk. 'Is your brother crazy?'

She gulped. 'He – is, in a sense. A mania, collecting. But they all have it. This Psi mysticism. There was such a blob on your -gram; it tipped him across.'

'How about you?'

'I suppose I'm not so clever either.' Her voice was thin, brittle. 'I've had four days travelling in to think about it. As soon as I saw you were gone, I followed. I – really thought you'd come back to the house. Wishful thinking . . . it was so damn nice and cozy.' Suddenly she lashed out furiously. 'You stupid bastard!'

Allen looked at his watch and saw that Harry Priar would be another ten minutes. Probably he was just now backing the sliver onto the roof field of the Agency.

'What are you going to do with me?' Gretchen said.

'Drive you out somewhere and dump you.' He wondered if Gates could help. Maybe she could be detained at Hokkaido. But that was their gimmick. 'Didn't it seem a little unfair to me?' he said. 'I went to you for help; I acted in good faith.'

Staring at the floor, Gretchen said: 'My brother's responsible. I didn't know in advance; you were starting out the door to leave, and then you keeled over. He gas-pelleted you. Somebody was detailed to get you to Other World; they were going to ship you there by freight, in a cataleptic state. I – was afraid you might die. It's risky. So I accompanied you.' She raised her head. 'I wanted to. It was a terrible thing to do, but it was going to happen anyhow.'

He felt less hostility, since it was probably true. 'You're an opportunist,' he murmured. 'The whole affair was ingenious. Especially that bit when the house dissolved. What's this blob on my -gram?'

'My brother puzzled over it from the time he got it. He never figured it out, and neither did the Dickson. Some psionic talent. Precognition, he thinks. You japed the statue to prevent your own murder at the hands of the Cohorts. He thinks the Cohorts kill people who rise too high.'

'Do you agree?'

'No,' she said, 'because I know what the blob means. You do have something in your mind nobody else has. But it's not precognition.'

'What is it?'

Gretchen said: 'You have a sense of humor.'

The office was quiet as Allen considered and Gretchen sat smoothing her skirt.

'Maybe so,' Allen said finally.

'And a sense of humor doesn't fit in with Morec. Or with us. You're not a "mutant"; you're just a balanced human being.' Her voice gained strength. 'The japery, everything you've done. You're just trying to re-establish a balance in an unbalanced world. And it's something you can't even admit to yourself. On the top you believe in Morec. Underneath there's that blob, that irreducible core, that grins and laughs and plays pranks.'

'Childish,' he said.

'Not at all.'

97

'Thanks.' He smiled down at her.

'This is such a goddamn mess.' From her purse she got her handkerchief; she wiped her eyes and then stuffed the handkerchief into her coat pocket. 'You've got this job, Director of Telemedia, the high post of morality. Guardian of public ethics. You *create* the ethics. What a screwy, mixed-up situation.'

'But I want this job.'

'Yes, your ethics are very high. But they're not the ethics of this society. The block meetings – you loathe them. The faceless accusers. The juveniles – the busybody prying. This senseless struggle for leases. The anxiety. The tension and strain; look at Myron Mavis. And the overtones of guilt and suspicion. Everything becomes – tainted. The fear of contamination; fear of committing an indecent act. Sex is morbid; people hounded for natural acts. This whole structure is like a giant torture chamber, with everybody staring at one another, trying to find fault, trying to break one another down. Witchhunts and star chambers. Dread and censorship. Mr Bluenose banning books. Children kept from hearing *evil*. Morec was invented by sick minds, and it creates more sick minds.'

'All right,' Allen said, listening. 'But I'm not going to lie around watching girls sun-bathe. Like a salesman on vacation.'

'That's all you see in the Resort?'

'That's all I see in Other World. And the Resort is a machine to process people there.'

'It does more than that. It provides them with a place they can escape to. When their resentment and anxiety starts destroying them—' She gestured. 'Then they go over.'

'Then they don't smash store windows. Or jape statues. I'd rather jape statues.'

'You came to us once.'

'As I see it,' Allen said, 'the Resort acts as part of the system. Morec is one half and you're the other. Two sides of the coin: Morec is all work and you're the badminton and checkers set. Together you form a society; you uphold and support each other. I can't be in both parts, and of the two I prefer this.'

'Why?'

'At least something's being done, here. People are working. You tell them to go out and fish.'

'So you won't go back with me,' she said reasonably. 'I didn't really think you would.'

'Then what did you show up here for?'

'To explain. So you'd understand how that whole damn foolish business happened, and what my part was. Why I got involved. And so you'd understand about yourself. I wanted you to be aware of your feelings . . . the hostility you feel toward Morec. The deep outrage you have for its cruelties. You're moving in the direction of integration. But I wanted to help. Maybe it'll pay you back for what we took. You did ask us for help. I'm sorry.'

'Being sorry is a good idea,' he said. 'A step in the right direction.'

Gretchen got up and put her hand on the doorknob. 'I'll take the next step. Goodbye.'

'Just sit down.' He propelled her back to the chair but she disengaged her arm. 'What now?' he demanded. 'More speeches?'

'No.' She faced him. 'I give up. I won't cause you any more trouble. Go back to your little worrying wife; that's where you belong.'

'She's younger than you,' Allen said. 'As well as smaller.'

'How wonderful,' Gretchen said lightly. 'But – does she understand about you? This core you have that makes you different and keeps you out of the system? Can she help bring that out as it should be? Because that's important, more important than anything else. Even this heroic position, this new job, isn't really—'

'Still the welfare worker,' he said. He was only partly listening to her; he was watching for Harry Priar.

'You do believe what I say, don't you? About you; about what's inside you.'

'OK,' he said. 'I'm taken in by your story.'

'It's true. I – really care about you, Allen. You're a lot like Donna's father. Equivocating about the system, leaving it and then going back. The same doubts and mistrusts. Now he's back here for good. I said goodbye to him. I'm saying goodbye to you, the same way.'

'One last thing,' Allen said. 'For the record. Do you honestly suppose I'm going to pay that bill?'

'It does seem stupid. There's a routine procedure, and it was marked "for services rendered," so nobody would identify it. I'll have the account voided.' She was suddenly shy. 'I'd like to ask for something. Possibly you'll laugh.'

'Let's hear it.'

'Why don't you kiss me goodbye?'

'I hadn't thought about it.' He made no move.

Stripping off her gloves, Gretchen laid them with her purse and raised her bare, slim fingers to his face. 'There really isn't anybody named Molly, is there? You just made her up.' She dug her nails into his neck, tugging him down against her. Her breath, as she kissed him, was faintly sweet with peppermint, and her lips were moist. 'You're so good,' she said, turning her face away.

She screamed.

On the floor of the office was a metal earwig-shaped creature, its receptor stalks high and whirring. The juvenile scuttled closer, then retreated in a dash of motion.

Allen grabbed up a paper weight from the desk and threw it at the juvenile. He missed, and the thing kept on going. It was trying to get back out the window, through which it had come. As it scooted up the wall he lifted his foot and smashed it; the juvenile fell broken to the floor and crawled in a half-circle. Allen found a typewriter and dropped it on the crippled juvenile. Then he began searching for its reservoir of tape.

While he was searching, the office door fell open and a second juvenile spurted in. Behind it was Fred Luddy, snapping pictures with a flash camera. With him were Blake-Moffet technicians, trailing wires and earphones and lenses and mikes and batteries. After the Blake-Moffet people came a horde of T-M employees, screeching and fluttering.

'Sue us for the lock!' Luddy shouted, tripping on a mike cable. 'Somebody get the tape from that busted juve—'

Two technicians jumped past Gretchen and swept up the remains of the demolished juvenile. 'Looks intact, Fred.'

As Luddy snapped pictures, tape transports revolved and the surviving juvenile whirred exultantly. The office was jammed with people and equipment; Gretchen stood huddled in a corner, and somewhere far off burglar alarms were ringing.

'We reamed out the lock!' Luddy shouted, rushing up to Allen with his camera. 'You didn't hear it; you were killing that juve we sent in through the window. Up six flights – those things *climb*!'

'Run,' Allen said to Gretchen, pushing people out of her way. 'Get downstairs and out of here.'

She broke from her paralysis and started toward the open door. Luddy saw and yelped with dismay; he shoved his camera into a subordinate's arm and hurried after. As he caught hold of her arm, Allen reached him and socked him on the jaw. Luddy collapsed, and Gretchen, with a wail of despair, disappeared down the corridor.

'Oh boy,' one of Blake-Moffet's men chortled, helping Luddy up. 'Have we got pictures.'

There were now three juveniles, and more were on the way. Allen seated himself on an air conditioner and rested. Turmoil surged everywhere; the Blake-Moffet people were still taking pictures and his own T-M people were trying to restore order.

'Mr Purcell,' one of his secretaries – probably Vivian – was shrilling in his ear. 'What'll we do? Call the police?'

'Get them out,' Allen grunted. 'Bring up people from the other departments and throw them out. They're trespassing.'

'Yes, sir,' the secretary said, and darted off.

Luddy, propped up by two of his compatriots, approached. He was fingering his chin and he had got back his camera. 'The first tape's intact. You and that gal clinching; it's all down. And the rest, too; you busting the juve up and hitting me, and sending her off. And the door locked, the intercom ripped out – the whole works.'

From the confusion Harry Priar emerged. 'What happened, Allen?' He saw Luddy and the juveniles. 'Oh no,' he said. 'No.'

'You didn't last long,' Luddy said to Allen. 'You—' He ducked off as Priar started at him.

'I guess,' Priar said, 'I didn't get here in time.'

'How'd you come? On your hands?' Some of the chaos was dying down. The Blake-Moffet people, and their equipment, were being forcibly ushered out. They were all smiles. His own staff was gathering in gloomy bunches, glancing at him and exchanging mutters. A T-M repairman was inspecting the hole in the office door where the lock had been. Blake-Moffet had carried the lock off with them, probably as a trophy.

'Invasion,' Priar said. 'I never would have thought Luddy had the guts.'

'Blake's idea,' Allen said. 'And Luddy's vendetta. So now it comes full cycle. I got Luddy, now he gets me.'

'Did they – I mean, they got what they wanted, didn't they?'

'Drums of it,' Allen said. 'I did the ultimate; I stamped on a juvenile.'

'Who was the girl?'

Allen grimaced. 'Just a friend. A niece visiting from the country. My daughter. Why do you ask?'

18

Late that night he sat with Janet in the darkness, listening to the noises filtering through the walls from other apartments. The murmur of voices, faint music, rattle of dishes and pans, and indiscriminate globs of sound that could be anything.

'Want to go for a walk?' he asked.

'No.' Janet stirred a little beside him.

'Want to go to bed?'

'No. Just sit.'

Presently Allen said: 'I ran into Mrs Birmingham on my way to the bathroom. They brought the reports in a convoy of Getabouts. Six men guarding it. Now she's got it all hidden somewhere, probably in an old stocking.'

'You're going into the block meeting?'

'I'll be there, and I'm going to fight with everything I've got.'

'Will it do any good?'

He reflected. 'No.'

'Then,' Janet said, 'we're washed up.'

'We'll lose our lease, if that's what you mean. But that's all Mrs Birmingham can do. Her authority ends when we leave here.'

'You've resigned yourself to that,' Janet said.

'I might as well.' He searched for his cigarettes, then gave up. 'Haven't you?'

'Your family worked for decades for this lease. All those years your mother was with the Sutton Agency before it merged. And your father in T-M's art department.'

'Pooled status,' he said. 'You don't have to remind me. But I'm still Director of Telemedia. Maybe I can wangle a lease out of Sue Frost. Technically I'm entitled to one. We should be living in Myron Mavis' apartment, within walking distance of my work.'

'Would she give you a lease now? After this business today?'

He tried to imagine Sue Frost and the expression on her face. The sound of her voice. The rest of the day he had hung around his office at T-M expecting her to call, but she hadn't. No word had arrived from above; the powers had remained mum.

'She'll be disappointed,' he said. 'Sue had the kind of hopes for me only a mother could invent.'

Up the ladder generation by generation. The schemings of old women, the secret ambitions and activity of parents boosting their children one more notch. Exhaustion, sweat, the grave.

'We can assume Blake-Moffet briefed her,' he said. 'I guess it's time to tell you what happened last night at her apartment.'

He told Janet, and she had nothing to say. There wasn't enough light in the apartment to see her face, and he wondered if she had passed out with wretchedness. Or if some primordial storm were going to burst over him. But, when he finally nudged her, she simply said: 'I was afraid it was something like that.'

'Why the h—l why?'

'I just had a feeling. Maybe I'm clairvoyant.' He had told her about Doctor Malparto's Psionic-testing. 'And it was the same girl?'

'The girl who got me to the Health Resort; the girl who helped kidnap me; the girl who leaned her bosom in my face and said I was the father of her child. A very pretty black-haired girl with a big lovely house. But I did come back. Nobody seems to care about that part.'

'I care,' Janet said. 'Do you think she was in on the frame-up?'

'The idea entered my mind. But she wasn't. There was nothing to be gained, except by Blake-Moffet. And the Resort isn't part of

Blake-Moffet. Gretchen was just witless and irresponsible and full of feminine vigor. Young love, they call it. And the idealism of her calling. Her brother's the same way: idealism, for the benefit of the patient.'

'It's so sort of crazy,' Janet protested. 'All she did was walk into your office, and all you did was kiss her when she left. And you're completely ruined.'

'The word is "vile enterprise," ' Allen said. 'It'll be showing up Wednesday, about nine a.m. I wonder what Mr Wales can do in my defence. It should pose quite a challenge to him.'

But the block meeting wasn't really important. The unknown was Sue Frost, and her reaction might not be in for days. After all, she had to confer with Ida Pease Hoyt: the reaction needed the stamp of absolute finality.

'Didn't you say something about bringing home a quart of ice cream?' Janet asked wanly.

'Seems sort of silly,' Allen said. 'Everything considered.'

19

On Wednesday morning the first-floor chamber of the housing unit was crammed to bursting. The gossip relay had carried the news to everybody, mostly through the wives. Stale cigarette smoke hung in its cloud and the air conditioning system was making no progress. At the far end was the platform on which the wardens sat, and they were all present.

In a freshly-starched dress, Janet entered slightly ahead of him. She went directly to a vacant table and placed herself before the microphone. The table, by an unverbalized protocol, was purposely untaken; in times of real crisis the wife was expected to aid her husband. To deprive her of that right would have been an affront to Morec.

Last time, no table had been left vacant. Last time had not been a crisis.

'This is serious,' Allen said to his wife, stationing himself behind her. 'And this long is; this vindictive is; and this going to lose is. So don't get too involved. Don't try to save me, because I can't be saved. As we said last night.'

She nodded sightlessly.

'When they start burying their teeth in me,' he continued softly, as if humming a tune, 'don't spring up and take them all on. This is so rigged it's ready to burst. For example, where's little Mr Wales?'

The man who had faith in Allen Purcell was not present. And the doors were being closed: he was not coming.

'They probably discovered a loophole in his lease,' Allen said. Now Mrs Birmingham was rising to her feet and accepting the agenda. 'Or it turned out that he's the owner of a chain of w—e houses stretching from Newer York to Orionus.'

Janet still continued to face front, with a rigidity he had never before seen. She seemed to have created an exoskeleton for herself, a containing envelope through which nothing entered and nothing escaped. He wondered if she were saving herself for one grand slam. Perhaps it would appear when the ladies read their decision.

'It's dusty in here,' Allen said, as the room dwindled into silence. A few persons glanced at him, then looked away. Since he was coasting downhill it was a poor idea to associate themselves with him.

At the end of the room the juveniles were surrendering their tapes. Seven tapes in all. Six, he conjectured, were for him. And one for everybody else.

'We will first undertake the case of Mr A.P.,' Mrs Birmingham announced.

'Fine,' Allen said, relieved. Again heads turned, then swiveled back. A murmur drifted up and joined the haze of cigarette smoke.

In a sardonic way he was amused. The rows of solemn, righteous faces . . . this was a church, and these were the members of the congregation in pious session. With long strides he made his way to the defendant's stage, hands in his pockets. In the rear, at her table, Janet sat wooden-faced, as stiff and unyielding as a carved stick. He nodded to her, and the session began.

*

'Mr A.P.,' Mrs Birmingham said, in her noisy, authoritative voice, 'did willingly and knowingly on the afternoon of October 22, 2114, in his place of business and during the working hours of the day, engage in a vile enterprise with a young woman. Further, Mr A.P. did willingly and knowingly destroy an official monitoring instrument to avoid detection, and to further avoid detection he did strike the face of a Morec citizen, damage private property, and in every possible fashion seek to conceal his actions.'

A series of clicks bounced from the loudspeaker, as the voice warmed up. The interconnecting network was in operation: the speaker hummed, buzzed and then spoke.

'Definition. Be specific. Vile enterprise.'

Mrs Birmingham adjusted her glasses and read on. 'Mr A.P. did welcome the young woman – not his lawful wife – into his office at the Committee Telemedia Trust, and there he did lock himself in with her, did take precautions to guarantee that he not be discovered, and, when discovered, *was in the act of petting and embracing and sexually fondling the young woman about the shoulder and face*, and had so placed his body *that it was in contact with that of hers*.'

'Is this the same Mr A.P. who was up before us the week before last?' the voice asked.

'It is,' Mrs Birmingham said, without reluctance.

'And this last week he was not present at the meeting?' The voice then declared: 'Mr A.P. is not being judged for his absence last week, and his lapse of the previous week has already been dealt with by this gathering.'

The mood of the gathering was now varied. As always, many of the members were curious; some were bored and not particularly concerned. A few appeared unusually interested, and it was those to whom Allen paid attention.

'Mr A.P.,' the voice said. 'Was this the first time you had met the young woman?'

'No,' he said. 'I'd seen her before.' It was a trap, practised as a matter of routine: if his reply was that yes, this was the first time, he was open for the charge of promiscuity. Sexual misconduct was better understood if it was confined to one partner; Miss J.E. had been cleared by that point, and he intended to use it, too.

'Often?' the voice asked, infinitely toneless.

'Not in excess. We were good friends. We still are. I think a great deal of Miss G.M. I have the highest respect for her, and so does my wife.'

'Your wife knows her?' the voice asked. It answered its own question: 'He just said so.'

Allen said: 'Let me make this clear. Miss G.M. is a responsible woman, and I have absolute faith in her moral integrity. Otherwise I wouldn't have admitted her to my office.' His job was a matter of public knowledge, so he took the plunge. 'In my position as Director of Telemedia, I must be highly careful of my choice of friends. Therefore—'

'How long have you been Director?'

He hesitated. 'Monday was my first day.'

'And that was the day this young woman appeared?'

'People streamed in and out all day. Bundles of "flowers" arrived; you're familiar with the protocol of congratulation. I was besieged by well-wishers. Miss G.M. was one of them. She dropped by to wish me luck.'

The voice said: 'A great *deal* of luck.' Several persons smirked knowingly. 'You locked the door, did you? You ripped out the intercom? You phoned for a Getabout to pick the two of you up as soon as possible?'

To his knowledge this information wasn't available on the official report. He felt uneasy. 'I locked the door because people had been barging in all day. I was nervous and irritable. Frankly, I was a little overwhelmed by the job, and I didn't care to see anybody. As to the intercom—' He lied shamelessly, without conscience. Under the system there was no choice. 'Being unfamiliar with my new office I inadvertently tripped over the wires. The wires broke. Anybody in business is aware that such things happen frequently – and at exactly such times.'

'Indeed,' the voice said.

'Miss G.M.,' Allen went on, 'stayed about ten minutes. When the monitoring device entered, I was saying goodbye to her. As she left she asked if she could kiss me, as a token of congratulation. Before I could say no, she had done so. That was what happened, and that was what the monitor saw.'

'You tried to destroy the monitor.'

'Miss G.M. screamed; she was taken unawares. It had entered by the window and neither of us noticed it. To be honest, we both imagined it was some sort of menace. I'm not clear now as to exactly what I thought it was. I heard Miss G.M. scream; I saw a blur of motion. Instinctively I kicked out, and my foot connected with it.'

'This man you hit.'

'At Miss G.M.'s scream the door was forced and a number of hysterical people burst in. There was bedlam for a time, which is reported. A man ran up and started to grab at Miss G.M. I thought it was an attack aimed at Miss G.M., and I had no choice but to defend her. As a gentleman it was incumbent on me.'

'Does the record bear that out?' the voice asked.

Mrs Birmingham consulted. 'The individual who was struck was attempting physically to apprehend the young woman.' She turned a page. 'However, it is stated that Mr A.P. had instructed the woman to flee the scene.'

'Naturally,' Allen said. 'Since I feared an attack on her I wanted her to escape to safety. Consider the situation. Miss G.M. enters my office to wish me—'

'This is the same Miss G.M.,' the voice interrupted, 'with whom you spent four days and *nights* on an inter-S ship? The same Miss G.M. who registered under a phony name in order to conceal her identity? Is this not the same Miss G.M. with whom you have committed adultery at a number of times, in a number of places? Is it not true that all this has been concealed from your wife and that in reality your wife has never met this woman and could not possibly have any opinion of her except the normal opinion of a wife toward her husband's mistress?'

General pandemonium.

Allen waited for the noise to die down. 'I have never committed adultery with anybody. I have no romantic relationship with Miss G.M. I have never—'

'You fondled her; you kissed her; don't you call that romantic?'

'Any man,' Allen said, 'who is capable of sexual activity during his first day at a new job is an unusual man.'

Appreciative laughter. And a scatter of applause.

'Is Miss G.M. pretty?' This, in all probability, was a wife. The planted questioner, with extra information at his disposal, had temporarily retired.

'I suppose,' Allen said. 'Now that I think of it. Yes, she was attractive. Some men would think so.'

'When did you first meet her?'

'Oh, about—' And then he broke off. He had almost fallen on that one. Two weeks was the wrong answer. No friendship of two weeks included a hug and kiss, in the Morec world. 'I'll have to think back,' he said, as if it were decades. 'Let's see, when I first met her I was working for . . .' He let his voice trail off, until the questioner became impatient and asked:

'How did you meet her?'

In the back of his mind Allen sensed that the enemy was closing in. There were many questions he couldn't answer, for which no evasion would work. This was one of them.

'I don't remember,' he said, and saw the floor open to receive him. 'Some mutual friends, maybe.'

'Where does she work?'

'I don't know.'

'Why did you take a four-day trip with her?'

'Prove that I did.' He had a way out of that, at least. 'Is that in the report?'

Mrs Birmingham searched, and shook her head no.

'Mr A.P.,' the voice said. 'I'd like to ask you this.' He couldn't tell if this were the same accuser; warily, he assumed it was. 'Two weeks ago, when you arrived home drunk. Had you been with this woman?'

'No,' he said, which was true.

'Are you positive? You had been alone at your office; you took a sliver to Hokkaido; you showed up several hours later clearly having had—'

'I didn't even know her then,' he said. And realized his utter and final mistake. But now, alas, it was too late.

'You met her less than *two weeks ago*?'

'I had seen her before.' His voice came out insect-frail, weak with awareness of defeat. 'But I didn't know her well.'

'What happened between you and her during the last two weeks? Was that when the relationship grew?'

Allen reflected at length. No matter how he answered, the situation was hopeless. But it was bound to end this way. 'I'm not aware,' he said at last, half-idly, 'that it ever grew, then or any other time.'

'To you a relationship with a young woman not your wife that involves petting and fondling and the juxtaposition of bodies—'

'To a diseased mind any relationship is foul,' Allen said. He got to his feet and faced the people below him. 'I'd like to see who I'm talking to. Come on out from under your rock; let's see what you look like.'

The impersonal voice went on: 'Are you in the habit of putting your hands on the bodies of young women with whom you happen, during the course of the day, to come in contact? Do you use your job as a means by which—'

'I tell you what,' Allen said. 'If you'll identify yourself I'll knock the living Jesus out of you. I'm fed-up with this faceless accusation. Obscene, sadistic minds are using these meetings to pry out all the sordid details, tainting every harmless act by pawing over it, reading filth and guilt into every normal human relationship. Before I step off this stage I have one general, theoretical statement to make. The world would be a lot better place if there was no morbid inquisition like this. More harm is done in one of these sessions than in all the copulation between man and woman since the creation of the world.'

He reseated himself. No sound was audible anywhere. The room was totally silent. Presently Mrs Birmingham said: 'Unless anybody wishes to make any further statements, the Council will prepare its decision.'

There was no response from the impersonal voice of 'justice.' Allen, hunched over, realized that it had said not one word in his defense. Janet still sat like a stick of wood. Possibly she agreed with the accusations. At the moment it didn't really matter to him.

The council of ladies conferred for a period that seemed to him unnecessarily long. After all, the decision was foregone. He plucked at a thread on his sleeve, coughed, twisted restlessly on the chair. At last Mrs Birmingham stood.

'The block-neighbors of Mr A.P.,' she stated, 'regret that they are required to find Mr A.P. to be an undesirable tenant. This exceptionally unfortunate is, since Mr A.P. has been an exemplary tenant in this housing unit for many years, and his family before him. Mr A.P., in point of fact, was born in the apartment he now holds. Therefore it is with deep reluctance that the Council, speaking for Mr A.P.'s block-neighbors, declares his lease to be void as of the sixth day of November, 2114, and with even deeper reluctance petitions Mr A.P. to remove his person, family, and possessions from these premises by that date.' Mrs Birmingham was silent a moment and then concluded: 'It is also hoped that Mr A.P. will understand that given the circumstances the Council and his block-neighbors had no choice in the matter, and that they wish him the best of personal luck. In addition, the Council wishes to make clear its conviction that Mr A.P. is a man of greatest fortitude and perseverance, and it is the Council's belief that Mr A.P. will surmount this temporary difficulty.'

Allen laughed out loud.

Mrs Birmingham glanced at him quizzically, then folded up her statement and stepped back. Allen walked from the stage, down the steps and across the crowded room to the table at which his wife sat.

'Come on,' he said to her. 'We might as well leave.'

As the two of them pushed outside they heard Mrs Birmingham droning into the next indictment.

'We will now undertake the case of R.P., a boy, age nine, who did willingly and knowingly on the morning of October 21, 2114, scrawl certain pornographic words on the wall of the community bathroom of the second floor of this housing unit.'

'Well,' Allen said to his wife, as the door was locked after them, 'that's that.'

She nodded.

'How do you feel?' he asked.

'It seems so unreal.'

'It's real. We have two weeks to get out. Temporary difficulty.' He shook his head. 'What a travesty.'

Loitering in the corridor was Mr Wales, a folded newspaper under his arm. As soon as he saw Allen and Janet he walked hesitantly forward. 'Mr Purcell.'

Allen halted. 'Hello, Mr Wales. We missed you.'

'I wasn't in there.' Mr Wales seemed both apologetic and animated. 'Mr Purcell, my new lease came through. That's why I wasn't there; I'm not part of this unit any more.'

'Oh,' Allen said. So they hadn't eased him out; they had bought up a superior lease and presented it to him. Presumably Mr Wales was ignorant of the purpose of his good fortune; after all, he had his own problems.

'What was it like in there?' Mr Wales asked. 'Somebody told me you were up again.'

'I was,' Allen admitted.

'Serious?' Mr Wales was concerned.

'Not too serious.' Allen patted the little fellow on the arm. 'It's all over now.'

'I hope because I wasn't—'

'Made no difference at all. But thanks anyhow.'

They shook hands. 'Drop by and see us,' Mr Wales said. 'My wife and I. We'd be glad to have you.'

'Okay,' Allen said, 'we'll do that. When we're in the neighborhood.'

After returning Janet to the apartment, Allen walked the long way to Telemedia and his new office. His staff was subdued; they greeted him and swiftly returned to their work. His two-hour absence testified to a block-meeting; they all knew where he had been.

In his office he examined a summary of the day's schedule. The tree packet was in process, and for that he was glad. He called a few T-M officials in, discussed technical problems, then sat alone for awhile, smoking and meditating.

At eleven-thirty Mrs Sue Frost, in a long coat, looking handsome and efficient, bustled cheerfully in to pay a visit.

'I won't take up much of your time,' she announced. 'I realize how busy you are.'

'Just sitting here,' he murmured. But she went on:

'We were wondering if you and your wife are free, tonight. I'm having a little Juggle get-together at my place, just a few people; we'd particularly like you two to be there. Mavis will be there, so will Mrs Hoyt and perhaps—'

He interrupted: 'You want my resignation? Is that it?'

Flushing, she said: 'As long as we're going to be getting together I thought it might be a good opportunity to discuss further some of the—'

'Let's have a direct answer,' he said.

'All right,' she said. In a tight, controlled voice she said, 'We'd like your written resignation.'

'When?'

'As soon as possible.'

He said, 'You mean now?'

With almost perfect composure Sue Frost said, 'Yes. If it's convenient.'

'What if it isn't?'

For a moment she did not seem to understand.

'I mean,' he said, 'what if I refuse to resign?'

'Then,' she said, facing him calmly, 'you'll be discharged.'

'As of when?'

Now, for the first time, she floundered. 'Mrs Hoyt will have to approve. As a matter of fact—'

'As a matter of fact,' he said, 'it takes full Committee action. My lease is good until the sixth and it'll be at least that long before you can legally get me out of T-M. Meanwhile I'm still Director. If you want me you can call me here at my office.'

'You're serious?' she said, in a strained voice.

'I am,' Allen said. 'Has this ever happened before?'

'N-no.'

'I didn't think so.' He picked up some papers from his desk and began to study them; in the time he had left there was a great deal of work to be done.

20

All alone, Mr Wales surveyed his new apartment in unit R6 of leasing zone 28. A life-long dream was fulfilled. He had advanced not one but two zones toward *omphalos*. The Housing Authority had investigated his petition, seen the utter virtue of his life, his devotion to public good.

Moving about the room, Mr Wales touched walls, the floor, gazed out the window, inspected the closet. He ran his hands over the stove, marvelling at his gain. The former tenants had even left their Edufactured objects: clock, shaving wand, small appliances.

To Mr Wales it seemed unbelievable that his trivial person had been recognized. Petitions lay in ten-foot heaps on the desks at the Housing Authority. Surely there was a God. Surely this proved that the gentle and the meek, the unassuming won out in the end.

Seating himself, Mr Wales opened a package and brought forth a vase. He had acquired it as a gift for his wife, a celebration present. The vase was green and blue and speckled with light. Mr Wales turned it around, blew on the smooth glazed surface, held it tightly in his hands.

Then he thought about Mr Purcell. He remembered all the times Mr Purcell had stuck up for victims in the weekly block meetings. All the kind words he had put in. The encouragement he had given the tormented in their trial.

Mr Wales thought how Allen Purcell must have looked coming up before the last block meeting. The dogs tearing at him. The female bitches guzzling at his throat.

Suddenly Mr Wales shouted: 'I betrayed him! I let them crucify him!'

Anguished, he rocked back and forth. Then he sprang to his feet and hurled the vase against the wall. The vase burst, and bits of green and blue and speckled light danced around him.

'I'm a Judas,' Mr Wales said to himself. He covered his eyes with his fingers so he would not have to look at the apartment. He hated the apartment. Now he had what he had always wanted, and he didn't want it.

'I've changed my mind!' he shouted. But nobody heard him. 'You can have it back!'

The room was silent.

'Go away!' Mr Wales cried.

He opened his eyes. The room was still there. It did not respond; it did not leave.

Mr Wales began gathering up the fragments of vase. The bits of glass cut his fingers. He was glad.

21

The next morning Allen arrived promptly at eight o'clock at his office in the Telemedia building. As the staff appeared for work, he called them into his office until all thirty-three of them were present. The hundreds of assignment workers continued at their desks throughout the building as Allen addressed their executive department heads.

'Yesterday my resignation was requested. It's involved with the fracas that took place here Monday afternoon. I refused to resign, so I'm still Director, at least until the Committee can assemble and fire me.'

The staff took the news with aplomb. One member, head of the layout department, asked: 'How long will you remain in your estimation?'

'A week or so,' Allen answered. 'Maybe a little longer.'

'And you intend to continue work during that time?'

'I'll work to the best of my ability,' Allen said. 'There's plenty to do and I want to get into it. But you're entitled to know the situation.'

Another member of the staff, a trim woman with glasses, asked: 'You're the legal Director, is that correct? Until they fire you—'

'Until dismissal papers are served, I'm the sole legal Director of this Trust; I'm your boss, with the powers implicit and explicit in that capacity. Naturally my policies here will be highly suspect. Probably the next Director will cancel them all, straight across the board.'

The staff murmured among themselves.

'You should meditate over that,' Allen said, 'as I give you your assignments. How much trouble you'll get into for obeying and working with me I can't say. Your guess is as good as mine. Maybe the next Director will fire the lot of you. Probably not.'

'It's unlikely,' a staff member said.

'I'm going to give you a few hours to talk it over among yourselves. Let's say until noon. Those of you who would prefer not to take the risk can go home and wait out the period of my directorship. I'm positive that won't get you into trouble with the Committee; they may even suggest it.'

One staff member asked: 'What are your policies going to be? Maybe we should hear them before we decide.'

'I don't think you should,' Allen said. 'You should make your decision on other grounds. If you stay, you'll have to follow my orders no matter what they are. This is the important thing for you to decide: do you care to work for a man who's out of favor?'

The staff left his office, and he was alone. Outside in the corridor their mumbles reached him dully through the closed door.

By noon virtually all the department heads had discreetly gone home. He was without an executive staff. The various operations went on, but the ranks were thinning. An unearthly loneliness hung around the building. The din of machines echoed in the empty offices and halls, and nobody seemed to feel like talking.

To the intercom he said: 'Vivian, come in here a moment.'

A rather drab young woman entered with pencil and pad. 'Yes, Mr Purcell. My name is Nan, Mr Purcell. Vivian left.'

'You're staying?' he asked.

'Yes, sir.' She put on her thick glasses and made ready to take dictation.

'I want you to canvass the departments. It's noon, so presumably those remaining will be with us during the next week. Find out where the depletions are.'

'Yes, sir.' She scribbled notes.

'Specifically I'll need to know which departments can function and which can't. Then send me the highest ranking staff member left. If no staff members are left, send in whoever you think is most familiar with general operations.'

'Yes, sir.' She departed. An hour later a tall, gangling middle-aged party entered shyly.

'Mr Purcell,' he said. 'I'm Gleeby. They said you wanted me. I'm head of music.' He tilted his right ear with his thumb, conveying the interesting bit of news that he was deaf.

'Sit down,' Allen said, pleased by the man, and pleased, also, that one of the staff remained. 'You were in here at eight? You heard my speech?'

'Yes. I heard.' Evidently the man lip-read.

'Well? Can we function?'

Gleeby pondered and lit his pipe. 'Well, that's hard to say. Some departments are virtually closed down. We can redistribute personnel. Try to even up the losses. Fill in some of the widest gaps.'

Allen asked: 'Are you really prepared to carry out my orders?'

'Yes. I am.' Gleeby sucked on his pipe.

'You may be held Morecly responsible.'

'I'd become psychotic loafing around my apartment a week. You don't know my wife.'

'Who here does the research?'

Gleeby was puzzled. 'The Agencies handle that.'

'I mean real research. Checking for historical accuracy. Isn't machinery set up to go over projections point by point?'

'A gal named Phyllis Frame does that. She's been around here thirty years. Has a big desk down in the basement, millions of files and records.'

'Did she leave? If not, send her up.'

Miss Frame hadn't left, and presently she appeared. She was a heavy, sturdy-looking, iron-haired lady, formidable and taciturn. 'You wanted me, Director?'

'Be seated.' He offered her his cigarette case, which she declined. 'You understand the situation?'

'What situation?'

He explained. 'So bear that in mind.'

'I'll bear it in mind. What is it you want? I'm in a hurry to get back to my work.'

'I want,' Allen said, 'a complete profile of Major Streiter. Not derived from packets or projections, but the actual facts as are known about his life, habits, character, and so forth. I want unbiased material. No opinions. Material that is totally authentic.'

'Yes, Director.'

'How soon can you have the profile?'

'By six.' She was starting from the office. 'Should this project include material on the Major's immediate family?'

Allen was impressed. 'Yes. Very good.'

'Thank you, Director.' The door closed and she was gone.

At two o'clock Gleeby re-appeared with the final list of workers remaining. 'We could be worse off. But there's almost nobody capable of making decisions.' He rattled the list. 'Give these people something to do and they'll go into action. But what'll we give them?'

'I have some ideas,' Allen said.

After Gleeby had left the office, Allen phoned his old Agency.

'I have vacancies here,' he said, 'that need to be filled. I think I'll draw from the Agency. I'll put our people on the T-M payroll and try to get funds from the paymaster. If not, then I'll cover with Agency funds. Anyhow, I want people over here, and I'm sending my want-list to you.'

'That'll deplete us,' Harry Priar pointed out.

'Sure. But it's only for a week or so. Give our people the situation about me, see who's willing to come. Then fill as best you can. A dozen should do. What about you personally?'

'I'll work for you,' Priar said.

'I'm in big disfavor.'

Priar said: 'When they ask, I'll say you brainwashed me.'

Toward four in the afternoon the first trickle of Agency personnel began to show up. Gleeby interviewed each person and assigned him to a department. By the end of the day a make-shift working staff had been built up. Gleeby was optimistic.

'These are policy-making people,' he said to Allen. 'And they're used to working with you. We can trust them, too. Which is good. I suppose the Committee has a few of its creatures lurking around. Want us to set up some sort of loyalty review board?'

'Not important,' Allen said. 'As long as we see the finished products.' He had studied the statement of projections in process; some were now scratched off, some had been put ahead, and most had been rerouted into dead-ends. The assembly lines were open and functioning, ready to undertake fresh material.

'What's that?' Gleeby asked, as Allen brought out sheets of lined paper.

'My preliminary sketches. What's the normal span required from first stage to last?'

'Well,' Gleeby said, 'say a packet is approved on Monday.

Usually we take anywhere from a month to five months, depending on the medium it's to be projected over.'

'Jesus,' Allen said.

'It can be cut. For topical stuff we prune down to—' He computed. 'Say, two weeks.'

Allen turned to Harry Priar, who stood listening. 'How's that strike you?'

'By the time you're out of here,' Priar said, 'you won't have one item done.'

'I agree,' Allen said. 'Gleeby, to be on the safe side we'll have to prune to four days.'

'That only happened once,' Gleeby said, tugging at the lobe of his ear. 'The day William Pease, Ida Pease Hoyt's father, died. We had a huge projection, on all media, within twenty-four hours.'

'Even woven baskets?'

'Baskets, handbills, stenciled signs. The works.'

Priar asked: 'Anybody else going to be with us? Or is this the total crew?'

'I have a couple more people,' Allen said. 'I won't be sure until tomorrow.' He looked at his watch. 'They'd be at the top, as original idea men.'

'Who are they?' Gleeby asked. 'Anybody we know?'

'One of them is named Gates,' he said. 'The other is a man named Sugermann.'

'Suppose I asked you what you're going to do?'

Allen said: 'I'd tell you. We're going to do a jape on Major Streiter.'

He was with his wife when the first plug was aired. At his direction a portable TV receiver was set up in their one-room apartment. The time was twelve-thirty at night; most of Newer York was asleep.

'The transmitting antenna,' he told Janet, 'is at the T-M building.' Gleeby had collected enough video technicians to put the transmitter – normally closed down at that hour – back on the air.

'You're so excited,' Janet said. 'I'm glad you're doing this; it means so much to you.'

'I only hope we can pull it off,' he said, thinking about it.

'And afterward?' she said. 'What happens then?'

'We'll see,' he said. The plug was unfolding.

A background showed the ruins of the war, the aftermath of battle. The tattered rags of a settlement appeared; slow, halting motion of survivors creeping half-starved, half-baked through the rubble.

A voice said: 'In the public interest a Telemedia discussion program will shortly deal with a problem of growing importance for our times. Participants will analyze the question: Should Major Streiter's postwar policy of active assimilation be revived to meet the current threat? Consult your area log for time and date.'

The plug dissolved, carrying the ruins and desolation with it. Allen snapped off the TV set, and felt tremendous pride.

'What'd you think of it?' he asked Janet.

'Was that it?' She seemed disappointed. 'There wasn't much.'

'With variations, that plug will be repeated every half hour on all channels. Mavis' hit 'em, hit 'em. Plus plants in the news-papers, mentions on all the news programs, and minor hints scattered over the other media.'

'I don't remember what "active assimilation" was. And what's this "current threat"?'

'By Monday you'll have the whole story,' Allen said. 'The slam will come on "Pageant of Time." I don't want to spoil it for you.'

Downstairs on the public rack, he bought a copy of tomorrow's newspaper, already distributed. There, on page one, in the left-hand column, was the plant developed by Sugermann and Priar.

TALK OF REVIVING ASSIMILATION

Newer York Oct. 29 (T-M): It is reliably reported that a number of persons high in Committee circles who prefer to remain anonymous at this time favor a revival of the postwar policy of active assimilation developed by Major Streiter to cope with the then-extensive threats to Moral Reclamation. Growing out of the current menace this revived interest in assimilation expresses the continued uneasiness of violence and lawlessness, as demonstrated by the savage assault on the Park of the Spire monument to Major Streiter. It is felt that the therapeutic method of Mental Health, and the efforts of the Mental Health Resort to cope with current instability and unrest, have failed to

Allen folded up the newspaper and went back upstairs to the apartment. Within a day or so the domino elements of the Morec society would be tipped. 'Active assimilation' as a solution to the 'current threat' would be the topic of discussion for everybody.

'Active assimilation' was his brain child. He had made it up. Sugermann had added the idea of the 'current threat.' Between them they had created the topic out of whole cloth.

He felt well-pleased. Progress was being made.

22

By Monday morning the projection was complete. T-M workers, armed, carried it upstairs to the transmitter and stood guard over it. The Telemedia building was sealed off; nobody came and nobody went. During the day the hints, spots, mentions on various media dinned like pond frogs. Tension began to build, a sense of expectancy. The public was alive to the topic of 'active assimilation,' although nobody knew what it meant.

'Opinion,' Sugermann said, 'runs about two to one in favor of restoring a cautious policy of active assimilation.' A poll had been taken, and the results were arriving.

'Active assimilation's too good for those rascals,' Gates announced. 'Let's have no coddling of traitors.'

At a quarter of eight that evening, Allen assembled his staff in his office. The mood was one of optimism.

'Well,' Allen said, 'it won't be long. Another fifteen minutes and we're on the air. Anybody feel like backing out?'

Everybody grinned inanely.

'Got your dismissal notice yet?' Gates asked him.

The notice, from the Committee, had arrived registered mail.

Now Allen opened the envelope and read the brief, formal statement. He had until noon Thursday. Then he was no longer Director of Telemedia.

'Give me the story on the follow-ups,' he said to Gleeby.

'Pardon? Yes, um.' From a prepared list, Gleeby read him the total projected coverage. 'Up to now it's been ground breakers. Tonight at eight comes the actual discussion. Tomorrow night a repeat of the discussion program will be aired, by "public demand." '

'Better move that up,' Allen said. 'Allows too much time for them to act.'

'Make it later tonight,' Sugermann suggested. 'About ten, as they're all popping into bed.'

Gleeby scribbled a few words. 'We've already mailed out duplicate films to the colonies. The discussion has been written up and will be printed in full in Tuesday morning's newspapers, plus comments pro and con. Late news programs tonight will give resumes. We've had the presses run off paper-bound copies to be sold in commissaries at magazine slots. Youth editions for school use have been prepared but, frankly, I don't imagine we can distribute them in time. It'll take another four days.'

'And the poll,' Sugermann added.

'Fine,' Allen said. 'For less than a week that's not bad.'

A T-M employee entered. 'Mr Purcell, something's come up. Secretary Frost and Mrs Hoyt are outside in a Committee Getabout. They want to be admitted.'

'Peace party,' Priar said.

'I'll talk to them outside,' Allen said. 'Show me where they are.'

The employee led him to the ground floor and outside through the barricade erected before the entrance. In the back seat of a small blue Getabout sat the two women, bolt-upright, their faces pinched. Ralf Hadler was behind the tiller. He pretended not to notice or in any way conceive of Allen. They were not in the same world.

'Hi,' Allen said.

Mrs Hoyt said: 'This is unworthy. I'm ashamed of you, Mr Purcell. I really am.'

'I'll make a note of that,' Allen said. 'What else?'

'Would you have the decency to tell us what you're doing?' Sue Frost demanded in a low, choked voice. She held up a newspaper. ' "Active assimilation." What in the name of heaven is this? Have you all completely lost your minds?'

'We have,' Allen admitted. 'But I don't see that it matters.'

'It's a fabrication, isn't it?' Sue Frost accused. 'You're inventing it all. This is some sort of horrible prank. If I didn't know better I'd say you had a hand in the japery of Major Streiter's statue; I'd say you're involved in this whole outbreak of anarchistic and savage lawlessness.'

Her choice of words showed the potency of the campaign. It made him feel odd to hear her speaking right out of the plug.

'Now look,' Mrs Hoyt said presently, in a tone of forced amiability. 'If you'll resign we'll see that you regain your lease. You'll be able to continue your Agency; you'll be exactly where you were. We'll prepare a guarantee, written, that Telemedia will buy from you.' She hesitated. 'And we'll undertake to expose Blake-Moffet for their part in the frame-up.'

Allen said: 'Now I know I'm on the right track. And try to watch TV tonight; you'll get the full story on "active assimilation." '

Re-entering the building he halted to watch the blue Getabout steam away. Their offer had genuinely surprised him. It was amazing how much moral righteousness the breath of scandal could blow down. He ascended by the elevator and joined the group waiting in his office.

'Almost time,' Sugermann said, consulting his watch. 'Five more minutes.'

'At a rough guess,' Gleeby said, 'dominos representing seventy percent of the population will be watching. We should achieve an almost perfect saturation on this single airing.'

From a suitcase Gates produced two fifths of Scotch whiskey. 'To celebrate,' he said, opening both. 'Somebody get glasses. Or we can pass them around.'

The phone rang, and Allen answered it.

'Hello, Allen,' Myron Mavis' creaky voice came. 'How're things going?'

'Absolutely perfect,' Allen answered. 'Want to stop by and join us?'

'Sorry. Can't. I'm bogged down in leaving. All my stuff to get packed for the trip to Sirius.'

'Try to catch the projection tonight,' Allen said. 'It starts in a couple of minutes.'

'How's Janet?'

'Seems to be feeling pretty fair. She's glad it's out in the open.' He added, 'She's watching at the apartment.'

'Say hello to her,' Mavis said. 'And good luck on your lunacy.'

'Thanks,' Allen said. He said goodbye and hung up.

'Time,' Sugermann said. Gates turned on the big TV receiver and they gathered around it. 'Here we go.'

'Here we go,' Allen agreed.

Mrs Georgina Birmingham placed her favorite chair before her television set and anticipated her favourite program, *The Pageant of Time*. She was tired from the hectic activities of the day, but a deep spiritual residuum reminded her that work and sacrifice were their own reward.

On the screen was an inter-program announcement. A large decayed tooth was shown, grimacing with pain. Next to it a sparkling healthy tooth jeered sanctimoniously. The two teeth engaged in Socratic dialogue, the upshot of which was the rout and defeat of the bad tooth.

Mrs Birmingham gladly endured the inter-program announcements because they were in a good cause. And the program, *Pageant of Time*, was well worth any reasonable effort. She always hurried home early on Monday evening; in ten years she hadn't missed an edition.

A shower of brightly-colored fireworks burst across the screen, and from the speaker issued the rumble of guns. A jagged, slashing line of words cut through the blur of war:

THE PAGEANT OF TIME

Her program had begun. Folding her arms, leaning her head back, Mrs Birmingham now found herself viewing a table at which sat four dignified gentlemen. A discussion was in progress, and dim words were audible. Over them was superimposed the announcer's voice.

'Pageant of Time. Ladies and gentlemen, at this table sit four men, each a distinguished authority in his field. They have come together to discuss an issue vital to every citizen of the Morec society. In view of the unusual importance of this program there will be no interruptions, and the discussion, which is already in progress, will proceed without pause until the end of the hour. Our topic for tonight . . .' Visible words grew on the screen.

ACTIVE ASSIMILATION IN THE WORLD TODAY

Mrs Birmingham was delighted. She had been hearing about active assimilation for some time, and this was her opportunity to learn once and for all what it was. Her lack of information had made her feel out of touch.

'Seated at my right is Doctor Joseph Gleeby, the noted educator, lecturer, writer of numerous books on problems of social values.' A lean middle-aged man, smoking a pipe and rubbing his ear, was shown. 'To Doctor Gleeby's right is Mr Harold Priar, art critic, architect, frequent contributor to the *Encyclopedia Britannica*.' A smaller individual was shown, with an intense, serious face. 'Seated next to Mr Priar is Professor Sugermann, whose historical studies rank with those of Gibbon, Schiller, Toynbee. We are very fortunate to have Professor Sugermann with us.' The camera moved forth to show Professor Sugermann's heavy, solemn features. 'And next to Professor Sugermann sits Mr Thomas L. Gates, lawyer, civic leader, consultant to the Committee for a number of years.'

Now the moderator appeared, and Mrs Birmingham found herself facing Allen Purcell.

'And I,' Mr Purcell said, 'am Allen Purcell, Director of Telemedia.' He seated himself at the end of the table, by the water pitcher. 'Shall we begin, gentlemen, with a few words about the etymology of active assimilation? Just how did Major Streiter develop the policy that was to prove so effective in his dealings with opposition groups?'

'Well, Mr Purcell,' Professor Sugermann began, coughing importantly and fingering his chin, 'the Major had many opportunities to see first-hand the ravages of war on principally agricultural and food-producing areas, such as the livestock regions of the West, the wheat fields of Kansas, the dairy industry of New England. These were all but wiped out, and naturally, as we all know, there was intensive deprivation if not actual starvation. This contributed to a decline of over-all productivity affecting industrial reconstruction. And during this period, of course, communications broke down; areas were cut off; anarchy was common.'

'In that connection,' Doctor Gleeby put in, 'many of the problems of decline of moral standards inherent in the Age of Waste were vastly intensified by this collapse of what little government there was.'

'Yes indeed,' Professor Sugermann agreed. 'So in following this historic pattern, Major Streiter saw the need of finding new sources of food . . . and the soil, as we know, was excessively impregnated with toxic metals, poisons, ash. Most domestic herds had died off.' He gazed upward. 'I believe by 1975 there were less than three hundred head of cattle in North America.'

'That sounds right,' Mr Purcell said agreeably.

'So,' Professor Sugermann continued, 'Moral Reclaimers as they operated in the field in the form of teams—' He gestured. 'More or less autonomous units; we're familiar with the technique . . . Encountered a virtually insoluble problem, that of feeding and caring for the numbers of persons coming across from hostile groups operating in the same area. In that connection I might add that Major Streiter seems to have foreseen long in advance the continual decline of animal husbandry that was to occur during the next decade. He took steps to anticipate the decline, and of course historians have made a big point of the aptness of those steps.'

Professor Sugermann sighed, contemplated his clasped hands, then went on.

'To fully grasp their situation, we must picture ourselves as living essentially without government, in a world of brute force. What concepts of morality existed were found only within the Reclaimers' units; outside of that it was dog-eat-dog, animal against animal. A kind of jungle struggle for survival, with no holds barred.'

The table and five men dissolved; in their place appeared familiar scenes of the first postwar years. Ruins, squalor, barbarians snarling over scraps of meat. Dried pelts hanging from slatternly hovels. Flies. Filth.

'Large numbers of opposition groups,' Professor Sugermann continued, 'were falling into our hands daily, thus complicating an already catastrophic problem of creating a stable diet in the devastated areas. Morec was on the ascendancy, but nobody was so idealistic as to believe the problem of creating a unified cultural milieu could be solved overnight. And the really sobering factor, evidently recognized early by the Major, was the so-called "impossible" faction: those groups who could never be won over, and who were doing the most harm. Since Reclaimers were principally operating against those "impossibles," it was only natural that in the plan worked out by Major Streiter these "impossibles" would be the most natural sources for assimilation. Further—'

'I must disagree,' Mr Gates interrupted, 'if I may, Professor Sugermann. Isn't it true that active assimilation had already occurred, *prior* to the Morec Plan? The Major was fundamentally an empiricist; he saw assimilation occurring spontaneously and he was quick to take advantage of it.'

'I'm afraid that doesn't do justice to the Major's planning ability,' Mr Priar spoke up. 'That is, you're making it sound as if active assimilation just – happened. But we know active assimilation was basic, preceding the autofac system which eventually supplanted it.'

'I think we have two points of view here,' Mr Purcell, the moderator, said. 'But in any case we agree that Major Streiter did utilize active assimilation early in the postwar years to solve the problem of feeding rural populations and of reducing the numbers of hostile and "impossible" elements.'

'Yes,' Doctor Gleeby said. 'By 1997 at least ten thousand "impossibles" had been assimilated. And numerous by-products of economic value were being obtained: glue, gelatins, hides, hair.'

'Can we fix a date for the first official assimilation?' Mr Purcell asked.

'Yes,' Professor Sugermann said. 'It was May of 1987 that one hundred Russian "impossibles" were captured, killed, and then processed by Reclaimers operating in the Ukrainian area. I believe Major Streiter himself divided an "impossible" with his family, on the Fourth of July.'

'I suppose boiling was the usual processing method,' Mr Priar commented.

'Boiling, and of course, frying. In this case Mrs Streiter's recipe was used, calling for broiling.'

'So the term "active assimilation,"' Mr Purcell said, 'can historically be used to encompass any form of killing, cooking, and eating of hostile groups, whether it be by boiling, or frying, or broiling, or baking; in short, any culinary method apropos, with or without the preserving of by-products such as skin, bones, fingernails, for commercial use.'

'Exactly,' Doctor Gleeby said, nodding. 'Although it should be pointed out that the indiscriminate eating of hostile elements without an official—'

Whamp! went the television set, and Mrs Birmingham sat up with dismay. The image had gone dead; the screen was dark.

The discussion of 'active assimilation' had been plunged abruptly off the air.

23

Allen said: 'They cut off our power.'

'The lines,' Gleeby answered, fumbling around in the darkness of the office. All the lights of the Telemedia building had vanished; the TV transmitter above them was silent, and projection had ceased. 'There's emergency generating equipment, independent of city power.'

'Takes a lot to run a transmitter,' Sugermann said, pulling aside the window blinds and peering out at the evening lanes below. 'Getabouts everywhere. Cohorts, I think.'

Allen and Gleeby made their way down the stairs to the emergency generators, guided by Allen's cigarette lighter. Gates followed; with him was a technician from the transmitter.

'We can have it back on in ten or fifteen minutes,' the TV

technician said, inspecting the generator capacities. 'But it won't hold. The drain's too great for these; it'll be on for awhile and then – like now.'

'Do the best you can,' Allen said. He wondered how much of the projection had been understood. 'You think we made our Morec?' he asked Sugermann.

'Our un-Morec,' Sugermann said. He smiled crookedly. 'They were standing by for the point-of-no-return. So we must have made it clear.'

'Here goes,' Gates said. The generators were on, and now the overhead lights flickered. 'Back in business.'

'For awhile,' Allen said.

The screen of Janet Purcell's television set was small; it was the portable unit that Allen had brought. She lay propped up on the couch in their one-room apartment, waiting for the image to return. Presently it did.

'. . . d,' Professor Sugermann was saying. The image faded and darkened, then ebbed into distortion. 'But broiling was favored, I believe.'

'Not according to my information,' Doctor Gleeby corrected.

'Our discussion,' the moderator, her husband, said, 'really concerns the use of active assimilation in the present-day world. Now it has been suggested that active assimilation as a punitive policy be revived to deal with the current wave of anarchy. Would you care to comment on that, Doctor Gleeby?'

'Certainly.' Doctor Gleeby knocked dottle from his pipe into the ash tray in the center of the table. 'We must remember that active assimilation was primarily a solution to problems of nutrition, not, as is often supposed, a weapon to convert hostile elements. Naturally I'm gravely concerned with the outbreak of violence and vandalism today, as epitomized by this really dreadful japery of the Park statue, but we can scarcely be said to suffer from a nutritional problem. After all, the autofac system—'

'Historically,' Professor Sugermann interrupted, 'you may have a point, Doctor. But from the standpoint of efficacy: what would be the effects on these present-day "impossibles"? Wouldn't the threat of being boiled and eaten act as a deterrent to their hostile impulses? There would be a strong subconscious inhibitory effect, I'm sure.'

'To me,' Mr Gates agreed, 'it seems that allowing these anti-social individuals merely to run away, hide, take refuge at the Health Resort, has made it far too easy. We've permitted our dissident elements to do their mischief and then escape scot-free. That's certainly encouraged them to expand their activities. Now, if they knew they'd be eaten—'

'It's well known,' Mr Priar said, 'that the severity of punitive action doesn't decrease the frequency of a given crime. They once hanged pickpockets, you realize. It had no effect. That's quite an outmoded theory, Mr Gates.'

'But, to get back to the main discussion,' the moderator said, 'are we certain that no nutritional effects would accrue from the eating, rather than the expulsion, of our criminals? Professor Sugermann, as an historian, can you tell us what the general public attitude was toward the use, in everyday cookery, of boiled enemy?'

On the TV screen appeared a collection of historical relics: six-foot broiling racks, huge human-sized platters, various cutlery. Jars of spices. Immense-pronged forks. Knives. Recipe books.

'It was clearly an art,' Professor Sugermann said. 'Properly prepared, boiled enemy was a gourmet's delight. We have the Major's own words on this subject.' Professor Sugermann, again visible, unfolded his notes. 'Toward the end of his life the Major ate only, or nearly only, boiled enemy. It was a great favorite of his wife's, and, as we've said, her recipes are regarded as among the finest extant. E. B. Erickson once estimated that Major Streiter and his immediate family must have personally assimilated at least six hundred fully-grown "impossibles". So there you have the more or less official opinion.'

Whamp! the TV screen went, and again the image died. A kaleidoscopic procession of colors, patterns, dots passed rapidly; from the speaker emerged squawks of protest, whines, squeals.

'. . . a tradition in the Streiter family. The Major's grandson is said to have expressed great preference for . . .'

Again silence. Then sputters, garbled visual images.

'. . . so I cannot over-emphasize my support of this program.

130

The effects—' More confusion, sounds and flickers. A sudden roar of static. '. . . would be an object lesson as well as the contemporary restoration of boiled enemy to its proper place on—'

The TV screen gurgled, died, returned briefly to life.

'. . . may be the test one way or another. Were there others?'

Allen's voice was heard: 'Several, supposedly now being rounded up.'

'But they caught the ringleader! And Mrs Hoyt herself has expressed—'

More interference. The screen showed a news announcer standing at the table with the four participants. Mr Allen Purcell, the moderator, was examining a news dispatch.

'. . . assimilation in the actual historic vessels employed by her family. After tasting a carefully-prepared sample of boiled conspirator, Mrs Ida Pease Hoyt has pronounced the dish "highly savory," and "fit to grace the tables of—"'

Again the image died, and this time for good. Within a few moments a mysterious voice, not part of the discussion, became suddenly audible, declaring:

'Because of technical difficulties it is suggested that viewers turn off their sets for the balance of the evening. There will be no further transmission tonight.'

The statement was repeated every few minutes. It had the harsh overtones of the Cohorts of Major Streiter. Janet, propped up on the couch, understood that the powers had regained control. She wondered if her husband was all right.

'Technical difficulties,' the official voice said. 'Turn off your sets.'

She left hers on, and waited.

'That's it,' Allen said.

From the darkness Sugermann said: 'We got it over, though. They cut us off, but not in time.'

Cigarette lighters and matches came on, and the office re-emerged. Allen felt buoyed up with triumph. 'We might as well go home. We did our job; we put the japery through.'

'May be sort of hard to get home,' Gates said. 'The Cohorts

are hanging around out there, waiting for you. The finger's on you, Allen.'

Allen thought of Janet alone in the apartment. If they wanted him they'd certainly try there. 'I should go after my wife,' he said to Sugermann.

'Downstairs,' Sugermann said, 'is a Getabout you can use. Gates, get down there with him; show him where it is.'

'No,' Allen said. 'I can't walk out on you people.' Especially on Harry Priar and Joe Gleeby; they had no Hokkaido to lose themselves in. 'I can't leave you to be picked off.'

'The biggest favor you can do us,' Gleeby said, 'is to get out of here. They don't care about us; they know who thought this japery up.' He shook his head. 'Cannibalism. Gourmet's delight. Mrs Streiter's own recipes. You better get moving.'

Priar added: 'That's the price you pay for talent. It shows a mile off.'

Getting a firm grip on Allen's shoulder, Sugermann propelled him to the office door. 'Show him the Getabout,' he ordered Gates. 'But keep him down while you're out there; the Cohorts are the wrath of God.'

As Allen and Gates descended the long flight of stairs to the ground floor, Gates said: 'You happy?'

'Yes, except for Janet.' And he would miss the people he had assembled. It had been satisfactory and wonderful to concoct the japery with Gates and Sugermann, Gleeby and Priar.

'Maybe they caught her and boiled her,' Gates giggled, and the match he held swayed. 'That isn't probable. Don't worry about it.'

He wasn't worried about that, but he wished he had planned for the Committee's prompt reaction. 'They weren't exactly asleep,' he murmured.

A herd of technicians raced past them, shining flashlights ahead along the stairs. 'Get out,' they chanted. 'Get out, get out.' The racket of their descent echoed and faded.

'All finished,' Gates snickered. 'Here we go.'

They had reached the lobby. T-M employees milled in the darkness; some were stepping through the barricade out into the evening lane. The headlights of Getabouts flashed, and voices called back and forth, a confusion of catcalls and fun. The indistinct activity was party-like; but now it was time to leave.

'Here,' Gates said, pushing through a gap in the barricade. Allen followed, and they were on the lane. Behind them the Telemedia building was huge and somber, deprived of its power: extinguished. The parked Getabout was moist with night mist as Gates and Allen climbed into it and slammed the doors.

'I'll drive,' Allen said. He snapped on the motor, and the Getabout glided steamily out onto the lane. After a block he switched on the headlights.

As he turned at an intersection another Getabout rolled out after him. Gates saw it and began whooping with glee.

'Here they come – let's go!'

Allen pushed the Getabout to its top speed, perhaps thirty-five miles an hour. Pedestrians ran wildly. In the rear-view mirror he could make out faces within the pursuing Getabout. Ralf Hadler was driving. Beside him was Fred Luddy. And in the back seat was Tony Blake of Blake-Moffet.

Leaning out, Gates shouted back: 'Boil, bake, fry! Boil, bake, fry! Try and catch us!'

His face expressionless, Hadler lifted a pistol and fired. The shot whistled past Gates, who ducked instantly in.

'We're going to jump,' Allen said. The Getabout was nearing a sharp curve. 'Grab hold.' He forced the tiller as far as it would go. 'We have to stop first.'

Gates pulled his knees up and wrapped himself head-down in a fetal posture. As the Getabout completed the curve, Allen slammed down on the brake; the little car screamed and shuddered, bucked from side to side, and then wandered tottering into a rail. Gates half-rolled, half-fell from the swinging and open door, struck the pavement and bounded to his feet. Dizzy, his head ringing, Allen stumbled after him.

The second Getabout hurtled around the curve and without slowing – Hadler was still the bum driver – struck its stalled quarry. Parts of Getabout flew in all directions; the three occupants disappeared in the rubbish. Hadler's gun skidded across the lane and bounced noisily from a lamp-post.

'See you,' Gates panted to Allen, already loping off. He

grinned back over his shoulder. 'Boil, bake, fry. They won't get us. Say hello to Janet.'

Allen hurried through the semi-gloom of the lane, among the pedestrians who seemed to be everywhere. Behind him Hadler had emerged from the wreckage of the two Getabouts; he picked up his gun, inspected it, lifted it uncertainly in Allen's direction, and then shoved it away inside his coat. Allen continued on, and the figure of Hadler fell away.

When he reached the apartment, he found Janet fully dressed, her face white with animation. The door was locked, and he had to wait while she untangled the chain. 'Are you hurt?' she asked, seeing blood on his cheek.

'Jarred a little.' He took hold of her arm and led her out into the hall. 'They'll be here any minute. Thank God it's night.'

'What was that?' Janet asked, as they hurried downstairs. 'Major Streiter didn't really *eat* people, did he?'

'Not literally,' he said. But in a sense, a very real sense, it was true. Morec had gobbled greedily at the human soul.

'How far are we going?' Janet asked.

'To the field,' he grunted, holding on tightly to her. Fortunately it wasn't far. She seemed in good spirits, nervous and excited, and not depressed. Perhaps much of her depression had come from sheer boredom . . . from the ultimate emptiness of a drab world.

Holding hands they trotted onto the field, gasping for breath.

There, outlined with lights, was the great inter-S ship preparing for its flight from the Sol System to the Sirius System. Passengers were clustered at the foot of the lift, saying goodbye.

Running across the gravel field, Allen shouted: 'Mavis! Wait for us!'

Among the passengers stood a dour, slumped-over man in a heavy overcoat. Myron Mavis glanced up, peered sourly.

'Stop!' Allen shouted, as Mavis turned away. Clutching his wife's fingers Allen reached the edge of the passenger platform and halted, wheezing. 'We're going along.'

Mavis scrutinized the two of them with bloodshot eyes. 'Are you?'

'You've got room,' Allen said. 'You own a whole planet. Come on, Myron. We've got to leave.'

'Half a planet,' Mavis corrected.

'What's it like?' Janet gasped. 'Is it nice, there?'

'Cattle, mostly,' Mavis said. 'Orchards, plenty of machinery crying to be used. Lots of work. You can tear down mountains and drain swamps. You'll both sweat; you won't be sitting around sun-bathing.'

'Fine,' Allen said. 'Exactly what we want.'

In the darkness above them a mechanical voice intoned: 'All passengers step onto lift. All visitors leave the field.'

'Take this,' Mavis instructed, pushing a suitcase into Allen's hands. 'You, too.' He handed Janet a box tied with twine. 'And keep your mouths shut. If anybody asks you anything, let me do the talking.'

'Son and daughter,' Janet said, pressing against him and holding onto her husband's hand. 'You'll take care of us, won't you? We'll be as quiet as mice.' Breathless, laughing, she hugged Allen and then Mavis. 'Here we go – we're leaving!'

At the edge of the field, at the railing, was a clump of shapes. Clutching Mavis' suitcase, Allen looked back and saw the teenagers. There they were, clustered in the usual small, dark knot. Silent, as always, and following the progress of the ship. Weighing, speculating, imagining where it was going . . . picturing the colony. Was it crops? Was it a planet of oranges? Was it a world of growing plants, hills and pastures and herds of sheep, goats, cattle, pigs? Cattle, in this case. The kids would know. They would be saying it now, speaking it back and forth to one another. Or not speaking it. Not having to, because they had watched so long.

'We can't leave,' Allen said.

'What's the matter?' Janet tugged at him urgently. 'We have to stay on the lift; it's going up.'

'Ye gods!' Mavis groaned. 'Changed your mind?'

'We're going back,' Allen said. He set down Mavis' suitcase and took the package from Janet's hands. 'Later, maybe. When we're finished here. We still have something to do.'

'Lunacy,' Mavis said. 'Lunacy on top of lunacy.'

'No,' Allen said. 'And you know it isn't.'

'Please,' Janet whispered. 'What is it? What's wrong?'

'You can't do anything for those kids,' Mavis said to him.

'I can stay with them,' Allen said. 'And I can make my feelings clear.' That much, at least.

'It's your decision.' Mavis threw up his arms in disgust and dismissal. 'The hell with you. I don't even know what you're talking about.' But the expression on his face showed that he did. 'I wash my hands of the whole business. Do what you think is best.'

'All right,' Janet said. 'Let's go back. Let's get it over with. As long as we have to.'

'You'll keep a place for us?' Allen asked Mavis.

Sighing, Mavis nodded. 'Yes, I'll be expecting you.'

'It may not be for awhile.'

Mavis thumped him on the shoulder. 'But I'll see both of you.' He kissed Janet on the cheek, and then very formally, and with emphasis, he shook hands with both of them. 'When the time comes.'

'Thanks,' Allen said.

Surrounded by his luggage and fellow passengers, Mavis watched them go. 'Good luck.' His voice followed after them, and then was lost in the murmur of machinery.

With his wife, Allen walked slowly back across the field. He was winded from the running, and Janet's steps dragged. Behind them, with a growing roar, the ship was rising. Ahead of them was Newer York, and sticking up from the expanse of housing units and office buildings was the spire. He felt sobered, and a little ashamed. But now he was finishing what he had begun that Sunday night, in the darkness of the Park. So it was good. And he could stop feeling ashamed.

'What'll they do to us?' Janet asked after while.

'We'll survive.' In him was an absolute conviction. 'Whatever it is. We'll show up on the other side, and that's what matters.'

'And then we'll go to Myron's planet?'

'We will,' he promised. 'Then it'll be all right.'

Standing at the edge of the field were the teenagers, and a varied assortment of people: relatives of passengers, minor field officials, passers-by, an off-duty policeman. Allen and his wife approached them and stopped by the rail.

'I'm Allen Purcell,' he said, and he spoke with pride. 'I'm the person who japed the statue of Major Streiter. I'd like everybody to know it.'

The people gaped, murmured together, and then melted off to safety. The teenagers remained, aloof and silent. The off-duty policeman blinked and started in the direction of a telephone.

Allen, his arm around his wife, waited composedly for the Getabouts of the Cohorts.

DR FUTURITY

1

The spires were not his own. The colors were not his own. He had a moment of shattering, blinding terror – and then calmness. He took a long breath of cold night air and began the job of working out his bearings.

He seemed to be on some kind of hillside, overgrown with brambles and vines. He was alive – and he still had his gray metal case. Experimentally, he tore the vines away and inched cautiously forward. Stars glittered above. Thank God for that. Familiar stars . . .

Not familiar.

He closed his eyes and hung on until his senses came trickling back. Then he pushed painfully down the side of the hill and toward the illuminated spires that lay perhaps a mile ahead, his case clutched in his hand.

Where was he? And why was he here? Had somebody *brought* him here, dumped him off at this spot for a reason?

The colors of the spires shifted and he began to work out, in a vague fashion, the equation of their pattern. By the time he was halfway he had it down fairly well. For some reason it made him feel better. Here was something he could predict. Get hold of. Above the spires, ships swirled and darted, swarms of them, catching the shifting lights. How beautiful it was.

This scene wasn't his, but it looked nice. And that was some-thing. So this hadn't changed. Reason, beauty, cold winter air late at night. He quickened his pace, stumbled, and then, pushing through trees, came out onto the smooth pavement of a highway.

He hurried.

As he hurried he let his thoughts wander around aimlessly.

Bringing back the last fragments of sound and being, the final bits of a world abruptly gone. Wondering, in a detached, objective way, exactly what had happened.

Jim Parsons was on his way to work. It was a bright sunny morning. He had paused a moment to wave to his wife before getting into his car.

'Anything you want from town?' he called.

Mary stood on the front porch, hands in the pockets of her apron. 'Nothing I can think of, darling. I'll vid you at the Institute if I remember anything.'

In the warm sunlight Mary's hair shone a luminous auburn, a flashing cloud of flame which, this week, was the new fashion among the wives. She stood small and slender in her green slacks and close-fitting foilite sweater. He waved to her, grabbed one final vision of his pretty wife, their one-story stucco house, the garden, the flagstone path, the California hills rising up in the distance, and then hopped into the car.

He spun off down the road, allowing the car to operate on the San Francisco guide-beam north. It was safer that way, especially on U.S. 101. And a lot quicker. He didn't mind having his car operated from a hundred miles off. All the other cars racing along the sixteen-lane highway were guide-operated, too, those going his way and those heading in the opposite direction, on the analog south highway to Los Angeles. It made accidents almost impossible, and meant he could enjoy the educational notices which various universities traditionally posted along the route. And, behind the notices, the countryside.

The countryside was fresh and well cared for. Attractive, since President Cantelli had nationalized the soap, tire, and hotel industries. No more ads to ruin the hills and valleys. Wouldn't be long before all industries were in the hands of the ten-man Economics Planning Board, operating under the Westinghouse research schools. Of course, when it came to doctors, that was another thing.

He tapped his instrument case on the seat beside him. Industry was one thing; the professional classes another. Nobody was going to nationalize the doctors, lawyers, painters, musicians. During the last decades the technocratic and professional classes had gradually gained control of society. By 1998, instead of business-men and politicians, it was scientists rationally trained to—

Something picked up the car and hurled it from the road.

Parsons screamed as the car spun dizzily onto the shoulder and careened into the brush and educational signs. *The guide has failed.* That was his last thought. *Interference.* Trees, rocks came looming up, bursting in on him. A shrieking crash of plastic and metal fused together, and his own voice, a chaotic clatter of sound and movement. And then the sickening impact that crumpled up the car like a plasti-carton. All the safety devices within the car – he dimly felt them scrambling into a belated action. Cushioning him, surrounding him, the odor of antifire spray . . .

He was thrown clear, into a rolling void of gray. He remem-bered spinning slowly, coming to earth like a weightless, drifting particle. Everything was slowed down, a tape track brought almost to a halt. He felt no pain. Nothing at all. An enormous formless mist seemed all around him.

A radiant field. A beam of some kind. The power which had interfered with the guide. He realized that – his last conscious thought. Then darkness descended over him.

He was still gripping his gray instrument case.

Ahead the highway broadened.

Lights flickered around him, geared to his presence. An advan-cing umbrella of yellow and green dots that showed him the way. The road entered and mixed with an intricate web of other roads, branches that faded into the darkness. He could only guess their directions. At the hub of complex he halted and examined a sign which immediately came alive, apparently for his benefit. He read the unfamiliar words aloud:

'DIR 30c N; ATR 46c N; BAR 100c S; CRP 205s S; EGL 67c N.'

N and S no doubt were north and south. But the rest meant nothing. The C was a unit of measurement. That had changed; the mile was no longer used. The magnetic pole was still used as a reference point, but that did not cheer him much.

Vehicles of some sort were moving along the roads that lifted above and beyond him. Drops of light. Similar to the spires of the city itself, they shifted hues as they altered space relationship with him.

Finally, he gave up on the sign. It told him only what he knew already, nothing more. He had gone ahead. A considerable jump. The language, the mensural system, the whole appearance of society had changed.

He hoisted himself from the lowest road up the steps of a hand-ramp to the next level. Quickly, he swung up to a third and then a fourth. Now he could see the city with ease.

It was really something. Big and beautiful. Without the con-stellation of industrial outfits ringing it, the chimneys and stacks that had made even San Francisco ugly. It took his breath away. Standing on the ramp in the cold night darkness, the wind rustling around him, the stars overhead, the moving drops of color that were the shifting vehicles, Parsons was overcome with emotion. The sight of the city made his heart ache. He began to walk again, buoyed up with vigor. His spirits were rising. What would he find? What kind of world? Whatever it was, he'd be able to function. The thought drummed triumphantly in his brain: *I'm a doctor. A heck of a good doctor. Now, if it were anybody else . . .*

A doctor would always be needed. He could master the language – an area in which he had always shown skill – and the social customs. Find a place for himself, survive while he dis-covered how he had gotten here. Eventually get back to his wife, of course. Yes, he thought, Mary would love this. Possibly reutilize the forces that had brought him here; relocate his family in this city . . .

Parsons gripped his gray metal case and hurried. And while he was hurrying breathlessly down the incline of the road, a silent drop of color detached itself from the ribbon beneath him, rose, and headed straight for him. Without hesitation, it aimed itself in his direction. He had time only to freeze; the color *whooshed* toward him – and he realized that it did not intend to miss.

'Stop!' he shouted. His arms came up reflexively; he was waving frantically at the burgeoning color, the thing so close now that it filled his eyes and blinded him.

It passed him, and as the hot wind blew around him, he made

out a face which peered at him. Peered in mixed emotions. Amusement – and astonishment!

Parsons had an intuition. Difficult to believe, but he had seen it himself. The driver of the vehicle had been surprised at his reaction to being run down and killed.

Now the vehicle returned, more slowly this time, with the driver hanging his head out to stare at Parsons. The vehicle coasted to a stop beside him, its engine murmuring faintly.

'*Hin?*' the driver said.

Foolishly, Parsons thought, *But I didn't even have my thumb out.* Aloud he said, 'Why, you tried to run me down.' His voice shook.

The driver frowned. In the shifting colors his face seemed first dark blue, then orange; the lights made Parsons shut his eyes. The man behind the wheel was astonishingly young. A youth, hardly more than a boy. The whole thing was dreamlike, this boy who had never seen him before trying to run him down, then calmly offering him a ride.

The door of the vehicle slid back. '*Hin,*' the boy repeated, not in a commanding voice but with politeness.

At last, almost as a reflex, Parsons got shakily in. The door slammed shut and the car leaped forward. Parsons was crushed back against the seat by the velocity.

Beside him, the boy said something that Parsons could not understand. His tone suggested that he was still amazed, still puzzled, and wanted to apologize. And the boy continued to glance at Parsons.

It was no game, Parsons realized. This boy really meant to run me down, to kill me. If I hadn't waved my arms—

And as soon as I waved my arms the boy stopped.

The boy thought I wanted to be run down!

2

Beside him, the boy drove with easy confidence. Now the car had turned toward the city; the boy leaned back and released the controls. His curiosity about Parsons clearly was growing stronger. Turning his seat so that he faced Parsons, he studied him. Reaching up, he snapped on an interior light that made both of them more visible.

And, in the light, Parsons got his first real look at the boy. And what he saw jarred him.

Dark hair, shiny and long. Coffee-colored skin. Flat, wide cheek bones. Almond eyes that glinted liquid in the reflected light. A prominent nose. Roman?

No, Parsons thought. Almost Hittite. And his black hair . . .

The man was certainly multiracial. The cheek bones suggested Mongolian. The eyes were Mediterranean. The hair possibly Negroid. The skin color, perhaps, had an underglint of reddish brown. Polynesian?

On the boy's shirt – he wore a dark red, two-piece robe, and slippers – an embroidered herald caught Parson's attention. A stylized eagle.

Eagle. *Egl*. And the others. *Dir* was deer. *Bar* was bear. The rest he couldn't guess. What did this animal nomenclature mean? He started to speak, but the youth cut him off.

'*Whur venis a tardus?*' he demanded in his not entirely grown-up voice.

Parsons was floored. The language, although unfamiliar, was not alien. It had a bafflingly natural ring; something almost understood, but not quite.

'What?' he asked.

The youth qualified his question. '*Ye kleidis novae en sagis novate. Whur iccidi hist?*'

Now he began to get the drift. Like the boy's racial cast, the language was a polyglot. Evidently based on Latin, and possibly an artificial language, a lingua franca; made up of the most familiar bits possible. Pondering the words, Parsons came to the conclusion that the boy wanted to know why he was out so late and why he dressed so strangely. And why he spoke as he did. But at the moment he did not feel inclined to give answers; he had questions of his own.

'I want to know,' he said slowly and carefully, 'why you tried to run me down.'

Blinking, the boy said haltingly, '*Whur ik . . .*' His voice trailed off. Obviously, he did not understand Parson's words.

Or was it that the words were understood, but the question was incomprehensible? With a further chill, Parsons thought, maybe it's supposed to be self-evident. Taken for granted. Of course he tried to kill me. Doesn't everybody?

Feeling a profound resurgence of alarm, he settled down to get at the language barrier. I'm going to have to make myself understood, he realized. And right away.

To the boy, he said, 'Keep talking.'

'*Sag?*' the boy repeated. '*Ik sag yer, ye meinst?*'

Parsons nodded. 'That's right,' he said. Ahead of them, the city came closer and closer. 'You've got it.' We're making progress, he thought grimly. And he stiffened himself to listen as carefully as possible as the boy, haltingly, prattled on. We're making progress, but I wonder if there's going to be enough time.

A broad span carried the car over a moat which surrounded the city, a purely ornamental moat, from the brief glimpse that Parsons caught of it. More and more cars became visible, moving quite slowly, and now people on foot. He made out the sight of crowds, great masses moving along ramps, entering and leaving the spires, pushing along sidewalks. All the people that he saw seemed young. Like the boy beside him. And they, too, had the dark skin, the flat cheek bones, and the robes. He saw a variety of emblems. Animal, fish and bird heralds.

Why? Society organized by totem tribes? Or different races? Or was some festival in progress? But they were physically alike, and that made him discard the theory that each emblem represented a different race. An arbitrary division of the population?

Games?

All wore their hair long, braided, and tied in back, both men and women. The men were considerably larger than the women. They had stern noses and chins. The women hurried along, laughing and chattering, bright-eyed, lips luminous and striking, unusually full. But so young – almost children. Merry, laughing boys and girls. At an intersection a hanging light gave off the first full-spectrum white that he had seen in this world, so far; in its stark glare he saw that the lips of both men and women had a black color, not red at all. And it's not the light, he decided.

Although it could be a dye. Mary used to show up with those fashionable hair dyes . . .

In this first genuinely revealing light, the boy beside him was staring at him with a new expression. He had halted the car.

'Agh,' the boy gasped. And on his face the expression became obvious. Drawing back, he shrank against the far door of the car. '*Ye*—' He stammered for words, and at last burst out chokingly, and so loudly that several passers-by glanced up, '*Ye bist sick!*'

That word was a remnant of Parsons' language: it could not be mistaken. The tone itself, and the boy's expression, removed any doubt.

'Why sick?' Parsons answered, nettled and defensive. 'I can tell you for a certainty—'

Interrupting him, the boy spat out a series of rapid-fire accusations. Some of the words – enough – were understandable. Finally he was beginning to catch the pattern of speech. And this was what he got: realization that now, having seen him clearly for the first time, the boy was overcome with aversion and disgust. The accusations poured out at Parsons in an almost hysterical tirade, while he sat helpless. And outside the car, a group of people had gathered to listen.

The door on Parsons' side of the car slid open; the boy had jabbed at a button on the control panel. I'm being ejected, Parsons realized. Protestingly, he tried to break into the tirade once more.

'Look here,' he began. At that point he broke off. Standing on the pavement outside the car, the people who had caught sight of him had the same expression on their faces. The same horror and dismay. The same disgust as the boy. The people murmured, and he saw a woman raise her hand and indicate something to those behind who couldn't quite see. The woman indicated her own face.

My white skin! Parsons realized.

'Are you going to drop me out there?' he said to the boy, and indicated the murmuring crowd.

The boy hesitated. Even if he did not quite grasp Parsons' words he could follow his meaning. There was hostility in the crowd as it jostled for a better look at Parsons, and the boy saw that; both he and Parsons heard the angry tones and saw the movement of more definite purpose.

With a whirr, the door beside Parsons slid shut. It locked, with him still inside the car. Bending forward, the boy caught hold of the car's controls; the car at once moved rapidly forward.

'Thanks,' Parsons said.

Without answering him, or even paying any attention to him, the boy made the car pick up speed. Now they had reached an ascending ramp; the car shot up it and leveled off at the top. Glancing out, the boy slowed the car almost to a halt. To their left Parsons made out a less brightly lighted avenue. The car moved in that direction and came to rest in half-shadows. The structures here seemed poorer, less ornate. And no people were in sight.

Again the door slid open.

Parsons said, 'I appreciate it.' Shakily, he stepped out.

The boy shut the door, and then the car shot off and out of sight. Parsons found himself standing alone, still trying to frame a statement or ask some question – he did not know which. Suddenly the car reappeared; without slowing it hurtled by him, once again breathing its hot exhaust breath at him, sending him spinning back to escape its gleaming lights. From the car something sailed out and crashed at Parsons' feet.

His instrument case. He had left it in the car.

Seated in the shadows, he opened his instrument case and inspected the contents. Nothing appeared broken or damaged. Thank God for that.

Mercifully, the boy had let him off in a warehouse district. The buildings had a massive quality, with enormous double doors clearly not intended for human traffic but for some kind of over-sized vehicles. And, on the pavement around him, he saw the dim outline of refuse.

He picked up a piece of written material. A political pamphlet, evidently. Denouncing someone or some party. He recognized words here and there – the syntax seemed easy enough; the language was inflected, along the lines of Spanish or Italian, not distributive, but with occasional English words. Seeing it written made the problem of understanding it much easier for him. He recalled the medical texts in Russian and Chinese that had been required reading, the twice-monthly journal with abstracts in six languages. Part of being a medical man. At the University of La Jolla he had had to read not only German, Russian, Chinese, but also French – a language of no real current importance, but forced on them by tradition. And his wife, as a cultural asset, had been learning classic Greek.

Anyhow, he realized, that's all solved now. They have their one synthetic language. And this is it.

What I need is a place to hide, he decided. While I orient myself – a breathing-spell, where I'm less vulnerable. The buildings, dark and silent around him, appeared deserted. At the end of the street, a variety of lights and the tiny, distant shapes of people indicated a commercial section, open in the night to do business.

A dim street light lit the way ahead of him as he walked cautiously among the discarded cartons heaped by a loading platform. Now he stumbled over a series of waste-cans, from which a muted churning became audible. The overflowing waste began to stir, and he discovered that by knocking against the cans he had started the mechanism back into operation. No doubt it was supposed to be automatic, consuming trash as fast as it was put in, but it hadn't been kept in good repair.

A flight of cement steps led down to a doorway. He descended and tried the rusty handle of the door. Locked, of course. A storage area, probably.

Kneeling down in the semidarkness he opened his instrument case and got out the surgical packet. Its power supply was self-contained, and he clicked it on. The basic tools lit up; for emergency operations they cast enough light to work by. Expertly, he fitted a cutting blade into the drive-gear socket and cinched it up. Whining faintly, the blade cut into the lock of the door. He stood close to it, muffling the sound.

The blade crunched loose; the lock had been cut away from the door. Hastily, he disassembled the surgical tools, stuffed them back into the instrument case. With both hands he gently tugged at the door.

The door opened, squeaking on its hinges.

Now, he thought. A place to hide. In his case he had a number of dermal preparations, for use in treating burns. Already he had selected in his mind the combination of aseptic sprays that would yield a darker color; he could lower his skin hue to one indistinguishable from that of . . .

In sudden bright light he stood blinking. Not a deserted store-room at all. Warm air greeted him, smells of food. A man stood with a decanter in his hand, stopped in the act of pouring a woman's drink.

Seven or eight people faced him. Some sitting in chairs, a couple standing. They regarded him placidly, without surprise. They had obviously been aware of him while he cut away the lock; they had heard him outside, working.

The man resumed pouring the woman's drink. Now a low-pitched murmur of talk picked up. His presence – manner of entry – did not seem to perturb these people at all.

A woman, seated near him, was saying something to him. The musical flow of words repeated themselves several times, but he could not catch the meaning. The woman smiled up at him, without rancor, again speaking, but now more slowly. He caught one word, then another. She was telling him firmly but politely that it was up to him to replace the door lock.

'. . . and please shut it,' she concluded. 'The door.'

Foolishly, he reached behind him and pulled the door shut.

A dapper-looking youth, leaning toward him, said, 'We know who you are.' At least, so Parsons interpreted his statement.

'Yes,' another man said. Several of them nodded.

The woman near the door said, 'You're the—' And a word followed that he could make no sense of. It had a totally artificial ring, jargon rather than language.

'That's right,' another echoed. 'That's what you are.'

'But we don't care,' a boy said.

They all agreed to that.

'Because,' the boy continued, his white teeth sparkling, 'we're not here.'

A chorus of agreement. 'No, not here at *all*!'

'This is a delusion,' a slender woman said.

'Delusion,' two men repeated.

Parsons said unsteadily, 'Who am I, did you say?'

'So we're not afraid,' one of them said, or at least so he understood that person to say.

'Afraid?' Parsons said. That caught his attention at once.

'You came to get us,' a girl said.

'Yes,' they all agreed, with evident delight, their heads nodding up and down. 'But you can't.'

He thought, *They think I'm somebody else.*

'Touch me,' the woman by the door said. She set down her drink and rose from her chair. 'I'm not actually here.'

'None of us are,' several people agreed. 'Touch her. Go on.'

Unable to move, Parsons stood where he was. *I don't get it*, he thought. *I just don't.*

'All right,' the woman said. 'I'll touch you. My hand will pass right through yours.'

'Like air,' a man said happily.

The woman reached out her slim, dark fingers, closer and closer to his arm. Smiling, her eyes alive with delight, she put her fingers on his arm.

Her fingers did not pass through. At once, her mouth fell open with shock. 'Oh,' she whispered.

The room became silent. They all stared at him.

Finally one of the men said faintly, 'He's genuinely found us.'

'He really is here,' a woman murmured, her eyes wild with fear. 'Here where we are. In the basement.'

They gazed at Parsons numbly. He could do nothing but gaze back.

3

After a terrible silence, one of the women sank down in a chair and said, 'We thought you were up on Fingal Street. We have a projection on Fingal Street.'

'How did you find us?' a man said. Their rather adolescent voices mingled in a chorus.

Of the welter of talk he could make out a reasonable portion. A meeting. Secret, down here in the warehouse district. So sure of their seclusion that his coming hadn't registered.

Shupo. That had been the word for him.

With great care, Parsons said, 'I'm not *shupo*.' Whatever that was.

At once, they perked up. All eyes again fixed on him, the black, large, youthful eyes.

A man said, with bitterness, 'Who else drills through doors?'

'Not only does he drill,' a girl said, 'but he's enmask.'

They nodded. Their anxiety had become tinged with resentment.

'That incredible white mask,' a girl said.

'We had masks,' a man said. 'The last time.'

'Oftentimes,' another said, 'we wear masks when we're out.'

He had, apparently, stumbled onto a marginal, covert group that operated outside the law. Conspiring, possibly political . . . in danger. Certainly in no position to menace him. Good luck for me, he decided.

'Let's see your real face,' a man said. Now they all clamored, with mounting indignation.

'This is my real face,' he said.

'All *white* like that?'

'And listen to him talk,' another said. 'Speech impediment.'

'Partly deaf, too,' another said, a girl. 'In that he doesn't get half of what's said.'

'A real *quivak*,' a boy said scathingly.

A small, sharp-faced youth swaggered up to Parsons. With contempt, in a drawling, insinuating voice, he said close to Parsons' face, 'Let's get it over with.' He held up his right thumb.

'Cut it off,' a girl said, her eyes flashing. She also held out her right thumb. 'Go ahead. Cut it off right now!'

So, Parsons thought. Political criminals are maimed in this society. Ancient punishment. He felt deep revulsion. Barbaric . . . and these animal totems. Reversion to tribes.

And on the highway, the boy who thought I wanted to be killed. Who tried to ride me down and was perplexed when I tried to escape.

He thought, And the city looked so beautiful to me.

Off in the corner stood a man who had said nothing, who sipped his drink and watched. His dark, heavy features had an

153

ironic expression; of them all, he seemed the only one who had control of his emotions. Now he moved toward Parsons and for the first time spoke up.

'You expected to find nobody here,' he said. 'You thought this was an empty warehouse.'

Parsons nodded.

'The only complexion of your type,' the man continued, 'in my experience, is the result of a highly contagious plague. But you seem healthy. I notice also that you have unpigmented eyes.'

'Blue,' a girl corrected.

'That is unpigmented,' the heavy-set man continued. 'What interests me most is your clothing. I'd guess 1910.'

With care, Parsons said, 'More like 2010.'

The man smiled slightly. 'Not far off, though.'

'What's this, then?' Parsons asked.

The black eyes flickered. 'Ah,' he said. Turning to the group he said, 'Well, *amici*, this is less threatening than you imagine. We have here another botch tempus-wise. I suggest we get the door relocked, and then sit down and cool.' To Parsons, he said, 'This is 2405. You're the first person that I know of. Up to now it's been *things*. Displacements. Said to be natural but freak. Frogs fall in the street, an extinct species. That tips off our scientific men. Stones. Debris. Bric-a-brac. You see?'

'Yes,' Parsons said hesitantly.

The man shrugged. 'But who can tell why.' Again he smiled at Parsons. 'Name's Wade,' he said. 'Yours?'

'Parsons.'

'Hail,' Wade said, lifting his open palm. 'Or what is it? Noses? No matter. You care to join our party? Not frolic, but the other usage.'

'Political,' Parsons said.

'Yes, to change – not understand – society. I lead, here. The – what is your old word? Sill? Sold?'

'Cell,' Parsons said.

'Quite right,' Wade said. 'As in bees, honey. Care to hear our program? Couldn't possibly mean anything to you. I suggest you exit. There is some danger to us.'

Parsons said, 'I've had trouble outside. For me there's danger

154

'out there, too.' He indicated his face. 'At least give me time to work on my color.'

'Caucasic,' Wade said, tasting the word as he said it, scowling.

'Give me half an hour,' Parsons said tightly.

Wade made a gesture of largess. 'Be our guest.' He eyed Parsons. 'We – they, if you will – have rigid standards. Maybe we can fit in. Unfortunately, no middle ground. Law of the excluded middle, sort of.'

'In other words,' Parsons said, feeling his tension and aversion rise, 'it's like all primitive societies. The stranger isn't considered human. Killed on sight, is he? Anything unfamiliar.' His hands were shaking; getting out a cigarette he lit it, trying to steady himself. 'Your totem-device,' he said, gesturing at Wade. 'The eagle. You exalt eagle qualities? Ruthlessness and quickness?'

'Not exactly,' Wade said. 'All tribes are unified, with common world view. We know nothing about eagles. Our tribal names came out of the Age of Darkness that followed the H-War.'

Kneeling down, Parsons opened his instrument case. As quickly as possible he laid out his dermal sprays. Wade and the others watched for a few moments, and then seemed to lose interest. Their talk resumed. He thought, Short span of attention. Like children.

Not even like. Are. As yet he hadn't seen anyone over twenty or so. Wade had the most mature manner, the grave, educated pomposity of a left-wing college sophomore. Of course, he hadn't as yet seen a real sample. This group, the boy on the highway . . .

The door opened suddenly. A woman entered. At sight of Parsons she stopped. 'Oh,' she gasped. Her dark eyes widened with astonishment. 'Who . . . ?'

Wade greeted her. 'Icara. This is not illness. This is one of those frogs. Displacement named Parsons.' To Parsons he said, 'She is – my doxy? Bawd? Great and good friend? *Puella*.'

The woman nodded nervously. She set down an armload of packages, which the other persons immediately gathered up. 'Why is your skin chalk-colored?' she asked, bending down beside him, slender, breathing a little rapidly, her black lips twisting with concern.

'In my times,' he said with difficulty, 'we were divided into white, yellow, brown, black races. All varieties of sub-species within the species. It's obvious there was a fusion sometime later on.'

Icara's finely-shaped nose wrinkled. 'Separate? How awful. And your language is foul. Full of lapses. Why is the door hanging open?'

'He cut the lock,' Wade sighed.

'Then he should fix it,' the woman said with no hesitation. Still bending down beside him, watching him work, she said, 'What's that gray box? Why are you opening those tubes? Are you going to travel back in time? Can we watch?'

'He's spraying himself,' Wade said. 'Darker.'

Her shining dark hair came closer to him as she leaned forward and delicately sniffed. In a low voice she said to him, 'Also, you should do something about your smell.'

'What?' he said, jolted on several levels.

Studying him, she said, 'You smell bad. Like mold.'

The others, overhearing, came over to see and then give their opinions. 'More like vegetables,' one man said. 'Maybe it's his clothes. Vegetable fiber, possibly.'

Icara said, 'We bathe.'

'So do we,' Parsons said, with anger.

'Every day?' She drew back. 'I believe it's your clothes, not you.' She eyed him as he sprayed on his skin-coloring. 'That's a good deal better. God, you looked like a grub. Not—'

'Not human,' Parsons finished ironically.

Standing up, Icara said to Wade, 'I don't see – I mean, it's going to be such a problem. The Soul Cube will be thrown off. And how can he possibly be fitted with the Fountain? He's so very different, and anyhow we don't have time for this; we have to get on with the meeting. And there our door is, hanging open.'

'Is that bad?' Parsons demanded.

'The door?' she said.

'To be different.'

'Why, of course it's bad. If you're different then you don't belong. But you can learn. Wade will give you the right clothing. You can learn to speak correctly. And look – those dyes of yours are working quite well.' She smiled at him hopefully.

'Real problem,' Wade said, 'is orientation. He can't possibly learn. Basic concepts lacking; we got as babies.' Raising an eyebrow he said to Parsons. 'How old are you?'

'Thirty-two,' Parsons said. He had almost finished spraying his face, neck, hands and arms; now he had begun removing his shirt.

Wade and Icara exchanged glances. 'Oh, dear,' Icara said. 'You mean it? Thirty-two?' Evidently to change the subject she said, 'What is that clever little gray box, and those objects in it?'

'My instruments,' Parsons said, his shirt off now.

'And what about the Lists?' Wade said, half to himself. 'The government won't like it.' He shook his head. 'He can't be fitted into any of the tribes. He'll throw the count off.'

Parsons shoved the open instrument case toward Wade. 'Look,' he said harshly. 'I don't give a damn about your tribes. You see these? They're the finest surgical tools developed in twenty-six centuries. I don't know how good or how extensive your own medical work is, but I can hold my own in any culture, past or present. With my kind of knowledge and skill, I can be of value anywhere. I know that, if nothing else. My medical knowledge will always find me a place!'

Icara and Wade looked blank. 'Medical knowledge?' Icara faltered. 'What's that?'

Parsons, appalled, said, 'I'm a physician.'

'You're a—' Icara searched for the word. 'What was it I read in the history tape? Alchemist? No, that's earlier. Sorcerer? Is a physician a sorcerer? Does he predict events by examining the motion of the stars, and consulting with spirits and so on?'

'How dull,' Wade murmured. 'There are no spirits.'

Now Parsons had sprayed his chest, shoulders and back; as rapidly as possible he rebuttoned his shirt, hoping that the film had dried. He put on his coat, tossed his instruments back in the case, and started toward the half-open door.

Wade said, '*Salvay, amicus.*' He sounded gloomy.

Pausing at the door, Parsons turned to speak, but the door, on its own, whipped away from him. Half falling, he lurched, caught himself – and looked down into a grinning, sardonic little face that peered up at him gleefully. A child, he thought. A ghastly carica-ture of a child, and more of them, all wearing the same dainty green cap . . . costumes in a grammar school play. Pointing a metal tube at him, the first child shrilled:

'*Shupo!*'

He managed to kick the first *shupo*; his toe caught it and lifted it up. It still shrilled, even as it crashed into the cement wall that rose from the entranceway. But while he kicked it, the others swarmed past him, between his legs, up him and over him, their nails tearing at him, as they scrabbled on by, into the meeting room.

His arms in front of his face, he plowed his way up the steps, to the street.

Below him, the *shupos* clustered at the door like venomous green wasps. He could not make out what was happening inside; he saw only their backs, and he could hear nothing but their shouts. They had the political people trapped. They did not care about him, or, if they did, they had not had time to snare him. Now, he saw their vehicles. Several had been placed to block the street. Possibly the unlocked, half-open door had let out light, which had attracted a routine patrol. Or they had followed the woman, Icara. He did not know. Perhaps they had even followed him, all the way from the start.

They lose their thumbs, do they? he wondered. And voluntarily? It did not sound as if the group had decided to submit; the uproar was growing. If I brought the *shupos* here, he thought, I'm responsible; I can't run off. Hesitantly, he started back.

From the undulating mass in the shadows at the base of the stairs, two full-grown shapes split apart and emerged. A man and a woman, fighting their way up, gasping. He saw, with horror, trails of blood dripping and glistening on their faces. Not thumbs, he thought. They're fighting, and it doesn't end. That's the sacrifice, but if they won't make it, then – their lives?

The man, Wade, called hoarsely up to him, 'Parsons!' His arms lifted; he tried to propel the girl up the steps. *Shupos* clung to every part of him. 'Please!' he called, his eyes blind, agonized.

Parsons came back. Dropping down the stairwell, both feet stamping, he caught hold of the girl.

Sinking back, Wade again merged, pulled back by the *shupos*, into the darkness and noise; the green shapes gleamed, shrieking in triumph. Blood, Parsons thought. They're getting blood. Holding the girl against him he struggled up the stairs, gasping; he reached the street, staggered. Blood ran down his wrists, from the girl's body. Warm, boneless, she slipped closer to him as he walked. Her head lolled. Her untied hair, shimmering, spread out. Icara. Not surprising, he thought in a dulled fashion. Love before politics.

Here, in the darkness of the street, he wandered along, panting for breath, his clothing torn, carrying Wade's doxy, or girl, or whatever. Do they have last names? he asked himself.

The noise of the fracas had attracted passers-by; they flocked, calling excitedly. Several glanced at Parsons as he carried the unconscious girl. Dead? No. He could feel her heart beating. The passers-by hurried on in the opposite direction, to the scene of the fighting.

Worn out, he halted to gather up the girl and hoist her up onto his shoulder. Her face brushed his, the excellent smooth skin. Lips, he thought, warm and moist . . . what a pretty woman. Twenty or so.

Turning the corner he continued on, almost unable to proceed. His lungs hurt and he had trouble seeing. Now he had come out onto a brightly lighted street. He saw many people, a glimpse of stores, signs, parked vehicles. Activity, and the pleasant background of leisure. From the doorway of a store – a dress shop, by the looks of the window display – music swirled, and he recognized it: the Beethoven *Archduke Trio*. Bizarre, he thought.

Ahead, a hotel. At least, a great many-storied building, with trees, wrought-iron railing, vehicles in rows before it. Reaching the steps, he ascended into a lobby in which people moved about. What he meant to do he did not know, for all at once, against him, the girl's heartbeat fluttered, became irregular.

He had his instrument case, didn't he? Yes, he had managed to hold onto it. Setting the girl down, he opened the case.

People milled around him. 'Get the hotel euthanor!'

'Her own. She has her own euthanor.'

Parsons said, 'No time.' And he began to work.

4

Close by his ear, a polite but authoritative voice said, 'Do you need assistance?'

Parsons said, 'No. Except—' He glanced up from his work for a moment. Into the girl's chest he had plugged a Dixon pump; it had taken over temporarily the job of her uneven heart.

Beside him stood a man wearing a nondescript white robe, without emblem. Like the others, he was in his twenties. But his voice and manner were not the same, and in his hand he held a flat, black-bordered card.

'Keep the people back,' Parsons said, and resumed work. The throb of the robot pump gave him confidence; it had been inserted very well, and the load had left the girl's circulatory system.

Over her lacerated right shoulder he sprayed art-derm; it sealed off the open wound, halted bleeding and prohibited infection. The most serious damage was to her windpipe. He turned the little art-derm nozzle on an exposed section of rib, wondering what the *shupos* had that worked so well. It had carved her open expertly, whatever it was. Now he turned his attention to her windpipe.

Beside him the polite official put away his identification card and said, 'Are you certain you know what you're doing?' He had, at least, cleared away the people. Evidently his rank affected them; the lobby had become empty. 'Maybe we should call the building euthanor.'

The hell with him, Parsons thought. 'I'm doing fine,' he said aloud. His fingers flew. Twisting, cutting, spraying, breaking open plastic tubes of tissue graft, fitting them into place.

'Yes,' the official said. 'I can see. You're an expert. By the way, my name's Al Stenog.'

At last, Parsons thought, a man with a last name.

'This furrow,' Parsons said, tracing the line that crossed the girl's stomach. He had coated it with airproof plastic. 'It looks bad, but it's merely into the fatty wall, not the abdominal cavity.' He showed Stenog the damaged windpipe. 'That's the worst.'

'I think I see the building euthanor,' Stenog said in an affable voice. 'Yes. Somebody must have called him. Do you want him to assist you?'

'No,' Parsons said.

'It's your decision,' Stenog said. 'I won't interfere.' He was staring at Parsons with curiosity.

My speech, Parsons thought. But he could not worry about that, now. At least he had altered the color of his skin. My eyes! he realized suddenly. As Wade said: unpigmented.

I have to save this girl's life, he decided. That's first.

With the official watching over his shoulder, he continued his job of healing the girl.

'I failed to catch your name,' Stenog said unobtrusively.

'Parsons,' he answered.

'That's an odd name,' Stenog said. 'What does it mean?'

'Nothing,' Parsons said.

'Oh?' Stenog murmured. He was silent, then, for a time, as Parsons worked. 'Interesting,' he said at last.

A second shape appeared beside Stenog. Parsons, taking a moment to glance up, saw a carefully groomed, handsome man with something under his arm, a kit of some kind. The euthanor.

'It's all over,' Parsons said. 'I took care of her.'

'I'm a little late,' the euthanor admitted. 'I was out of the building.' His eyes strayed, as he took in the sight of the girl. 'Did this occur here? In the hotel?'

Stenog said, 'No, Parsons brought her in from the street.' To Parsons he said in his smooth voice, 'A vehicle accident? Or an assault? You neglected to say.'

Parsons simply didn't answer; he concentrated on the final portion of the job.

The girl would live. In another half minute her life would have ebbed out of her throat and chest, and then nothing would have saved her. His skill, his knowledge, had saved her life, and these two men – evidently respected individuals in this society – were witnesses to it.

'I can't follow your work,' the euthanor admitted. 'I've never seen anything like it. Who are you? Where did you come from?

How did you learn techniques like that?' To Stenog he said, 'I'm completely baffled. I don't recognize any of his accessories.'

'Perhaps Parsons will tell us,' Stenog said softly. 'Of course, this is hardly the time. A little later, no doubt.'

'Does it matter,' Parsons said, 'where I come from, or who I am?'

Stenog said, 'I've been informed that there's police action going on around the corner. This girl might be from that event, possibly. You were passing nearby, found the girl injured on the street, brought her . . .'

His voice trailed off questioningly, but Parsons said nothing.

Now Icara was beginning to regain consciousness. She gave a faint cry and moved her arms.

There was a moment of stunned silence. 'What does this mean?' the euthanor demanded.

'I've been successful,' Parsons said irritably. 'Better get her into a bed. There's damage that'll have to heal over a period of weeks.' What did they expect, a miracle? 'But there's no longer any danger.'

'No longer any danger?' Stenog repeated.

'That's right,' Parsons said. What was the matter with them? 'She'll recover. Understand?'

In a slow, cautious voice, Stenog said, 'Then in what sense have you been successful?'

Parsons stared at him, and Stenog stared back with a faintly contemptuous expression.

Examining the girl, the euthanor began to tremble. 'I understand,' he said in a choked voice. 'You pervert! You maniac!'

As if he were enjoying the situation, Stenog said in a pleasant, light voice, 'Parsons, you've blatantly healed the girl. Isn't that a fact? These are therapeutic devices you have here. I'm amazed.' He seemed almost to laugh. 'Well, of course you're under arrest. You realize that.' With firmness, he moved the furious-faced euthanor back. 'I'll handle this,' he said. 'This is my business, not yours. You can go. If you're needed as a witness, my office will get in touch with you.'

As the euthanor reluctantly left, Parsons found himself facing

Stenog alone. Leisurely, Stenog brought forth what looked to Parsons like an eggbeater. Touching a raised spot on its handle, Stenog sent the blades into spinning motion; the blades disappeared and from it came a high-pitched whine. Obviously, it was a weapon.

'You're under arrest,' Stenog said. 'For a major crime against the United Tribes. The Folk.' The words had a formal sound, but not the man's tone; he spoke them as if they had no importance to him; it was a mere ritual. 'Follow me, if you will.'

Parsons said, 'You're serious?'

The younger man raised a dark eyebrow. He motioned with the eggbeater. He *was* serious. 'You're lucky,' he said to Parsons, as they moved toward the entrance to the hotel. 'If you had healed her there, with those tribe people . . .' Again he eyed Parsons with curiosity. 'They would have torn you apart. But of course you knew that.'

This society is insane, Parsons thought. This man and this society together.

I am really afraid!

In the dimly lighted room the two shapes watched the glowing procession of words avidly, leaning forward in their chairs, powerful bodies taut.

'Too late!' the strong-faced man cursed bitterly. 'Everything was out of phase. No accurate junction with the dredge. And now he's trapped in an intertribal area.' Pressing a control, he speeded up the flow of words. 'And now, someone from the government.'

'What's the matter with the emergency team?' the woman beside him whispered. 'Why aren't they there? They could have got him on the street. The first flash was sent out as soon as—'

'It takes time.' The strong-faced man paced restlessly back and forth, feet lost in the thick carpets that covered the floor. 'If only we could have come out in the open.'

'They won't get there soon enough.' The seated woman struck out savagely, and the flow of illuminated words faded. 'By the time they get there he'll be dead – or worse. So far we've completely failed, Helmar. It's gone wrong.'

*

Noise. Lights and movement around him. For an instant he opened his eyes. A shattering blaze of white poured remorselessly down on him from all sides; once more he shut his eyes. It hadn't changed.

'Your name again?' a voice said. 'Name, please.'

He did not answer.

'James Parsons,' another voice said. A familiar voice. As he heard it he wondered dully whose voice it was. He could almost place it. Almost, but not quite.

'Old?'

'Thirty-two,' the voice said, after a pause. And this time he recognized it; the voice was his, and he was answering their questions without volition. Off somewhere, machinery hummed.

'Born?' the voice asked.

Once more he struggled to open his eyes. His hand came up to shield his eyes from the glare, and he saw, for a moment, the blur of objects and people. A clerk, bored, empty-faced, seated at a recording machine, writing down the answers that were given. A bureaucrat. A functionary in a clean office. No force, no violence. The answers came, however. *Why do I tell them?*

'Chicago, Illinois,' his voice, from some other point in the room, answered. 'Cook County.'

The clerk said presently, 'What month, date?'

'October 16,' his voice answered. '1980.'

On the clerk's face the expression remained the same. 'Brothers or sisters?'

'No,' his voice said.

On and on the questions went. And he answered each one of them.

'All right, Mr Parsons,' the clerk said at last.

'Dr Parsons,' the voice – his voice – corrected, from a learned reflex.

The clerk paid no attention. 'You're through,' he said, removing a spool from the recording machine. 'Will you go across the hall to Room 34, please?' With a nod of his chin he indicated the direction. 'They'll take care of you there.'

Stiffly, Parsons rose. A table, he discovered. He had been sitting on a table, and he had on only his shorts. Like a hospital –

aseptic, white, professional looking. He began to walk. And, as he did so, he saw his white legs, unsprayed, a strange contrast to his dyed arms, chest, back, and neck. So they know, he thought. But he kept on walking. In him there was no desire either to comply or to resist; he simply walked from the interrogation room, down a well-lit hall, to Room 34.

The door opened as he approached. Now he found himself standing in what appeared to be a personal apartment. He saw, with amazement, a harpsichord. Cushions upon a window seat, a window that overlooked the city. Midday, by the looks of the sun. Books here and there, and, on the wall, a reproduction of a Picasso.

While he stood there, Stenog appeared, leafing through a clipboard of papers. Glancing at Parsons he said, 'Even the deformed? The congenitally deformed? You healed *them* too?'

'Sure,' Parsons said. Now, some sense of control had begun to filter back into him. 'I—' he began haltingly, but Stenog broke in.

'I have read about your period on the history tapes,' Stenog said. 'You're a *doctor*. Well, that term is clear. I understand the function you performed. But I can't grasp the ideology behind it. *Why?*' His face became animated with emotion. 'That girl, Icara. She was dying, and yet you deliberately made skillful alterations to her system for the purpose of keeping her alive.'

Parsons answered with an effort. 'That's right.'

Now he saw that several other persons had accompanied Stenog into the room. They hung back, out of the way, letting Stenog do the talking.

'In your culture this had a positive value?' Stenog said. 'Such an act was officially sanctioned?'

A person in the background said, 'Your profession was honored? A valued social role, with plaudits?'

Stenog said, 'I find it impossible to believe a whole society could have been oriented around such behavior. Surely it was a splinter group that sanctioned you.'

Parsons heard them, but their words made no sense. Everything was out of focus. Distorted. As if turned out by some warped mirror. 'Healing was respected,' he managed to say. 'But you people seem to think it's somehow wrong.'

165

A furious rustle leaped through the circle of listeners. 'Wrong!' Stenog snapped. 'It's madness! Don't you see what would happen if everybody were healed? All the sick and injured? The old?'

'No wonder his society collapsed,' a harsh-eyed girl said. 'It's amazing it stood so long. Based on such a perverted system of values.'

'It demonstrates,' Stenog said thoughtfully, 'the almost infinite variety of cultural formations. That a whole society could exist oriented around such drives seems to us beyond belief. But from our historical reconstruction we know such a thing actually went on. This man here is not an escaped lunatic. In his own time he was a valued person. His profession had not only sanction – it gave him prestige.'

The girl said, 'Intellectually, I can accept it. But not emotionally.'

A cunning expression appeared on Stenog's face. 'Parsons, let me ask you this. I recall a pertinent fact. Your science was also devoted to keeping new life from appearing. You had contraceptives. Chemical and mechanical agents preventing zygote formation within the oviduct.'

Parsons started to answer. 'We—'

'*Rassmort!*' the girl snarled, pale with fury.

Parsons blinked. What did that mean? He couldn't convert it into his own semantic system.

'Do you remember the average age of your population?' Stenog asked.

'No,' Parsons muttered. 'About forty, I believe.'

At that, the roomful of persons broke into jeers. 'Forty!' Stenog said, with disgust. '*Our* average age is fifteen.'

It meant nothing to Parsons. Except that, as he had already seen, there were few old people. 'You consider that something to be proud of?' he said wonderingly.

A roar of indignation burst from the circle around him. 'All right,' Stenog said, gesturing. 'I want you all to leave; you're making it impossible for me to perform my job.'

They left reluctantly.

When the last had gone, Stenog walked to the window and stood for a moment.

'We had no idea,' he said at last to Parsons, over his shoulder. 'When I brought you in here, it was for a routine examination.' He paused. 'Why didn't you dye your body all over? Why just in parts?'

Parsons said, 'No time.'

'You've just been here briefly.' Stenog glanced over the written material on his clipboard. 'I see that you claim no knowledge of how you got from your time segment to ours. Interesting.'

If it was all there, there was no point in him saying anything. He remained silent. Past Stenog he could see the city, and he began to take an interest in it. The spires . . .

'What bothers me,' Stenog said, 'is that we dropped experimentation with time travel something like eight years ago. The government, I mean. A principle was put forth, showing that time travel was a limited application of perpetual motion, and hence a contradiction of its own working laws. That is, if you wanted to invent a time machine, all you'd have to do was swear or prophesy that when you got it working, the first use you'd put it to would be to go back into time, to the point at which you got interested in the idea.' He smiled. 'And give your earlier self the functioning, finished piece of equipment. This has never happened; evidently there can be no time travel. By definition, time travel is a discovery that, if it could be made, *would already have been made*. Perhaps I oversimplified the proof, but substantially—'

Parsons interrupted. 'That assumes that if the discovery had already been made, it would be publicly known. Recognized. But nobody saw me leave my own world.' He gestured. 'And do you think they realize now what's happened? All they know is that I disappeared, with no trace. Would they infer that I was carried into time?' He thought of his wife. 'They don't know,' he said. 'There was no warning.' Now he told Stenog the details; the younger man listened attentively.

'A force field,' Stenog said presently. With a sudden shudder of anger he said, 'We shouldn't have given up experimentation; we had a good deal of basic research done, hardware constructed.' Now, he pondered. 'That hardware – God knows what became of it. The research never was kept secret. Presumably the hardware was sold off; a lot of valuable components were involved. That was last year or so. We had it so clearly in mind that time travel would show up in some vast historic way, interfere with the collapse of the Greek City States, assist the success of Napoleon's European plan and thereby obviate the following wars. But you're implying a *secret*, limited time travel. For some personal reasons. Not official, not for social aims.' His boyish face drew into a troubled scowl.

'If you recognize that I'm from another time,' Parsons said, 'from another culture, how can you convict me for what I did?'

To that, Stenog nodded. 'You had no knowledge, of course. But our law has no clause about "persons from another culture." There is no other culture, no diversity whatever. Ignorant or not, you have to stand trial for sentence. There's a historic concept: Ignorance of the law is no excuse. And isn't that what you're claiming?'

The patent injustice of it staggered Parsons. Yet he could not tell from Stenog's tone just how serious the man was; the faintly detached, ironical quality could not be interpreted. Was Stenog mocking himself?

Parsons said stiffly, 'Can't you use your reason?'

Chewing his lip, Stenog said, 'You have to abide by the laws of the community in which you live. Whether you came voluntarily or not. But' – he now appeared to be genuinely concerned; the irony had gone – 'possibly some suspension can be worked out. The motions could be gone through.'

Going from the room, he left Parsons alone for a time. When he returned he carried a polished oak box with a lock on it. Seating himself, he produced a key from his robe and unlocked the box. Out of it he lifted a massive white wig. With solemnity, he placed the wig on his head; at once, with his dark hair concealed, and the heavy rolls of the wig outlining his face, he lost the appearance of youth. A gravity and importance entered his appearance.

Stenog said, 'As Director of the Fountain, I have the authority to pass judgment on you.' From beneath his peruke, he scrutinized Parsons. 'What we mainly have to consider is the formal procedure of exile.'

'Exile!' Parsons echoed.

'We don't maintain our prison colonies here. I forget what system your culture employed. Work camps? C.C.C. in Soviet Asia?'

After a pause, Parsons managed to say, 'By my time the C.C.C. camps were gone. So were the slave labor camps in Russia.'

'We make no attempt to rehabilitate the criminal,' Stenog said. 'That would be an invasion of his rights. And, from a practical standpoint, it doesn't work. We don't want substandard persons in our society.'

'The *shupos*,' Parsons said, with dread. 'They're involved in these colonies?'

Stenog said, 'The *shupos* are too valuable to be sent off Earth. A good deal of them are our youth, you understand. Especially the active element. The *shupo* organization maintains youth hostels and schools set apart from society, operated in the Spartan manner. The children are trained both in body and in mind. They're hardened. The activity that you saw, the raid on the illegal political group, is incidental, a sort of field expedition. They're quite zealous, the boys from the hostels. On the streets they have the right, as individuals, to challenge any person they feel is not acting properly.'

'What are the prison colonies like?'

'They're city sized. You'll be free to work, and you'll have a separate dwelling of the apartment type where you can pursue various hobbies or creative crafts. The climate, of course, isn't favorable. Your life-span will be cut down enormously. Much depends on your own stamina.'

'And there's no way I can appeal your decision?' Parsons demanded. 'No trial system? The government brings the charges and then acts as the judge? Merely by putting on a medieval periwig—'

'We have the girl's signed complaint,' Stenog said.

At that, Parsons stared at him. He could not believe it.

'Oh, yes,' Stenog said. 'Come along.' Rising, he opened a side door, beckoning Parsons to follow him. Formidable and solemn in his wig, he said, 'Possibly this will tell you more about us than anything you have seen so far.'

They passed by door after door; Parsons, in a daze, followed

169

the bewigged younger man, barely able to keep up with his springy step. At last Stenog halted at a door, unlocked it, and stepped aside for Parsons to enter.

On the first of several small stages lay a body, partly covered by a white sheet. Icara. Parsons walked toward her. Her eyes were shut and she did not move. Her skin had a faded, washed-out quality.

'She filed the complaint,' Stenog said, 'just before she died.' He switched on a light; gazing down. Parsons saw that beyond any doubt the girl was dead, possibly had been for several hours.

'But she was recovering,' he said. 'She was getting well.'

Reaching down, Stenog lifted the sheet back. Along the side of the girl's neck, Parsons saw a careful, precise slash. The great carotid arteries had been cut, and expertly.

'In her complaint, she charged you with deliberately obstructing the natural process of seelmotus,' Stenog said. 'As soon as she had filled out this form she called her residential euthanor and underwent the Final Rite.'

'Then she did it herself,' Parsons said.

'It was her pleasure. By her own will she undid the harm you had attempted.' Stenog shut off the light.

5

In his own personal car, Stenog took him to his house for dinner.

As they drove through the afternoon traffic, Parsons tried to see as much of the city as possible. Once, when the car halted for a three-level bus, he rolled down the window and leaned out. Stenog made no move to inhibit his actions.

'There's where I work,' Stenog said once. He slowed the car and pointed. A flat building, larger than any others that Parsons had seen, lay to their right. 'That's where we were – in my office at the Fountain. That means nothing to you, but you were at the most highly guarded spot we possess. We've been all this time getting through the check-stations.' They had been in the car now for almost half an hour. 'Every day I have to go through this,'

Stenog said. 'And I'm the Director of the Fountain. But they check me, too.'

A final uniformed guard halted the car, took the flat black card that Stenog showed him, and then the car started up onto a through ramp. The city fell below them.

'The Soul Cube is at the Fountain,' Stenog said, by way of explanation. 'But that makes no sense to you either, does it?'

'No,' Parsons said. His mind was still on the girl, and on her death.

'Concentric rings,' Stenog continued. 'Zones of importance. Now, of course, we're out in the tribal areas again.' The brightly colored dots that Parsons had first seen now passed by them at high velocity; Stenog did not appear to be a fast driver. In the daylight, Parsons noticed that each passing car had one of the tribal totem animals painted on its door, and, on the hoods, metal and plastic ornaments that might have been totem – the cars moved by too fast for him to be certain.

'You'll stay with me,' Stenog said, 'until time for your emigration to Mars. That should be in a day or so; it takes a little time to arrange transportation, what with all the red tape and government forms.'

The house, small, part of a group of many houses built along the same lines, reminded Parsons of his own house. On the front steps he halted for a moment.

'Go in ahead,' Stenog said. 'The car parks itself.' His hand on Parsons' shoulder, he steered him up the steps and onto the porch. The front door, open, let out the sound of music. 'You lived before the age of radio, didn't you?' Stenog said as they entered.

'No,' Parsons said. 'We had it.'

'I see,' Stenog said. He seemed tired, now, at the end of the day. 'Dinner should be ready,' he murmured; sitting down on a long low couch he removed his sandals.

As Parsons moved about the living room he realized that Stenog was gazing at him oddly.

'Your shoes,' Stenog said. 'Didn't you people take off your shoes when you entered a house?'

After Parsons had removed his shoes Stenog clapped his hands.

A moment later a woman appeared from the back of the house, wearing a flowing, brightly colored robe, her feet bare. She paid no attention to Parsons. From a low cabinet set against the wall she brought forth a tray on which stood a ceramic pot and a tiny glazed cup; Parsons smelled tea as the woman set the tray down on a table near the couch on which Stenog sat. Without a word, Stenog poured himself tea and began to drink.

None for me, Parsons thought. Because he was a criminal? Or were all guests treated this way? The differing customs. Stenog had not introduced the woman to him. Was she his wife? His maid?

Gingerly, Parsons seated himself on the far end of the couch. Neither Stenog nor the woman gave any sign that he had done rightly or wrongly; the woman kept her black eyes fixed on Stenog while he drank. She, too, like all the others Parsons had seen in this world, had the long shiny hair, the dark coloring; but in her he thought he saw one difference. This woman seemed less dainty, more heavily built.

'This is my *puella*,' Stenog said, having finished his cup of tea. 'Let's see.' He relaxed, yawned, obviously glad to be out of his office and in his own home. 'Well, there's probably no way I can express it to you. We have a legal relationship, recorded by the government. It's voluntary. I can break it; she can't.' He added, 'Her name is Amy.'

The woman held out her hand to Parsons; he took it, and found himself shaking hands. This hadn't changed, this custom. The sense of continuity raised his morale slightly, and he found himself, too, relaxing.

'Tea for Dr Parsons,' Stenog said.

While the two men sipped tea, Amy fixed dinner somewhere out of sight, behind a fragile-looking screen that Parsons recognized as distinctly Oriental. And here, as in his office, Stenog had a harpsichord; on this one stood a stack of sheet music, some of it very old looking.

After dinner, Stenog rose and said, 'Let's take a run down to the Fountain.' He nodded to Parsons. 'I want you to understand our point of view.'

172

Together, in Stenog's car, they drove through the night darkness. The air, fresh and cold, blew around Parsons; the younger man kept the windows down, clearly from habit. He seemed withdrawn into himself, and Parsons did not try to talk to him.

As they were being processed through the check-stations once more, Stenog abruptly burst out, 'Do you consider this society morbid?'

'There are strains of it,' Parsons said. 'Visible to an outsider. The emphasis on death—'

'On life, you mean.'

'When I first got here, the first person who saw me tried to run me down and kill me. Thinking I wanted to be killed.' *And Icara*, he thought.

'That person probably saw you roaming around alone at night, on foot, on the public highway.'

'Yes,' Parsons said.

'That's one of the favorite ways for certain types of dashing individuals with a flair for the spectacular. They go out on the highway, outside the city, and it's the custom that the cars that see them run over them. It's time-honored, established. Didn't persons in your society go out at night, onto bridges, and throw themselves off?'

Parsons said, 'But they were a trivial few, a mentally disturbed minority.'

'Yet the custom, even so, was established within society! It was *understood*. If you decided to kill yourself, that was the proper way.' Now, working himself up emotionally, Stenog said, 'Actually, you know nothing about this society – you just came here. Look at this.'

They had come out in a huge chamber. Parsons halted, impressed by the maze of corridors that stretched off in all directions. Even at night, work continued; the corridors were active and alight.

One wall of the chamber looked onto the edge of a cube. Going in that direction, Parsons discovered with a shock that he was seeing only a slice of the cube; virtually all of it lay buried in the ground, and he could only infer dimly what its full size might be.

The cube was alive.

The ceaseless undercurrent drummed up from the floor itself; he felt it moving through his body. An illusion, created by the countless technicians hurrying back and forth? Self-regulated freight elevators brought up empty containers, loaded themselves with new material and descended again. Armed guards prowled back and forth, keeping an eye on things; he saw them watching even Stenog. But the sense of life was not an illusion; he felt the emanation from the cube, the churning. A controlled, measured metabolism, but with a peculiar overtone of restlessness. Not a tranquil life, but with the tidal ebb and flow of the sea. Disturbing to him, and also to the other people; he caught, on their faces, the same fatigue and tension that he had seen with Stenog.

And he felt coldness rising from the cube.

Odd, he thought. Alive and cold . . . not like our life, not warm. In fact, he could see the breaths of the individuals in the corridors, his own, Stenog's, the white fog blown out by each of them. The pneuma.

'What is in it?' he asked Stenog.

Stenog said, 'We are.'

At first, he did not understand; he assumed the man meant it metaphorically. Then, by degrees, he began to see.

'Zygotes,' Stenog said. 'Arrested and frozen in cold-pack by the hundred billion. Our total seed. Our horde. The *race* is in there. Those of us now walking around—' He made a motion of dismissal. 'A minute fraction of what's contained in there, the future generations to come.'

So, Parsons thought, their minds aren't fixed on the present; it's the future that's real to them. Those to come, in a sense, are more real than those who are walking around now.

'How is it regulated?' he asked Stenog.

'We keep a constant population. Roughly, two and three-quarter billion. Each death automatically starts a new zygote from cold-pack along its regular developmental path. For each death there is an instantaneous new life; the two are interwoven.'

Parsons thought, So out of death comes life. In their view, death is the cause of life.

'Where do the zygotes come from?' he inquired.

'Contributed according to a specific and very complex pattern. Each year we have Lists. Contest examinations between the tribes. Tests that cover all phases of ability, physical fitness, mental faculties, and intuitive functioning at every level and of every description and orientation. From the most abstract to the object-correlatives, the manual skills.'

With comprehension, Parsons said, 'The contribution of gametes is proportional to the test ratings of each tribe.'

Stenog nodded. 'In the last Lists the Wolf Tribe gained sixty victories out of two hundred. Therefore it contributed thirty percent of the zygotes for the next period, more than the three next highest-scoring tribes. As many gametes as possible are taken from the actual high-scoring men and women. The zygotes are always formed here, of course. Unauthorized zygote formation is illegal . . . but I don't want to offend your sensibilities. Extremely talented persons have made substantial contributions, even where their particular tribes have scored low. Once a gifted individual is located, all efforts are made to obtain his or her total supply of gametes. The Mother Superior of the Wolf Tribe, for example. None of Loris' gametes are lost. Each is removed as it is formed and immediately impregnated at the Fountain. Inferior gametes, the seed of low-scores, are ignored and allowed to perish.'

Now, with first real clarity, Parsons grasped the underlying scheme of this world. 'Then your stock is always improving.'

'Of course,' Stenog said, surprised.

'And the girl, Icara. She wanted to die because she was maimed, disfigured. She knew she would have had to compete in the Lists that way.'

'She would have been a negative factor. She was what we call substandard. Her tribe would have been pulled down by her entry. But as soon as she was dead, a superior zygote, from a later stock than her own, was released. And at the same time a nine month embryo was brought out and severed from the Soul Cube. A Beaver died. Therefore this new baby will wear the emblem of the Beaver Tribe. It will take Icara's place.'

Parsons nodded slowly. 'Immortality.' Then death, he realized, has a positive meaning. Not the end of life. And not merely because these people *wish* to believe, but because *it is a fact*. Their world is constructed that way.

This is no idle mysticism! he realized. *This is their science.*

On the drive back to Stenog's house, Parsons contemplated the bright-eyed men and women along the route. Strong noses and chins. Clear skins. A handsome race of imposing men and full-breasted young women, all in the prime of youth. Laughing, hurrying through their fine city.

He caught a glimpse, once, of a man and woman passing along a spidery ramp, a strand of shimmering metal connecting two spires. Neither of them was over twenty. Holding hands as they rushed along, talking and smiling at each other. The girl's small, sharply-etched face, slender arms, tiny feet in sandals. A rich face, full of life and happiness. And health.

Yet, this was a society built on death. Death was an everyday part of their lives. Individuals died and no one was perturbed, not even the victims. They died happily, gladly. But it was wrong. It was against nature. A man was supposed to defend his life instinctively. Place it before everything else. This society denied a basic drive common to all forms.

Struggling to express himself, he said, 'You invite death. When someone dies, you're glad.'

'Death,' Stenog said, 'is part of the cycle of existence, as much so as birth. You saw the Soul Cube. A man's death is as significant as his life.' He spoke disjointedly, as traffic ahead of him caused him to turn his attention back to driving.

And yet, Parsons thought, this man does everything he can to avoid piling up his car. He's a careful driver. A contradiction.

In my own society—

Nobody thought about death. The system in which he had been born, in which he had grown up, had no explanation for death. A man simply lived out his life and tried to pretend that he wouldn't die.

Which was more realistic? This integration of death into the society, or the neurotic refusal of his own society to consider death *at all*? Like children, he decided. Unable and unwilling to imagine

176

their own deaths . . . that's how my world operated. Until mass death caught up with us all, as apparently it did.

'Your forefathers,' Stenog said, 'the early Christians, I mean, hurled themselves under chariot wheels. They sought death, and yet out of their beliefs came your society.'

Parsons said slowly, 'We may ignore death, we may immaturely *deny* the existence of death, but at least we don't court death.'

'You did indirectly,' Stenog said. 'By denying such a powerful reality, you undermined the rational basis of your world. You had no way to cope with war and famine and overpopulation because you couldn't bring yourselves to discuss them. So war *happened* to you; it was like a natural calamity, not man-made at all. It became a force. We control our society. We contemplate all aspects of our existence, not merely the good and pleasant.'

For the rest of the trip they drove in silence.

After they had gotten out of the car, and had started up the front steps of the house, Stenog paused at a shrub that grew by the porch. In the porchlight he directed Parsons' attention to the various blooms.

'What do you notice growing?' he said, lifting a heavy stalk.

'A bud.'

Stenog lifted another stalk. 'And here is a blooming flower. And over here, a dying flower. Past its bloom.' He took a knife from his belt and with one swift, clean swipe he severed the dying flower from the shrub and dropped it over the railing. 'You saw three things: the bud, which is the life to come. The blossom, which is the life going on now. And the dead flower, which I cut off so that new buds could form.'

Parsons was deep in thought. 'But somewhere in this world, there's someone who doesn't think like you do. That must be why I was brought here. Sooner or later—'

'They'll show up?' Stenog finished, his face animated.

All at once Parsons understood why no attempt had been made to keep him under careful guard. Why Stenog drove him so openly and readily about the city, brought him to his house, to the Fountain itself.

They *wanted* the contact made.

Inside the house, in the living room, Amy sat at the harpsichord. At first the music did not seem familiar to Parsons, but after a time he became aware that she was playing Jelly Roll Morton tunes, but in some strange, inaccurate rhythm.

'I got to looking for something from your period,' she said, pausing. 'You didn't happen ever to see Morton, did you? We consider him on a par with Dowland and Schubert and Brahms.'

Parsons said, 'He lived before my time.'

'Am I doing it wrong?' she said, noticing his expression. 'I've always been fond of music of that period. In fact, I did a paper on it, in school.'

'Too bad I can't play,' he said. 'We had TV, in our period. Learning to play a musical instrument had just about vanished as either a social or a cultural experience.' In fact, he had never played a musical instrument of any kind; he recognized the harpsichord only from having seen one in a museum. This culture had revived elements from centuries previous to his own, had made them a part of their world; for him, music had been important, but it had come from recordings, or, at best, concerts. The idea of playing music in the home was as incredible as owning one's own telescope.

'I'm surprised you don't play,' Stenog said. He had produced a bottle and glasses. 'What about this? Fermented drink, made from grains.'

'I think I recall that,' Parsons said with amusement.

Still very seriously, Stenog said, 'As I understand it, liquor was introduced to take the place of drugs popular during your period. It has fewer toxic side-effects than the drugs you're probably familiar with.' He opened the bottle and began to pour. From the color and smell, Parsons guessed that the stuff was a sour-mash bourbon.

He and Stenog sat drinking, while Amy played her eerie version of Dixieland jazz at the harpsichord. The house had a deeply peaceful air, and he felt himself becoming a little more calm. Was this, after all, so vile a society?

How, he thought, can a society be judged by an individual

created by another society? There's no disinterested standard. I'm merely comparing this world to mine. Not to a third.

The bourbon seemed to his taste unaged; he drank only a little. Across from him, Stenog filled his own glass a second time, and now Amy came over. He watched her go to the cupboard for a glass; Stenog had not gotten one out for her. The status of women . . . and yet, in his contact with Wade and Icara, he had not been conscious of this disparity.

'That illegal political group,' he said. 'What did they advocate?'

Stenog stirred. 'Voting rights for women.'

Although she had her drink, Amy did not join them. She retired to a corner and seated herself, small and quiet and thoughtful.

But she did mention going to school, Parsons remembered. So women aren't excluded from educational opportunities. Perhaps education itself, especially non-scientific education, such as a degree in history, has no status here. Something appropriate for women: a mere hobby.

Studying his glass, Stenog said, 'Do you like my *puella*?'

Embarrassed, Parsons said, 'I—' He could not keep himself from glancing in her direction. She showed no emotion.

'You're staying here tonight,' Stenog said. 'You can sleep with Amy if you want.'

To that, Parsons could say nothing. Guardedly, he looked from Stenog to Amy, trying to make out what actually was meant. Here, the language barrier had betrayed him – and the difference in customs.

'That's not done in my time segment,' he said finally.

'Well, you're here now,' Stenog said with a touch of ire.

Certainly, that was true. Parsons considered, and then said, 'I should think this practice would upset your careful control of zygote formation.'

At once, both Stenog and Amy started. 'Oh,' Amy said. 'Of course.' To Stenog she said, 'Remember, he didn't go through the Initiation.' With visible uneasiness she added, 'It's a good thing he spoke up. This could be a very dangerous situation. I'm surprised none of you thought about it.'

Drawing himself up, Stenog said with pride, 'Parsons, prepare to have your sensibilities offended.'

'That isn't important,' Amy said to him. 'I'm thinking of situations he might get into.'

Paying no attention to her, Stenog focussed his attention on Parsons. 'All males are sterilized at the inception of puberty,' he said, an expression of deep satisfaction on his face. 'Myself, included.'

'So you can see,' Amy said, 'why this custom causes no particular trouble. But in your case—'

'No, no,' Stenog said. 'You can't sleep with her, Parsons. In fact, you can't sleep with any of the women.' Now he, too, had become disturbed. 'You should be gotten to Mars, I think. As soon as it's feasible. A thing like this . . . it could cause great problems.'

Approaching Parsons, Amy said, 'More to drink?' She started to refill his glass. He did not protest.

6

It became feasible at four that morning. Suddenly Jim Parsons found himself on his feet, out of bed; his clothes were handed to him, and before he had even gotten half-dressed the several men, wearing government uniforms of some kind, had him in motion, out of the house to a parked car. No one spoke to him. The men worked fast, and with skill. A moment later the car carried him at high speed along the empty highway, away from the city.

At no time did he see any sign of Stenog. Or of Amy.

The field, when they reached it, surprised him by its size: no larger than the back yard of an ordinary upper-middle-class home, and not even fully level. On it a ship, like an egg, painted originally a dark blue but not pitted and corroded, was in the process of being prepared. Several field lights had been trained on it, and in the glare technicians were going over it, making what he guessed to be final examinations.

Almost at once he found himself being propelled up a ramp and through the porthole entrance of the ship. There, in a single compartment, he was seated in a reinforced chair, clamped so that he could not stir – and at that point the men let go of him.

The compartment contained, besides himself, a single entity. He had never seen such an object before; he stared at it, feeling a pervasive dread.

The machine stood almost as high as a man, built partly of opaque metals and plastic, and partly – near the top – of a transparent membrane through which he could see activity taking place. In a fluid, something soft, on the order of gray organic material, floated. Out of the top of the machine several delicate projections sprouted, reminding him of the below-surface portions of mushrooms. Fine interlacing of fibres almost too tenuous to be visible.

Pausing at the entrance porthole, one of the government men turned and said, 'It's not alive. That business floating around up top, that's a section cut out of a rat brain. It's growing in the medium, but it's not conscious; it's just to simplify building them.'

'Easier to cut a section from a rat brain than build a control,' another man said, and then both of them disappeared; the lock slipped into place and the hull of the ship became sealed.

Immediately the machine in front of Parsons whirred, clicked, and said in a calm, distinctly human voice, 'The trip to the Martian settlements takes approximately seventy-five minutes. You will be supplied with adequate ventilation and heat, but there is no provision for food except in emergency.'

The machine clicked off. It had spoken its piece.

Now the ship shuddered. Parsons shut his eyes as the ship began to lift, very slowly at first, and then, abruptly, at enormous speed. The far section of wall had a wide slot for viewing purposes; he saw the surface of Earth rush away, the stars swirl as the ship changed course. Nice of them to let me see, he thought in a dazed, remote way.

Now the machine spoke again. 'This ship is so constructed that tampering with any portion of it will produce a detonation that will destroy both the ship and occupant. The trajectory of flight is prearranged, and any tampering with the automatic self-contained beam will cause the same detonating mechanism to become active.' After a moment the machine repeated its message.

The swirl of stars that he faced gradually settled down. One spot of light began to grow, and he identified it as Mars.

'By your left hand you will find an emergency button,' the machine said suddenly. 'If you find yourself deprived of either adequate ventilation or warmth, press that button.'

For other kinds of situations, Parsons thought, there probably are no provisions. This ship carries me to Mars, blows up if anyone tries to interfere, gives me air and heat, and that's its job.

The interior, as well as the exterior, had a worn, used quality. It's made this trip many times, he decided. It's carried quite a few people between Earth and the Martian settlements. Back and forth. A shuttle-service, leaving at odd hours.

Mars continued to grow. He guessed at the time. Half an hour possibly had gone by. It makes good speed, he thought. Perfected.

And then Mars, on the screen, disappeared.

The stars leaped; he felt a vacuum within him, as if he were falling. The stars settled into place and the feeling departed almost as quickly as it had come.

But, on the screen, he saw no destination. Only black emptiness and the far-off stars. The ship continued to move, but now he had no constant by which to measure.

Across from him, the machine clicked and said in its recorded human voice, 'We have passed approximately half-way on the trip.'

Something has gone wrong, Parsons realized. *This ship is no longer heading toward Mars.* And it did not seem to bother the robot self-regulating mechanism.

He thought in panic, *Mars is gone!*

Slightly over half an hour later the machine announced, 'We are about to land. Be prepared for a series of concussions as the ship adjusts itself.'

Beyond the ship – only void.

This is what they had in mind, Parsons thought. Stenog and the government men. No intention of taking me to any 'prison colonies.' This is a shuttle that drops me off to die, out in space.

'We have landed,' the machine said. And then it corrected itself. 'We are about to land.' Several humming sounds issued from it and, although the voice had the same measured confidence, Parsons had the intuition that the machine, too, had been thrown off. Perhaps this situation hadn't been intentional – at least, not intended by the designers of the ship.

It's confused, he realized. It doesn't know what to do.

'This isn't Mars,' Parsons said aloud. But, even as he spoke, he realized that it couldn't hear him; it was only a self-regulating device, not alive. 'We're in the void,' he said.

The machine said, 'From here on you will be remanded to the local authorities. The trip is over.' It fell silent then; he saw its swirling interior die off into immobility. It had done its job – or at least it imagined that it had done its job.

The entrance lock of the ship swung back, and Parsons gazed out into nothingness. Around him, the atmosphere of the ship began to shriek away, rushing out through the open lock. At once, a helmetlike unit sprang from the chair to which he was strapped; the unit dropped into his lap. And, at the same time, the machine returned to life.

'Emergency,' the machine said. 'Immediately don the protective equipment which has been put within your reach. Do not delay!'

Parsons did so. The straps that held him barely permitted him to get the unit into place. As the last air rushed from the ship, he had the unit over him. Already it had begun pumping; he tasted the stale, cool air.

The walls of the ship glowed red. Undoubtedly, an emergency mechanism was trying to make up for the dissipating heat.

For what he judged to be fifteen minutes the lock of the ship remained open. Then, all at once, the lock slid shut.

Across from him the machine clicked, and inside it the sentient tissue eddied about in its medium. But the machine had nothing to say. No passengers go back, he decided. The ship shuddered, and, through the viewing slot, he saw a flash of light. Some kind of jets had gone into action.

With horror he realized that he was on his way across space once more. From one empty point to another. How many times? Would it go on and on, this meaningless shuttle-service?

Through the viewing slot the stars altered positions as the ship adjusted itself onto its return course. Hope entered him. Maybe, at the other end, he would find Earth. Through some mechanical failure the ship had taken him, not to Mars, but to a random, alternate point; but now the mistake would be rectified. Now he would find himself back where he had started.

Seventy-five minutes later – at least, he presumed it to be – the ship shuddered and once again unfastened its entrance lock. Once more he gazed out into the void. Oh, God, he thought. And not even the physical sense of motion; only the intellectual realization that I have traveled between far-distant points. Millions and millions of miles.

After a time the lock slid shut. Again, he thought. The nightmare. The terrible dream of motion. If he shut his eyes, did not look at the viewing slot, and if he could keep his mind from working . . .

That would be insanity, he decided.

How easy it would be. To sink into an insane withdrawal, sitting here in this chair. Ignore what I know to be true.

But in a few more hours he would be hungry. Already his mouth had become dry; he would die of thirst long before he died of hunger.

The machine said in the calm voice so familiar to him now, 'The trip to the Martian settlements takes approximately seventy-five minutes. You will be supplied with adequate ventilation and heat, but there is no provision for food except in emergency.'

Isn't this an emergency? Parsons thought. Will it recognize it as such? When I begin to die of thirst, perhaps?

Will it squirt me with water from taps somewhere in the walls of the ship? Across from him the bit of gray rat tissue floated in its medium. You're not alive, Parsons said to himself. You're not suffering; you're not even aware of this.

He thought about Stenog. Did you plan this? I can't believe it. This is some hideous freak accident. Nobody planned this.

Someone took away Mars and the Earth, he thought. And forgot about me. Take me too, he thought. Don't forget me; I want to go along.

The machine clicked and said, 'This ship is so constructed that tampering with any portion of it will produce a detonation.'

He felt a surge of bizarre hope. Better if the ship blew up, than this. Perhaps he could get loose . . . anything would be better.

In the viewing slot, the distant stars. Nothing to notice him.

While he stared at the viewing slot, a star detached itself. It was not a star. It was an object.

The object grew.

Coming closer, Parsons thought. For what seemed to him an unbearable time the object remained virtually the same size, not getting either larger or smaller. He could not tell what it was. A meteor? Bit of space debris? A ship? Keeping its distance . . .

The machine said, 'We are about to land. Be prepared for a series of concussions as the ship adjusts itself.'

This time, Parsons thought, something is out there. Not Mars. Not a planet. But – something.

'We are going to land,' the machine said, and, as before, began a rapid series of uncertain noises. 'We have landed,' it said at last.

The lock slid open. Again the void. Where is it? Parsons asked silently. Has it gone? He could do nothing but sit, strapped to his chair. Please, he prayed. Don't go away.

In the entrance lock an opaque surface dropped into place, blocking the sight of stars.

'Help,' Parsons shouted. His voice rebounded deafeningly in his helmet.

A man appeared, wearing a helmet that made him look like a giant frog. Without hesitation he sprinted toward Parsons. A second man followed him. Expertly, obviously knowing exactly what to do, they began cutting through the straps that held him to the chair. Sparks from the seared metal showered throughout the ship – and then they had him loose.

'Hurry,' one of the men said, touching his helmet against Parsons' to make a medium for his voice. 'It's open only a few more minutes.'

Parsons, struggling painfully up, said, 'What went wrong?'

'Nothing,' the man said, helping him. The other, holding what Parsons recognized as a weapon, prowled about the ship watchfully. 'We couldn't show up on Earth,' the first man said, as he and Parsons moved toward the lock. 'They were waiting – the *shupos* are good at it. We moved this ship back into time.'

On the man's face, Parsons saw the grin of triumph. He and the man started from the ship, through the open lock. Not more than a hundred feet away a larger ship, like a pencil, hung waiting, its lock open, lights gleaming out. A cord connected the two ships.

Beside Parsons, his companion turned back for the other man. 'Be careful,' the man said to Parsons. 'You're not experienced in crossing. Remember, no gravity. You could sail off.' He clung to the cable, beckoning to his colleague.

His colleague took a step toward the lock. From the wall of the ship the muzzle of a gun appeared; the muzzle flashed orange, and the man pitched forward on his face. Beside Parsons, his companion gasped. His eyes met Parsons'. For an instant Parsons saw the man's face, distended with fear and comprehension; then the man had lifted a weapon and fired directly at the blank wall of the ship, at the spot where the gun muzzle had appeared.

A blinding pop made Parsons fall back. The helmet of the man beside him burst; bits of helmet cascaded against his own. And, at the same time, the far wall of the ship splintered; a crack formed and material rained in all directions.

Exposed, but obviously already dying, a *shupo* confronted Parsons. The dwarf figure gyrated slowly, in an almost ritualistic convulsion. The eyes bulged, and then the *shupo* collapsed. Its damaged body floated and eddied about the ship, mixing with the clouds of particles. Finally it came to rest against the ceiling, head down, arms dangling grotesquely. Blood from the wound in its chest gathered in an elongated ball of glistening, bright crimson that froze, expanded, and, as it drifted against the *shupo*'s leg, broke apart.

In Parsons' numbed brain the words that he had so recently heard returned. '*The* shupos *are good at it.*' Yes, he thought. Very good. The *shupo* had been aboard all the time. It made no sound. Had not moved. Had gone on waiting. Would it have died there, in the wall, if no one had appeared?

Both men lay dead. The *shupo* had killed them both.

Beyond the prison ship the pencil-shaped ship still drifted at the end of its cable. Lights still gleamed out. But now it's empty,

Parsons realized. They came for me, but too soon; they couldn't avoid the trap.

I wonder who they were.

Will I ever know?

Kneeling down, he started to examine the dead man nearest him. And then he remembered the lock. Any moment it would close – he would be sealed in here, and the ship would start back once more. Abandoning the two dead men he jumped through the lock, grasping the cable. His leap carried him farther than he had anticipated; for a moment he spun, sweeping away from the two ships, seeing them dwindle away from him. The bitter cold of space licked at him; he felt it seeping into his body. Struggling, he reached out, stretching his arms, fingers . . .

By degrees his body drifted toward the pencil-shaped ship. Suddenly it swept up at him; he smashed against it stunningly, and clung, spread out against its hull. Then, when his mind cleared, he began moving inch-by-inch toward the open entrance.

His fingers touched the cable. He dragged himself down and inside the ship. Warmth from the ship spread around him, and the chill began to depart.

Across the cable-length, at the far end, the entrance lock of the prison ship clicked shut.

Kneeling, Parsons found the origin of the cable. How firmly was it attached? Already, the prison ship's rockets had begun to fire; it was ready to start back. The cable became taut; the prison ship was pulling against it.

In panic, Parsons thought, *Do I want to go back? Or should I cut the cable?*

But the decision had been made. As the rockets fired, the cable snapped. The police ship, at terrific speed, shot away, became small, and then vanished.

Gone. Back to Earth. Carrying three corpses.

And where was he?

Closing the door by hand – it took considerable effort, but at last he had it in place – Parsons turned to examine the ship into which he had come. The ship that had been intended as his means of rescue, and which, for all practical purposes, had failed.

7

On all sides of him, meters and controls. The central panel glowed with data.

Parsons seated himself on one of two stools facing the panel. In an ash tray he saw a smoldering cigarette butt. Only a few minutes ago the two men had hurried out of here, across to the prison ship; now they were dead, and now he was here in their place.

He thought, *Am I much better off?*

The control panel hummed. Dials changed slightly. The man had said, *'We moved the ship back in time.'* How far in time?

But also, it must travel in space. It goes in both dimensions.

Examining the controls, he wondered. Which operates which? He could make out a division on the board, two hemispheres.

Somebody *was* trying to reach me, he realized. They brought me forward through time, hundreds of years. From my society to theirs. For some purpose. Will I ever know the purpose?

At least I saw them face to face. If only for a moment.

Good God, he thought. I'm lost in space and I'm lost in time. In both dimensions.

Above the hum of the panel he detected an intermittent crackle of static. Now he located the cloth grill of a speaker. A communication system? But connected to what?

Reaching out, he experimentally turned a knob. Nothing appreciable changed. He pressed a button near the edge of the board.

All the dials changed.

Around him the ship trembled. The muffled concussion of jets shook him. We're moving, he thought. Hands swept out clockfaces, counters vanished; no numbers at all showed. A red light winked on, and at once the dials slowed.

Some safety mechanism had come on.

The viewscreen over the controls showed stars. But now one bright dot had become larger. He saw in its color a clear tint of red. A planet. Mars?

Taking a deep, unsteady breath, he once again began experimenting with the controls.

Below him a parched red plain stretched out.

He did not recognize it.

Far to the right – mountains. Cautiously, he tried adjustments. The ship dropped sharply; he managed to steady it until it hung above the sun-cracked land. Corrosion . . . he saw limitless furrows gouged into the baked clay. Nothing moved. No life.

After many failures he managed to land the ship. With care he unbolted the door.

An acrid wind billowed into the ship and around him. He sniffed the smell of age and erosion. But the air, thin and weak, brought a faint trickle of warmth. Now Parsons stepped out onto the crumbling sand; his feet sank and he stumbled.

For the first time in his life he was standing on another planet.

Scanning the sky he made out dim clouds on the horizon. Did he see a bird among them? Black speck that disappeared.

The silence frightened him.

He began to walk. Beneath his feet, stones broke apart and puffed into particles. No water! Bending, he picked up a handful of sand. Rough against his skin.

To his right, a heap of slag and boulders.

There, in the cold shadows, gray lichens that seemed no more than stains on the rock. He climbed the largest of the boulders. Far off he saw what might have been an artificial construction. The remains of some massive trench cut deep into the desert. So he went that way.

He thought, I'd better not lose sight of the ship.

While he walked he saw his second sign of life. On his wrist, a fly. It danced off and disappeared. Most noxious of all pests, and yet preferable to the dead wastes. This meager life form, awesome and tragic in this context.

Yet surely if a fly could survive, there had to be organic matter.

Possibly on some other part of the planet, a settlement of some kind. The prison colonies – unless he had arrived long before or long after. Once he had mastered the controls of the ship . . .

In the distance, something sparkled.

He started in that direction. At last he came close enough to make out the sight of an upright slab. A marker? Breathless, he went up a slope, sliding in the loose sand.

In the weak, ruddy sunlight he saw before him a granite block set in the sand. Green patina covered it, almost obscuring that which had flashed: a metal plate bolted to the center.

On the plate – writing. Engraved deep into the metal at one time, but now scoured almost smooth. Squatting down, he tried to read. Most of it was obliterated or illegible, but at the top, in larger letters, a word that could still be read:

PARSONS

His own name. Coincidence? He stared at it, unbelieving. Then, pulling off his shirt, he began rubbing away the accumulation of sand and grime. Before his name, another word:

JIM

So there could be no doubt. This plaque, set here in this wasteland, had him as its topic. Into his mind came the mad, eerie notion that perhaps he had become some gigantic figure in history, known to all the planets. A legendary figure, commemorated in this monument, like some god.

But now, feverishly rubbing with his shirt, he managed to read the smaller engraving beneath. The plaque did not concern him; it was addressed to him. Foolishly, he sat in the sand, brushing at the letters.

The plaque told him how to operate the ship. A manual of instruction.

Each sentence was repeated, apparently to combat the ravages of time. He thought, they must have known that this block would stand here for centuries, perhaps thousands of years. Until I came along.

The shadows, on the far range of mountains, had become longer. Overhead, the sun had begun to decline. The day was ending. Now the air had lost all warmth. He shivered.

Gazing up at the sky he saw a shape half-lost in the haze. A gray disk sailed beyond the clouds. For a long time he watched it, his heart beating heavily. A moon, crossing the face of this world. Much closer than the Moon he knew; but perhaps its greater size was due to Mars being so much smaller. Shading his eyes against the long rays of the sun, he studied the face of this moon. The worn surface . . .

The moon was Luna.

That had not changed; the pattern on its visible side remained the same. This was not Mars. It was Earth.

Here he stood on his own planet, on the dying, ancient Earth. The waterless last age. It had, like Mars before it, ended in drought and weariness. With only black sand-flies and lichens. And rock. Probably it had been like this a long time, long enough to eradicate most of the remains of the human civilization that once existed. Only this plaque, erected by time travelers like himself; persons in search of him, tracking him down to re-establish the contact that had been lost. They had possibly put up many of these markers here and there.

His name, the final written words. To survive man, when everything else had gone.

At sunset he returned to the ship. Before entering it he paused, taking a last look behind him.

Better this, the night falling obscuring the plain. He could imagine animals stirring, night insects appearing.

Finally he shut the lock. He snapped on lights; the cabin of the ship filled with pale white, and the control panel glowed red. Overhead the loudspeaker crackled faintly to itself. The semblance, at least, of something alive.

And on the threshold, a creature that had crawled into the ship during his absence. A hard-to-kill form of life. An earwig.

He thought, That may survive everything else. The last to die. He watched this particular earwig crawl under a storage cupboard.

A few will probably still survive, he reflected, when the plaque with my name on it has crumbled to dust.

Seated at the controls he selected the keys which the instructions had described. Then, in the combination given him, he punched out the tape and started the transport feeding.

Dials changed.

Now he had turned control over to them, the people who

wanted him. He sat passive as the odd shudder again reached him, and, on the viewing screen, the nocturnal scene jumped. Daylight returned, and, after a time, hues of green and blue to replace the parched red.

Earth reborn, he thought somberly. The desert made fertile once more. Faster and faster the scenes blurred, altered. Thousands of years passing backward, no doubt millions. He could scarcely grasp it. In his attempts to operate the ship he had run out the string entirely; he had gone into the future as far as the ship was capable of carrying him.

Abruptly, the dials ceased their motion.

I'm back, Parsons thought. Reaching out his hand, he touched a switch on the panel. The machinery shut off. He rose and walked to the door of the ship. For a moment he hesitated. And then he unbolted the door and pushed it wide.

A man and woman faced him. Each held a gun pointed at him. He caught a glimpse of a lush green landscape, trees and a building, flowers. The man said, 'Parsons?' Golden, hot sunlight streamed down.

'Yes,' he said.

'Welcome,' the woman said in a husky, throaty voice. But the guns did not lower. 'Come out of the ship, Doctor,' the woman said.

He did so.

'You found one of those markers?' the man said. 'The instructions sent ahead for you?'

Parsons said, 'Apparently it had been up a long time.'

Going by him, the woman entered the ship. She inspected the meter readings on the panel. 'A very long time,' she said. To her companion, she said, 'Helmar, he went all the way.'

'You're lucky it was still usable,' the man said.

'Are you going to keep the guns pointed at me?' Parsons said.

The woman came to the doorway behind him and said over his shoulder, 'I don't see any *shupos*. I think it's all right.' She had put her gun away already, and now the man did so too.

The man put his hand out; he and Parsons shook.

'Do women shake hands too?' the woman asked, extending her hand. 'I hope this doesn't violate a custom of your period.'

The man – Helmar – said, 'How did the far future strike you?'

'I couldn't take it,' Parsons said.

'It's quite depressing,' Helmar said. 'But remember; it'll be a long time coming, and gradual. And by that time there'll be other planets inhabited.' Both he and the woman regarded him with expressions of deep emotion. And he, too, felt profoundly moved.

'Care for a drink, Doctor?' the woman asked.

'No,' he said. 'Thanks.' He saw bees at work in nearby vines, and, further along, a row of cypress trees. The man and woman followed after him as he walked in the direction of the trees. Halfway there he halted, taking in deep lungfuls of air. The pollen-laden air of midsummer . . . the odors of growing things.

'Time travel works erratically,' the woman said. 'At least for us. We've had bad luck striving for exactitude. I'm sorry.'

'That's all right,' Parsons said.

Now he surveyed the man and woman, aware of them more clearly.

The woman was beautiful even beyond what he had already seen in this world of youth and robust bodies. This woman was *different*. Copper-colored skin that shone in the midday sun. The familiar flat cheek bones and dark eyes, but a different kind of nose. Stronger. All her features had an emphatic quality new to his experience. And she was older. Perhaps in her middle thirties. A powerfully built creature, with cascades of black hair, a heavy torrent all the way down her shoulders to her waist.

On the front of her robe, lifted high by her breasts, was a herald, an intricate design woven into the rich fabric, that rose and fell with the motion of her breathing. A wolf's head.

'You're Loris,' Parsons said.

'That's right,' the woman answered.

He could see why she had become the Mother Superior of the society. Why her contribution to the Soul Cube was of supreme importance. He could see it in her eyes, in the firm lines of her body, her wide forehead.

Beside her, the man shared some of her characteristics. The same coppery skin, the starkly etched nose, the mass of black hair. But with subtle, crucial differences. A mere mortal, Parsons thought. Yet even so, impressive. Two fine and handsome individuals, returning his gaze with intelligence and sympathy, alert to his needs. A high emphatic order, he decided. Their dark eyes had a depth to which he felt his own psyche respond; the strength of their personalities forced his, too, to rise to a higher level of cognition.

To him Helmar said, 'Let's go inside.' He indicated the gray stone building nearby. 'It's cooler, and we can sit down.'

As they walked up the path, Loris said, 'And more private.'

A collie, wagging its great tail, approached them, its elongated muzzle raised. Helmar paused to thump the dog. As they turned the corner of the building, Parsons saw descending terraces, a well-tended garden that merged with trees and wilder shrubs.

'We're quite secluded here,' Loris said. 'This is our Lodge. It dates back three hundred years.'

In the center of an open field, Parsons saw a second time travel ship and several men at work on it.

'You may be interested in this,' Loris said. Leading the way, she brought Parsons over to the ship; there she took a smooth, shiny sphere from one of the technicians. The sphere, the size of a grapefruit, lifted of its own accord from her hands; she caught hold of it at once. 'It's all set to go,' she said. 'We're in the process of taking these into the future.' She pointed; the ship had been filled with these spheres.

Helmar said, 'I presume by the time you came onto it, the thing was rather shabby looking.'

Parsons took the sphere from Loris. 'I don't recognize it,' he said, examining it.

Helmar and Loris exchanged glances. 'These are the markers,' Loris said. 'One of these contacted you in the far future.'

'These transmit for hundreds of miles,' Helmar said. 'To your ship's radio.' They both stared at him. 'Didn't you get your instructions through the loudspeaker? Didn't you hear one of these telling you how to operate the ship to bring it back here?'

'No,' Parsons said. 'I found a granite monument with a metal plaque. The instructions were engraved in the metal.'

Silence.

At last Loris said quietly, 'We know nothing about that. We constructed no such device. And it gave you *instructions*?'

Helmar said, 'For operating our time ship?'

'Yes,' Parsons said. 'And it was addressed to me. It had my name on it.'

Helmar said, 'We've sent out hundreds of these markers. You never encountered *one*?'

'No,' Parsons said.

The man and woman had lost their air of confidence. And Parsons, too, wondered the same thing. What had become of these spheres? And if these people hadn't erected the plaque, *then who had*?

8

Parsons said, 'Why did you bring me to your time?'

After a pause, Loris said, 'We have a medical problem. We've tried to solve it, but we've failed. More accurately, we've had only a limited success. Our medical knowledge falls short, and in our world there's no better knowledge that we can draw on.'

'How many of you are there?' Parsons said.

Loris smiled. 'Just ourselves and a few others. A few who are sympathetic.'

'Within your tribe?'

'Yes,' she said.

'What will the government think happened to me? They know something happened to the prison rocket.'

'The rocket disappeared,' Helmar said. 'Very common. That's why the prisoner is sent unescorted. Travel between planets is as erratic as time travel. Like the early days of travel between Europe and the New World . . . tiny ships setting out into the void.'

Parsons said, 'But they'll suspect that—'

'Suspecting is not the same as knowing,' Loris said. 'What information does it give them about us? Not even that we exist, let alone who we are or what we are trying to do. At best, they know no more than they did already.'

'Then they do suspect you,' Parsons said. 'Already.'

'The government suspects that someone has been able to make use of the time-travel experiments which they abandoned. Our early efforts were unfortunate. We dumped telltale material where they could find it and study it. They've had clues for some time.' Her fierce, compelling eyes blazed. 'But they wouldn't dare accuse me. They can't come here; this is sacred land. Our land. Our Lodge.' Under her robes her breasts rose and fell.

Parsons said, 'Is this medical problem getting worse while we stand here?'

'No,' Helmar said. 'We've managed to bring it to a stasis.' His calm came as a contrast to Loris' fervor. 'Remember, Doctor, *we have gained control of time.* If we're careful, no one can defeat us. We have a unique advantage.'

'No group in history,' Loris breathed, 'has ever had our weapon, our opportunity.'

As the three of them entered the Wolf Lodge, ascending a flight of wide stairs, Parsons thought to himself, But one of the principal discoveries in science is the demonstration that a thing is possible. Once that's been done, then half the work is over. These people have proved to the government that a time-travel machine can be built. The government now knows that it made an error in dropping its experiments. It doesn't know *how* the experiments were successfully completed, or by whom. But it does know – or at least, has good reason to presume – that time travel is possible. And that alone is a uniquely important discovery.

Both Loris and Helmar strode ahead with such determination that Parsons got only a glimpse of the long, dark-paneled hall. A double door slid back, and he was led into a luxurious alcove. Helmar seated him in a leather-covered armchair, and then, with a flourish, placed an ash tray beside him – and a package of Lucky Strike cigarettes.

'From your century,' Helmar said. 'Correct?'

'Yes,' Parsons said, with gratitude.

'What about a beer?' Helmar said. 'We have several beers from your period, all ice cold.'

'This is fine,' Parsons said, lighting one of the cigarettes and inhaling with enjoyment.

Loris, seating herself opposite, said, 'And we've brought

magazines forward. And clothing. And a variety of objects, some of which we can't identify. Chance plays quite a role, as you might guess. The time dredge scoops up more than three tons; we often get mere debris, however, especially in the earlier stages.' She also took one of the cigarettes.

'Have you been able to orient yourself to our world?' Helmar said, seating himself and crossing his legs.

Parsons said, 'The government official I ran into—'

'Stenog,' Loris said. Her face showed her aversion. 'We know him. Technically, he's in charge of the Fountain, but we have reason to believe he's tied up with the *shupos*. Of course, he disavows that.'

'They harness what would be delinquent children,' Helmar said. 'Putting their energies and talents at the disposal of the government. The desire to maim and kill and fight. They train the youth to have contempt for death, which, as you have learned, is a valuable point of view to have in our society.' His eyes had a deep grimness in them.

'You must realize,' Loris said, 'that this society has been long established. This way of life has the sanction of years. This is not a momentary abnormality in history. Human beings are a cheap commodity in history; we've seen quite a panorama come and go, during our work with the dredge. It gives one a rather different point of view, to go back and forth into time. Both Helmar and I can see – at least intellectually – the tribes' concept of the inevit-ability of life. They do not encourage life in the same way as they encourage death. They limit birth, for instance, to achieve a static population.'

Helmar said: 'Had they not limited birth, there would be by now a valuable human population on Mars and Venus. But as you know, Mars is used only as a prison. Venus is used as a source of raw materials. Sapped, year after year. Plundered.'

'As the New World was plundered by the Spanish and French and English,' Loris said.

She pointed upward, and Parsons saw that along one wall of the room hung large framed portraits, ancient faces familiar to him. Portraits of Cortez, Pizarro, Drake, Cabrillo, and others that

197

he could not manage to identify. But all wore the ruffles of the sixteenth century; all were noblemen and explorers of that period.

Those were the only pictures in the room.

'Why your interest in sixteenth century explorers?' he asked.

Loris said, 'You'll learn about that in due time. The point which I mean to stress is this. Despite the morbid strain in this society, there is no reason to expect it to expire and decline from its own imbalances. Having looked ahead, we can see that there's a life expectancy for it of several centuries. We share your aversion to its dynamics, but—' She shrugged. 'We're more stoic about it. As you will be, finally.'

Rome, Parsons thought, didn't decline in a day.

'What about my own society?' he said.

'It depends on what you identify as the authentic values of your society. Some, of course, still survive and may always survive. The superiority of the white nations, Russia, Europe and North American democracies, lasted about a century after your time; then Asia and Africa emerged as the dominant areas, with the so-called "colored" races acquiring their rightful heritage.'

Helmar said, 'In the wars of the twenty-third century, all races blended together, you understand. So, from that time on, it was not meaningful to speak of "white" or "colored" races.'

'I see,' Parsons said. 'But the appearance of this Soul Cube, and these tribes—'

'That, of course,' Loris said, 'was not connected with the blending of the several races. The division into tribes is purely artificial, as you've probably concluded. It stems from a twenty-third century innovation, a great world-wide competition along the olympics line – but with the victors becoming eligible for national office. At that time, there were still nations, and the participants at first came as representations of their nations.'

'The Communist youth festivals,' Helmar said, 'were one of the historic sources of the custom. And of course the medieval jousts.'

Loris said, 'But the principal origin of the Soul Cube, and the planned manipulation of zygotes, doesn't lie in any source that you would be aware of.' Facing Parsons, her eyes intense, she said, 'You must understand that for centuries the colored races of the world had been told they were inferior, that they couldn't control their own destinies. There is in all of us this lingering sense that we have to prove we're better, prove we're able to construct a society and a population far more advanced than any seen in the past.'

Helmar said, 'We've made our point, but we've achieved a calcified society that spends its time meditating about death; it has no plans, no direction. No desire for growth. Our nagging sense of inferiority has betrayed us; it's made us expend our energies in recovering our pride, in proving our ancient enemies false. Like the Egyptian society – death and life so interwoven that the world has become a cemetery, and the people nothing more than custodians living among the bones of the dead. They are virtually the pre-dead, in their own minds. So their great heritage has been frittered away. Think what they – we – might have become.' He broke off, his face a study of conflicting emotions.

For a time none of them spoke. Then Parsons, eager to change the subject, said, 'What's your medical problem?' He wanted, now, to see it at once. To find out what it was.

'Turn your chair,' Loris said. She and Helmar turned until they faced the far wall of the room. Parsons did so, too.

Breathing quickly, her lips half-parted, her fists clenched at her sides, Loris stared at the wall.

'Watch,' she said. She pressed a stud.

The wall dimmed. It flickered and was gone. Parsons found himself looking into another room. Familiar, he thought. A place he had been. Was it – the Fountain!

Not quite. Everything here was minute. This chamber was a replica of what he had seen at the Fountain. The same syndromes of equipment, power cables, freight elevators. And at the far end, the gleaming blank surface of a cube – a scaled down cube, perhaps ten feet high and three feet in depth.

'What is it?' Parsons demanded.

Loris hesitated.

'Go ahead,' Helmar said.

Now she touched the stud again. The blank face of the cube faded. They were looking inside, into its depths. Into the swirling liquid that filled it.

A man stood upright, suspended in the medium of the cube.

He lay motionless, arms at his sides, eyes shut. With a shock, Parsons realized that the man was dead. Dead – and somehow preserved within the cube. He was tall, powerfully built, with a great gleaming copper-colored torso. His nude body was maintained uncorrupted by this miniature Soul Cube, this small version of the great government cube at the Fountain.

Instead of a hundred billion zygotes and developed embryos, this small cube contained the preserved body of a single man, a fully developed male perhaps thirty years old.

'Your husband?' Parsons asked Loris, without thinking.

'No. We have no husbands.' Loris gazed at the man with great emotion. She seemed in the grip of a swelling tide of feeling.

Parsons persisted. 'You had an emotional relationship? He was your lover?'

Loris shuddered, then abruptly laughed. 'No, not my lover.' Her whole body swayed, trembled, as she rubbed her forehead and turned away a moment. 'Although we have lovers, of course. Quite a few. Sexual activity continues, independent of reproduction.' She seemed almost in a trance. Her words came slowly, tonelessly.

In his chair, Helmar said, 'Go closer, Doctor. You'll see how he met his death.'

Getting up, Parsons walked toward the wall. What at first appeared to be a small spot on the left breast of the man turned out to be something quite different. Here, beyond a doubt, was the cause of death. How out of place in this world, Parsons thought. He gazed up at it, amazed. But there was no doubt.

From the dead man's chest protruded the feathered, notched end of an arrow.

9

At a signal from Loris, a servant approached Parsons. Bowing formally, the servant set down an object at Parsons' feet. He recognized it at once. Dented, stained, it was still familiar. His gray instrument case.

'We were not able to get you,' Helmar said, 'but we managed

to pick this up. In the hotel lobby. During the confusion, after the government understood that the girl would recover.'

With tension, they watched as he opened the instrument case and began inspecting the contents.

'We examined those instruments,' Loris said, from over his shoulder. 'But none of our technicians could make use of them. Our orientation does not equip us – we lack the basic principles. If you don't have all you need, we can supply you with other medical material which we dredged from the past. Originally, we imagined that if we had the material, we could make use of it ourselves.'

Parsons said, 'How long has this man been in the cube?'

'He has been dead thirty-five years,' Loris said matter-of-factly.

Parsons said, 'I'll know more once I've been able to examine him. Can he be brought out of the cold-pack?'

'Yes,' Helmar said. 'For no more than half an hour at a time, however.'

'That should be enough,' Parsons said.

Almost altogether, Helmar and Loris said, 'Then you'll do it?'

'I'll try,' he answered.

A wave of relief ran between the two of them; relaxing, they smiled at him. The tension in the room waned.

'Is there any reason,' Parsons said, 'why you can't tell me your relation to this man?' He faced Loris squarely.

After a pause, she said, 'He's my father.'

For a moment, the significance did not register. And then he thought, *But how can she know?*

Loris said, 'I'd prefer not to tell you any more. At least not now. Later.' She seemed tired out by the situation. 'Let me have a servant show you to your apartment, and then perhaps we can—' She glanced at the man in the cube. 'Perhaps you could begin your examination of him.'

'I'd like to get some rest first,' Parsons said. 'After a good night's sleep I'd be in better shape.'

Their disappointment showed clearly. But immediately Loris nodded, and then, more reluctantly, Helmar. 'Of course,' she said.

A servant came to show him to his apartment. Carrying

Parsons' gray case, the servant preceded him up a wide flight of stairs. The man glanced back once, but said nothing. In silence they reached the apartment; the servant held the door open for Parsons, and he entered.

What luxury, he thought. Beyond doubt, he was the honored guest of the Lodge.

And with good reason!

At dinner that night he learned, from Loris and Helmar, the physical layout of their Lodge. They were slightly over twenty miles from the city which he had first encountered, the capital, at which the Soul Cube and Fountain were located. Here in the Lodge, Loris, as the Mother Superior, lived with her entourage. Like some great, opulent queen bee, Parsons thought. In this busy hive. Beyond that area controlled by the government; this was sacred land.

The Lodge, like a Roman demesne, was self-contained, independent economically and physically. Underneath the buildings were giant power turbines, atomic generators a century old. He had briefly glimpsed the subterranean landscape of drive-trains and whirring spheres, in some cases rust-covered masses of machines that still managed to roar and throb. But, as he had tried to penetrate further, he had been firmly turned back by armed uniformed guards, youths wearing the familiar Wolf emblem.

Food was grown artificially in subsurface chemical tanks. Clothing and furniture were processed from plastic raw materials by robots working somewhere on the grounds. Building materials, industrial supplies, everything that was needed, was manufactured and repaired on the Lodge grounds. A complete world, the core of which, like the city, was the cube. The miniature 'soul' with which he would soon be working. He didn't have to be told how carefully the secret of its existence was kept. Probably only a few persons knew of it; probably not more than a fraction of those living and working at the Lodge. And how many of them understood its purpose, the reason for its existence? Perhaps only Loris and Helmar knew.

As they sat at the table, sipping after-dinner coffee and brandy, he asked Helmar bluntly, 'Are you related to Loris?'

'Why do you ask?' Helmar said.

'You resemble the man in the cube – her father. And you resemble her, faintly.'

Helmar shook his head. 'No relation.' His earlier excitement and eagerness now seemed masked over by politeness. And yet Parsons felt it still there, still smoldering.

There were so many things that Parsons did not understand. Too much, he decided, was being kept back. He had accepted the obvious: Loris and Helmar were acting illegally. Had been for some time. The very possession of the miniature cube was clearly a crime of the first magnitude. The maintenance of the body, the attempt to restore it to life – all were part of a painstakingly guarded and constructed plan of which the government and certainly the other tribes knew nothing.

He could understand Loris' desire to see her father alive. It was a natural emotion, common possible to all societies, including his own. He could understand the elaborate lengths she had gone to, in attempting to realize that wish. With her great influence and power, it might actually be possible to do this – as contrary as it was to everything the society stood for. After all, the man had been preserved uncorrupted for all of Loris' lifetime. The cube, the complex maintenance equipment, the whole Lodge itself, was geared to this task. The development and use of the time dredge, no doubt. If so much had already been done, the rest might follow.

But out of all this, one element still made no sense. In this society, all zygotes were developed and preserved by the Fountain, a purely artificial process.

Parsons chose his words carefully. 'This man,' he said to Loris. 'Your father. Was he born at the Fountain?'

Both she and Helmar regarded him with equal caution. 'No one is born outside the Fountain,' Loris said in a low voice.

Helmar, with impatience, said, 'What does such information have to do with your work? We have complete data on his physical condition at the time of his death. It's his death that's germane to you, not his birth.'

'Who built the cube?' Parsons demanded bluntly.

'Why?' Loris said, almost inaudibly. She glanced at Helmar.

'The design,' Helmar explained slowly, 'is the same as the Fountain the government operates. No special knowledge was required to duplicate on a small scale what the government operates on a large scale.'

'Somebody brought schematics here and constructed all this,' Parsons persisted. 'Obviously at great risk, and for considerable purpose.'

Loris said, 'To preserve *him*. My father.'

At once, Parsons pounced; he felt his pulse race. 'Then the cube was built *after* his death?'

Neither of them answered.

'I don't see,' Loris said finally, 'what this has to do with your work. As Helmar says.'

'I'm a hired employee, then?' Parsons said. 'Not a genuine equal who can communicate with you as equals?'

Helmar glared at him, but Loris seemed more troubled than angry. Falteringly, she said, 'No, not at all. It's just that the risk is so great. And it actually doesn't concern you, does it? Why should it, Doctor? When you treat a patient, a person who's sick or injured, do you inquire into his background, his beliefs, his purpose in life, his philosophy?'

'No,' he admitted.

'We'll repay you,' Loris said. 'We can place you in any time period that you desire.' Across the table from him, she smiled hopefully, coaxingly.

But Parsons said, 'I have a wife whom I love. All I want to do is get back to her.'

'That's so,' Helmar said. 'We noticed her while we were out scouting you.'

'And knowing that,' Parsons said, 'you still brought me here, without my knowledge or permission. I gather that my personal feelings are of no concern to you.' He hesitated. 'In your estimation, I'm no better than a slave!'

'That's not true,' Loris said. And he saw tears in her eyes. 'You don't have to help us. You can go back to your own time if you want. It's your choice.' Suddenly she rose from the table. 'Excuse me,' she said in a choked voice, and ran at once from the room.

Presently Helmar said, 'You can sympathize with her feelings.'

He sat stoically sipping his coffee. 'There's never been any chance before your coming. Let's acknowledge that you don't particularly care for me. But that's not the issue. You're not doing this for me. You're doing it for her.'

The man had a point there.

And yet, even Loris had hung back, had not given him honest answers. The whole atmosphere was pervaded with this sense of the hidden, the concealed. Why from him? If they trusted him enough to show him the man in the cube, to reveal the cube itself, then what more could there be? Did they suppose that if he knew more about them, he would not co-operate?

He filed his suspicions away, and sat, like Helmar, sipping his coffee royal. Unobtrusively, servants came and departed.

Neither he nor Helmar said anything; they sipped in silence. The brandy was very good, an authentic cognac. At last Helmar put down his cup and stood up.

'Ready, Doctor?' he said. 'To make your initial exploratory examination?'

Parsons, too, stood. 'Yes,' he said. 'Let's go.'

10

The three of them stood together, watching tensely as automatic machinery moved the cube forward, toward them. The cube came directly in front of them and stopped there.

The chamber was a blaze of lights. In the glare, Parsons watched the cube gradually tip backward until it came to rest. Within its depths the inert figure drifted quietly, eyes closed, body relaxed. The dead god, suspended between worlds, waiting to return . . .

And in the chamber, his people.

The chamber was crowded. Men who had stayed in the shadows until now were beginning to emerge. Parsons had not realized the extent of the project. He paused to take in the sight of this first appearance in real force, the actual strength that operated the Lodge.

Was it his imagination, or did they resemble one another? Of course, all members of this society had some similar characteristics, the same general skull formation and hair texture. And the clothing of this group was identical throughout, the gray robe and chest-emblem of the Wolf Tribe.

But there was more. The ruddy cast to the skin. A certain heaviness of the brow. Wide forehead. Flaring nostrils. As if they were of one family.

He counted forty men and sixteen women and then lost track. They were moving about, murmuring to one another. Taking places where they could watch him as he worked. They wanted to see every move he made.

Now the cube had been opened by Lodge technicians. The cold-pack was being sucked out greedily by plastic suction tendrils. In a moment the body would be exposed.

'These people shouldn't be here,' Parsons said nervously. 'I'll have to open his chest and plug in a pump. Danger of infection will be enormous.'

The men and women heard him, but none of them budged.

'They feel they have a right to be here,' Helmar said.

'But you people admittedly know nothing about medicine, about hygiene—'

'You worked on the girl Icara in public,' Helmar said. 'And you have numerous sterilizing agents in your case; we were able to identify them.'

Parsons cursed under his breath. He turned away from Helmar and slid on his plastic protective gloves. Now he began arranging his instruments on a portable worktable. As the last of the cold-pack was drained off by the suction tendrils, Parsons flicked on a high-frequency field and placed the potentials on each side of the cube. The terminals hummed and glowed as the field warmed. Now the inert body was within a zone of bacteria-destroying radiation. He concentrated the field briefly on his instruments and gloves. The watching men and women took everything in without expression, faces blank with concentration.

Abruptly the cold-pack was gone. The body was exposed.

Parsons moved into activity. There had been no tangible decay. The body appeared perfectly fresh. He touched the lifeless wrist. It was *cold*. A chilling effluvium that trickled up his arm and made him quickly let go. The utter cold of outer space. He shivered and wondered how he was going to work.

'He will warm rapidly,' Helmar grated. 'It's no form of refrigeration you're familiar with. Molecular velocity has not been reduced. It has been differently phased.'

The body was now warm enough to touch. Whatever alteration had been made in the vibrational pattern, the molecules were already beginning to return to their natural rate.

With scrupulous care, Parsons locked a mechanical lung in place and activated it. While the lung exerted rhythmic pressure on the immobile chest, he concentrated on the heart. He punctured the rib cage and plugged the Dixon pump into the vascular system, bypassing the suspended heart. The pump went immediately to work. Blood flowed. Both respiration and circulation resumed in this body that had died thirty-five years ago. Now, if there hadn't been much tissue deterioration from lack of oxygen and nutrition, especially in the brain . . .

Unnoticed, Loris had come over beside him, so that now her body pressed against him. Rigid as stone, she peered down.

'Instead of removing the arrow from the heart,' Parsons said, 'I have gone around the heart. Temporarily, at least.' Now he inspected the injured organ itself.

The arrow had penetrated accurately. Probably there was little he could do to restore the organ. But, with the proper tool, he plucked the arrow out and tossed it to the floor. Blood oozed.

'It can be repaired,' he said to Loris. 'But the big question has to do with brain damage. If it's too great, I recommend that we destroy him.' The alternative, letting him live, would not be pleasant.

'I see,' she said in a stricken voice. No more than a whisper.

'In my opinion,' Parsons said, addressing both her and the group, 'we should proceed now.'

'You mean try to revive him?' she said. He had to catch hold of her; she had begun to sway, and he saw that her eyes were almost blind with fear.

'Yes,' he said. 'May I?'

'Suppose you fail,' she whispered, appealing to him.

'I have as much chance of success as I will ever have,' he said frankly. 'Every time he's revived, there will be some further deterioration of brain tissue.'

'Then go ahead,' she said in a stronger voice.

Helmar, behind them, said, 'And don't fail.' He did not say it as a threat; his voice had more a patently fanatical tone. As if, to him, failure simply could not occur; it was not possible.

Parsons said, 'With the pump operating, he should revive very shortly.' With instruments, he listened for a pulse, for the man's breathing. That is, if he ever does, he thought to himself.

The man stirred. His eyelids fluttered.

A gasp came from the watchers. A simultaneous expression of amazement and joy.

'He is living by use of the mechanical pump,' Parsons said to Loris. 'Of course, if everything goes well—'

'Ultimately you will stitch the heart fiber and attempt to remove the pump,' Loris finished.

'Yes,' he said.

Loris said, 'Doctor, would you please do that now? There are conditions that you know nothing about; please believe me when I say that if there's any possibility that you could perform the surgery on the heart at this time . . .' Pleadingly, she caught hold of his hands; he felt her strong fingers dig into his flesh. Gazing up at him she said, 'For my sake. Even if there's more risk this way, I feel convinced that you should go ahead. I have good reasons. Please, Dr Parsons.'

Reluctantly, studying the pulse and respiration of the patient, he said, 'He will have to mend over a period of weeks. You understand that. He can't take any strain, of any sort, until the fiber—'

'You'll do it?' she said, her eyes shining.

Assembling his instruments, he began the grueling task of repairing the ruptured heart.

When he had finished, he discovered that only Loris remained in the chamber; the others had been sent out, undoubtedly on her order. She sat silently across from him, her arms folded. Now she seemed more composed. But her face still had the rigidity, the fear.

'All right?' she said with a tremor.

'Evidently,' he said. Exhausted, he started putting away his instruments.

'Doctor,' she breathed, rising and approaching him, 'you have done a profound thing. Not only for us, but for the world.'

Too worn-out to pay much attention to her, he stripped off his gloves. 'I'm sorry,' he said. 'I'm too tired to talk. I'd like to go up to my apartment and go to bed.'

'You'll be on call? If anything goes wrong?' As he started from the chamber, Loris hurried after him. 'What should we watch for? We'll have attendants on hand at all times, of course . . . I realize that he's quite feeble, and will be for some time.' Now she made him halt. 'When will he be conscious?'

'Probably in an hour,' he said, at the door.

That apparently satisfied her. Nodding in a preoccupied fashion, she started back to the patient.

By himself, he ascended the stairs, and, after getting the wrong room several times, at last managed to find his own apartment. Inside, he shut and locked the door and sank down on the bed to rest. He felt too weary to undress or get under the covers.

The next he knew, the door was open. Loris stood in the entrance, gazing down at him. The room had become dark – or had he lain down with the light off? Groggily, he started to sit up.

'I thought you might want something to eat,' she said. 'It's after midnight.' As she switched on a lamp and went over to pull the drapes, he saw that a servant had followed her into the apartment.

'Thanks,' he said, rubbing his eyes.

Loris dismissed the servant and began lifting the pewter covers from the dishes. He could smell the warm, rich odors of food.

'Any change in your father?' he asked.

Loris said, 'He became conscious for a moment. At least, he opened his eyes. And I had a distinct impression that he was aware of me. And then he went to sleep; he's sleeping now.'

'He'll sleep a lot,' Parsons said. But he thought, That may indicate possible brain damage.

She had arranged two chairs at a small table, and now she let him seat her. 'Thank you,' she said. 'You put everything you had into what you did. Such an impressive spectacle for us to see – a

209

doctor and his devotion to healing.' She smiled at him; in the half-light of the room her lips were full and moist. Since he had last seen her she had changed to a different dress, and her hair, now, was tied back, held in place by a clasp. 'You're a very good man,' she said. 'A very kind and worthy man. We're ennobled by your presence.'

Embarrassed, he shrugged, not knowing what to say.

'I'm sorry to make you uncomfortable,' she said. She began to eat, and he did so too. But after a few bites he realized that he was not hungry. Feeling restless, he got to his feet, excusing himself. Walking to the veranda of the apartment he opened the glass door and stepped outside, into the cold night air.

Luminous night moths fluttered beyond the railing, among the trees and moist branches. Somewhere in the forest small animals crashed about, growled, moved sullenly off. Sounds of breaking twigs, stealthy footpads. Hissing.

'Cats,' Loris whispered. 'Domestic cats.' She had come out, too, to stand beside him in the darkness.

'Gone wild?'

She turned toward him. 'You know, Doctor, there is a basic fallacy in their thinking.'

'Who do you mean by "they"?'

Waving her hand vaguely she said, 'The government. The whole system, here. The Soul Cube, the Lists. That girl, Icara. The one you saved.' Her voice became firm. 'She killed herself because she had been disfigured. She knew she'd drag down the tribe when List time came. She knew she'd score badly because of her physical appearance. *But such things aren't inherited!*' Bitterness swept through her voice. 'She sacrificed herself for nothing. Who gained? What good did her death do? She was certain it was for the benefit of the tribe – for the race. I've seen enough of death.'

He knew, hearing her, that she was thinking about her father. 'Loris,' he said. 'If you can go back into the past, why didn't you try to change it? Prevent his death?'

'You don't know what we know,' she said. 'The possibility of changing the past is limited. It's very hard.' She sighed. 'Don't you suppose we tried?' Her voice rose now. 'Don't you think we went back again and again, trying to make it come out differently? And it never did.'

'The past is immutable?' he said.

'We don't understand it quite. Some things can be changed. But not this. Not the thing that matters! There's some kind of central force that eludes us. Some power working . . .'

'You really love him,' he said, moved by her emotion.

She nodded faintly. Now he saw her hand lift; she wiped at her eyes. Dimly, he could make out her face, her trembling lips, long lashes, the great black eyes sparkling with tears.

'I'm sorry,' Parsons said. 'I didn't mean to—'

'It's all right. We've been under so much strain. For so long. You understand, I've never seen him alive. And, to look at him day after day, suspended in there, beyond reach – utterly remote from us. All the time, when I was a child, growing up, I thought of nothing else. To bring him back. To have him again, to possess him. If he could be made to live again—' Her hands opened, reached out, yearning, groping, closing again on nothing. 'And now that we do have him back—' Abruptly, she broke off.

'Go on,' Parsons prompted.

Loris shook her head and turned away. Parsons touched her soft black hair, moist with the night mist. She did not protest. He drew her close to him; still she did not protest. Her warm breath drifted up in a cloud, rising around him, mixing with the sweet scent of her hair. Against him her body vibrated, intense and burning with suppressed emotion. Her bosom rose and fell, outlined against the starlight, her body trembling under the silk of her robe.

His hand touched her cheek, then her throat. Her full lips were close to him. Her eyes were half-closed, head bent back, breath coming rapidly. 'Loris,' he said softly.

She shook her head. 'No. Please, no.'

'Why don't you trust me? Why don't you want to tell me? What is there you can't—'

With a convulsive moan she broke away and ran toward the doorway, robes fluttering after her.

Catching up with her, he put his arms around her, holding her from escaping. 'What's the matter?' he said, trying to see her, trying to read the expression on her face. Wanting to make her look at him.

'I—' she began.

The door to the apartment flew open. Helmar, his face distorted, said, 'Loris. He—' Seeing Parsons he said, 'Doctor. Come.'

They ran, the three of them, down the corridor to the stairs, down the stairs; gasping, they reached the room in which Loris' father lay. Attendants ushered them in. Parsons caught sight of elaborate equipment, unfamiliar to him, in the process of being assembled.

On the bed lay Loris' father, his lips parted, his eyes glazed. His eyes, sightless in death, stared up at the ceiling.

'Cold-pack,' Loris was saying, somewhere in the background, as Parsons grabbed out his instruments.

Lifting aside the sheet, Parsons saw the feathered, notched end of an arrow protruding from the dead man's chest.

'Again,' Helmar said, in a tone of absolute hopelessness. 'We thought . . .' His voice trailed off, baffled and wretched. 'Get the pack around him!' he shouted suddenly, and attendants pushed between Parsons and the bed. He saw them expertly lift the corpse and slide it into the vacant cube; cold-pack poured in and surrounded the form until it became blurred and obscured.

After a time Loris said bitterly, 'Well, we were right.' The fury in her voice shocked Parsons; he turned involuntarily, and saw an expression he had never before witnessed on a woman's face. A complete and absolute hate.

'Right about what?' he managed to ask.

Lifting her head, she gazed at him; her eyes seemed to have shrunk so that the pupils gleamed like tiny, burning points, no longer located in space but somehow hovering before him, blinding him almost. 'Someone is working against us,' she said. 'They have it, too. Control of time. Thwarting us, enjoying it . . .' She laughed. 'Yes, *enjoying* it. Mocking us.' Abruptly, with a swing of her robes, she turned away from Parsons and disappeared past the ring of attendants.

Parsons, stepping back, saw the final surface of the Soul Cube slide into place. Once again the figure floated in eternal stasis. Dead and silent. Beyond the reach of the living.

11

Standing beside Parsons, Helmar muttered, 'It's not your fault.' Together, they watched the cube being lifted upright. 'We have enemies,' Helmar said. 'This happened before, when we went back into time and tried to recreate the situation. But we thought it was a natural force, a phenomenon of time. Now we know better. Our worst fears are justified. This did not happen through an impersonal force.'

'Perhaps not,' Parsons said. 'But don't see motive where there is none.' They are a little paranoid, he decided. Possibly rightly so. 'As Loris told me,' he continued, 'none of you fully comprehend the principles that lie behind time. Isn't it still possible that—'

'No,' Helmar said flatly. 'I know. We all know.' He started to speak further, and then, seeing something, he stopped.

Parsons turned. He, too, had meant to go on, but his words choked off.

For the first time he had noticed her.

She had entered silently, a few moments ago. Two armed guards stood on each side of her. A stir went through the room, among the people present.

She was old. The first old person that Parsons had seen in this world.

Approaching the old woman, Loris said, 'He is dead again. They managed to destroy him once again.'

The old woman advanced silently toward the cube, toward the dead man who lay within. She was, even at her age, strikingly handsome. Tall and dignified. A mane of white hair down the back of her neck . . . the same broad forehead. Heavy brows. Strong nose and chin. Stern, powerful face.

The same as the others. This old woman, the man in the cube, everybody at the Lodge – all partook of the same physical characteristics.

The stately old woman had reached the rim of the cube. She gazed at it, unspeaking.

Loris took her arm. 'Mother—'

There it was. The old woman was Loris' mother. The wife of the man in the cube.

It fitted. He had been in the cube thirty-five years. The old woman was probably seventy. *His wife!* This pair, this couple, had spawned the powerful, full-breasted creature who ruled the Wolf Tribe, the most potent human being alive.

'Mother,' Loris said. 'We'll try once more. I promise.'

Now the old woman had noticed Parsons. Instantly, her face became fierce. 'Who are you?' she asked in a deep, vibrant voice.

Loris said, 'He's the doctor who tried to bring Corith back.'

The old woman was still looking frigidly at Parsons. Gradually her features softened. 'It's not your fault,' she said at last. For a moment she lingered by the cube. 'Later,' she said. 'Once more.' She turned for a last look at Parsons, then at the man in the cube. And then the old woman and her attendants moved away, back toward the lift from which they had emerged. She had come up from the subsurface levels that honeycombed the ground beneath their feet – unguessed regions that he had never seen and probably would never see. The guarded, secret core of the Lodge.

All the men and women stood silently as the old woman passed among them. Heads bowed slightly. Reverence. They were all acknowledging her, Loris' mother. The regal, white-haired old woman who moved slowly and calmly across the room, away from the cube. Her face creased and frozen in grief. The mother of the Mother Superior—

The mother of them all!

At the lift she halted and half-turned. She made a faint motion with her hand, a motion that took them all in. She was recognizing them. Her children.

It was clear. Helmar, Loris, all the rest of them, all seventy or so, were descended from this old lady, and from the man who lay in the cube. Yet one thing did not fit.

The man in the cube and this old woman. If they were man and wife—

'I'm glad you saw her,' Loris said, from beside him.

'Yes,' he said.

'Did you see how she took it? She was an inspiration to us, in our deprivation. A model for us to follow.' Now Loris, too, seemed to have regained her poise.

'Good,' Parsons murmured. His mind was racing. *The old woman and the man in the cube.* Corith, she had called him. Corith – her father. That made sense. Everything made sense but one thing. And that one thing was a little difficult to get past.

Both Corith and the old woman, his wife, showed identical physical characteristics.

'What is it?' Loris was demanding. 'What's wrong?'

Parsons shook himself and forced his mind to turn outward. 'I'm having trouble,' he said. 'To have him die again, and in the same way.'

'Always,' Loris said. 'It's always the same way. The arrow driven through his heart, killing him instantly.'

'No variation?'

'None of importance.'

He said, 'When did it happen?' His question did not seem to be clear to her. 'The arrow,' he said. 'There are no such weapons in use in this time period, are there? I assume it happened in the past.'

'True,' she admitted with a shake of her head. 'Our work with time, our explorations—'

'Then you had the time-travel equipment first,' he said. 'Before his death.'

She nodded.

Parsons said, 'At least thirty-five years ago. Before your birth.'

'We have been at it a long time.'

Why? What are you trying to do? He shot the question at her, forcing it on her. 'What's this scheme you all have? Tell me. If you expect me to help you—'

'We don't expect you to help us,' she said bitterly. 'There's nothing you can do for us. We'll send you back. Your efforts are over; you have no further job here.' Leaving him, she moved away, her head bowed, lost in contemplation of the disaster that had befallen them all.

The whole family, Parsons thought as he watched her thread her way among the others. Brothers and sisters. But that still did

215

not explain the physical resemblance between Corith and his wife; the thing had to be carried back to another level.

And then he saw something that made him shrink into immobility. This time, he was the only one who had seen. The others were too wrapped up in their problems. Even Loris hadn't noticed.

Here was the missing element. The basic key that had been lacking.

She was standing in the shadows at the very edge of the room. Out of sight. She had come up with the other old woman, Loris' mother. But she had not emerged from the darkness. She remained hidden, watching everything that happened from her place of concealment.

She was unbelievably old. A tiny shriveled-up thing. Wizened and bent, claw-like hands, broomstick legs beneath the hem of her dark robe. A dry little bird face, wrinkled skin, like parchment. Two dulled eyes, set deep in the yellowing skull, a wisp of white hair like a spider web.

'She's completely deaf,' Helmar said softly, close by him. 'And almost blind.'

Parsons started. '*Who is she?*'

'She's almost a century old. She was the first. The very first.' Helmar's voice broke with emotion. He was shaking visibly, in the possession of primordial tidal surges that vibrated through his entire body. 'Nixina – the mother of them both. The mother of Corith and Jepthe. She is the *Urmutter.*'

'Corith and Jepthe are brother and sister?' Parsons demanded.

Helmar nodded. 'Yes. We're all related.'

His mind spun wildly. Inbreeding. But why? And in this society, how?

How was inbreeding accomplished in a world where the racial stock was thrown into one common pool? How had this magnificent family, this genuine family, been maintained?

Three generations. The grandmother, the mother and father. Now the children.

Helmar had said: *She was the first.* The tiny shriveled-up creature was the first – *what?*

Now the frail shape moved forward. The eyes lost their dulled

216

film, and Parsons saw that she was looking directly at him. The shrunken lips trembled, and then, in a voice audible to him, she said, 'Do I see a white person over there?' Step by step, as if blown gradually forward by some invisible wind, she approached him. Helmar at once hurried to her side, to assist her.

Holding out her hand to Parsons, the old woman said, 'Welcome.' He found himself taking the hand; it felt dry and cold and rough. 'You're the – what is the word?' For a moment the alertness faded from the eyes. And then it returned. 'The doctor who tried to bring my son back to life.' The old woman paused, her breath coming irregularly. 'Thank you for your efforts,' she finished in a hoarse whisper.

Not certain what to reply, Parsons said, 'I'm sorry it wasn't successful.'

'Perhaps . . .' Her voice ebbed, like the rise and fall of a far-off sea. 'The next time.' She smiled vaguely. And then, as before, her faculties focused; the brightness returned. 'Isn't it an irony, that a white person would be involved in this . . . or haven't they told you what we are trying to do?'

The whole room had become silent. All eyes had become fixed on Parsons and the ancient little woman. No one spoke; no one dared try to hinder her. Parsons, too, felt some of their veneration.

He said, 'No. No one has told me.'

'You should know,' Nixina said. 'It's not just unless you know. I'll tell you. My son Corith is responsible for the idea. Many years ago, when he was a young man like yourself. He was very brilliant. And so ambitious. He wanted to make everything right, erase the Terrible Five Hundred Years . . .'

Parsons recognized the term. The period of white supremacy. He found himself nodding.

'You saw the portraits?' the old woman breathed, gazing past Parsons. 'Hanging in the central hall . . . the great men in their ruffled collars. The noble explorers.' She chuckled, a dry laugh, like leaves blowing in the wind. Dried-up, fallen leaves of nightfall. 'Corith wanted to go back. And the government knew how to go back, but it didn't realize that it knew.'

Still no one spoke. No one tried to stop her. It was impossible; they could not presume.

Nixina said, 'So my son went back. To the first New England. Not the famous one, but the other one. The real one. In California. Nobody remembers . . . but Corith read all the records, the old books.' Again she chuckled. 'He wanted to start there, in Nova Albion. But he didn't get very far.' The dulled eyes blazed. Like Loris', Parsons thought. For a moment he caught the heritage, the resemblance. Bending, he listened to the dry whisper as it went on, only half directed to him, more a kind of remembering rather than any communication. 'On June 17,' she said. 'In 1579. He sailed into a port to work on his ship. He claimed the land for the Queen. How well we all know.' She turned to Helmar.

'Yes,' Helmar agreed quietly.

'For a little more than a month,' the old woman said. 'He was there. They careened their ship.'

Parsons said, 'The *Golden Hind*.' He understood now.

'And Corith came down,' the old woman whispered, smiling at Parsons. 'And instead . . . they shot him. Through his heart, with an arrow. And he died.' Her eyes faded, and then became opaque.

'She'd better rest,' Helmar said. Gently, he led the old woman away; the other gray-clad shapes closed in, and she was gone. Parsons no longer saw her.

That was their great plan. To change the past by going back centuries, before the time of the white empires. To find Drake encamped in California, helpless while his ship was being repaired. To kill him, the first Englishman to claim part of the New World for England.

They had special hatred for the English; of all the colonial powers, the English had been the most conscious of race. The most certain of their superiority to the Indians. They had not interbred.

Parsons thought, They wanted to be there, on the shore, to meet the English. Waiting. To shoot them down with equal weapons, or possibly even superior weapons. To make it a fair contest – or an unfair contest, but the other way.

How could he blame them? They had come back, centuries

later, regrouped, to regain control of their own lives. But the memory had not died. Revenge. To avenge the crimes of the past.

But Drake – or somebody at the time of Drake – had shot first.

By himself, Parsons found his way to the central hall in which the portraits of the sixteenth century explorers hung. For a time he studied them. One after another, he thought. Drake would have been first, and then – Cortez? Pizarro? And so on, down the line. As they landed with their helmeted troops, they would be wiped out – the conquerors, the plunderers and the pirates. Prepared to find a passive, helpless population, they would instead come face-to-face with the calculating, advanced descendants of that population. Grim and ready. Waiting.

There certainly was justice to it. Harsh, cruel. But he could not hold back his tacit sympathy.

Returning to the portrait of Drake, he scrutinized it more closely. The sharp, well-trimmed beard. High forehead. Wrinkles at the outer corners of the eyes. The well-chiseled nose. The Englishman's hand attracted Parsons' attention. Tapered, elongated fingers, almost feminine. The hand of a sailor? More the man of noblemen. An aristocrat. Of course, the portrait was idealized.

Going on, he found a second portrait, this one an engraving. This one showed Drake's hair as curly. And the eyes much larger and deeper colored. Rather fleshy cheeks. A less expertly done portrait, but perhaps more accurate. And in this one, the hands small and even weak looking. The hands of a ship's captain?

Something about the portrait struck him as familiar. Lines of the face. The curly hair. The eyes.

For a long time he studied the portrait, but he could not pin down the familiarity. At last, reluctantly, he gave up.

He hunted throughout the Lodge until he managed to locate Helmar. He found him conferring with several of his brethren, but at sight of Parsons, Helmar broke off.

Parsons said, 'I'd like to see something.'

'Of course,' Helmar said formally.

'The arrow that I removed from Corith's chest.'

'It has been taken below,' Helmar said. 'I can have it brought up, if you feel it's important.'

'Thanks,' Parsons said. He waited tensely while two servants were sent off. 'Have you given it a thorough examination?' he asked Helmar.

'For what?'

He did not answer. At last the arrow, in a transparent bag, was brought to him. Eagerly, he unfastened the wrapping and seated himself to study the thing.

'Could I have my instrument case?' he asked presently.

The servants were dispatched; they soon returned with the dented gray case. Opening it, Parsons lifted out various tools; before long he had begun cutting microscopic sections from the wood of the arrow, and then the feathers, and, at last, the flint point. Using chemicals from his supply, he arranged first one test and then another. Helmar watched. After a time Loris appeared, evidently summoned.

'What are you looking for?' Loris asked, her face still strained.

Parsons said, 'I want this flint analysed. But I can't do it.'

'I suppose we have the equipment to do it,' Helmar said. 'But it would take up quite a time to get the results.'

Slightly more than an hour later, the results were brought to him. He read the report, and then passed it on to Loris and Helmar.

Parsons said, 'The feathers are artificial. A thermoplastic. The wood is yew. The head is flint, but chipped with a metal tool, such as a chisel.'

They stared at him in bewilderment. 'But we saw him die,' Loris said. 'Back in the past – in 1579. In Nova Albion.'

'*Who* shot him?' Parsons said.

'We never saw. He started down the cliff and then he fell.'

'This arrow,' Parsons said, 'was not produced by New World Indians of the sixteenth century or by anyone of that century. It was made later than 1930, considering the substance from which the feathers were made.'

Corith had not been killed by someone from the past!

12

It was evening. Jim Parsons and Loris were standing on the balcony of the Lodge, watching the distant lights of the city. The lights shifted and moved constantly. An ever-changing pattern that glittered and winked through the clear darkness of the night. Like man-made stars, Parsons thought. And all colors.

'In that city,' Loris said. 'Somebody there. Some person down among those lights made that arrow and shot it into my father's chest. And the second arrow, too. The one that still is buried in him.'

And, Parsons thought, whoever it is has machinery for moving into time. Unless these people are misleading me. How do I know Corith died in Nova Albion, in 1579? He could have been shot down here, and the story could have been a concoction, put together by these people. But then, why would they have gone to the trouble to summon a doctor from the past? To heal a man whom they themselves had murdered?

'If you went back two times,' he said aloud, 'after he was shot originally, why didn't you see his attacker? Arrows don't carry far.'

'It's quite rocky,' Loris said. 'Cliffs all along the beach. And my father—' She hesitated. 'He kept himself apart, even from us. We were directly above the *Golden Hind*, looking down on Drake and his men while they worked.'

'They didn't see you?'

'We put on clothing of the period. Fur wrappers. And they were busy working on their little ship. Working very industriously.'

He said, 'An arrow. Not a musket shot.'

'We could never account for that,' Loris said. 'But Drake was not on the ship. He and a group of his men had gone off; that made my father's task more difficult. He had to wait. And then Drake appeared down the beach a distance, and held some sort of conference. So my father hurried down that way, out of our immediate sight.'

'What would Corith have killed Drake with?'

'A force tube, like this.' She went to her room and returned to the balcony, carrying a weapon familiar to Parsons. The *shupos* had had them, and so had Stenog. Evidently this was the standard hand weapon of this period.

'What would his crew have thought? They knew what weapons the Indians had.'

Loris said, 'The more mysterious it was to Drake's crew, the better. All we cared about was getting at Drake. And making sure that they should know that Drake died at the hands of a red man.'

'But would they know?'

'My father had made certain that they would know him to be an Indian. He worked for months on his disguise. At least, so my mother and grandmother tell me. I, of course, was not yet born. He had a special workroom down below, with all sorts of tools and materials. He kept his preparations secret, even from his mother and wife. From everyone. In fact' – her brow wrinkled with uneasiness as she remembered – 'he didn't put on his costume until he was back at Nova Albion, out of the time ship and away from them. He claimed it was dangerous to let even his family see him in advance.'

'Why?' Parsons said.

'He didn't trust anyone. Not even Nixina. Or so they say. Doesn't that seem odd to you? Surely he must have trusted them; he must have trusted his mother. But—' Awkwardly, she went on, her brow furrowed. 'Anyhow, he worked by himself down below, telling nobody anything. He's supposed to have gotten incoherent with rage if anybody asked him questions. And Jepthe says he several times accused her of trying to spy on him. He was sure that someone was watching him at work, trying to gain entrance into his workroom for some evil purpose. So of course he kept it locked; he even locked himself in while he worked. I know he believed that almost everyone was against him, especially the servants. He refused to have any.'

The man had been virtually a paranoid, Parsons thought. But it would fit with the grand scheme, the sense of heroic injustice and hate. How close the idealist, with his fanatical passion, was to the mentally disturbed.

'Anyhow,' Loris said, 'he intended finally to display himself. To be quite conspicuous as he killed Drake. So the crew would carry report back to Elizabeth that the red men had weapons superior to the English.'

To him, the logic was fuzzy. And yet, what did it matter? Details did not concern them; the overall scheme, dazzling them, led them on, not such picayune matters as the incongruity of a twenty-fifth century hand weapon used in the sixteenth century. And certainly the English would be impressed.

'Why can't you continue without Corith?' he said.

Loris said, 'Because you know only one part of our program.'

'And what's the other part?'

'Do you want to know? Does it matter?'

He said, 'Tell me.'

Beside him, the woman sighed, shivering in the night air. 'I want to go in,' she said. 'The darkness . . . it depresses me. All right?'

Together, they left the balcony and entered Loris' apartment.

This was the first time that Parsons had been invited here. At the threshold he paused. Through a half-opened closet door he made out the indistinct shapes of a woman's clothing. Robes and gowns. Slippers. And, on the far side of the room, satin covers on the wide bed. Lush wine-colored drapes. Thick multi-colored carpet which he knew at once had been pilfered from the Middle Eastern past. Someone had used the time dredge to its best advantage, furnishing the apartment in excellent taste.

Loris seated herself in an easy chair, and Parsons came up close behind her and put his hands on her warm, smooth shoulders. 'Tell me about the part I don't know,' he said. 'About your father.'

Loris, her back to him, said, 'You know that all the males are sterile.' She raised her head, shaking her mane of black hair aside. 'And you know that Corith is not. Otherwise, how could I exist?'

'True,' he said.

'Nixina, my grandmother, was the Mother Superior at her time, decades ago. She managed to get him past the sterilization procedures; it was almost impossible because they're so careful. But she was able to, and in the records he was listed as sterilized.' Under his hands her body trembled. 'The women are not, as you

223

know. So there was no difficulty in his mating with my mother, Jepthe. The union took place here, in secret. Then the zygote was taken, in cold-pack, to the great central Fountain and placed in the Soul Cube. Jepthe was the Mother Superior at that time, you understand. She kept the zygote separate until it had developed into a fetus . . . in fact, all along its trip to full embryo and at last birth.'

'And this was done with the rest of your family?'

'Yes. My brother, Helmar. But—' Now she got up from the chair and moved away from him. 'You see, they managed to sterilize all the males who came after Corith. He was the only one who escaped.' Now she was silent.

Parsons said, 'Then for further reproduction of your family, you're dependent on Corith.'

The woman nodded.

'Including your own. If you choose to continue.'

'Yes,' she said. 'But that's not important now.'

'Why was it ever important? What did you mean to do with this family?'

Raising her head she confronted him proudly. 'We're not like the others, Doctor. Nixina tells us that she's a full-blooded Iroquois Indian. We're practically pure. Couldn't you see?' She put her hand to her cheek. 'Look at my face. My skin. Don't you think it's true?'

'Possibly,' he said. 'It would be almost impossible to verify, though. Such a claim as that – it sounds more mystical than practical.'

'I prefer to believe it,' she said. 'Certainly it's spiritually true. We are the spiritual heirs, their blood brothers in any and all meaningful senses. Even if it's only a myth.'

Parsons reached out and touched her jaw, the firm boneline. She did not move back or protest.

'What we are going to do,' she said, her face close to his, her breath stirring against his mouth, 'is as follows. We intended to preempt your ancestors, Doctor. Unfortunately, it didn't work out. But if we had been successful, if we had been able to assassinate the white adventurers and pirates who came to the New World and established footholds, we would have installed our own stock –

ourselves! What do you think of that?' A taunting smile appeared on her lips.

'Are you serious?' he said.

'Of course.'

'You would have been the vanguard of civilization, then. Instead of the Elizabethans and Spanish gentry and Dutch traders.'

Now, with deep seriousness, she said, 'And it would not have been masters over slaves. The supremacy of one race over another. It would have been a natural relationship: *the future guiding the past.*'

He thought, Yes, it would have been more humane. No tribes to be wiped out, no concentration camps – euphemistically referred to as 'reservations.' Too bad, he thought. He felt real regret.

'You're sorry,' she said, peering at him. 'And you're white. How odd.' It seemed to disconcert her. 'You don't identify with those conquerors, do you? And yet they built your civilization. We plucked you from the latter part of that world.'

Parsons said, 'I didn't burn witches, either. I have no sense of identification with many of those things. Are all whites alike?'

'No,' she said. But she had become colder, now. The friendliness was gone. From beneath his hands she slipped away; all at once she had left him and was walking off.

Following her, he took hold of her, turned her toward him, and kissed her. Her eyes, dark and full, were fixed on him. But she did not try to draw away.

'You were protesting,' she said, when he released her, 'that we had kidnapped you away from your wife.' She said it with hostility.

It was hard for him to defend himself. So he said nothing.

'Well,' she said, 'it's absurd anyhow. You'll be going back, wife or not.'

'And you're full-blooded Indian and I'm white,' he added ironically.

She said in a quiet voice, 'Don't vilify me, Doctor. I'm not a fanatic. We're not contemptuous of you.'

'Do you see me as a person?'

'Oh, you definitely bleed when cut,' she said, laughing now but with no unkindness. At that, he had to smile too. Suddenly she threw her arms around him and hugged him with amazing vitality. 'Well, Doctor,' she said, 'do you want to be my lover? Make up your mind.'

Tightly, he said, 'Remember, I'm not sterile.'

'That's no problem for me. I'm the Mother Superior. I have access to every part of the Fountain. We have our regular procedure; if I become pregnant I can introduce the zygote into the Soul Cube, and' – she made a gesture of resignation – 'plop. Lost forever, into the race.'

He said, 'All right, then.'

At once she tore herself away from him. 'Who said you could be my lover? Did I give you permission? I was just curious.' She retreated from him, her lovely face alive with glee. 'You don't want a fat squaw, anyhow.'

Moving quickly, he caught her. 'Yes, I do,' he said.

Later, as they lay together in the darkness, Loris whispered, 'Is there anything else you want?'

Parsons had lit a cigarette. Smoking, meditating, he said, 'Yes, there is.'

Beside him, the woman rolled closer; pressing against him she said, 'What is it?'

'I want to go back to see his death,' he said.

'My father? Back to Nova Albion?' She sat up, brushing her long, untied hair back from her face.

'I want to be there,' he said calmly.

In the dark he could feel her staring at him. And he could hear her breathing, the long, unsteady inhalations and then the rush with which she breathed out. 'We weren't planning to try again,' she murmured. Now she slid from the bed, and, in the gloom, padded barefoot in search of her robe. Outlined against the faint light from the window, she stood buttoning her robe around her and tying the sash.

'Let's try,' he said.

She did not answer. But he knew, intuitively and with certitude, that they would.

*

Toward morning, as the first insipid gray appeared outside, filtering into the apartment through the drapes, he and Loris sat facing each other across a small glass-topped table on which were a stainless steel coffeepot, china cups and saucers, an overflowing ash tray. Her face fatigued, but still strong and vital, Loris said:

'You know, your willingness to do this – your desire to do this – makes me wonder about our whole plan.' Smoke drifted from her lips, she set her cigarette down and began rubbing her throat. 'I wonder if we're right. It's a little late to wonder that, isn't it?'

'A paradox,' he said.

'Yes,' she said. 'We can only eradicate the whites by prevailing on a white to help us. But we recognized that when we first began scouting you.'

'But at that time,' he said, 'you were making use of my special talent. Now—' What was it now? He thought, More the whole person. Myself as an individual, not as a doctor. The person, not the skill. Because I am doing this knowingly. Deliberately. With full awareness of what the issues are.

This is my choice.

'Let me ask you something,' he said. 'Suppose you are successful. Won't that alter history? Won't Drake's death wipe out all of us, as products of a process that includes Drake? You, me, every one of us.'

Loris said, 'You must understand that we are not ignorant of these massive paradoxes. Since my father's time there has been continual experimentation with the results of altering the past, seeing exactly how the historic process proceeds after a change – even a minute one – has been made. There is a general tendency for the vast, inertial flow to rectify itself. To seek a sort of level. It's almost impossible to affect the far future. Like rocks thrown in a river . . . a series of ripples that finally die. To do what we want, we must manage to assassinate fifteen or sixteen major historic figures. Even so, we do not end European civilization. We do not fundamentally alter it. There will still be telephones and motorcars and Voltaire – we presume.'

'But you're not sure.'

'How could we be? We have reason to believe that, generally, the same persons who now exist will exist after our plan works out. Their condition, their status, will be different. Looking backward, the conditions become more affected the closer you get to the original moment. The sixteenth century will be completely different. The seventeenth, not completely but very much so. The eighteenth, different but recognizable. Or so we hypostatize. We could be wrong. There's much guesswork in this maneuvering with history. But—' Her voice became firm. 'We've been back many times, and so far we've been able to make no changes whatsoever. Our problem is not that we risk altering the present, but that we've been unable to alter anything at all.'

'It's possible,' Parsons said, 'that it can't be altered. That the paradox obviates any meddling with the past – by definition.'

'That may be. But we want to try.' She pointed a coppery, tapered finger at him. 'You must carry your paradox to its logical conclusion. If we obviate ourselves by succeeding in the past, then the agent that alters the past will have ceased to exist; hence, no alteration will have occurred. The worst that can happen is that we will wind up where we are now; unable to budge what has already occurred.'

He had to admit that their reasoning was sound.

There was simply no complete theory about time, he realized. No hypothesis by which results could be anticipated.

Only experiment – and guesswork.

But, he thought, billions of human lives, complete civilizations, depend on how accurately these people have guessed. Wouldn't it be better not to risk further attempts to tamper? Shouldn't I, for the sake of centuries of human achievement and suffering, stay away from Nova Albion and 1579?

He had a theory, however. A theory that had entered his mind when he saw the plastic feathers of the arrow.

In fact, a theory that had come to mind when he had noticed something familiar in the engraving of Sir Francis Drake.

All the tampering had already been done. That was his theory. And, by going back, he would simply observe, not alter. The past had been tampered with up to the hilt, but none of them, not Loris, nor even Corith, had recognized it.

The portrait of Drake, with the skin darkened, the beard and mustache removed, would have looked very much like a portrait of Al Stenog.

13

In the wheel chair, the ancient, tattered figure sat huddled in a heavy wool blanket. At first Nixina did not seem aware of him. She stood by the doorway, waiting. Then, at last, the eyes opened. Up from the depths swam a fragment of personality; he saw the consciousness there, in the expression. The coming to the surface, from sleep. For her, at her age, sleep was perpetual and natural; it ended only at unusual moments. And, before long, it would never end.

'Madam,' he said.

Beside him, an armed attendant said, 'Remember, she is deaf. Go closer and she'll be able to read your lips.'

He did so.

'So you're going to try again,' Nixina said, her voice a dry, rasping whisper.

'Yes,' he said.

'Did you know,' she whispered, 'that I was along the other times?'

He could hardly believe it. Surely the strain—

'I intend to come this time,' she told him. 'It's my son, you recall.' Her voice gained sudden vigor. 'Don't you think if anyone can protect him, I can?'

There was nothing he could say to that.

'Helmar built me a special chair,' she said, and in her tone he heard something that told him a great deal. He heard authority.

She had not always been old. Once she had been young, not blind and not deaf, and not infirm. This woman kept the rest of them going. She did not – and would never – permit them to stop. As long as she lived, she would keep them at her task. As she had kept her son at the task, until the moment of his death.

Now her voice sank back to the labored whisper. 'So,' she went on, 'I'll be perfectly safe. I don't intend to interfere with what you're going to do.' Plaintively, she asked, 'Do you mind . . . can you tell me what you think you can do? They say you have a notion that you might do some good.'

'I hope so,' he said. 'But I don't know.' He became silent, then. There was nothing to tell her, actually. It was all vague.

The tired lips moved. 'I will see my son alive,' she said. 'He starts down the cliff. There's that weapon in his hand; he goes down to kill that man—' Hate and loathing filled her voice. 'That *explorer*.' Smiling, she shut her eyes, and, imperceptibly, passed back into sleep. The energy, the authority, had ebbed away. It could not be sustained, now.

After a moment Parsons tiptoed away, and out of the room.

Outside, Loris met him. 'She's an incredibly strong person,' he murmured, still under her spell.

'You told her?' Loris said.

'There was damn little to tell her,' he said, feeling futile. 'Except that I want to go back.'

'Does she intend to try to come this time?'

'Yes,' he said.

'Then we'll have to let her. Nobody would go against her decision. You know her; you've felt her power.' Loris raised her hands in bitter resignation. 'You can't blame her. We all want to see him, I, Jepthe, the old lady . . . we get a second to see him in all his glory, running down the cliff with that gun. And then—' She shuddered.

Parsons thought, But it's hard to feel sorry for a man who had murder in mind. After all, Corith was on his way down to kill.

On the other hand, Drake had certainly sent a good number of heavily armored Spanish soldiers over the side to drown; weighed down, those men had had no chance. Drake, to them, was simply a pirate. And in a sense they were right.

'We've made good progress in getting ready,' Loris said, as they walked together along the corridor. 'We've had more experience, now.' Her voice was heavy with despair. 'Do you want to see?'

This time, he was permitted to descend to the subsurface levels. At last he had been let in on all that the Wolf Clan had; nothing was kept back.

'You'll have to go further than the rest of us,' Loris said, as they stepped from the lift. 'In the way of altering your appearance. Because of your white skin. Our problem is one of costume. And keeping our equipment out of sight.'

Ahead of him stood a group of men and women wearing furs and moccasins. It was difficult to accept the fact that such primitive-looking people were spurious. With a shock he identified Helmar among the group. All of them, their faces somber, hair braided back, had an ominous, warlike cast, an air of anger and distrust about them. An illusion, he decided, produced by their costumes.

The burnished red of their skins glowed in the artificial light that reflected throughout this subsurface chamber. That was natural, the fine, impressive red. He glanced at his own arms. How different he felt from them . . . what a contrast.

'You'll be all right,' Loris said. 'We have pigments.'

'I have my own,' he said. 'In my instrument case.'

By himself, in a side room, he removed all his clothing. This time he rubbed the pigment onto every part of him; he did not leave the telltale middle area white, as he had before. Then, with the help of several servants, he dyed his hair black.

'That isn't enough,' Loris said, entering the room.

Startled, he said, 'I haven't got anything on.' He stood naked, the reddish pigment drying on him, with the servants braiding artificial hair into his, to give length to it. Loris, however, did not seem to care. She paid scarcely any attention to him.

'You must remember your eyes,' she said. 'They are blue.'

With contact lenses, the pupils of his eyes were given a dark brown cast.

'Now look at yourself in the mirror,' Loris said. A full-length mirror was produced, and Parsons studied himself in it. Meanwhile, the servants began to dress him in the furs. Loris watched critically, seeing to it that each part of his garments was placed on him properly.

'How about it?' he said. The man in the mirror moved when he moved; he had trouble accepting the image as his, this frowning, bare-armed, bare-legged warrior, with his coppery skin, his greasy-looking uncut hair falling down the back of his neck.

'Fine,' Loris said. 'It isn't important that we be authentic, but that we fit the sixteenth century English stereotype of Indians – they're the ones we have to deceive. They kept several armed scouts posted here and there on the cliffs overlooking their careened ship.'

'What's the relationship between Drake's party and the local Indians?' Parsons asked.

'Evidently good. He has been plundering Spanish ships to his heart's content, so there is plenty of valuable material aboard – no need of ravaging the countryside. To him and his men, the California Coast area has no value; he's there because after he successfully plundered the Spanish ships near Chile and Peru, he went north seeking a passage to the Atlantic.'

'So in other words,' Parsons said, 'he's not there for conquest. At least, not against the Indians. It's been other whites that he's preyed on.'

'Yes,' she admitted. 'And now that you are all ready, I think we had better be getting back to the others.'

As they walked back to join the group, Loris asked, 'In case of emergency, you're familiar enough with the controls of our time ship so that you could operate it?'

'I hope so,' he said.

Loris said, 'You can be killed there, in Nova Albion.'

'Yes,' he said, thinking of the lifeless figure floating and drifting silently, unchangingly, in the cold-pack. And, he thought, if anything went wrong, if we're not able to get back to our own centuries . . .

We would be catching abalone and mussels. Living on elk and deer and quail.

These people could extol the virtues of Indian culture, but certainly they themselves would be unable to endure it. With an eerie awareness he thought, They would probably try to get back to England with Drake's men.

And, he thought, *so would I.*

The 'Plate of Brasse' which Drake's men had left on the California Coast had been found forty miles north of San Francisco Bay. The *Golden Hind* had cruised up and down a considerable part of the coast before Drake, an expert and provident seaman, had found a harbor that suited him. The ship needed its rotten planks repaired, its bottom breamed, for the voyage across the Pacific back to England; it was loaded with enormous treasure, enough to transform the economy of the home country. To insure safety for the men and ship during the careenage, Drake needed a harbor that would give him as much privacy and freedom as possible. At last he found that harbor, with white cliffs, fog, much like the Sussex Coast that he knew so well. The ship was brought into the Estero, its cargo removed, and the careening begun.

Standing on the cliff, several miles from the Estero, Jim Parsons watched the work through high-powered prismatic binoculars.

Ropes from the ship trailed out into the water where they were attached to stakes driven deep and out of sight. The ship, on its side, lay like some injured animal washed up onto the beach, helpless and unable to get back to its element. Out in the water, several winches controlled the angle of the ship. The seamen at work replacing rotten planks stood on a wooden platform that kept them, at high tide, above the water level. Through his binoculars, Parsons saw them working with what appeared to be pots of tar or pitch; fires smoldered beneath the pots, and the men carried the tar to the side of the ship by means of broomlike poles. The men wore cloth trousers, rolled up, and cloth shirts, washed a light blue. Their hair, in the warm, midday sun, shone yellow.

To his ears came the distant, faint noises of their voices.

He saw no sign of Drake himself.

Surveying the Estero, Parsons tried to recall what had become of this region in his own time. A subdivision of tract houses called Oko Village, named after the twentieth century realtor who had financed it. And a resort frontage along the water's edge: private beaches and boats.

'Where is Drake?' he said, crouching down beside Helmar and Loris and the others in their fur wrappers.

'Off somewhere in a dinghy,' Helmar said. 'Scouting.'

Behind them, the time ship had been hidden among trees, covered with shrubbery and branches to disguise its metal exterior. Now, as Parsons glanced back at it, he saw that they were bringing out the old woman in her chair. With her was her daughter, Jepthe, the wife of her son. The old woman, wrapped in a black wool shawl, complained in a shrill peevish voice as the chair bumped over the uneven ground.

'Can't she be kept more quiet?' he said softly to Loris.

'This excites her,' Loris said. 'They won't hear. Sound travels up here because it's reflected by the water and cliffs. She knows that she has to be careful.'

The old woman, as her chair neared the cliff edge, became silent.

'What are we supposed to do?' Loris said to Parsons.

He said, 'I don't know.' He did not know what he himself was supposed to do. If he could sight Drake . . . 'You're sure he's not aboard the ship,' he said.

With a sardonic twitch of his lips, Helmar said, 'Look along the cliff.'

Turning his glasses, Parsons saw, hidden among the rocks, a small group of figures. Red arms, shiny black hair, the gray fur of their garments. Both men and women.

'Ourselves,' Helmar said hoarsely. 'The previous time.'

In the binoculars, Parsons saw a woman rise up slightly, a powerfully built woman whose strong neck glistened in the heat. Her head turned and he recognized Loris.

And, further along, also perched in a declivity of rock, another group. Through the glasses he once more identified Loris and, with her, Helmar and the others. Beyond that, he could not see.

He said to Loris beside him, 'Where is your father?'

'He left Nixina and Jepthe at the time ship,' she said tonelessly. 'He made them wait there while he started along the cliff. For quite a time they lost sight of him. When he reappeared he had changed to his costume and he was about one-third of the way down the face of the cliff. He disappeared behind some rocks, and then—' Her voice broke. Presently she resumed. 'Anyhow, they saw him jump up, just for a second, and go over head-first with a yell. Whether the arrow had gotten him at that point we don't know. They next saw him roll down until he came to rest against a shrub growing from the face of the cliff. They hurried to the edge

234

and managed to get down to him. And of course when they got to him they found him with the arrow in his heart.'

Now she ceased talking. Helmar finished, 'They saw no one else. But of course they were too busy trying to get the ship close enough to get him into it. They managed to land the ship on the cliff face, using its jets to support it until they had him inside.'

'Was he dead?' Parsons asked.

'Dying,' Helmar said matter-of-factly. 'He lived for several minutes. But he wasn't conscious.'

Loris touched Parsons' arm. 'Look down again,' she said.

Again he studied the Estero far below.

A small boat with five men in it had appeared from the far side of the careened ship. Methodically, it moved along, with four of the men working long oars. The fifth man, bearded, had some kind of metal instrument in his hand; Parsons saw it glint in the sun.

The man was Drake.

Yes, Parsons thought. But was it Stenog? He saw only the head, the beard, and the man's clothes; the face was obscured, and too far away. If that is Stenog, he said to himself, then this is a trap, a fake. They are waiting. And they have weapons as good as ours.

'What weapons do they have?' he asked.

Loris said, 'We understand that they have cutlasses, of course. And wheel-lock rifles, or possibly the older matchlock rifles. It is possible that some rifles have spiral grooves in the barrels, but that's only conjecture. They can't possibly fire this far in any case. There are a few cannon, removed from the ship – or at least we assume there are. We have seen none on the beach, however, and if they're still aboard the ship they certainly can't be fired. Not with the ship on its side. They took everything possible off to lighten the ship, so it would draw the least water. In any case, they have never fired on us, either with hand weapons or cannon.'

They didn't have to, Parsons thought. At least, not with the weapons that Loris supposed. He said aloud, 'So Corith went down the cliff assuming he was not in jeopardy.'

'Yes,' she said. 'But Drake's men wouldn't be using an Indian weapon, would they?' The doubt, the bewilderment, showed in both her voice and face. This catastrophe made no sense to her; now, as before, it was beyond them. With the information they had, they could not deal with it. 'Anyway, why would a native kill him?' Loris demanded.

Below them, the small boat had begun pushing away from the *Golden Hind*. It moved gradually to the south, in their direction. Presently it would pass directly beneath their spot.

Parsons said, 'I'm going down.' Handing her the binoculars, he took the coil of rope that they had brought and began lashing one end to a well-secured rock. Helmar helped him, and together they got the rope tight. Then, taking the coil, Parsons started away from the group.

Almost at once he realized that he could not descend directly. Even if the rope were long enough to let him down to the beach, he would be conspicuous, dangling against the white cliff; the men in the boat would be aware of him. Leaving the rope, he scrambled back up to the top of the cliff and began to run. Ahead of him he made out a deep cleft, overgrown with shrubbery, a tangle of broken rocks and roots that dipped out of sight beneath him.

Catching hold, he crept down, step by step. Below, the Pacific seemed perfectly flat, spread out as far as the eye could see; the ocean and the cliffs – nothing else. The blue of the water, the crumbling rock in his hands as he clawed his way down. Now, for an instant, he caught sight of the small boat once more. The men rowing. Ribbon of sand, with foam and breakers, driftwood washed up. The disorderly collections of seaweed . . .

He stumbled and almost fell. Head-first, he hung, clutching at roots. Rocks and bits of shrubbery rained past him, falling some-where. He could hear the sound echo.

Far below, the boat continued on. Silently. None of the tiny figures seemed to hear or notice.

Parsons, by degrees, righted himself. Facing the cliff, not look-ing at the ocean below, he again descended.

When next he halted, getting his wind, he saw that the boat had come closer to shore. Two of the men had gotten out and were wading in the surf.

Had they seen him?

Swiftly, he made his way down. The rock surface became smooth; he clung for an interval, and then, taking a deep, prayerful breath, he released his grip and dropped. Beneath him, the sand rose. He struck and fell, his legs thrashing with pain. Rolling, he slid down among the seaweed and lay, wheezing, enduring the gradually declining numbness of impact.

The boat had been dragged up onto the shore. The men were searching for something on the beach, kicking at the sand. Some lost tool or instrument, Parsons thought. He lay stretched out, watching.

One of the men came toward him. And, after him, Drake. Both men passed directly in front of Parsons, and as Drake turned, Parsons saw his face clearly, outlined against the sky.

Scrambling up, Parsons said, 'Stenog!'

The bearded man turned. His mouth fell open with astonishment. The other men froze.

'You *are* Stenog,' Parsons said. It was true. The man stared at him without recognition. 'Don't you remember me?' Parsons said grimly. 'The doctor who cured the girl, Icara.'

Now recognition came. The expression on the bearded man's face changed.

Stenog smiled.

Why? Parsons wondered. Why is he smiling?

'They got you out of the prison rocket, did they?' Stenog said. 'We thought so. One dead *shupo* and two unidentified corpses out of nowhere, sealed in and traveling back and forth.' His smile grew, a knowing, confident smile. 'I'm surprised to see you – you completely threw me off. How interesting . . . you here.' His white, even teeth showed; he had begun to laugh.

'Why are you laughing?' Parsons demanded.

'Let's see your friend,' Stenog said. 'The one who's going to do the killing. Send him down.' He put his hands on his hips, his legs wide apart. 'I'm waiting.'

14

Like a voice in a nightmare, the laughter followed after Parsons as he raced along the base of the cliff.

I was right, he thought.

Pausing once, he looked back. There on the beach, Stenog and his men waited for Corith. From the sand they had fished up what they had been searching for, a deadly, gleaming little weapon.

They had managed to complete the time-travel experiments.

Catching hold of roots and branches, Parsons scrambled up the cliff wall. I have to get to him first, he thought. I have to warn him. Rocks tumbled away; he sprawled and rolled back, clutching.

The figures below became smaller. They made no move to follow him.

Why don't they shoot me? he asked himself.

Now a ledge of rock came between him and Stenog. Gasping, he rested for a minute, out of sight, protected. But he had to go on. Struggling up, he seized a tree root and continued on up.

Don't they think I can stop him? he wondered. Is it foreordained that he will go through his cycle, be killed no matter what I do?

Am I going to fail?

Now, reaching out, he managed to catch hold of the turf at the crest of the cliff. He was able to pitch himself up onto the level ground. But at once he was up again, on his feet.

Where was Corith?

Somewhere. Not far off.

Trees grew ahead, a grove of wind-bent pines. He entered the grove, panting for breath. Back and forth he ran, searching among the trees.

I can't blame Stenog, he thought. He's protecting his society. It's his job.

And this is my job, he realized. To save my patient. The man I was called on to heal.

He stopped now, winded, unable to go on. Sinking down, he sat in the damp grass, in the shadows, resting and recovering. His fur garments were torn from scrambling up the cliff. Drops of blood oozed from his arm; he wiped it off on the grass.

Strange, he thought. Stenog, with his dark skin dyed white, masquerading as a white man. And myself, with my white skin dyed dark, masquerading as an Indian.

And – a white man struggling to help Corith kill Drake. And Stenog on the other side, taking Drake's place.

Or not taking Drake's place. But actually Drake. Is there an authentic Drake? Or is Stenog Drake? Was there another man, actually born in England in the early sixteenth century, named Francis Drake? Or has Stenog always been Drake? And there is no other person.

If there is another Drake, a real Drake, then where is he?

One thing he knew: the engraving and portrait had been made of Al Stenog, with beard and white skin, in Drake's place. So Stenog, not Drake, had come back to England from the New World with the plunder, and been knighted by the Queen. But had Stenog then continued to be Drake for the rest of his life?

Had that been Stenog who fought the Spanish warships, later on, in the war against Spain?

Who had been the great navigator? Drake or Stenog?

An intuition . . . the exploits of those explorers. The fantastic navigation and courage. Each of them: Cortez, Pizarro, Cabrillo . . . each of them a man transplanted from the future, an impostor. Using equipment from the future.

No wonder a handful of men had conquered Peru. And another handful, Mexico.

But he did not know. If Corith died while trying to reach Drake, there would be no reason for Stenog, for the government of the future, to go on. The man could die only once.

Parsons got shakily to his feet. He began to walk, preserving his strength. The man is here somewhere, he told himself. If I keep looking, I'll eventually find him. There's no need for a panic reaction; it's only a question of time.

Ahead of him, among the trees, someone moved.

Cautiously, he approached. He saw several figures . . . reddish skin, furs. Had he found him? Reaching out, he spread apart the foliage.

On the far side of a rise the metallic sphere of a time ship caught the afternoon sun.

One of them, he realized. But which one?

Not the one he himself had come in; that was hidden elsewhere, disguised with mud and branches. This one sat out in the open.

There would be at least four time ships.

Assuming that this trip was the last.

I wonder if I will ever make any more, he thought. If, like Loris and Nixina, I will come again and again. Like a ghost. Haunting this spot, seeking a way to change the flow of past events.

One of the figures turned, and Parsons saw – who? A woman he did not recognize. A handsome woman, in her thirties . . . like Loris, but not Loris. The woman's black hair tumbled down her bare shoulders, her strong chin raised as she stood listening. She wore a skirt of hide around her waist, an animal pelt. Her naked breasts glistened, swayed as she turned her body. A wild-eyed, fierce woman who now dropped, crouching, alert.

A second woman appeared. Elderly and frail. Hesitantly stepping from the time ship. Wrapped in heavy robes.

The younger woman was Jepthe. Loris' mother. At an earlier time. When she was here before.

Nixina said, in a voice familiar to Parsons, 'Why did you let him get out of sight?'

'You know how he is,' Jepthe shot back in a husky voice. 'How could I stop him?' She leaped up, tossing her mane of hair back. 'Maybe we should go to the cliff. We might find him again there.'

I am back thirty-five years, Parsons realized. Loris has not been born.

Barefoot, Jepthe hurried from the ship, into the trees. Her long legs carried her quickly; she vanished almost at once, leaving the old woman to catch up.

'Wait for me!' Nixina called anxiously.

Reappearing, Jepthe said, 'Hurry.' She emerged from the trees to help her mother. 'You shouldn't have come.'

Watching the supple body, the energetic loins, Parsons thought, But she has already conceived. Loris is in her womb now, as I'm looking at her. And one day she will nurse at those superb breasts.

He began to hurry through the trees, back in the direction of the cliff. Corith had left his time ship; at least he knew that. The man was on his way, approaching what he imagined to be Drake.

Ahead of him, he saw the Pacific. He emerged on the cliff once more. The sunlight momentarily blinded him and he halted, shielding his eyes.

Far off, also on the cliff edge, he saw a single figure. A man, standing on the edge.

The man wore a loincloth. On his head a horned buffalo skull jutted up, covering him almost to his eyes. Black hair hung down from beneath the buffalo skull.

Parsons ran toward him.

The man did not seem aware of him. He bent down, gazing over the edge of the cliff, at the ship below. His enormous copper-colored body was splashed with paint streaks of blue and black and orange and yellow across his chest, his thighs, his shoulders, even his face. Over his back a pelt-covered mass was tied to him by a thong that passed over his chest and strapped beneath his armpits. Weapons there, Parsons decided. And binoculars. The man whipped a pair of binoculars from the pack on his back, and, squatting down, studied the beach.

Of all of them, Parsons thought, Corith had by far the best disguise. It was worthy of his great preparation, his months of secret effort. The magnificent buffalo skull, with tatters of skin flapping in the ocean wind. The blazing bands of paint slashed across his body. A warrior in the prime of life.

Now, lifting his head, Corith noticed him. Their eyes met. Parsons was face to face with him – with the living man, for the first time.

And, he wondered, the last?

Seeing him, Corith stuck the binoculars back into his pack. He did not seem alarmed; there was no fear on his face. His eyes flashed. The man's mouth was set, the teeth showing, almost a grin. Suddenly he sprang to the edge of the cliff. In an instant he had gone over the side; he had vanished.

'Corith!' Parsons shouted. The wind whipped his voice back at him. His lungs labored as he reached the spot, dropped down, saw the loose rock sliding where Corith had gone. The fanatic, cunning assassin had gotten away. Without knowing – or caring – who Parsons was or why he wanted him. Or how he had known his name.

Corith did not intend to stop for anything. He could not take the chance.

Making his way down, Parsons thought, I've lost him. The man had already gotten past him. Down the cliff side.

Why did I think I could stop him? he asked himself. When they failed. His mother, his son, his wife, his daughter – the family itself, the Wolf Tribe.

Sliding, half-falling, he reached a projection and halted. He could see no sign of the man.

On the beach, the small boat was still drawn up in the surf. The five men had collected by their weapon, concealing it. The bearded man wandered away, glanced up, continued to roam. Pretending that he doesn't know, Parsons thought. The decoy.

Taking hold of an outcropping, Parsons started cautiously on. He turned about, to face the cliff . . .

A few feet from him, Corith crouched. The relentless eyes bored at him; the face, inflamed with conviction, glowed. Corith held a tube in his hands. An elongated version of the weapon familiar to Parsons. With this, no doubt, he intended to kill Drake.

'You called me by name,' Corith said.

Parsons said, 'Don't go down there.'

'How do you know my name?'

'I know your mother,' he said. 'Nixina. Your wife, Jepthe.'

'I've never seen you before,' Corith said. His eyes flickered; he studied Parsons, licking at his lower lip. Poised to spring, Parsons realized. Ready to leap away and on down the cliff. But, he thought, he will kill me first. With that tube.

'I want to warn you,' Parsons said. He felt dizzy; for a moment black flecks passed in front of him, and the cliff wavered and began receding. The glare of the sun, the stark white sand, the ocean . . . he sat listening to the noise of the surf. Over it he could hear Corith's breathing. The rapid, constricted spasms.

'Who are you?' Corith said.

'You don't know me,' he said.

'Why shouldn't I go down there?'

'It's a trap. They're waiting for you.'

The massive face quivered. Corith raised the tube that he held. 'It doesn't matter.'

'They have the same weapons you have,' Parsons said.

To that, Corith said nothing. He did not seem to react.

'The Director of the Fountain,' Parsons said.

After a long time, Corith said, 'The Director of the Fountain is a woman named Lu Farns.'

At that, Parsons stared.

Corith said, 'You're lying to me. I've never heard of anybody named Stenog.'

They sat crouched against the rock surface of the cliff, facing each other silently.

'Your speech,' Corith said. 'You have an accent.'

Parsons' mind raced. The whole thing had a ring of madness in it. Who was Lu Farns? Why had Corith never heard of Stenog? And then he understood.

Thirty-five years had passed since Corith's death. Stenog was a young man, no more than twenty. He had not become Director until long after Corith's death; in fact, he had not even been alive when Corith died. The woman, Lu Farns, was undoubtedly the Director of the Fountain during Corith's lifetime.

Relaxing a little, Parsons said, 'I'm from the future.' His hands were still shaking; he tried to quiet them. 'Your daughter—'

'My *daughter*,' Corith echoed, with a mocking grimace.

'If you go any further down,' Parsons said, 'you'll be shot through the chest. Killed. Your body will be taken back to your own time, to the Wolf Lodge, and put into cold-pack. For thirty-five years your mother and your wife, and finally your daughter, will try to undo your death; they'll give up eventually and call me in.'

Corith said, 'I don't have any daughter.'

'But you will,' he said. 'You do now, in fact, but you don't know it. Your wife has conceived.'

With no indication that he had heard him, Corith said, 'I must go down there and kill that man.'

'If you want to kill him,' Parsons said, 'I'll tell you how you can do it. Not by going down there.'

'How?' Corith said.

'In your own time. *Before he solves the problem of time travel and comes back here.*' That was the only way; he had worked it out in his mind, examined the alternatives. 'Here, he knows. There, if you go back, he doesn't. He didn't know about you when I was with him; all he had was a series of conjectures to go on. Shrewd guesses. But he was able to put them together; they resumed time-travel experimentation, and finally they were successful.' Leaning urgently toward Corith, he went on, 'Those weapons that you have won't help you here because—'

He broke off. From the pack strapped to Corith's body something stuck up – something that made cold, bleak fright rise inside him.

'Your costume,' he managed to say. 'You constructed it yourself. No one else saw it.' He reached toward Corith. Toward the pack. From the pack he took—

A handful of arrows. With flint tips. And feathered with familiar colors.

'Fakes,' Parsons said. 'Which you made as part of your disguise. To come back here.'

Corith said, 'Look at your arm.'

'What?' he said, dazed.

'You're a white man,' Corith said. 'The dye has rubbed off where you got scratched.' Suddenly he seized hold of Parsons' arm and rubbed at his flesh. The dye, moistened, rubbed away, leaving a spot of grayish white. Letting go of his arm, he caught hold of the artificial hair braided into Parsons'; in an instant he had torn the artificial hair away. He sat holding it in his hand.

And then, without a word, he sprang at Parsons.

Now I see, Parsons thought. He tumbled back over the lip of the rock and down the cliff side. Snatching, scrabbling, he managed to catch hold; his body dragged agonizingly against the rock. And then, above him, Corith appeared. The massive body descending.

Parsons rolled away, trying to avoid him. *No*, he thought. *I don't want to.* The copper-colored hands closed around his throat, and he felt the man's knee dig into him . . .

Against him, Corith sagged. Blood gushed, staining the ground as it gurgled and became pools. Parsons, with a violent effort, managed to struggle out from beneath the man. He held, now, only one arrow. And he did not have to turn Corith over to see where the other was. As the man had dropped onto him, he had propped the arrow upright and it had gone into his heart.

I killed him, Parsons thought. By accident.

Above, on the edge of the cliff, Jepthe appeared. They'll know, he realized. In a moment. And when they find out—

Pressing against the cliff, he moved away from the dying man, crawling along the rock surface until he could no longer see either the woman or Corith. Then, step by step, he began ascending the cliff.

He reached the top. No one was in sight. They had gone down to Corith, but they would be back up immediately.

His mind empty, he ran from the cliff, toward the grove of trees. Presently he was out of sight among them. Safe, he thought. No one will know; now they won't know.

The mystery of his death. They will never find out.

I did not intend to, he thought, but that makes no real difference. No wonder Stenog laughed. He knew it was going to be I who killed Corith.

Stopping, he stood deep in frantic thought.

I can go back to Loris and Helmar, he decided. Tell them that I saw only what they saw: Corith on the cliff, going down, and then Corith die. No one else. Nobody came up the cliff from below. The only ones who came down were Jepthe and Nixina. I don't know any more than they do.

And Corith will never tell, because he is dead.

Hiding, he heard voices. He saw Nixina and Jepthe rushing through the trees, searching for their time ship, their faces blank with grief. Going to get the ship, put him into it, take him back and get him into cold-pack.

Corith is dead, but thirty-five years from now he will be brought back to life. I will do it. I will be there, in the Lodge, responsible for his rebirth.

He knew, now, why the second arrow had appeared in Corith's chest. Why he had not remained alive.

The first time, he had killed Corith by accident. But not the second time. That would be on purpose.

I must have come back, he realized, in one of the time ships. That night that I revived Corith, while he lay unconscious, recuperating. While I was with Loris, I was also downstairs with him.

But why with an arrow?

He looked down at his hand. He still clutched one arrow. Scrambling up the cliff, he had hung onto it. Why? he asked himself

Because the arrows saved my life. If I hadn't had them, Corith would have killed me. I was defending myself.

There had been no choice.

And yet, he felt dread, the horror of responsibility. He had been trapped, drawn into it against his will. Corith had leaped on him, and he had done nothing but struggle to protect himself.

What else could I have done? he asked himself. Surely it isn't my fault. But if not, then whose fault is it?

Who really was responsible for the crime? And it was a crime. Any killing is a crime. I'm a doctor, he said to himself. My job is to save human life. Especially this man's life.

But at the cost of my own? Because, when I revive him at the Lodge, he will point me out. And I will be helpless. Because I will not know; this has not happened to me yet.

15

Standing alone in the woods, Parsons thought, I am the man they are searching for. Thirty-five years.

The people at the Lodge would kill him at once, as soon as Corith indicted him. They would show no mercy – and why should they?

Had he, himself?

Perhaps he could break the sequence at some point. Catch myself before I come back here, he thought. Before I kill him the first time.

Above his head, a metallic object moved swiftly, leaving the woods and going to the cliff. The object dropped beyond the edge of the cliff; he heard its jets roaring as it stabilized itself near Corith. The old woman and her daughter had gone to collect the dying man.

In the vicinity, he realized, there were three other time ships; four, if Stenog's was included. This one had already gone into motion, but the others remained. Or did they?

I have to get to one of them, he thought. He began running aimlessly, in panic. But the ships from past time-segments – he could not approach them without disrupting history. That left only Stenog's ship, and the one that he had arrived here in. Could he go back and face Loris and the others? Knowing that he had killed Corith?

He had to.

Coming out on the cliff, he began running back the way he had originally come. As far as they're concerned, he told himself, this trip has simply been a failure. As before, no one has been able to make out what happened. I've given them no help. My plan was a failure. There is no choice but to give up and return to the future.

While he ran he saw, over the cliff, the tiny figures on the beach below. Stenog's men, at the boat.

The men, with their oars, were tracing huge letters in the sand. Parsons paused. And saw that the letters spelled out his name. Stenog was trying to signal him. With great speed, as if by some prearranged system, the men got their message completed as he stood gazing down.

PARSONS. THEY SAW, KNOW.

Warning him. That this time the trip had not been a total failure. So he could not go back after all.

Turning, he sprinted across the open space, back into the woods. Once they see me, he realized, they'll kill me. Or – his heart sank. They don't even have to do that. All they have to do is go back to the future without me. Leave me here.

But then I can go down to Stenog's ship, he realized.

Go down – and find himself in the hands of the government once more, to be shipped out to the prison colonies. Was that what he wanted? Was that better than remaining here, a cast-away? At least he would be free here; he could certainly contact

247

an Indian tribe in the area, survive with them . . . and, later on, when a ship from Europe arrived, he could go back with them. He racked his brains. What was the next contact between this region, Nova Albion, and the Old World? Something like 1595. A captain named Cermeno had wrecked – *would* wreck – his vessel off the entrance to the Estero. That was – sixteen years.

Sixteen years here, living on clams and deer, squatting around a fire, huddled in a tent made of animal hide, scratching at the soil for roots. This was the superlative culture that Corith wanted to preserve, in place of Elizabethan England.

Better, Parsons thought, to turn myself over to Stenog. He started back in the direction of the cliff.

Ahead of him, a figure emerged, stepped into his path. For one terrible instant he thought it was Corith. The powerful shoulders, the grim, rigid features, the sharp, hawklike nose . . .

It was Helmar. Corith's son.

Halting, Parsons faced him. Now Loris and Jepthe appeared.

By the expression on their faces, he saw that Stenog had not lied to him.

'He was on his way down to them,' Helmar said to Loris.

Loris, her face stark, said, 'You betrayed us.'

'No,' Parsons said. But he knew that it was pointless to try to talk to them.

'When did the idea come to you?' Loris said. 'Back at the Lodge? Did you get us to bring you here so you could do it? Or did the idea come to you when you saw him?'

Parsons said, 'The idea never came to me.'

'You intercepted him,' Loris said. 'You went down and talked to Drake – you conferred with him. We saw you. And then you came up the cliff and stopped Corith and murdered him. And then you were going back down to Drake, to go back with him. He warned you that we saw; he had his men write in the sand. So you knew you couldn't go back to us.'

To that, Parsons said nothing. He faced them silently.

Pointing his weapon at Parsons, Helmar said, 'We're going back to the time ship.'

'Why?' Parsons said. Why not kill me here? he wondered.

'Nixina has made the decision,' Loris said.

'What decision?'

Loris, in a choked, constricted voice, said, 'She thinks you didn't mean to do it. She says—' She broke off. 'If you had meant to do it, you would have brought some kind of weapon with you. She thinks you stopped Corith to argue with him, and that he wouldn't listen to you. And you fought each other, and in the fight Corith was stabbed.'

Parsons said, 'I warned him not to go down.' They were listening, at least for a moment. 'I told him,' he said, 'that it's not Drake down there. It's Stenog, waiting for him.'

After a pause, Loris said, 'And of course my father had never heard of Stenog. He didn't know what you meant.' Bitterly, her lips twisting, she said, 'And he saw the white showing on your arm. He knew you were a white man, and he didn't trust you; he wouldn't listen to you, and it cost him his life.'

'Yes,' Parsons said.

All of them were silent now.

'He was too suspicious,' Loris said at last. 'Unwilling to trust anyone. Nixina was right. You didn't mean to. It wasn't your fault. Any more than it was his.' She raised her dark, grief-stricken eyes. 'It *was* his fault in a sense. For being the way he was.'

'There's no use thinking about that now,' Jepthe said curtly.

'No,' Loris agreed. 'Well, there's nothing to do but go back. We failed.'

Helmar said, 'At least we know how it happened.' He eyed Parsons with scorn and loathing.

'We'll abide by Nixina's decision,' Jepthe said to him in a sharp, commanding voice.

'Yes,' Helmar said, still staring fixedly at Parsons.

Loris said, 'We'll—' She hesitated. 'Even if it was an accident,' she said woodenly, 'we feel that you should make some sort of atonement for it. We're going to leave you here. But not at this point in time.' Her voice grew fainter. 'A little further along.'

With comprehension, Parsons said, 'You mean after Drake's ship has left.'

Helmar said, 'You can spend your time trying to find that out.' With his weapon, he indicated that he wanted Parsons to come toward them.

Together, they walked back along the cliff, to the time ship. Sitting in front of the ship, in her special chair, Nixina waited for them unseeingly. Several of the Wolf Tribe stood around her.

When they reached her, Parsons stopped. 'I'm sorry,' he said.

The old woman's head moved slightly, but she said nothing.

'Your son wouldn't listen to me,' Parsons said.

After a time, Nixina said, 'You shouldn't have stopped him. You weren't worthy to stop him.'

Parsons thought, The blame has to be on me. For them to admit that Corith was responsible, through his fanaticism and paranoia – that would be too much for them. Psychologically, they could not stand it. So, he thought, I'm the scapegoat. I must be punished, as proof of my guilt.

Wordlessly, he entered the ship.

Trees.

He stood looking around him, trying to catch some indication of change. Blue sky, the distant boom of the surf . . .

All the same. Except—

As fast as possible, he made his way to the cliff. Below, the beach, sand, seaweed, the Pacific. Nothing else.

The careenage had ended. The *Golden Hind* had gone.

Or – had not yet come.

How could he tell? Marks in the sand? The remains of the wooden stakes to which the ropes had been tied? Some debris of some sort would remain . . .

But what did it matter?

Maybe, he thought, I can find some way of getting south, down into Mexico, Cortez . . . when he landed?

The best I can hope for is to reach a friendly Indian tribe. If I'm lucky I can either live with them or persuade them to help me get south. But I can't remember if there are Spanish settlements yet. And I don't know what year this is, so even if I remembered, it would not help me. They could have moved me back a century. Or even several centuries. Ocean, rocks, trees – those remain the same for a thousand years.

I may be standing here two hundred years before the first white man lands in the New World.

He thought, In fact *I* may be the first white man in the New World.

At least he could go down to the beach and see. If there were any debris left from the *Golden Hind*, it would prove that they had not moved him back in time. And that would be something. A faint hope – the Spanish colonies to the south. And then a ship back to Europe.

Once again, he began the slow, dangerous descent to the beach.

For an hour he searched up and down the beach, seeing no sign of the ship or the men ever having been there. No marks, no refuse. What about the brass plate? he asked himself. Where had Drake actually left it? Lying in the sand? Buried in the face of the cliff? He searched for that, but by now he had covered so much of the beach that he no longer had a central point from which to work. Possibly he had wandered a mile or so from his original spot. The beach all looked alike, now; cliff and sand and seaweed . . .

Suddenly he stopped in his tracks. *If he was stranded here, how did he manage to get back to the Wolf Lodge to kill Corith a second time?* All this had no importance; obviously he did get back to the Lodge. If not, then he would be removed from this place anyhow, by the new time-sequence set up by his failure to reach the recuperating Corith. And the only way he could get back to the Wolf Lodge was by means of a time ship. Obviously, someone came back to get him – would come back.

But how soon? He could spend years here, decades, become an old man, and then, after all that, one of them could return in a time ship and pick him up. Near the end of his life.

For instance, he might, over a period of years, work his way south to a Spanish settlement, and then back to Spain, up to England, where he would manage to make contact with Stenog. Eventually, in that manner, he could regain access to the future . . . a worn-out, fever-ravaged old man whose life was over. A man who had wandered the face of the globe, who had used up his life.

And of course it was always possible that someone else killed Corith the second time.

He noticed, now, that the day was ending. The air had become cold and the sun had moved to the edge of the sky. A few gulls flapped by overhead; their mournful cry, like the rubbing of ropes, made the scene even more lonely.

Night would come on soon. What would he do? He couldn't spend the night on the beach. Better to trudge back up and start inland, back across the peninsula; as he recalled, there had been Indian settlements on the inner bay, Tomales Bay, where it was more sheltered.

Standing on the beach, looking up at the cliff, he did not see a way to ascend; he would have to go along the beach, searching for one of the declivities, or a spot where trees and shrubs had grown. But he was too tired. I'll have to wait until tomorrow, he decided. He seated himself on a log that had been washed up on the beach, unlaced his moccasins, and rested his head on his arms. Closing his eyes, he listened to the surf and the croaking gulls. The inhuman, inhospitable sound . . . how many millions of years, more or less, had this sound gone on? Long before there had been any men. And long after.

He thought. It would be so easy to walk out into the water and not come back. Simply start walking.

The chill wind blew about him; he shivered. How long could he sit here? Not much longer. Opening his eyes he saw that it had become appreciably darker; the sun had now disappeared. Far off, a flight of birds disappeared beyond the hills to the north.

Like children, he thought. Punishing me by exiling me here. Unable to bear the blame themselves. And yet, in a sense, they were right. I should bear the blame; I was the agent responsible for his death. And if I had a chance to kill him again, I would. I wish to God I had that chance, he thought. He got up from the log and began walking along aimlessly, kicking at shells on the sand ahead of him.

A large rock crashed noisily down the cliff side; involuntarily, he jumped away. The rock rolled out onto the beach, along with a shower of smaller stones. Shading his eyes, he peered up.

A figure stood at the top of the cliff, waving to him. The figure cupped its hands to its mouth and called something, but the boom of the surf blotted it out. He saw only the outline of the figure; he could not tell if it was a man or a woman or what it wore. At once he began frantically waving back.

'Help!' he shouted. He ran toward the cliff, indicating that he could not climb up. Now he scampered along, half-falling, trying to find a way up.

Above him, the figure made motions that he could not grasp. He halted, panting for breath, trying to make out what it was telling him. Then the figure abruptly disappeared. One moment it was there; the next it was gone. He blinked in bewilderment, feeling slow terror creep over him. The person had turned away from the cliff and gone off.

Frozen with disbelief, he remained where he was, unable to stir. And, while he stood there, a metallic sphere rose from the top of the cliff and rapidly floated down to the beach.

The time ship landed on the sand ahead of him. Who would come out? He waited, his heart laboring.

The door opened and Loris appeared. She did not wear the Indian costume now; she had changed back to the gray robe of the Wolves. Her face had lost most of its shock and grief; he realized that for her considerable time had passed.

'Hello, Doctor,' she said.

He could only gaze mutely at her.

'I came back for you,' she said. She added, 'It's a month or so later. I'm sorry it took so long. How long has it been for you? You haven't got any beard, and your clothes look about the same . . . I hope it's the same day.'

'Yes,' he said, hearing his voice grate out harshly.

'Come on,' she said, beckoning him toward her. 'Get in. I'll take you back, Doctor. To your own time. To your wife.' She smiled at him, a forced smile. 'You don't deserve to be left here.' She added, 'Nobody from your civilization would ever find you here. Helmar saw to that. This is 1597. No one will come here for a long, long time.'

Trembling, he stepped into the time ship.

After she had closed the door behind him, he said, 'What made you change your mind?'

Loris said, 'You'll find out some day. It has to do with something that you and I did together. Something that didn't seem

253

important at the time.' Again she smiled at him, but this time it was an enigmatic, almost caressing smile on her full, dark lips.

'I appreciate it,' he said.

'Do you want me to take you directly back?' she asked, as he began to operate the controls. 'Or is there anything from our period that you need? I have your instrument case here.' She pointed, and he saw, on the floor of the time ship, his familiar gray case.

With difficulty, he said, 'I'd like to go back to the Lodge for a little while. To get cleaned up. Change my clothes, rest. I don't want to return to my family this way.' He indicated the ragged fur costume, the remains of the dye. 'They'll think it's a wild man escaped from the zoo.'

'Of course,' Loris said, in the formal, civil way that he had become familiar with. The aristocratic politeness. 'We'll go back to my time; you'll be given whatever you need. Of course, you'll have to stay out of sight. No one else must see you. But you understand that. I'll take you directly to my apartment.'

'Fine,' he said. And he thought with a rush of misery, It's her father that I'm going back for. To complete what I have to do. How will she feel if she ever finds out? Maybe she never will. If I can get use of the time machine for even a second . . .

She saved me, he thought, so that I can murder her father. For the second time.

Silently, he sat watching her manipulate the controls.

16

The time ship came to rest in an enclosed courtyard paved with cobblestones. Parsons, as he stepped from the ship, saw the iron railings of vaulted balconies, damp foliage of plants, and then Loris led him through a doorway and along a deserted corridor.

'This part of the Lodge,' she said over her shoulder to him, 'is mine. So you don't need to worry; no one will interfere with us.'

Soon he lay in a bathtub of hot water, his head against the porcelain side, eyes shut, enjoying the smell of soap and the peace and silence of the room.

Almost at once the door opened and Loris entered with an armload of washcloths and towels. 'Sorry to bother you,' she said, folding a fluffy white bathtowel over a rack on the wall.

He did not answer. He did not even open his eyes.

'You're tired,' she said. Lingering, she said, 'I know now why none of our signal markers reached you.'

At that, he opened his eyes.

'That first trip you took,' she said. 'To the far future. When you didn't know how to operate the ship.'

'What happened to the markers?'

She said, 'Helmar destroyed them.'

'Why?' he said, wide awake.

Brushing her long black hair from her eyes she said calmly, 'We sought any possible way to break the chain at some point. You understand – very few of us have any well-disposed feelings toward you.' She hesitated, considering him as he lay in the tub. 'Odd,' she said, 'to have you back here. You're going to spend the night with me, aren't you?'

He said, 'So Helmar did what he could to leave me trapped in the future.' He thought, It was not bad enough for me, back in the past, in Nova Albion. Recalling the desolate plains of the future, his body and mind recoiled. And they had done their best. If it had not been for the plaque . . . Abruptly he said, 'And he tried to find the granite plaque, too?'

'He searched,' Loris said. 'But he failed to find it. There was some doubt in our minds – quite a bit in Helmar's – that there ever was any plaque. All the signal markers were located; there was no real trouble in doing that, since we knew exactly where they were, and how many we had sent out. Helmar returned, but it made no difference. My father—' She shrugged, her arms folded. 'It had no effect on him.'

After his bath, he dried himself. He shaved, and then, putting on a silk robe that Loris had presented to him, came out of the bathroom.

On a chair in the corner of the bedroom, Loris sat curled up, her feet bare; she wore Chinese coolie trousers and a white cotton shirt. On her wrists were heavy silver bracelets. And she had tied her hair back in a pony tail. She seemed pensive and taciturn.

'What is it?' he said.

She glanced up. 'I'll be sorry to see you go. I wish—' All at once she slid from the chair and paced about the room, her fingers stuck in the side pockets of her light blue trousers. 'I want to tell you something, Doctor. But I shouldn't. Maybe some day.' Turning swiftly, she said, 'I think a great deal of you. You're a fine person.'

He thought, She is making it hard for me. Excruciatingly hard. I wonder if I can do it. But there is no alternative that I know of.

His clothes had been carefully put up on a shelf of the closet. Now he got them down.

'What are you going to do?' Loris said, watching him. 'Aren't you going to bed?' She showed him the pajamas that she had for him.

'No,' he said, 'I want to be up awhile.'

After he had dressed he stood indecisively at the door of the apartment.

'You're so tense,' Loris said. 'Does it frighten you to be here, in the Lodge? You're not afraid Helmar will come bursting in, are you?' Going past him – he smelled the warm fragrance of her hair – she bolted the door to the outer hall. 'Nobody can come in here; this is sacred. The queen's bedroom.' She smiled, showing her regular, white teeth. 'Enjoy yourself,' she said gently, putting her hand on his arm. 'This will be your last time, my dear.' Leaning forward, she kissed him on the mouth with great tenderness.

'I'm sorry,' he said. And unbolted the door.

'Where are you going?' Now her face filled with wariness. 'You're going to do something. What is it?' At once she slipped by him, catlike, barring his passage. Her eyes glowing, she said, 'I won't let you go. You want to get revenge on Helmar, do you? Is that it?' She studied him. 'No, that's not it. But what can it be?'

Putting his hands on her shoulders, he moved her aside. Her powerful, healthy body resisted; for a moment she tugged at his hands, and then suddenly, on her face, comprehension appeared.

'Oh God,' she whispered. The color left her face; the burnished red faded, and he saw, for an instant, the haggard, desolate face of an old woman. 'Doctor,' she said. 'Please don't.'

He started to open the door.

At once she was on him. Her fingers raked at his face, tearing at his flesh, clawing at his eyes. His arms came up instinctively and he flung her backward; she clung to him, pulling him down, dragging at him with the strength and weight of her body. Her white teeth flashed; she bit him frenziedly on the neck. With his other arm he struck her across the face and she dropped away, gasping hoarsely.

Rapidly, he stepped out of the apartment, into the hall.

'Stop,' she snarled, coming after him. From her shirt she tugged something, a slender metal tube; he saw it, and then he lashed out. His fist caught her on the side of the jaw, but she avoided the force of the blow; her eyes glazed with pain, but she did not fall. The tube wavered, and he grabbed at it. Instantly she yanked back, away from him; he saw the tube pointed at him, and the look on her face. The suffering. Raising her hand, drawing it back, she flung the tube at him, sobbing.

The tube fell to the floor near his feet and rolled away.

'Goddamn you,' she moaned, covering her face with her hands. She turned away, her back to him; he saw the convulsions that racked her. 'Go on,' she cried, again turning toward him, tears spilling down her cheeks.

Swiftly, he ran down the hall, the way they had come. He came out onto the darkened courtyard. There, dimly, he saw the outline of the metal ship. As quickly as possible he entered it, slammed and locked the door.

Could he operate it? Seating himself, he inspected the dials. Then, summoning his memory, he clicked on a toggle switch.

The machinery hummed. Dials swung to register.

He closed a switch and then, hesitating, pressed a button.

A dial showed that he had gone back half an hour in time. That gave him half an hour to make a thorough study of the dials, to recover his earlier knowledge.

Calming himself, he began his scrutiny.

At a period of one day and a half in the past, he stopped the mechanism. With caution, he unlocked the door of the ship and swung it open.

No one was in sight.

257

Stepping out, he made his way across the courtyard. He swung up onto a balcony and stood, pondering.

First, he had to get one of Corith's arrows.

Down beneath the ground, in the first subsurface level, he would find the workroom in which Corith had constructed his costume. But did the arrows still exist there? A few were far back in the past, at Nova Albion. One, which he had pulled from Corith's chest, was here somewhere in the Lodge, unless it had been destroyed.

Did Corith die the second time from the *same* arrow?

Now he remembered. That arrow had been disassembled; he had removed the flint head, the feathers, to analyse them. So his second death could not have come from that arrow; it had to be one of the others. And that second arrow was not, like the first, removed. At least, not to his knowledge.

The time was evidently quite late at night. Almost morning. The halls, artificially lighted, seemed deserted.

With infinite caution, he made his way down to the first subsurface level.

For an hour he searched in vain for one of Corith's arrows. At last he gave up. Now the clocks on the walls of the various chambers read five-thirty; the Lodge would soon be awake.

He had no choice but to go back into the past for the arrow.

Returning to the time ship, he locked himself inside and again seated himself at the controls.

This time he sent himself and the ship back thirty-five years. Before Loris' birth. Before either she or Helmar existed. And, he hoped, before Corith left for his ill-fated encounter in the far past.

Again, he had arrived late at night. He had no difficulty locating the Lodge's subsurface work area of that period, its machine shops. But Corith's workroom was, of course, securely locked. It took skillful use of the time ship before he located a moment at which he could enter. But he at last found such a moment. The door of the workroom hung open, and no one was inside. In need of a particular tool, Corith had gone off; he caught a glimpse of the man leaving, and an inspection of the near future showed that he would not return for at least two hours.

Entering, he found half-finished costumes here and there, and, on a work bench, the buffalo head. Pigments, photographs of the Indian tribes of the past – he roamed about, examining everything. There, by a lathe, he found three arrows. Only one had its flint head in place. With an odd feeling he picked up a chisel that Corith had been using. And here was the raw flint, too. He noticed the textbook on Stone Age artifacts that Corith had employed as his guide; the heavy book was propped up against the wall, held open with a block of wood.

The book – written in English – had been pilfered from the library of the University of California. It was due back on March 12, 1938, and after that the borrower would be fined.

Instead of the one finished arrow, he selected one in process, reasoning that Corith would not as readily notice its absence. By scrutinizing the book and the finished arrows, he was able to see how the flint and the feathers were secured in place.

Seating himself at the bench, he finished making the arrow. It took him well over an hour. I wonder if I've done as good a job as Corith, he asked himself.

Taking his completed arrow, he cautiously left the workroom and made his way from the subsurface level, up the ramp and along the corridors, to the time ship. Again, no one saw him; he reached the ship safely and re-entered.

And now, he thought, there is nothing more. Only the act itself. Can I do it? I have to, he realized.

I already have done it.

With precision, he selected the exact time, the period in which Corith lay recuperating from the operation which Parsons himself had performed. Again and again, he checked the settings on his dials. If he made an error at this point . . .

But he knew, with leaden hopelessness, that he would not – had not – made an error.

Wrapping the arrow, he placed it inside his shirt.

This trip he had to move in space as well as time. The room in which Corith lay was well guarded; he could not get in without being noticed and recognized. Of course, the guards would admit him, but later they would remember. He had to emerge within the room itself, close by the patient's bed.

Now, with equal precision, he began setting the controls that would relocate the ship in space. A nexus of the two, time and space, a point on the graph . . .

The control board hummed. Dials registered. And then the self-regulating banks of equipment clicked off. The trip had ended; according to the indicators, he had arrived.

At once he flung open the door of the time ship.

A room, familiar, with white walls. To his left, a bed on which lay a man, a dark-faced man with powerful features, eyes shut.

He had succeeded!

Going to the bed, Parsons bent down. He had only seconds; he could not pause. Now he brought out the arrow and stripped the wrappings from it.

On the bed, the man breathed shallowly. His large, strong hands lay at his sides, copper against the white of the sheets. His thick black hair spilled down over the pillow.

Again, Parsons thought. As if once was not enough, for both of us. Shaking, he raised the arrow back, gripping its shaft with both hands. Can I penetrate the ribs this way? he asked himself. Yes. The soft, vulnerable area around the heart . . . he had laid it open in order to perform the operation.

Good God, he realized with horror. He had to drive the arrow into that spot, into the newly-stitched tissue that he had only a short while ago repaired. The sardonic irony . . .

Below him, Corith's eyes fluttered. His breathing changed. And, as Parsons stood holding the arrow, Corith opened his eyes.

He gazed up at Parsons. The eyes, empty, saw nothing at first. And then, imperceptibly, consciousness came. The slack lines of the man's tired face altered, gained force.

Parsons started to bring the arrow down. But his hand wobbled; he had to draw the arrow back once again, to start over.

Now the dark eyes fixed themselves on him. The man's mouth opened; the lips drew back as Corith tried to speak.

After thirty-five years, Parsons thought. To come back to life, for this.

Corith lifted his hand from the sheet, raising it an inch and then letting it fall back. 'You, once more . . .' Corith whispered.

'I'm sorry,' Parsons said.

There was comprehension in the dark eyes. He seemed aware of the arrow. Again he put up his hand, as if reaching for it. But he did not take his eyes from Parsons. Faintly, he said, 'You've been against me . . . from the start.' The frail chest heaved beneath the sheet. 'Spying on me as I worked . . . lying to me . . . pretending to be on my side.' Now the weak, trembling hands touched the arrow, and then fell away. Consciousness ebbed; he gazed at Parsons wonderingly, with the vacant, troubled gaze of a child.

I can't do it, Parsons realized.

My entire life, everything that I've ever been and stand for, prohibits me. Even if it means my own death; even though, when this man awakens, he will name me, point me out, get his fanatic, paranoid revenge. Parsons lowered the arrow, and then dropped it to the floor, away from the bed.

He felt utter, numbing fear. And defeat.

So now this man can go on, he thought. Standing by the bed, looking down at Corith, he thought, There is nothing to stop him. A madman. He will destroy me first, and then go on to the rest of his 'enemies.' But I still can't do it.

Turning from the bed, he walked unsteadily back to the time ship, entered, and bolted the door after him. But there's no safety in here, he realized. Snapping on the bank of controls, he moved the ship ahead in time two hours. Two hours or two thousand years; it made no difference. Not with Corith alive. Not for that other, earlier Parsons, sitting with Loris, waiting for his patient to regain consciousness.

Now the past can unravel. Now the new chain of cause and effect can begin. Starting from that moment, at the bed, when I failed to drive the arrow into the man's chest. When I let him live. A whole new world, built up from that moment on. Unwinding, carrying itself forward with its own dynamic force.

Shutting off the controls of the time ship, he stood hesitantly at the door. Shall I see? he asked himself. Corith regaining consciousness, his wife and son and daughter and mother around him . . . and myself there, too. All of us pleased. Gratified. Bending to hear his every word.

Can I watch?

Strange . . . that he was still here. He had expected the change to set in at once, as soon as he moved away from the bed.

Now he had to look – without delay.

Tearing open the door of the time ship, he peered out at a scene that he had lived through once before. People at the bedside, their backs to him, paying no attention to him. The elaborate machinery of the Lodge's soul cube, the pumps that activated the cold-pack. Already, they had gotten Corith back into the cold-pack; he saw their grief-stricken faces, and then the man himself, drifting in the familiar medium.

The arrow, as before, projected from his chest.

Instantly, Parsons slammed the door of the time ship; he punched dials and sent the ship randomly into time, away from the scene. Had they noticed him? Evidently not; the room had been chaotic with activity, men coming and leaving, and himself – he had seen himself standing by the soul cube with Loris, both of them lost in the shock of the moment. Neither of them able to understand or explain – or even accept – what had happened.

He felt that way now.

Shaken, he sat at the controls. So it was not I, he realized. I didn't kill him. Someone else did, the second time.

But who?

He had to go back. To see. After he had left the room, gone back into his time ship, someone else had arrived. Loris? But she had been with him during that period, they had been together when Helmar brought the news. Helmar?

If Corith returned to life, Helmar would be supplanted. For the first time in his life. His potent father, returning . . . and Corith would easily dominate the Wolf Tribe; Helmar would shrink to nothing. Or—

Step by step, he began methodically setting the controls of the time ship.

Who would he see when he opened the door? He steeled himself against the sight. Calculating down to seconds, he brought the ship to a point in time immediately following the moment at which he had left. There would be no gaps; he would be present during the whole sequence. It must have happened almost at once, he decided. As soon as I left, someone else came in. Someone opened the door of the room and slipped inside. Possibly they saw me; he or she was waiting for me to leave.

Throwing the controls to *off*, he jumped to his feet, ran to the door of the ship and opened it, looked out into the room.

At the bed two figures stood. A man and a woman, bending over the prone figure of Corith. The man's arm flashed up; it came down, and the act had been accomplished. Swiftly, the man and the woman retreated from the bed, silently, already in flight. They wasted no time; their movements were expert and orderly. Obviously, every step had been well planned long in advance. Their tense, strained faces confronted him as they turned.

He had never seen either of them before. Both the man and the woman were total strangers to him.

They were young. No more than eighteen or nineteen, with firm, smooth faces, skin almost as light as his own. The woman's hair was wheat-colored, her eyes blue. The man, somewhat darker, had heavier brows and almost black hair. But both of them had the same finely-made cheek bones and molded jaw-lines; he saw the resemblance between them. The spark, the alertness and clarity, in their gaze. The high order of intelligence.

The woman – or girl – reminded him of Loris. She had Loris' carriage, her well-made shoulders and hips. And the man also had familiar lines in his body.

'Hello,' the girl said.

Both of them wore the gray robes of the Wolf Tribe. But not the emblem. On their breasts a new emblem stood out: crossed snakes twining up a staff topped by open wings. The caduceus. The ancient sign of the medical profession.

The boy said, 'Doctor, we should get out of here at once. Will you let my sister go in your ship?' He pointed, and Parsons saw, beside his own ship, a second identical metallic sphere with its door hanging open. 'We'll meet ahead in time; Grace knows the point.' He smiled briefly at Parsons as he raced past him and into his own ship. The door shut and the ship at once vanished.

'Please, Doctor,' the girl said, touching his arm. 'Will you let

263

me operate the controls? I can do it more quickly, rather than telling you—' She had already started into his ship; he followed mutely, letting her shut the door after them.

After a pause, Parsons said, 'How is your mother?'

'You'll be seeing her,' the girl said. 'She's fine.'

Parsons said, 'You're Loris' children. From the future.'

'Your children, too,' the girl said. 'Your son and daughter.'

17

As the time ship moved into the future, Parsons understood at last why Loris had changed her mind. Why she had returned to Nova Albion for him, knowing that he had killed her father.

In the month that had followed, she had discovered that she was pregnant. Possibly she had even gone ahead into the future and seen their children. In any case, she had let the children be born; she had not had the zygotes removed and put covertly into the great Soul Cube, to merge with the hundreds of millions already there.

Realizing that, he felt a profound, humble emotion toward her, and, at the same time, pride.

'What's your brother's name?' he asked the girl. His daughter, he realized with a further deepening of emotion.

Grace said, 'Nathan. She – our mother – wanted us to have names that you would approve of.' She lifted her head and studied him. 'Do you think we look like you? Would you have recognized us?'

'I don't know,' he said. He was too overcome to think about it right now.

'We knew you,' Grace said. 'But of course we expected to see you; we knew that you came there, to do what had to be done. And we knew that you were unable to go through with it.'

And so, he thought, you came back and did it for me. Both of you. Aloud, he said, 'How does your mother feel about what you did?'

'She understands that it's necessary. It would not have worked out, for her to have children by Corith. There was already too much interbreeding. She was aware of that, even in your time. But there did not seem to be any alternative, and the old lady – our great grandmother, Nixina – would not permit anything else. Of course in our time she's long since dead.'

Parsons said, 'Tell me why you have the caduceus emblem on your clothing.'

'I'd rather wait,' she said. 'Until we get back. So we can all be there, my mother and my brother and you and I.'

He thought, The family in its entirety.

'She told you about me?' he asked the girl.

'Oh, yes,' she said. 'All about you. We've waited a long time to see you face-to-face.' Her even white teeth flashed as she smiled at him. Exactly as Loris had smiled at him, he thought.

History repeats itself, he thought. And this woman waiting year after year, all her life, until this moment: seeing her father for the first time. But, in contrast to Corith, I was not entombed in a transparent cube.

As he and his daughter stepped from the time ship, Loris came to meet them. Gray-haired, a handsome middle-aged woman . . . in her late fifties, he realized. Still the strong face, the erect posture. Her hand came out, and he saw the pleasure in her eyes, her dark, full eyes.

'The last time I saw you,' she said huskily, 'I cursed you. I'm sorry, Jim.'

'I couldn't bring myself to do it,' he said. 'I got there, but that was all.' He became silent again.

'For me, that was a long time ago,' Loris said. 'What do you think of our children?' She drew Grace over to her, and now, from the other ship, Nathan appeared. 'They're almost nineteen,' she said. 'Don't they look healthy and sound?'

'Yes,' he agreed tightly, surveying the three of them. This is so much like *his* situation, he thought. If he had returned to life. His wife much older, his two children – which he did not even know he had. He said, 'The combination of my racial heritage and yours make an attractive amalgam.'

'The union of the opposites,' Loris said. 'Come along, so we can sit down and talk. You can stay awhile, can't you? Before you go back to your own time?'

To my wife, he thought. How hard it is to reconcile that with this. With what I see here.

The Wolf Lodge did not seem to have changed in appearance in twenty years. The same dark, massive, aged beams. The wide stairs. The stone walls that had impressed him so much. This building would continue to stand a long, long time. The grounds, too, remained the same. The lawns and trees, the flower beds.

'Stenog remained in Drake's place for ten years or so,' Loris said. 'In case my father made a second try. Stenog had no way of telling what our circumstances were. He believed that Corith could still make an assassination attempt, but of course my father has been buried now for almost the full twenty years. We did not make any more attempts to revive him. Nixina died soon after our return from Nova Albion, and without her, much of the impetus dwindled away.'

The power behind it all, Parsons thought. The savage, relentless schemes of a dried-up little old lady, who imagined herself as the protagonist of an ancient race reborn.

Loris said, 'It was a fatal blow to us to discover that the man whom we had selected as the epitome of the conquering whites was actually a man from our own times. Born in our culture, adhering to its values. Stenog went back into time to protect our culture. That is, the aspect of our culture that he had taken the job of supporting. Our tribe, as you know, does not follow their system of birth or death.' She added, 'I have something to tell you about that, Jim.'

Later, the four of them sat drinking coffee and facing one another.

'What is the caduceus?' Parsons asked. By now, he had begun to get an inkling.

His daughter said, 'We're following in your footsteps, sir.'

'That's right,' Nathan said with agitation. 'It's still illegal, but not for long – in another ten years we know it'll be accepted. We've looked ahead.' His young face gleamed with pride and determination. Parsons saw some of the family's fanaticism, the desire to prevail at all costs. But in this boy, there was a fuller grasp on reality. He and his sister were not so far removed from the world as it actually was; the near-paranoid dreams were gone.

At least he hoped they were gone. Shifting his gaze, he studied Loris. The older Loris.

Can she manage them? he wondered. The image of the boy and girl at Corith's bedside remained in his mind. The swift act, completed in a matter of seconds; he had not been able to do it, and so they had, in his place. Because they believed that it had to be done. Possibly they were right. But—

'I'd like to know about your illegal group,' he said, indicating the caducei.

With enthusiasm, the boy and girl spilled out their accounts, interrupting each other in their eagerness. Loris, silent, watched them with an expression that Parsons could not read.

They had, they told him, about a hundred and forty members in their profession (as they called it). Several had been caught by the government and exiled to the Martian prison colonies. The group distributed inflammatory propaganda, demanding the end of the euthanors and the resumption of natural birth – at the very least, the freedom of women to conceive and give birth, or to turn their zygote over to the Soul Cube if they preferred. The element of *choice*. And, as an essential, the end of enforced sterilization for the young men.

Breaking into her children's account, Loris said, 'You understand that I'm still Mother Superior. I've been able to get a small number of males out of the hands of the sterilization agency . . . not many, but enough to give us hope.'

Parsons thought, Maybe they have to be fanatics. In a world like this, where they're fighting compulsory sterilization, exile to prison camps without trial, vicious *shupos*. And, underneath it all, the ethos of death. A system devoted to the extinction of the individual, for the sake of the future.

Whatever virtues it might have, whatever good aspects—

'I guess there's no chance that you could stay here,' Grace said. 'With mother and us.'

Awkwardly, Parsons said, 'I don't know if you know it, but in my own time I have a wife.' He felt his face flush, but neither of the children seemed embarrassed or surprised.

'We know,' Nathan said. 'We've gone back several times to have a look at you. Mother took us back when we were younger; we persuaded her to. Your wife seems very nice.'

Loris said, in a practical tone, 'Let's be realistic. Jim, at this point, is twenty years my junior.' But something in her eyes, a certitude, made Parsons wonder what she was thinking.

Does she know something important about me? he asked himself. Something that I have no way of knowing? They have use of their time-travel equipment for any purpose that they want.

In a low voice, Loris said, 'I know what makes you look so worried, Jim. You saw them kill my father. I want to tell you why they did it. You're afraid it's the maniacal fanaticism of the family showing itself in one more generation. You're wrong. They killed Corith to save your life. If he had lived, he would have had you destroyed; I knew it, and so did the children. They saw you unable to do it, and they admire you more. It was the highest morality possible. But your life is worth too much to them to let anything happen to you. Their whole outlook is based on what I've told them about you, and what they've seen for themselves. You, with your system of values, your humane ethics, your sense of others, have formed them. And, through their profession, you will alter this society. Even if you yourself are not here.'

None of them spoke, for a time.

'You were a powerful and unanswerable lesson for this society,' Loris said.

To that, Parsons could say nothing.

Loris said, 'And so was your profession.'

'Thanks,' he said finally.

The three of them smiled at him with great tenderness. And with love. My family, he said to himself. And, in these children, the best of both of us, of Loris and me.

'Do you want to go back to your own time now?' Loris said, in her considerate, mature manner.

He nodded. 'I suppose I should.'

Disappointment, crushing and bleak, appeared on the children's faces. But they said nothing. They accepted it.

Later on, Loris sent both Grace and Nathan off, so she and Parsons could be alone for a time.

'Will I ever be back here?' he asked her bluntly.

With composure, she said, 'I won't tell you.'

'But you know.'

'Yes,' she said.

'Why won't you tell me?'

'I don't want to rob you of the power of choosing for yourself. If I tell you, it will seem determined. Out of your hands. But of course, it would still be your choice – as it was your choice not to kill my father.'

'Do you believe that choice actually exists? That it's not an illusion?'

She said, 'I believe it's authentic.'

He let it go at that.

'In one matter, however,' she continued, 'you have no choice. You know about that – what remains to be done. Of course, you can do it here as well as back in your own time.'

'Yes,' he said. 'But I'd rather do it back there.'

Rising, Loris said, 'I'll take you back. Do you want to see the children again before you go?'

He hesitated, considering. 'No,' he decided. 'I feel that I have to go back. And if I see them again, I probably won't.'

Matter-of-factly, Loris said, 'We've been without you for their lifetime. But for you, only an hour or so passed. If you decide to come back to us, it will follow a twenty year period for you. But—' She smiled. 'For us, it will probably be during the next few days. You see?'

'You won't have to wait,' he said.

Loris nodded.

'How strange,' he said. 'Having two families, at different periods in history.'

'Do you consider that you have two? I see only one. Here, with the children. You have a wife back in your own time, but no family.' Her eyes flared with the familiar determination.

Parsons said, 'You would be a difficult person to live with.' He spoke half-jokingly, but with more than a little seriousness.

'This is a difficult period in time,' Loris said.

He could hardly argue with that.

As they walked toward the time ship, Loris said, 'Would you be afraid of the problems here? No, I know you wouldn't. There's no fear on your part. You would be a lot of help to us.'

At the ship, as he shut the door after them, he said, 'What about Helmar? Is he still around?'

Loris said, 'He went over to the government, to join them.'

That did not surprise him. 'And Jepthe?'

'She's with us here. But in retirement. She's gotten quite feeble; in her old age she has none of Nixina's strength.'

Presently she switched on the controls. He was on his way back, at last, to his own time.

'I'm afraid your car was wrecked,' Loris said. 'When the dredge picked you up. We hadn't had the experience we needed then.'

He said, 'That's all right. I have insurance.'

Once more, the highway with its educational signs. Cars moving toward San Francisco, and, on the other side, the traffic on its way to Los Angeles. He stood uncertainly on the shoulder of the road, smelling the oleander that the public roads department had planted, miles of it between the two strips. Then he began to walk.

Trudging along, wondering if any of the cars would stop – it meant unhooking from the automatic beam – he considered the work that lay ahead of him. He did not have to undertake it at once; in fact, he had years to accomplish it. Most of his lifetime.

He thought of his house, Mary standing on the front porch as he had last seen her. Image of her waving, pert and fresh in her green slacks . . . hair shining in the early-morning sunlight as he set off to his office.

How will I feel when I see her? he asked himself.

I wonder how soon I'll be going back into the future. A method of communicating with Loris had been arranged between them. How easy it would be . . .

A car slowed, left the lane, and coasted to a halt on the shoulder. 'Engine trouble?' the driver called to him.

'Yes,' he said. 'I'd appreciate a ride into San Francisco.'

A moment later he had gotten in; the car started up and rejoined the beam.

'Strange looking outfit you have on,' the driver remarked politely, but with curiosity.

Parsons realized that he had come back to his time wearing clothes from another world entirely. And he had left his gray instrument case somewhere. This time it really was lost.

The ring of industrial installations around San Francisco appeared ahead. He watched the factories, tracks, towers and sheds go by beneath the highway.

I wonder where I can get the materials, he said to himself. And where it should be placed. But evidently the placing was not a problem; he had found it, and that was what mattered. Can I do the work myself? he wondered. He had never done anything with stone before. Of course, the inscription itself was cut directly into the metal. Probably, after practice, he could manage it; he would not have to hire the job out.

If I can, he decided, I want to do it myself. To be sure there is no slip-up. After all, my life depends on it.

It would be interesting to see the plaque come into existence, here in his own time. Contrast to the eroded, damaged monument that had greeted him in the future, countless centuries hence . . .

But a job well done. And it had outlasted all his other acts in this world.

Maybe it should be buried, he decided. Sunk deep into the earth, out of sight. After all, it won't be needed for a long, long time.

VULCAN'S
HAMMER

1

Arthur Pitt was conscious of the mob as soon as he left the Unity office and started across the street. He stopped at the corner by his car and lit a cigarette. Unlocking the car, he studied the mob, holding his brief case tightly.

There were fifty or sixty of them: people of the town, workers and small businessmen, petty clerks with steel-rimmed glasses. Mechanics and truckdrivers, farmers, housewives, a white-aproned grocer. The usual – lower middle-class always the same.

Pitt slid into his car, and snapping on the dashboard mike, called his highest ranking superior, the South American Director. They were moving fast, now, filling up the street and surging silently toward him. They had, no doubt, identified him by his T-class clothes – white shirt and tie, gray suit, felt hat. Brief case. The shine of his black shoes. The pencil beam gleaming in the breast pocket of his coat. He unclipped the gold tube and held it ready. '*Emergency,*' he said.

'Director Taubmann here,' the dashboard speaker said. 'Where are you?' The remote, official voice, so far up above him.

'Still in Cedar Groves, Alabama. There's a mob forming around me. I suppose they have the roads blocked. Looks like the whole town.'

'Any Healers?'

Off to one side, on the curb, stood an old man with a massive head and short-cropped hair. Standing quietly in his drab brown robe, a knotted rope around his waist, sandals on his feet. 'One,' Pitt said.

'Try to get a scan for Vulcan 3.'

'I'll try.' The mob was all around the car now. Pitt could hear their hands, plucking and feeling at the car, exploring it carefully and with calm efficiency. He leaned back and double-locked the doors. The windows were rolled up; the hood was down tight. He snapped on the motor which activated the defense assembly built into the car. Beneath and around him the system hummed as its feedback elements searched for any weak links in the car's armor.

On the curb, the man in brown had not moved. He stood with a few others, people in ordinary street clothing. Pitt pulled the scanner out and lifted it up.

A rock at once hit the side of the car, below the window. The car shuddered; in his hands the scanner danced. A second rock hit directly against the window, sending a web of cracks rippling across it.

Pitt dropped the scanner. 'I'm going to need help. They mean business.'

'There's a crew already on the way. Try to get a better scan of him. We didn't get it well.'

'Of course you didn't,' Pitt said with anger. 'They saw the thing in my hand and they deliberately let those rocks fly.' One of the rear windows had cracked; hands groped blindly into the car. 'I've got to get out of here, Taubmann.' Pitt grinned bleakly as he saw, out of the corner of his eye, the car's assembly attempting to repair the broken window – attempting and failing. As new plastiglass foamed up, the alien hands grasped and wadded it aside.

'Don't get panicky,' the tinny dashboard voice told him.

'Keep the old-brain down?' Pitt released the brake. The car moved forward a few feet and stopped dead. The motor died into silence, and with it, the car's defense system; the hum ceased.

Cold fear slid through Pitt's stomach. He gave up trying to find the scanner; with shaking fingers he lifted out his pencil beam. Four or five men were astride the hood, cutting off his view; others were on the cab above his head. A sudden shuddering roar: they were cutting through the roof with a heat drill.

'How long?' Pitt muttered thickly. 'I'm stalled. They must have got some sort of interference plasma going – it conked everything out.'

'They'll be along any minute.' The placid, metallic voice, lacking fear, so remote from him and his situation. The organization voice. Profound and mature, away from the scene of danger.

'They better hurry.' The car shuddered as a whole barrage of rocks hit. The car tipped ominously; they were lifting it up on one side, trying to overturn it. Both back windows were out. A man's hand reached for the door release.

Pitt burned the hand to ash with his pencil beam. The stump frantically withdrew. 'I got one.'

'If you could scan some of them for us . . .'

More hands appeared. The interior of the car was sweltering; the heat drill was almost through. 'I hate to do this.' Pitt turned his pencil beam on his brief case until there was nothing left. Hastily, he dissolved the contents of his pockets, everything in the glove compartment, his identification papers, and finally he burned his wallet. As the plastic bubbled away to black ooze, he saw, for an instant, a photograph of his wife . . . and then the picture was gone.

'Here they come,' he said softly, as the whole side of the car crumpled with a hoarse groan and slid aside under the pressure of the drill.

'Try to hang on, Pitt. The crew should be there almost any—'

Abruptly the speaker went dead. Hands caught him, throwing him back against the seat. His coat ripped, his tie was pulled off. He screamed. A rock crashed into his face; the pencil beam fell to the floor. A broken bottle cut across his eyes and mouth. His scream bubbled into choked silence. The bodies scrambled over him. He sank down, lost in the clutching mass of warm-smelling humanity.

On the car's dashboard, a covert scanner, disguised as a cigar lighter, recorded the immediate scene; it continued to function. Pitt had not known about it; the device had come with the car supplied to him by his superiors. Now, from the mass of struggling people, a hand reached, expertly groped at the dashboard – tugged once, with great precision, at a cable. The covert scanner ceased functioning. Like Pitt, it had come to the end of its span.

Far off down the highway the sirens of the police crew shrieked mournfully.

The same expert hand withdrew. And was gone, back into the mass . . . once more mingled.

William Barris examined the photo carefully, once more comparing it with the second of scanning tape. On his desk his coffee cooled into muddy scum, forgotten among his papers. The Unity Building rang and vibrated with the sounds of endless calculators, statistics machines, vidphones, teletypes, and the innumerable electric typewriters of the minor clerks. Officials moved expertly back and forth in the labyrinth of officers, the countless cells in which T-class personnel worked. Three young secretaries, their high heels striking sharply, hurried past his desk, on their way back from their coffee break. Normally he would have taken notice of them, especially the slim blonde in the pink wool sweater, but today he did not; he was not even aware that they had passed.

'This face is unusual,' Barris murmured. 'Look at his eyes and the heavy ridge over the brows.'

'Phrenology,' Taubmann said indifferently. His plump, well-scrubbed features showed his boredom; *he* noticed the secretaries, even if Barris did not.

Barris threw down the photo. 'No wonder they get so many followers. With organizers like that—' Again he peered at the tiny fragment of scanning tape; this was the only part that had been clear at all. Was it the same man? He could not be sure. Only a blur, a shape without features. At last he handed the photo back to Taubmann. 'What's his name?'

'Father Fields.' In a leisurely fashion, Taubmann thumbed through his file. 'Fifty-nine years old. Trade: electrician. Top-grade turret-wiring expert. One of the best during the war. Born in Macon, Georgia, 1970. Joined the Healers two years ago, at the beginning. One of the founders, if you can believe the informants involved here. Spent two months in the Atlanta Psychological Correction Labs.'

Barris said, 'That long?' He was amazed; for most men it took perhaps a week. Sanity came quickly at such an advanced lab – they had all the equipment he knew of, and some he had only glimpsed in passing. Every time he visited the place he had a deep sense of dread, in spite of his absolute immunity, the sworn sanctity that his position brought him.

'He escaped,' Taubmann said. 'Disappeared.' He raised his head to meet Barris' gaze. 'Without treatment.'

'Two months there, and no treatments?'

'He was ill,' Taubmann said with a faint, mocking smile. 'An injury, and then a chronic blood condition. Then something from wartime radiation. He stalled – and then one day he was gone. Took one of these self-contained air-conditioning units off the wall and reworked it. With a spoon and a toothpick. Of course, no one knows what he made out of it; he took his results through the wall and yard and fence with him. All we had for our inspection were the left-over parts, the ones he didn't use.' Taubmann returned the photo to the file. Pointing at the second of scanning tape he said, 'If that's the same man, it's the first time we've heard anything about him since then.'

'Did you know Pitt?'

'A little. Nice, rather naive young fellow. Devoted to his job. Family man. Applied for field duty because he wanted the extra monthly bonus. Made it possible for his wife to furnish her living room with Early New England oak furniture.' Taubmann got to his feet. 'The call is out for Father Fields. But of course it's been out for months.'

'Too bad the police showed up late,' Barris said. 'Always a few minutes late.' He studied Taubmann. Both of them, technically, were equals, and it was policy for equals in the organization to respect one another. But he had never been too fond of Taubmann; it seemed to him that the man was too concerned with his own status. Not interested in Unity for theoretical reasons.

Taubmann shrugged. 'When a whole town's organized against you, it isn't so odd. They blocked the roads, cut wires and cables, jammed the vidphone channels.'

'If you get Father Fields, send him in to me. I want to examine him personally.'

Taubmann smiled thinly. 'Certainly. But I doubt if we'll get him.' He yawned and moved toward the door. 'It's unlikely; he's a slick one.'

'What do you know about this?' Barris demanded. 'You seem familiar with him – almost on a personal basis.'

Without the slightest loss of composure, Taubmann said, 'I saw him at the Atlanta Labs. A couple of times. After all, Atlanta is part of my region.' He met Barris' gaze steadily.

'Do you think it's the same man that Pitt saw slightly before his death?' Barris said. 'The man who was organizing that mob?'

'Don't ask me,' Taubmann said. 'Send the photo and that bit of tape on to Vulcan 3. Ask it; that's what it's for.'

'You know that Vulcan 3 has given no statement in over fifteen months,' Barris said.

'Maybe it doesn't know what to say.' Taubmann opened the door to the hall; his police bodyguard swarmed alertly around him. 'I can tell you one thing, though. The Healers are after one thing and one thing only; everything else is talk – all this stuff about their wanting to destroy society and wreck civilization. That's good enough for the commercial news analysts, but we know that actually—'

'What are they really after?' Barris interrupted.

'They want to smash Vulcan 3. They want to strew its parts over the countryside. All this today, Pitt's death, the rest – they're trying to reach Vulcan 3.'

'Pitt managed to burn his papers?'

'I suppose. We found nothing, no remains of him or any of his equipment.' The door closed.

After he had waited a careful few minutes, Barris walked to the door, opened it and peered out to be sure that Taubmann had gone. Then he returned to his desk. Clicking on the closed-circuit vidsender he got the local Unity monitor. 'Give me the Atlanta Psychological Correction Labs,' he said, and then instantly he struck out with his hand and cut the circuit.

He thought, It's this sort of reasoning that's made us into the thing we are. The paranoid suspicions of one another. Unity, he thought with irony. Some unity, with each of us eying the other, watching for any mistake, any sign. Naturally Taubmann had contact with a major Healer; it's his job to interview any of them that fall into our hands. He's in charge of the Atlanta staff. That's why I consulted him in the first place.

And yet – the man's motives. He's in this for himself, Barris thought grimly. But what about mine? What are my motives, that lead me to suspect him?

After all, Jason Dill is getting along in years, and it will be one of us who will replace him. And if I could pin something on Taubmann, even the suspicion of treason, with no real facts . . .

So maybe my own skirts aren't so clean, Barris thought. I can't trust myself because I'm not disinterested – none of us are, in the whole Unity structure. Better not yield to my suspicions then, since I can't be sure of my motives.

Once more he contacted the local monitor. 'Yes, sir,' she said. 'Your call to Atlanta—'

'I want that canceled,' he said curtly. 'Instead—' He took a deep breath. 'Give me Unity Control at Geneva.'

While the call was put through – it had to be cleared through an assortment of desks along the thousands of miles of channel – he sat absently stirring his coffee. A man who avoided psychotherapy for two months, in the face of our finest medical men. I wonder if I could do that. What skill that must have taken. What tenacity.

The vidphone clicked. 'Unity Control, sir.'

'This is North American Director Barris.' In a steady voice he said, 'I wish to put through an emergency request to Vulcan 3.'

A pause and then, 'Any first-order data to offer?' The screen was blank; he got only the voice, and it was so bland, so impersonal, that he could not recognize the person. Some functionary, no doubt. A nameless cog.

'Nothing not already filed.' His answer came with heavy reluctance. The functionary, nameless or not, knew the right questions; he was skilled at his job.

'Then,' the voice said, 'you'll have to put through your request in the usual fashion.' The rustling of sheets of paper. 'The delay period,' the voice continued, 'is now three days.'

In a light, bantering voice, Barris said, 'What's Vulcan 3 doing these days? Working out chess openings?' Such a quip *had* to be made in a bantering manner; his scalp depended on it.

'I'm sorry, Mr Barris. The time lag can't be cut even for Director-level personnel.'

Barris started to ring off. And then, plunging all the way into it, he said in a brisk, authoritative tone, 'Let me talk to Jason Dill, then.'

'Managing Director Dill is in conference.' The functionary was not impressed, nor disturbed. 'He can't be bothered in matters of routine.'

With a savage swipe of his hand, Barris cut the circuit. The screen died. Three days! The eternal bureaucracy of the monster organization. They had him; they really knew how to delay.

He reflectively picked up his coffee cup and sipped it. The cold, bitter stuff choked him and he poured it out; the pot refilled the cup at once with fresh coffee.

Didn't Vulcan 3 give a damn? Maybe it wasn't concerned with the world-wide Movement that was out – as Taubmann had said – to smash its metal hide and strew its relays and memory tubes and wiring for the crows to pick over.

But it wasn't Vulcan 3, of course; it was the organization. From the vacant-eyed little secretaries off on their coffee breaks, all the way up through the managers to the Directors, the repairmen who kept Vulcan 3 going, the statisticians who collected data. And Jason Dill.

Was Dill deliberately isolating the other Directors, cutting them off from Vulcan 3? Perhaps Vulcan 3 had responded and the information had been withheld.

I'm suspecting even him, Barris thought. My own superior. The highest official in Unity. I must be breaking down under the strain; that's really insane.

I need a rest, he thought wildly. Pitt's death has done it; I feel somehow responsible, because after all I'm safe here, safe at this desk, while eager youngsters like that go out in the country, out where it's dangerous. They get it, if something goes wrong. Taubmann and I, all of us Directors – we have nothing to fear from those brown-robed crack-pots.

At least, nothing to fear *yet.*

Taking out a request form, Barris began carefully to write. He wrote slowly, studying each word. The form gave him space for ten questions; he asked only two:

a) Are the Healers of real significance?
b) Why don't you respond to their existence?

Then he pushed the form into the relay slot and sat listening as the scanner whisked over its surface. Thousands of miles away, his questions joined the vast tide flowing in from all over the world, from the Unity offices in every country. Eleven Directorates – divisions of the planet. Each with its Director and staff and sub-directorate Unity offices. Each with its police organs under oath to the local Director.

In three days, Barris' turn would come and answers would flow back. His questions, processed by the elaborate mechanism, would be answered – eventually. As with everyone else in T-class, he submitted all problems of importance to the huge mechanical computer buried somewhere in the subsurface fortress near the Geneva offices.

He had no other choice. All policy-level matters were determined by Vulcan 3; that was the law.

Standing up, he motioned to one of the nearby secretaries who stood waiting. She immediately came toward his desk with her pad and writing stick. 'Yes, sir,' she said, smiling.

'I want to dictate a letter to Mrs Arthur Pitt,' Barris said. From his papers he gave her the address. But then, on second thought, he said, 'No, I think I'll write it myself.'

'In handwriting, sir?' the secretary said, blinking in surprise. 'You mean the way children do in school?'

'Yes,' he said.

'May I ask why, sir?'

Barris did not know; he had no rational reason. Sentimentality, he thought to himself as he dismissed the secretary. Throwback to the old days, to infantile patterns.

Your husband is dead in the line of duty, he said to himself as he sat at his desk meditating. Unity is deeply sorry. As Director, I wish to extend my personal sympathy to you in this tragic hour.

Damn it, he thought. I can't do it; I never can. I'll have to go and see her; I can't write a thing like this. There have been too many, lately. Too many deaths for me to stand. I'm not like Vulcan 3. I can't ignore it. I can't be silent.

And it didn't even occur in my region. The man wasn't even my employee.

Clicking open the line to his sub-Director, Barris said, 'I want you to take over for the rest of today. I'm knocking off. I don't feel too well.'

'Too bad, sir,' Peter Allison said. But the pleasure was obvious, the satisfaction of being able to step from the wings and assume a more important spot, if only for a moment.

You'll have my job, Barris thought as he closed and locked his desk. You're gunning for it, just as I'm gunning for Dill's job. On and on, up the ladder to the top.

He wrote Mrs Pitt's address down, put it in his shirt pocket, and left the office as quickly as he could, glad to get away. Glad to have an excuse to escape from the oppressive atmosphere.

2

Standing before the blackboard, Agnes Parker asked, 'What does the year 1992 bring to mind?' She looked brightly around the class.

'The year 1992 brings to mind the conclusion of Atomic War I and the beginning of the decade of international regulation,' said Peter Thomas, one of the best of her students.

'Unity came into being,' Patricia Edwards added. 'Rational world order.'

Mrs Parker made a note on her chart. 'Correct.' She felt pride at the children's alert response. 'And now perhaps someone can tell me about the Lisbon Laws of 1993.'

The classroom was silent. A few pupils shuffled in their seats. Outside, warm June air beat against the windows. A fat robin hopped down from a branch and stood listening for worms. The trees rustled lazily.

'That's when Vulcan 3 was made,' Hans Stein said.

Mrs Parker smiled. 'Vulcan 3 was made long before that; Vulcan 3 was made during the war. Vulcan 1 in 1970. Vulcan 2 in 1975. They had computers even before the war, in the middle of the century. The Vulcan series was developed by Otto Jordan, who worked with Nathaniel Greenstreet for Westinghouse, during the early days of the war . . .'

Mrs Parker's voice trailed off into a yawn. She pulled herself together with an effort; this was no time to be dozing. Managing Director Jason Dill and his staff were supposed to be in the school somewhere, reviewing educational ideology. Vulcan 3 was rumored to have made inquiries concerning the school systems; it seemed to be interested in knowing the various value biases that were currently being formulated in the pupils' basic orientation programs. After all, it was the task of the schools, and especially the grammar schools, to infuse the youth of the world with the proper attitudes. What else were schools for?

'What,' Mrs Parker repeated, 'were the Lisbon Laws of 1993? Doesn't anybody know? I really feel ashamed of you all, if you can't exert yourselves to memorize what may well be the most important facts you'll learn in your entire time of school. I suppose if you had your way you'd be reading those commercial comic books that teach adding and subtracting and other business crafts.' Fiercely, she tapped on the floor with her toe. 'Well? Do I hear an answer?'

For a moment there was no response. The rows of faces were blank. Then, abruptly, incredibly: 'The Lisbon Laws dethroned God,' a piping child's voice came from the back of the classroom. A girl's voice, severe and penetrating.

Mrs Parker awoke from her torpor; she blinked in amazement. 'Who said that?' she demanded. The class buzzed. Heads turned questioningly toward the back. 'Who was that?'

'It was Jeannie Baker!' a boy hollered.

'It was not! It was Dorothy!'

Mrs Parker paced rapidly down the aisle, past the children's desks. 'The Lisbon Laws of 1993,' she said sharply, 'were the most important legislation of the past five hundred years.' She spoke nervously, in a high-pitched shrill voice; gradually the class turned toward her. Habit made them pay attention to her – the training of years. 'All seventy nations of the world sent representatives to Lisbon. The world-wide Unity organization formally agreed that the great computer machines developed by Britain and the Soviet Union and the United States, and hitherto used in a purely advisory capacity, would now be given absolute power over the national governments in the determination of top-level policy—'

But at that moment Managing Director Jason Dill entered the classroom, and Mrs Parker lapsed into respectful silence.

This was not the first time she had seen the man, the actual physical entity, in contrast to the synthetic images projected over the media to the public at large. And as before, she was taken by surprise; there was such a difference between the real man and his official image. In the back of her mind she wondered how the children were taking it. She glanced toward them and saw that all of them were gazing in awe, everything else forgotten.

She thought, He's actually not so different from the rest of us. The highest ranking human being . . . and he's just a plain man. An energetic middle-aged man with a shrewd face, twinkling eyes, and a genial smile of confidence. He's short, she thought. Shorter than some of the men around him.

His staff had entered with him, three men and two women, all in the businesslike T-class gray. No special badges. No royal gear. If I didn't know, she thought, I wouldn't guess. He's so unassuming.

'This is Managing Director Dill,' she said. 'The Co-ordinating Director of the Unity system.' Her voice broke with tension. 'Managing Director Dill is responsible only to Vulcan 3. No human being except Director Dill is permitted to approach the computer banks.'

Director Dill nodded pleasantly to Mrs Parker and to the class. 'What are you children studying?' he asked in a friendly voice, the rich voice of a competent leader of the T-class.

The children shuffled shyly. 'We're learning about the Lisbon Laws,' a boy said.

'That's nice,' Director Dill affirmed heartily, his alert eyes twinkling. He nodded to his staff and they moved back toward the door. 'You children be good students and do what your teacher tells you.'

'It was so nice of you,' Mrs Parker managed to say. 'To drop by, so they could see you for a moment. Such an honor.' She followed the group to the door, her heart fluttering. 'They'll always remember this moment; they'll treasure it.'

'Mr Dill,' a girl's voice came. 'Can I ask you something?'

The room became abruptly silent. Mrs Parker was chilled. *The voice*. The girl again. Who was it? Which one? She strained to see, her heart thumping in terror. Good lord, was that little devil going to say something in front of Director Dill?

'Certainly,' Dill said, halting briefly at the door. 'What do you want to ask?' He glanced at his wrist watch, smiling rather fixedly.

'Director Dill is in a hurry,' Mrs Parker managed to say. 'He has so much to do, so many tasks. I think we had better let him go, don't you?'

But the firm little child's voice continued, as inflexible as steel. 'Director Dill, don't you feel ashamed of yourself when you let a machine tell you what to do?'

Director Dill's fixed smile remained. Slowly, he turned away from the door, back toward the class. His bright, mature eyes roved about the room, seeking to pinpoint the questioner. 'Who asked that?' he inquired pleasantly.

Silence.

Director Dill moved about the room, walking slowly, his hands in his pockets. He rubbed his chin, plucking at it absently. No one moved or spoke; Mrs Parker and the Unity staff stood frozen in horror.

It's the end of my job, Mrs Parker thought. Maybe they'll make me sign a request for therapy – maybe I'll have to undergo voluntary rehabilitation. No, she thought frantically. Please.

However, Director Dill was unshaken. He stopped in front of the blackboard. Experimentally, he raised his hand and moved it in a figure. White lines traced themselves on the dark surface. He made a few thoughtful motions and the date 1992 traced itself.

'The end of the war,' he said.

He traced 1993 for the hushed class.

'The Lisbon Laws, which you're learning about. The year the combined nations of the world decided to throw in their lot together. To subordinate themselves in a realistic manner – not in the idealistic fashion of the UN days – to a common supra-national authority, for the good of all mankind.'

Director Dill moved away from the blackboard, gazing thoughtfully down at the floor. 'The war had just ended; most of the planet was in ruins. Something drastic had to be done, because another war would destroy mankind. Something, some ultimate principle of organization, was needed. International control. Law, which no men or nations could break. Guardians were needed.

'But who would watch the Guardians? How could we be sure this supranational body would be free of the hate and bias, the animal passions that had set man against man throughout the centuries? Wouldn't this body, like all other man-made bodies, fall heir to the same vices, the same failings of interest over reason, emotion over logic?

'There was one answer. For years we had been using computers, giant constructs put together by the labor and talent of hundreds of trained experts, built to exact standards. Machines were free of the poisoning bias of self-interest and feeling that gnawed at man; they were capable of performing the objective calculations that for man would remain only an ideal, never a reality. If nations would be willing to give up their sovereignty, to subordinate their power to the objective, impartial directives of the—'

Again the thin child's voice cut through Dill's confident tone. The speech ceased, tumbled into ruin by the flat, direct interruption from the back of the classroom. 'Mr Dill, do you really believe that a machine is better than a man? That man can't manage his own world?'

For the first time, Director Dill's cheeks glowed red. He hesitated, half-smiling, gesturing with his right hand as he sought for words. 'Well . . .' he murmured.

'I just don't know what to say,' Mrs Parker gasped, finding her voice. 'I'm so sorry. Please believe me, I had no idea—'

Director Dill nodded understandingly to her. 'Of course,' he said in a low voice. 'It's not your fault. These are not *tabulae rasae* which you can mold like plastic.'

'Pardon?' she said, not understanding the foreign words. She had a dim idea that it was – what was it? Latin?

Dill said, 'You will always have a certain number who will not respond.' Now he had raised his voice for the class to hear. 'I'm going to play a game with you,' he said, and at once the small faces showed anticipation. 'Now, I don't want you to say a word; I want you to clap your hands over your mouths and be the way our police crews are when they're waiting to catch one of the enemy.' The small hands flew up to cover mouths; eyes shone with excitement. 'Our police are so quiet,' Dill continued. 'And they look around; they search and search to see where the enemy is. Of course, they don't let the enemy know they're about to pounce.'

The class giggled with joy.

'Now,' Dill said, folding his arms. 'We look around.' The children dutifully peered around. 'Where's the enemy? We count – one, two, three.' Suddenly Dill threw up his arms and in a loud voice said, 'And we *point* to the enemy. We point her *out*!'

Twenty hands pointed. In her chair in the back the small red-haired girl sat quietly, giving no reaction.

'What's your name?' Dill said, walking leisurely down the aisle until he stood near her desk.

The girl gazed silently up at Director Dill.

'Aren't you going to answer my question?' Dill said, smiling.

Calmly, the girl folded her small hands together on her desk. 'Marion Fields,' she said clearly. 'And you haven't answered *my* questions.'

Together, Director Dill and Mrs Parker walked down the corridor of the school building.

'I've had trouble with her from the start,' Mrs Parker said. 'In fact, I protested their placing her in my class.' Quickly, she said, 'You'll find my written protest on file; I followed the regular method. I knew that something like this was going to happen, I just knew it!'

'I guarantee you,' Director Dill said, 'that you have nothing to fear. Your job is safe. You have my word.' Glancing at the teacher he added reflectively, 'Unless, of course, there's more to this than meets the eye.' He paused at the door to the principal's office. 'You have never met or seen her father, have you?'

'No,' Mrs Parker answered. 'She's a ward of the government; her father was arrested and committed to the Atlanta—'

'I know,' Dill interrupted. 'She's nine, is she? Does she try to discuss current events with other children? I presume that you have some manner of monitoring equipment going at all times – in the cafeteria and on the playground especially.'

'We have complete tapes of all conversations among the pupils,' Mrs Parker said proudly. 'There's never a moment when they're not overheard. Of course, we're so rushed and overworked, and our budget is so low . . . frankly, we've had trouble finding time to replay the tapes. There's a backlog, and all of us teachers try to spend at least an hour a day in careful replaying—'

'I understand,' Dill murmured. 'I know how overworked you all are, with all your responsibilities. It would be normal for any child her age to talk about her father. I was just curious. Obviously—' He broke off. 'I believe,' he said somberly, 'that I'll have you sign a release permitting me to assume custody of her. Effective at once. Do you have someone you can send to her dorm to pick up her things? Her clothes and personal articles?' He glanced at his watch. 'I don't have too much time.'

'She has just the standard kit,' Mrs Parker said. 'Class B, which is provided for nine-year-olds. That could be picked up anywhere. You can take her right – I'll have the form made out at once.' She opened the door to the principal's office and waved to a clerk.

'You have no objection to my taking her?' Dill said.

'Certainly not,' Mrs Parker answered. 'Why do you ask?'

In a dark, introspective voice, Dill said, 'It would put an end to her schooling, for one thing.'

'I don't see that that matters.'

Dill eyed her, and she became flustered; his steady gaze made her shrink away. 'I suppose,' he said, 'that schooling for her has been a failure anyhow. So it doesn't matter.'

'That's right,' she said quickly. 'We can't help malcontents like her. As you pointed out in your statement to the class.'

'Have her taken down to my car,' Dill said. 'She's been detained by someone capable of restraining her, I presume. It would be a shame if she selected this moment to sneak off.'

'We have her locked in one of the washrooms,' Mrs Parker said.

Again he eyed her, but this time he said nothing. While she shakily made out the proper form he took a moment to gaze out the window at the playground below. Now it was recess; the faint, muffled voices of the children drifted up to the office.

'What game is that?' Dill said finally. 'Where they mark with the chalk.' He pointed.

'I don't know,' she said, looking over his shoulder.

At that, Dill was dumbfounded. 'You mean you let them play unorganized games? Games of their own devising?'

'No,' she said. 'I mean I'm not in charge of playground teaching; it's Miss Smollet who handles that. See her down there?'

When the custody transfer had been made out, Dill took it from her and departed. Presently she saw, through the window, the man and his staff crossing the playground. She watched as he waved genially to the children, and she saw him stop several times to bend down to speak to some individual child.

How incredible, she thought. That he could take the time for ordinary persons like us.

At Dill's car she saw the Fields girl. The small shape, wearing a coat, the bright red hair shimmering in the sun . . . and then an official of Dill's staff had boosted the child into the back of the car. Dill got in too, and the doors slammed. The car drove off. On the playground, a group of children had gathered by the high wire fence to wave.

Still trembling, Mrs Parker made her way back up the corridor to her own classroom. Is my job safe? she asked herself. Will I be investigated, or can I believe him? After all, he did give me his absolute assurance, and no one can contradict him. I know my record is clear, she thought desperately. I've never done anything subversive; I asked not to have that child in my class, and I never discuss current events in the classroom; I've never slipped once. But suppose—

Suddenly, at the corner of her eye, something moved.

She halted rigid where she was. A flicker of motion. Now gone. What was it? A deep, intuitive dread filled her; something had been there, near her, unobserved. Now swiftly vanished – she had caught only the most indistinct glimpse.

Spying on her! Some mechanism overhearing her. She was being watched. Not just the children, she thought in terror. But us, too. They have us watched, and I never knew for sure; I only guessed.

Could it read my thoughts? she asked herself. No, nothing can read thoughts. And I wasn't saying anything aloud. She looked up and down the corridor, striving to make out what it had been.

Who does it report to? she wondered. The police? Will they come and get me, take me to Atlanta or some place like that?

Gasping with fear, she managed to open the door of her classroom and enter.

3

The Unity Control Building filled virtually the whole business area of Geneva, a great imposing square of white concrete and steel. Its endless rows of windows glittered in the late afternoon sun; lawns and shrubs surrounded the structure on all sides; gray-clad men and women hurried up the wide marble steps and through the doors.

Jason Dill's car pulled up at the guarded Director's entrance. He stepped quickly out and held the door open. 'Come along,' he said.

For a moment Marion Fields remained in the car, unwilling to leave. The leather seats had given her a sense of security, and she sat looking out at the man standing on the sidewalk, trying to control her fear of him. The man smiled at her, but she had no confidence in the smile; she had seen it too many times on the public television. It was too much a part of the world that she had been taught to distrust.

'Why?' she said. 'What are you going to do?' But at last she slid slowly from the car onto the pavement. She was not sure where she was; the rapid trip had confused her.

'I'm sorry you had to leave your possessions behind,' Dill said to her. He took hold of her hand and led her firmly up the steps of the great building. 'We'll replace them,' he said. 'And we'll see that you have a pleasant time here with us; I promise you, on my word of honor.' He glanced down to see how she was taking it.

The long echoing hall stretched out ahead of them, lit by recessed lights. Distant figures, tiny human shapes, scampered back and forth from one office to another. To the girl, it was like an even larger school; it was everything she had been subjected to but on a much larger scale.

'I want to go home,' she said.

'This way,' Dill said in a cheerful voice, as he guided her along. 'You won't be lonely because there are a lot of nice people who work here who have children of their own, girls of their own. And they'll be glad to bring their children by so you can have someone to play with. Won't that be nice?'

'You can tell them,' she said.

'Tell them what?' Dill said, as he turned down a side passage. 'To bring their children, And they will. Because you're the boss.'

She gazed up at him, and saw, for an instant, his composure depart. But almost at once he was smiling again. 'Why do you always smile?' she said. 'Aren't things ever bad, or aren't you able to admit it when they're bad? On the television you always say things are fine. Why don't you tell the truth?' She asked these questions with curiosity; it did not make sense to her. Surely he knew that he never told the truth.

'You know what I think's wrong with you, young woman?' Dill said. 'I don't really think you're such a troublemaker as you pretend.' He opened the door to an office. 'I think you just worry too much.' As he ushered her inside he said, 'You should be like other children. Play more healthy outdoor games. Don't do so much thinking off by yourself. Isn't that what you do? Go off by yourself somewhere and brood?'

She had to nod in agreement. It was true.

Dill patted her on the shoulder. 'You and I are going to get along fine,' he said. 'You know, I have two children of my own – a good bit older than you, though.'

'I know,' she said. 'One's a boy and he's in the police youth, and your girl Joan is in the girls' army school in Boston. I read about it in a magazine they gave us at school to read.'

'Oh, yes,' Dill murmured. '*World Today*. Do you like to read it?'

'No,' she said. 'It tells more lies even than you.'

After that, the man said nothing; he concerned himself with papers on his desk, and left her to stand by herself.

'I'm sorry you don't like our magazine,' he said finally, in a preoccupied voice. 'Unity goes to a great deal of trouble to put it out. By the way. Who told you to say that about Unity? Who taught you?'

'Nobody taught me.'

'Not even your father?'

She said, 'Do you know you're shorter than you look on television? Do they do that on purpose? Try to make you look bigger to impress people?'

To that, Dill said nothing. At his desk he had turned on a little machine; she saw lights flash.

'That's recording,' she said.

Dill said, 'Have you had a visit from your dad since his escape from Atlanta?'

'No,' she said.

'Do you know what sort of place Atlanta is?'

'No,' she said. But she did know. He stared at her, trying to see if she was lying, but she returned his stare. 'It's a prison,' she said at last. 'Where they send men who speak their mind.'

'No,' Dill said. 'It's a hospital. For mentally unbalanced people. It's a place where they get well.'

In a low, steady voice, she said, 'You're a liar.'

'It's a psychological therapy place,' Dill said. 'Your father was – upset. He imagined all sorts of things that weren't so. There evidently were pressures on him too strong for him to bear, and so like a lot of perfectly normal people he cracked under the pressure.'

'Did you ever meet him?'

Dill admitted, 'No. But I have his record here.' He showed her a great mass of documents that lay before him.

'They cured him at that place?' Marion asked.

'Yes,' Dill said. But then he frowned. 'No, I beg your pardon. He was too ill to be given therapy. And I see he managed to keep himself ill the entire two months he was there.'

'So he isn't cured,' she said. 'He's still upset, isn't he?'

Dill said, 'The Healers. What's your father's relationship to them?'

'I don't know.'

Dill seated himself and leaned back in his chair, his hands

behind his head. 'Isn't it a little silly, those things you said? Over-throwing God . . . somebody has told you we were better off in the old days, before Unity, when we had war every twenty years.' He pondered. 'I wonder how the Healers got their name. Do you know?'

'No,' she said.

'Didn't your father tell you?'

'No.'

'Maybe I can tell you; I'll be a sort of substitute father, for a while. A "healer" is a person who comes along with no degree or professional medical training and declares he can cure you by some odd means when the licensed medical profession has given you up. He's a quack, a crank, either an out-and-out nut or a cynical fake who wants to make some easy money and doesn't care how he goes about it. Like the cancer quacks – but you're too young; you wouldn't remember them.' Leaning forward, he said, 'But you may have heard of the radiation-sickness quacks. Do you remember ever seeing a man come by in an old car, with perhaps a sign mounted on top of it, selling bottles of medicine guaranteed to cure terrible radiation burns?'

She tried to recall. 'I don't remember,' she said. 'I know I've seen men on television selling things that are supposed to cure all the ills of society.'

Dill said, 'No child would talk as you're talking. You've been trained to say this.' His voice rose. 'Haven't you?'

'Why are you so upset?' she said, genuinely surprised. 'I didn't say it was any Unity salesman.'

'But you meant us,' Dill said, still flushed. 'You meant our informational discussions, our public relations programs.'

She said, 'You're so suspicious. You see things that aren't there.' That was something her father had said; she remembered that. He had said, *They're paranoids. Suspicious even of each other. Any opposition is the work of the devil.*

'The Healers,' Dill was saying, 'take advantage of the super-stitions of the masses. The masses are ignorant, you see. They believe in crazy things: magic, gods and miracles, healing, the Touch. This cynical cult is playing on basic emotional hysterias familiar to all our sociologists, manipulating the masses like sheep, exploiting them to gain power.'

'You have the power,' she said. 'All of it. My father says you've got a monopoly on it.'

'The masses have a desire for religious certainty, the comforting balm of faith. You grasp what I'm saying, don't you? You seem to be a bright child.'

She nodded faintly.

'They don't live by reason. They can't; they haven't the courage and discipline. They demand the metaphysical absolutes that started to go out as early as 1700. But war keeps bringing it back – the whole pack of frauds.'

'Do you believe that?' she said. 'That it's all frauds?'

Dill said, 'I know that a man who says he has the Truth is a fraud. A man who peddles snake oil, like your—' He broke off. 'A man,' he said finally, 'like your father. A spellbinder who fans up the flames of hate, inflames a mob until it kills.'

To that she said nothing.

Jason Dill slid a piece of paper before her eyes. 'Read this. It's about a man named Pitt – not a very important man, but it was worth your father's while to have him brutally murdered. Ever hear of him?'

'No,' she said.

'Read it!' Dill said.

She took the report and examined it, her lips moving slowly.

'The mob,' Dill said, 'led by your father, pulled the man from his car and tore him to bits. What do you think of that?'

Marion pushed the paper back to him, saying nothing.

Leaning toward her, Dill yelled, 'Why? What are they after? Do they want to bring back the old days? The war and hatred and international violence? These madmen are sweeping us back into the chaos and darkness of the past! And who gains? Nobody, except these spellbinders; they gain power. Is it worth it? Is it worth killing off half of mankind, wrecking cities—'

She interrupted, 'That's not so. My father never said he was going to do anything like that.' She felt herself become rigid with anger. 'You're lying again, like you always do.'

'Then what does he want? You tell me.'

'They want Vulcan 3.'

'I don't get what you mean.' He scowled at her. 'They're wasting their time. It repairs and maintains itself; we merely feed it data and the parts and supplies it wants. Nobody knows exactly where it is. Pitt didn't know.'

'*You* know.'

'Yes, I know.' He studied her with such ferocity that she could not meet his gaze. 'The worst thing that's happened to the world,' he said at last, 'in the time that you've been alive, is your father's escape from the Atlanta Psych Labs. A warped, psychopathic, deranged madman . . .' His voice sank to a mutter.

'If you met him,' she said, 'you'd like him.'

Dill stared at her. And then, abruptly, he began to laugh. 'Anyhow,' he said when he had ceased laughing, 'you'll stay here in the Unity offices. I'll be talking to you again from time to time. If we don't get results we can send you to Atlanta. But I'd rather not.'

He stabbed a button on his desk and two armed Unity guards appeared at the office door. 'Take this girl down to the third subsurface level; don't let anything happen that might harm her.' Out of her earshot, he gave the guards instructions; she tried to hear but she could not.

I'll bet he was lying when he said there'd be other kids for me to play with, she thought. She had not seen another child yet, in this vast, forbidding building.

Tears came to her eyes, but she forced them back. Pretending to be examining the big dictionary in the corner of Director Dill's office, she waited for the guards to start ordering her into motion.

As Jason Dill sat moodily at his desk, a speaker near his arm said, 'She's in her quarters now, sir. Anything else?'

'No,' he said. Rising to his feet, he collected his papers, put them into his brief case and left his office.

A moment later he was on his way out of the Unity Control Building, hurrying up the ramp to the confined field, past the nests of heavy-duty aerial guns and on to his private hangar. Soon he was heading across the early evening sky, toward the underground fortress where the great Vulcan computers were maintained, carefully hidden away from the race of man.

Strange little girl, he thought to himself. Mature in some ways, in others perfectly ordinary. How much of her was derived from her father? Father Fields secondhand, Dill thought. Seeing the man through her, trying to infer the father by means of the child.

He landed, and presently was submitting to the elaborate examination at the surface check-point, fidgeting impatiently. The tangle of equipment sent him on and he descended quickly into the depths of the underground fortress. At the second level he stopped the elevator and got abruptly off. A moment later he was standing before a sealed support-wall, tapping his foot nervously and waiting for the guards to pass him.

'All right, Mr Dill.' The wall slid back. Dill hurried down a long deserted corridor, his heels echoing mournfully. The air was clammy, and the lights flickered fitfully; he turned to the right and halted, peering into the yellow gloom.

There it was. Vulcan 2, dusty and silent. Virtually forgotten. No one came here any more. Except himself. And even he not very often.

He thought, It's a wonder the thing still works.

Seating himself at one of the tables, he unzipped his brief case and got out his papers. Carefully, he began preparing his questions in the proper manner; for this archaic computer he had to do the tape-feeding himself. With a manual punch, he spelled out on the iron oxide tape the first series, and then he activated the tape transport. It made an audible wheezing sound as it struggled into life.

In the old days, during the war, Vulcan 2 had been an intricate structure of great delicacy and subtlety, an elaborate instrument consulted by the skilled technicians daily. It had served Unity well, in its time; it had done honorable service. And, he thought, the schoolbooks still laud it; they still give it its proper credit.

Lights flashed, and a bit of tape popped from the slot and fell into the basket. He picked it up and read:

Time will be required. Return in twenty-four hours, please.

The computer could not function rapidly, now. He knew that, and this did not surprise him. Again taking up the punch, he made the balance of his questions into feeding data, and then, closing his brief case, he strode rapidly from the chamber, back up the musty, deserted corridor.

How lonesome it is here, he thought. No one else but me.

And yet – he had the sudden acute sensation that he was not alone, that someone was nearby, scrutinizing him. He glanced swiftly about. The dim yellow light did not show him much; he ceased walking, holding his breath and listening. There was no sound except the distant whirl of the old computer as it labored over his questions.

Lifting his head, Dill peered into the dusty shadows along the ceiling of the corridor. Strands of cobweb hung from the light fixtures; one bulb had gone dead, and that spot was black – a pit of total darkness.

In the darkness, something gleamed.

Eyes, he thought, He felt chill fear.

A dry, rustling noise. The eyes shot off; he saw the gleam still, retreating from him along the ceiling of the corridor. In an instant the eyes had gone. A bat? Bird of some sort, trapped down here? Carried down by the elevator?

Jason Dill shivered, hesitated, and then went on.

4

From Unity records, William Barris had obtained the address of Mr and Mrs Arthur Pitt. It did not surprise him to discover that the Pitts – now just Mrs Pitt, he realized soberly – had a house in the expensive and fashionable Sahara region of North Africa. During the war that part of the world had been spared both hydrogen bomb explosions and fallout; now real estate there was priced out of the reach of most people, even those employed by the Unity system.

As his ship carried him from the North American landmass across the Atlantic, Barris thought, I wish I could afford to live there. It must have cost the man everything he had; in fact, he must have gone into debt up to his neck. I wonder why. Would it be worth it? Not to me, Barris thought. Perhaps for his wife . . .

He landed his ship at the fabulously illuminated Proust Field runways, and shortly thereafter he was driving by commercial robot taxi on the twelve-lane freeway to the Golden Lands Development, at which Mrs Pitt lived.

The woman, he knew, had been notified already; he had made sure that he would not be bringing her the first news of her husband's death.

On each side of the road, orange trees and grass and sparkling blue fountains made him feel cool and relaxed. As yet there were no multiple-unit buildings; this area was perhaps the last in the world still zoned for one-unit dwellings only. The limit of luxury, he thought. One-unit dwellings were a vanishing phenomenon in the world.

The freeway branched; he turned to the right, following the sign. Presently SLOW warnings appeared. Ahead he saw a gate blocking the road; astonished he brought his rented taxi to a halt. Was this development legally able to screen visitors? Apparently it was; the law sanctioned it. He saw several men in ornate uniforms – like ancient Latin American dictator garb – standing at stopped cars, inspecting the occupants. And, he saw, several of the cars were being turned back.

When the official had sauntered over to him, Barris said in a brusque voice, 'Unity business.'

The man shrugged. 'Are you expected?' he asked in a bored tone.

'Listen,' Barris began but the man was already pointing back at the through freeway. Subsiding, Barris said with great restraint, 'I want to see Mrs Arthur Pitt. Her husband was killed in line of duty and I'm here expressing official regrets.' That was actually not true, but it was near enough.

'I'll ask her if she wishes to see you,' the uniformed man, heavy with medals and decorations, said. He took Barris' name; the fact that he was a Director did not seem to impress him. Going off, he spent some time at a portable vidscreen, and then he returned with a more pleasant expression on his face. 'Mrs Pitt is willing to have you admitted,' he said. And the gate was drawn aside for Barris' rented taxi to pass.

Somewhat disconcerted by the experience, Barris drove on.

Now he found himself surrounded by small, modern, brightly colored houses, all neat and trim, and each unique; he did not see two alike. He switched on the automatic beam, and the taxi obediently hooked in to the circuit of the development. Otherwise, Barris realized, he would never find the house.

When the cab pulled over to the curb and stopped, he saw a slim, dark-haired young woman coming down the front steps of the house. She wore a wide-brimmed Mexican-style hat to protect her head from the midday African sun; from beneath the hat ringlets of black hair sparkled, the long Middle Eastern style so popular of late. On her feet she had sandals, and she wore a ruffled dress with bows and petticoats.

'I'm dreadfully sorry that you were treated that way, Director,' she said in a low, toneless voice as he opened the door of the cab. 'You understand that those uniformed guards are robots.'

'No,' he said. 'I didn't know. But it isn't important.' He surveyed her, seeing, he decided, one of the prettiest women that he had ever come across. Her face had a look of shock, a residue from the terrible news of her husband's death. But she seemed composed; she led him up the steps to the house, walking very slowly.

'I believe I saw you once,' she said as they reached the porch. 'At a meeting of Unity personnel at which Arthur and I were present. You were on the platform, of course. With Mr Dill.'

The living room of the house, he noticed, was furnished as Taubmann had said; he saw Early New England oak furniture on every side.

'Please sit down,' Mrs Pitt said.

As he gingerly seated himself on a delicate-looking straight-backed chair, he thought to himself that for this woman being married to a Unity official had been a profitable career. 'You have very nice things here,' he said.

'Thank you,' Mrs Pitt said, seating herself opposite him on a couch. 'I'm sorry,' she said, 'if my responses seem slow. When I got the news I had myself put under sedation. You can understand.' Her voice trailed off.

Barris said, 'Mrs Pitt—'

'My name is Rachel,' she said.

'All right,' he said. He paused. Now that he was here, facing this woman, he did not know what to say; he was not even sure, now, why he had come here.

'I know what's on your mind,' Rachel Pitt said. 'I put pressure on my husband to seek out active service so that we could have a comfortable home.'

To that, Barris said nothing.

'Arthur was responsible to Director Taubmann,' Rachel Pitt said. 'I ran into Taubmann several times, and he made clear how he felt about me; it didn't particularly bother me at the time, but of course with Arthur dead—' She broke off. 'It isn't true, of course. Living this way was Arthur's idea. I would have been glad to give it up any time; I didn't want to be stuck out here in this housing development, away from everything.' For a moment she was silent. Reaching to the coffee table she took a package of cigarettes. 'I was born in London,' she said, as she lit a cigarette. 'All my life I lived in a city, either in London or New York. My family wasn't very well off – my father was a tailor, in fact. Arthur's family has quite a good deal of money; I think he got his taste in interior decorating from his mother.' She gazed at Barris. 'This doesn't interest you. I'm sorry. Since I heard, I haven't been able to keep my thoughts in order.'

'Are you all by yourself here?' he said. 'Do you know anyone in this development?'

'No one that I want to depend on,' she said. 'Mostly you'll find ambitious young wives here. Their husbands all work for Unity; that goes without saying. Otherwise, how could they afford to live here?' Her tone was so bitter that he was amazed.

'What do you think you'll do?' he said.

Rachel Pitt said. 'Maybe I'll join the Healers.'

He did not know how to react. So he said nothing. This is a highly distraught woman, he thought. The grief, the calamity that she's involved in . . . or is she always like this? He had no way of telling.

'How much do you know about the circumstances surrounding Arthur's death?' she asked.

'I know most of the data,' Barris said cautiously.

'Do you believe he was killed by—' She grimaced. 'A mob? A

bunch of unorganized people? Farmers and shopkeepers, egged on by some old man in a robe?' Suddenly she sprang to her feet and hurled her cigarette against the wall; it rolled near him and he bent reflexively to retrieve it. 'That's just the usual line they put out,' she said. 'I know better. My husband was murdered by someone in Unity – someone who was jealous of him, who envied him and everything he had achieved. He had a lot of enemies; every man with any ability who gets anywhere in the organization is hated.' She subsided slightly, pacing about the room with her arms folded, her face strained and distorted. 'Does this distress you?' she said at last. 'To see me like this? You probably imagined some little clinging vine of a woman sobbing quietly to herself. Do I disappoint you? Forgive me.' Her voice trembled with fury.

Barris said, 'The facts as they were presented to me—'

'Don't kid me,' Rachel said in a deadly, harsh voice. And then she shuddered and put her hands against her cheeks. 'Is it all in my mind? He was always telling me about people in his office plotting to get rid of him, trying to get him in bad. Carrying tales. Part of being in Unity, he always said. The only way you can get to the top is push someone else away from the top.' She stared at Barris wildly. 'Who did you murder to get your job? How many men dead, so you could be a Director? That's what Arthur was aiming for – that was his dream.'

'Do you have any proof?' he said. 'Anything to go on that would indicate that someone in the organization was involved?' It did not seem even remotely credible to him that someone in Unity could have been involved in the death of Arthur Pitt; more likely this woman's ability to handle reality had been severely curtailed by the recent tragedy. And yet, such things had happened, or at least so it was believed.

'My husband's official Unity car,' Rachel said steadily, 'had a little secret scanning device mounted on the dashboard. I saw the reports, and it was mentioned in them. When Director Taubmann was talking to me on the vidphone, do you know what I did? I didn't listen to his speech; I read the papers he had on his desk.' Her voice rose and wavered. 'One of the people who broke into Arthur's car knew about that scanner – *he shut it off*. Only someone in the organization could have known; even Arthur didn't know. It had to be someone up high.' Her black eyes flashed. 'Someone at Director level.'

'Why?' Barris said, disconcerted.

'Afraid my husband would rise and threaten him. Jeopardize his job. Possibly eventually take his job from him, become Director in his place. Taubmann, I mean.' She smiled thinly. 'You know I mean him. So what are you going to do? Inform on me? Have me arrested for treason and carried off to Atlanta?'

Barris said, 'I – I would prefer to give it some thought.'

'Suppose you don't inform on me. I might be doing this to trap you, to test your loyalty to the system. You *have* to inform – it might be a trick!' She laughed curtly. 'Does all this distress you? Now you wish you hadn't come to express your sympathy; see what you got yourself into by having humane motives?' Tears filled her eyes. 'Go away,' she said in a choked, unsteady voice. 'What does the organization care about the wife of a dead minor petty field-worker?'

Barris said, 'I'm not sorry I came.'

Going to the door, Rachel Pitt opened it. 'You'll never be back,' she said. 'Go on, leave. Scuttle back to your safe office.'

'I think you had better leave this house,' Barris said.

'And go where?'

To that, he had no ready answer. 'There's a cumbersome pension system,' he began. 'You'll get almost as much as your husband was making. If you want to move back to New York or London—'

'Do my charges seriously interest you?' Rachel broke in. 'Does it occur to you that I might be right? That a Director might arrange the murder of a talented, ambitious underling to protect his own job? It's odd, isn't it, how the police crews are always just a moment late.'

Shaken, ill-at-ease, Barris said, 'I'll see you again. Soon, I hope.'

'Goodbye, Director,' Rachel Pitt said, standing on the front porch of her house as he descended the steps to his rented cab. 'Thank you for coming.'

She was still there as he drove off.

*

As his ship carried him back across the Atlantic to North America, William Barris pondered. Could the Healers have contacts within the Unity organization? Impossible. The woman's hysterical conviction had overwhelmed him; it was her emotion, not her reason, that had affected him. And yet he himself had been suspicious of Taubmann.

Could it be that Father Fields' escape from Atlanta had been arranged? Not the work of a single clever man, a deranged man bent on escape and revenge, but the work of dull-witted officials who had been instructed to let the man go?

That would explain why, in two long months, Fields had been given no psychotherapy.

And now what? Barris asked himself acidly. Whom do I tell? Do I confront Taubmann – with absolutely no facts? Do I go to Jason Dill?

One other point occurred to him. If he ever did run afoul of Taubmann, if the man ever attacked him for any reason, he had an ally in Mrs Pitt; he had someone to assist him in a counter-attack.

And, Barris realized grimly, that was valuable in the Unity system, someone to back up your charges – if not with evidence, at least with added assertion. Where there's smoke there's fire, he said to himself. Someone should look into Taubmann's relationship with Father Fields. The customary procedure here would be to send an unsigned statement to Jason Dill, and let *him* start police spies to work tracing Taubmann, digging up evidence. My own men, Barris realized, could do it; I have good police in my own department. But if Taubmann got wind of it . . .

This is ghastly, he realized with a start. I have to free myself from this vicious cycle of suspicion and fear! I can't let myself be destroyed; I can't let that woman's morbid hysteria infiltrate my own thinking. Madness transmitted from person to person – isn't that what makes up a mob? Isn't that the group mind that we're supposed to be combatting?

I had better not see Rachel Pitt again, he decided.

But already he felt himself drawn to her. A vague but nonetheless powerful yearning had come into existence inside him; he could not pin down the mood. Certainly she was physically attractive, with her long dark hair, her flashing eyes, slender, active body. But she is not psychologically well-balanced, he decided. She would be a terrible liability; any relationship with a woman like that might wreck me. There is no telling which way she might jump. After all, her tie with Unity has been shattered, without warning; all her plans, her ambitions, have been thrown back in her teeth. She's got to find another entree, a new technique for advancement and survival.

I made a mistake in looking her up, he thought. What would make a better contact than a Director? What could be of more use to her?

When he had gotten back to his own offices, he at once gave instructions that no calls from Mrs Arthur Pitt be put through to him; any messages from her were to be put through proper channels, which meant that regular agencies – and clerks – would be dealing with her.

'A pension situation,' he explained to his staff. 'Her husband wasn't attached to my area, so there's no valid claim that can be filed against this office. She'll have to take it to Taubmann. He was her husband's superior, but she's got the idea that I can help in some way.'

After that, alone in his office, he felt guilty. He had lied to his staff about the situation; he had patently misrepresented Mrs Pitt in order to insure protection of himself. Is that an improvement? he asked himself. Is that my solution?

In her new quarters, Marion Fields sat listlessly reading a comic book. This one dealt with physics, a subject that fascinated her. But she had read the comic book three times, now, and it was hard for her to keep up an interest.

She was just starting to read it over for the fourth time when without warning the door burst open. There stood Jason Dill, his face white. 'What do you know about Vulcan 2?' he shouted at her. '*Why did they destroy Vulcan 2?* Answer me!'

Blinking, she said, 'The old computer?'

Dill's face hardened; he took a deep breath, struggling to control himself.

'What happened to the old computer?' she demanded, avid with curiosity. 'Did it blow up? How do you know somebody did it? Maybe it just burst. Wasn't it old?' All her life she had read about, heard about, been told about Vulcan 2; it was an historic shrine, like the museum that had been Washington, D.C. Except that all the children were taken to the Washington Museum to walk up and down the streets and roam in the great silent office buildings, but no one ever had seen Vulcan 2. 'Can I look?' she demanded, following Jason Dill as he turned and started back out of the room. 'Please let me look. If it blew up it isn't any good any more anyhow, is it? So why can't I see it?'

Dill said, 'Are you in contact with your father?'

'No,' she said. 'You know I'm not.'

'How can I contact him?'

'I don't know,' she said.

'He's quite important in the Healers' Movement, isn't he?' Dill faced her. 'What would they gain by destroying a retired computer that's only good for minor work? Were they trying to reach Vulcan 3?' Raising his voice he shouted, 'Did they think it was Vulcan 3? Did they make a mistake?'

To that, she could say nothing.

'Eventually we'll get him and bring him in,' Dill said. 'And this time he won't escape psychotherapy; I promise you that, child. Even if I have to supervise it myself.'

As steadily as possible she said, 'You're just mad because your old computer blew up, and you have to blame somebody else. You're just like my dad always said; you think the whole world's against you.'

'The whole world is,' Dill said in a harsh, low voice.

At that point he left, slamming the door shut after him. She stood listening to the sound of his shoes against the floor of the hall outside. Away the sound went, becoming fainter and fainter.

That man must have too much work to do, Marion Fields thought. They ought to give him a vacation.

5

There it was. Vulcan 2, or what remained of Vulcan 2 – heaps of twisted debris; fused, wrecked masses of parts; scattered tubes and relays lost in random coils that had once been wiring. A great ruin, still smoldering. The acrid smoke of shorted transformers drifted up and hung against the ceiling of the chamber. Several technicians poked morosely at the rubbish; they had salvaged a few minor parts, nothing more. One of them had already given up and was putting his tools back in their case.

Jason Dill kicked a shapeless blob of ash with his foot. The change, the incredible change from the thing Vulcan 2 had been to *this*, still dazed him. No warning – he had been given no warning at all. He had left Vulcan 2, gone on about his business, waiting for the old computer to finish processing his questions . . . and then the technicians had called to tell him.

Again, for the millionth time, the questions scurried hopelessly through his brain. *How had it happened? How had they gotten it? And why?* It didn't make sense. If they had managed to locate and penetrate the fortress, if one of their agents had gotten this far, why had they wasted their time *here*, when Vulcan 3 was situated only six levels below?

Maybe they made a mistake; maybe they had destroyed the obsolete computer thinking it *was* Vulcan 3. This could have been an error, and, from the standpoint of Unity, a very fortunate one.

But as Jason Dill gazed at the wreckage, he thought, It doesn't look like an error. It's so damn systematic. So thorough. Done with such expert precision.

Should I release the news to the public? he asked himself. I could keep it quiet; these technicians are loyal to me completely. I could keep the destruction of Vulcan 2 a secret for years to come.

Or, he thought, I could say that Vulcan 3 was demolished; I could lay a trap, make them think they had been successful. Then maybe they would come out into the open. Reveal themselves.

They must be in our midst, he thought frantically. To be able to get in here – *they've subverted Unity*.

He felt horror, and, in addition, a deep personal loss. This old machine had been a companion of his for many years. When he had questions simple enough for it to answer he always came here; this visit was part of his life.

Reluctantly, he moved away from the ruins. No more coming here, he realized. The creaking old machine is gone; I'll never be using the manual punch again, laboriously making out the questions in terms that Vulcan 2 can assimilate.

He tapped his coat. They were still there, the answers that Vulcan 2 had given him, answers that he had puzzled over, again and again. He wanted clarification; his last visit had been to rephrase his queries, to get amplification. But the blast had ended that.

Deep in thought, Jason Dill left the chamber and made his way up the corridor, back to the elevator. This is a bad day for us, he thought to himself. We'll remember this for a long time.

Back in his own office he took time to examine the DQ forms that had come in. Larson, the leader of the data-feed team, showed him the rejects.

'Look at these.' His young face stern with an ever-present awareness of duty, Larson carefully laid out a handful of forms. 'This one here – maybe you had better turn it back personally, so there won't be any trouble.'

'Why do I have to attend to it?' Jason Dill said with irritation. 'Can't you handle it? If you're overworked, hire a couple more clerks up here, from the pool. There's always plenty of clerks; you know that as well as I. We must have two million of them on the payrolls. And yet you still have to bother me.' His wrath and anxiety swept up involuntarily, directed at his subordinate; he knew that he was taking it out on Larson, but he felt too depressed to worry about it.

Larson, with no change of expression, said in a firm voice, 'This particular form was sent in by a Director. That's why I feel—'

'Give it to me, then,' Jason Dill said, accepting it.

The form was from the North American Director, William Barris. Jason Dill had met the man any number of times; in his mind he retained an impression of a somewhat tall individual, with a high forehead . . . in his middle thirties, as Dill recalled. A

309

hard worker. The man had not gotten up to the level of Director in the usual manner – by means of personal social contacts, by knowing the right persons – but by constant accurate and valuable work.

'This is interesting,' Jason Dill said aloud to Larson; he put the form aside for a moment. 'We ought to be sure we're publicizing this particular Director. Of course, he probably does a full public-relations job in his own district; we shouldn't worry.'

Larson said, 'I understand he made it up the hard way. His parents weren't anybody.'

'We can show,' Jason Dill said, 'that the ordinary individual, with no pull, knowing no one in the organization, can come in and take a regular low-grade job, such as clerk or even maintenance man, and in time, if he's got the ability and drive, he can rise all the way up to the top. In fact, he might get to be Managing Director.' Not, he thought to himself wryly, that it was such a wonderful job to have.

'He won't be Managing Director for a while,' Larson said, in a tone of certitude.

'Hell,' Jason Dill said wearily. 'He can have my job right now, if that's what he's after. I presume he is.' Lifting the form he glanced at it. The form asked two questions.

a) Are the Healers of real significance?
b) Why don't you respond to their existence?

Holding the form in his hands, Jason Dill thought, One of the eternal bright young men, climbing rapidly up the Unity ladder. Barris, Taubmann, Reynolds, Henderson – they were all making their way confidently, efficiently, never missing a trick, never failing to exploit the slightest wedge. Give them an opportunity, he thought with bitterness, and they'll knock you flat; they'll walk right on over you and leave you there.

'Dog eat dog,' he said aloud.

'Sir?' Larson said at once.

Jason Dill put down the form. He opened a drawer of his desk and got out a flat metal tin; from it he took a capsule which he placed against his wrist. At once the capsule dissolved through the dermal layers; he felt it go into his body, passing into his blood stream to begin work without delay. A tranquilizer . . . one of the newest ones in the long, long series.

It works on me, he thought, and *they* work on me; it in one direction, their constant pressure and harassment in the other.

Again Jason Dill picked up the form from Director Barris. 'Are there many DQs like this?'

'No, sir, but there is a general increase in tension. Several Directors besides Barris are wondering why Vulcan 3 gives no pronouncement on the Healers' Movement.'

'They're all wondering,' Jason Dill said brusquely.

'I mean,' Larson said, 'formally. Through official channels.'

'Let me see the rest of the material.'

Larson passed him the remaining DQ forms. 'And here's the related matter from the data troughs.' He passed over a huge sealed container. 'We've weeded all the incoming material carefully.'

After a time Jason Dill said, 'I'd like the file on Barris.'

'The documented file?'

Jason Dill said, 'And the other one. The unsub-pak.' Into his mind came the full term, not usually said outright. *Unsubstantiated*. 'The worthless packet,' he said. The phony charges, the trumped-up smears and lies and vicious poison-pen letters, mailed to Unity without signature. Unsigned, sometimes in the garbled prose of the psychotic, the lunatic with a grudge. And yet those papers were kept, were filed away. We shouldn't keep them, Jason Dill thought. Or make use of them, even to the extent of examining them. But we do. Right now he was going to look at such filth as it pertained to William Barris. The accumulation of years.

Presently the two files were placed before him on his desk. He inserted the microfilm into the scanner, and, for a time, studied the documented file. A procession of dull facts moved by; Barris had been born in Kent, Ohio; he had no brothers or sisters; his father was alive and employed by a bank in Chile; he had gone to work for Unity as a research analyst. Jason Dill speeded up the film, skipping about irritably. At last he rewound the microfilm and replaced it in the file. The man wasn't even married, he reflected; he led a routine life, one of virtue and work, if the documents could be believed. If they told the full story.

And now, Jason Dill thought, the slander. The missing parts; the other side, the dark shadow side.

To his disappointment, he found the unsub-pak on William Barris almost empty.

Is the man that innocent? Dill wondered. That he's made no enemies? Nonsense. The absence of accusation isn't a sign of the man's innocence; to rise to Director is to incur hostility and envy. Barris probably devotes a good part of his budget to distributing the wealth, to keeping everybody happy. And quiet.

'Nothing here,' he said when Larson returned.

'I noticed how light the file felt,' Larson said. 'Sir, I went down to the data rooms and had them process all the recent material; I thought possibly there might be something not yet in the file.' He added, 'As you probably know, they're several weeks behind.'

Seeing the paper in the man's hand, Jason Dill felt his pulse speed up in anticipation. 'What came in?'

'This.' Larson put down a sheet of what appeared to be expensive watermarked stationery. 'I also took the measure, when I saw this, of having it analysed and traced. So you'd know how to assess its worth.'

'Unsigned,' Dill said.

'Yes, sir. Our analysts say that it was mailed last night, somewhere in Africa. Probably in Cairo.'

Studying the letter, Jason Dill murmured, 'Here's someone who Barris didn't manage to get to. At least not in time.'

Larson said, 'It's a woman's writing. Done with an ancient style of ball-point pen. They're trying to trace the make of pen. What you have there is actually a copy of the letter; they're still examining the actual document down in the labs. But for your purposes—'

'What are my purposes?' Dill said, half to himself. The letter was interesting, but not unique; he had seen such accusations made toward other officials in the Unity organization.

To whom it may concern:
  This is to notify you that William Barris, who is a Director, cannot be trusted, as he is in the pay of the Healers and has been for some time. A

*death that occurred recently can be laid at Mr Barris' door, and he should
be punished for his crime of seeing to it that an innocent and talented Unity
servant was viciously murdered.*

'Notice that the writing slopes down,' Larson said. 'That's
supposed to be an indication that the writer is mentally disturbed.'

'Superstition,' Dill said. 'I wonder if this is referring to the
murder of that field worker, Pitt. That's the most recent. What
connection does Barris have with that? Was he Pitt's Director?
Did he send him out?'

'I'll get all the facts for you, sir,' Larson said briskly.

After he had reread the unsigned letter, Jason Dill tossed it
aside and again picked up the DQ form from Director Barris.
With his pen he scratched a few lines on the bottom of the form.
'Return this to him toward the end of the week. He failed to fill in
his identification numbers; I'm returning it to be corrected.'

Larson frowned. 'That won't delay him much. Barris will
immediately return the form correctly prepared.'

Wearily, Jason Dill said, 'That's my problem. You let me
worry about it. Tend to your own business and you'll last a lot
longer in this organization. That's a lesson you should have
learned a long time ago.'

Flushing, Larson muttered, 'I'm sorry, sir.'

'I think we should start a discreet investigation of Director
Barris,' Dill said. 'Better send in one of the police secretaries; I'll
dictate instructions.'

While Larson rounded up the police secretary, Jason Dill sat
gazing dully at the unsigned letter that accused Director Barris
of being in the pay of the Healers. It would be interesting to know
who wrote this, he thought to himself. Maybe we will know, someday soon.

In any case, there will be an investigation – of William Barris.

After the evening meal, Mrs Agnes Parker sat in the school
restaurant with two other teachers, exchanging gossip and relaxing after the long, tense day.

Leaning over so that no one passing by could hear, Miss
Crowley whispered to Mrs Parker, 'Aren't you finished with that

313

book, yet? If I had known it would take you so long, I wouldn't have agreed to let you read it first.' Her plump, florid face trembled with indignation. 'We really deserve our turn.'

'Yes,' Mrs Dawes said, also leaning to join them. 'I wish you'd go get it right now. Please let us have it, won't you?'

They argued, and at last Mrs Parker reluctantly rose to her feet and moved away from the table, toward the stairway. It was a long walk up the stairs and along the hall to the wing of the building in which she had her own room, and once in the room she had to spend some time digging the book from its hiding place. The book, an ancient literary classic called *Lolita*, had been on the banned list for years; there was a heavy fine for anyone caught possessing it – and, for a teacher, it might mean a jail term. However, most of the teachers read and circulated such stimulating books back and forth among them, and so far no one had been caught.

Grumbling because she had not been able to finish the book, Mrs Parker placed it inside a copy of *World Today* and carried it from her room, out into the hall. No one was in sight, so she continued on toward the stairway.

As she was descending she recalled that she had a job to do, a job that had to be done before morning; the little Fields girl's quarters had not been emptied, as was required by school law. A new pupil would be arriving in a day or so and would occupy the room; it was essential that someone in authority go over every inch of the room to be certain that no subversive or illicit articles belonging to the Fields girl remained to contaminate the new child. Considering the Fields girl's background, this rule was particularly important. As she left the stairway and hurried along a corridor, Mrs Parker felt her heart skip several beats. She might get into a good deal of trouble by being forgetful in this area . . . they might think she wanted the new child contaminated.

The door to Marion Fields' old room was locked. How could that be? Mrs Parker asked herself. The children weren't permitted keys; they could not lock any doors anywhere. It had to be one of the staff. Of course she herself had a key, but she hadn't had time to come down here since Managing Director Dill had taken custody of the child.

As she groped in her pocket for her master key, she heard a sound on the other side of the door. Someone was in the room.

'Who's in there?' she demanded, feeling frightened. If there was an unauthorized person in the room, she would get into trouble; it was her responsibility to maintain this dorm. Bringing her key out, she took a quick breath and then put the key into the lock. Maybe it's someone from the Unity offices checking up on me, she thought. Seeing what I let the Fields girl have in the way of possessions. The door opened and she switched on the light.

At first she saw no one. The bed, the curtains, the small desk in the corner . . . the chest of drawers!

On the chest of drawers something was perched. Something that gleamed, shiny metal, gleamed and clicked as it turned toward her. She saw into two glassy mechanical lenses; something with a tubelike body, the size of a child's bat, shot upward and swept toward her.

She raised her arms. *Stop*, she said to herself. She did not hear her voice; all she heard was a whistling noise in her ears, a deafening blast of sound that became a squeal. *Stop!* she wanted to scream, but she could not speak. She felt as if she were rising; now she had become weightless, floating. The room drifted into darkness. It fell away from her, farther and farther. No motion, no sound . . . just a single spark of light that flickered, hesitated, and then winked out.

Oh dear, she thought. I'm going to get into trouble. Even her thoughts seemed to drift away; she could not maintain them. I've done something wrong. This will cost me my job.

She drifted on and on.

6

The buzzing of his bedside vidscreen woke Jason Dill from his deep, tranquilizer-induced sleep. Reaching, he reflexively snapped the line open, noticing as he did so that the call was on the private circuit. What is it now? he wondered, aware of a pervasive headache that he had been struggling with throughout hours of sleep. The time was late, he realized. At least four-thirty.

On the vidscreen an unfamiliar face appeared. He saw, briefly, a displayed identification-standard. The medical wing.

'Managing Director Dill,' he muttered. 'What do you want? Better check next time with the monitor; it's late at night here, even if it's noon where you are.'

The medical person said, 'Sir, I was advised by members of your staff to notify you at once.' He glanced at a card. 'A Mrs Agnes Parker, a schoolteacher.'

'Yes,' Dill said, nodding.

'She was found by another teacher. Her spinal column had been damaged at several points and she died at 1:30 a.m. First examination indicated that the injuries were done deliberately. There's indication that some variety of heat plasma was induced. The spinal fluid evidently was boiled away by—'

'All right,' Dill said. 'Thanks for notifying me; you did absolutely right.' Stabbing at a button he broke the connection and then asked the monitor for a direct line with Unity Police.

A placid, fleshy face appeared.

Dill said, 'Have all the men guarding the Fields girl removed and a new crew, picked absolutely at random, put in at once. Have the present crew detained until they can be fully cleared.' He considered. 'Do you have the information regarding Agnes Parker?'

'It came in an hour or two ago,' the police official said.

'Damn it,' Dill said. Too much time had passed. They could work a lot of harm in that time. *They?*

The enemy.

'Any word on Father Fields?' he asked. 'I take it for granted you haven't managed to round him up yet.'

'Sorry, sir,' the police official said.

'Let me know what you find on the Parker woman,' Dill said. 'Go over her file, naturally. I'll leave it to you; it's your business. It's the Fields girl I'm concerned about. Don't let anything happen to her. Maybe you should check right now and see if she's all right; notify me at once, either way.' He rang off then and sat back.

Were they trying to find out who took the Fields girl? he asked himself. And where? That was no secret; she was loaded into my car in broad daylight, in front of a playground of children.

They're getting closer, he said to himself. They got Vulcan 2 and they got that foolish, sycophantic schoolteacher whose idea of taking care of her children was to gladly sign them over to the first high official who came along. They can infiltrate our innermost buildings. They evidently know exactly what we're doing. If they can get into the schools, where we train the youth to believe . . .

For an hour or two he sat in the kitchen of his home, warming himself and smoking cigarettes. At last he saw the black night sky begin to turn gray.

Returning to the vidscreen he called Larson. The man, disheveled by sleep, peered at him grumpily until he recognized his superior; then at once he became businesslike and polite. 'Yes, sir,' he said.

'I'm going to need you for a special run of questions to Vulcan 3,' Jason Dill said. 'We're going to have to prepare them with utmost care. And there will be difficult work regarding the data-feeding.' He intended to go on, but Larson interrupted him.

'You'll be pleased to know that we have a line on the person who sent the unsigned letter accusing Director Barris,' Larson said. 'We followed up the lead about the "talented murdered man." We worked on the assumption that Arthur Pitt was meant, and we discovered that Pitt's wife lives in North Africa – in fact, she's in Cairo on shopping trips several times a week. There's such a high degree of probability that she wrote the letter that we're preparing an order to the police in that region to have her picked up. That's Blucher's region, and we'd better put it through his men so there won't be any hard feelings. I just want to get a clearance from you, so I won't have to assume the responsibility. You understand, sir. She may not have done it.'

'Pick her up,' Dill said, only half listening to the younger man's torrent of words.

'Right, sir,' Larson said briskly. 'And we'll let you know what we can get from her. It'll be interesting to see what her motive is for accusing Barris – assuming of course that it was she. My

317

theory is that she may well be working for some other Director who—'

Dill broke the connection. And went wearily back to bed.

Toward the end of the week, Director William Barris received his DQ form back. Scrawled across the bottom was the notation: '*Improperly filled out. Please correct and refile.*'

Furiously, Barris threw the form down on his desk and leaped to his feet. He snapped on the vidsender. 'Give me Unity Control at Geneva.'

The Geneva monitor formed. 'Yes, sir?'

Barris held up the DQ form. 'Who returned this? Whose writing is this? The feed-team leader?'

'No, sir.' The monitor made a brief check. 'It was Managing Director Dill who handled your form, sir.'

Dill! Barris felt himself stiffen with indignation. 'I want to talk to Dill at once.'

'Mr Dill is in conference. He can't be disturbed.'

Barris killed the screen with a savage swipe. For a moment he stood thinking. There was no doubt of it; Jason Dill was stalling. I can't go on like this any further, Barris thought. I'll never get any answers out of Geneva this way. *What is Dill up to, for God's sake?*

Why is Dill refusing to co-operate with his own Directors?

Over a year, and no statement from Vulcan 3 on the Healers. Or had there been, and Dill hadn't released it?

With a surge of disbelief, he thought, Can Dill be keeping back information from the computer? Not letting it know what's going on?

Can it be that Vulcan 3 does not know about the Healers *at all*?

That simply did not seem credible. What ceaseless mass effort that would take on Dill's part; billions of data were fed to Vulcan 3 in one week alone; surely it would be next to impossible to keep all mention of the Movement from the great machine. And if any datum got in at all, the computer would react; it would note the datum, compare it with all other data, record the incongruity.

And, Barris thought, if Dill is concealing the existence of the Movement from Vulcan 3, what would be his motive? What would he gain by deliberately depriving himself – and Unity in general – of the computer's appraisal of the situation?

But that has been the situation for fifteen months, Barris realized. Nothing has been handed down to us from Vulcan 3, and either the machine has said nothing, or, if it has, Dill hasn't released it. So for all intents and purposes, the computer has *not* spoken.

What a basic flaw in the Unity structure, he thought bitterly. Only the one man is in a position to deal with the computer, so that one man can cut us off completely; he can sever the world from Vulcan 3. Like some high priest who stands between man and god, Barris mused. It's obviously wrong. But what can we do? What can *I* do? I may be supreme authority in this region, but Dill is still my superior; he can remove me any time he wants. True, it would be a complex and difficult procedure to remove a Director against his will, but it has been done several times. And if I go and accuse him of—

Of what?

He's doing something, Barris realized, but there's no way I can make out what it is. Not only do I have no facts, but I can't even see my way clearly enough to phrase an accusation. After all, I did fill out the DQ form improperly; that's a fact. And if Dill wants to say that Vulcan 3 simply has said nothing about the Healers, no one can contradict him because no one else has access to the machine. We have to take his word.

Barris thought, But I've had enough of taking his word. Fifteen months is long enough; the time has come to take action. Even if it means my forced resignation.

Which it probably will mean, and right away.

A job, Barris decided, isn't that important. You have to be able to trust the organization you're a part of; you have to believe in your superiors. If you think they're up to something, you have to get up from your chair and do something, even if it's nothing more than to confront them face-to-face and demand an explanation.

Reaching out his hand, he relit the vidscreen. 'Give me the field. And hurry it up.'

After a moment the field-tower monitor appeared. 'Yes, sir?'

'This is Barris. Have a first-class ship ready at once. I'm taking off right away.'

'Where to, sir?'

'To Geneva.' Barris set his jaw grimly. 'I have an appointment with Managing Director Dill.' He added under his breath, 'Whether Dill likes it or not.'

As the ship carried him at high velocity toward Geneva, Barris considered his plans carefully.

What they'll say, he decided, is that I'm using this as a pretext to embarrass Jason Dill. That I'm not sincere; that in fact I'm using the silence of Vulcan 3 as a device to make a bid for Jason Dill's job. My coming to Geneva will just go to prove how ruthlessly ambitious I am. And I won't be able to disprove the charge; I have no way by which I can prove that my motives are pure.

This time the chronic doubt did not assail him; he *knew* that he was acting for the good of the organization. I know my own mind this time, he realized. In this case I can trust myself.

I'll just have to stand firm, he told himself. If I keep denying that I'm trying to undercut Dill for personal advantage—

But he knew better. All the denials in the world won't help me, he thought, once they loose the gods. They can get a couple of those police psychologists up from Atlanta, and once those boys have gone over me I'll *agree* with my accusers; I'll be convinced that I'm cynically exploiting Dill's problems and undermining the organization. They'll even have me convinced that I'm a traitor and ought to be sentenced to forced labor on Luna.

At the thought of the Atlanta psychologists, he felt cold perspiration stand out on his throat and forehead.

Only once had he been up against them, and that was the third year of his employment with Unity. Some unbalanced clerk in his department – at that time he had managed a small rural branch of Unity – had been caught stealing Unity property and reselling it on the black market. Unity of course had a monopoly on advanced technological equipment, and certain items were excessively valuable. It was a constant temptation, and this particular clerk had been in charge of inventories; the temptation had been coupled with opportunity, and the two together had been too much. The secret police had caught up with the man almost at once, had arrested him and gained the usual confession. To get himself in good, or what he imagined to be in good, the man had implicated several others in the branch office, including William Barris. And so a warrant had been served on him, and he had been hauled down in the middle of the night for an 'interview.'

There was no particular onus connected with being served with a police warrant; virtually every citizen became involved with the police at one time or another in his life. The incident had not hurt Barris' career; he had very quickly been released, and he had gone on at his job, and no one had brought the matter up when time came for his advancement to a high position. But for half an hour at police headquarters he had been worked over by two psychologists, and the memory was still with him to wake him up late at night – a bad dream but unfortunately one that might recur in reality at any time.

If he were to step out of line even now, in his position as North American Director with supreme authority over the area north of the Mason-Dixon Line . . .

And, as he was carried closer and closer to Unity Control at Geneva, he was decidedly sticking his neck out. *I should mind my own business*, he told himself. That is a rule we all learn, if we expect to get up the ladder or even keep out of jail.

But this *is* my business!

Not much later a recorded voice said pleasantly, 'We are about to land, Mr Barris.'

Geneva lay below. The ship was descending, pulled down by the automatic relays that had guided it from his field, across the Atlantic and over Western Europe.

Barris thought, Probably they already know I'm on my way. Some flunky, some minor informant, has relayed the information. Undoubtedly some petty clerk in my own building is a spy for Unity Control.

And now, as he rose from his chair and moved toward the exit, someone else was no doubt waiting at the Geneva terminal, watching to mark his arrival. I'll be followed the entire time, he decided.

At the exit he hesitated. I can turn around and go back, he said to himself. I can pretend I never started this trip, and probably no one will ever bring it up; they will know I started to come here, got as far as the field, but they won't know why. They'll never be able to establish that I intended to confront my superior, Jason Dill.

He hesitated, and then he touched the stud that opened the door. It swung aside, and bright midday sunlight spilled into the small ship. Barris filled his lungs with fresh air, paused, and then descended the ramp to the field.

As he walked across the open space toward the terminal building, a shape standing by the fence detached itself. There's one, he realized. Watching for me. The shape moved slowly toward him. It was a figure in a long blue coat. A woman, her hair up in a bandanna, her hands in her coat pockets. He did not recognize her. Sharp, pale features. Such intense eyes, he thought. Staring at him. She did not speak or show any expression until the two of them were separated by only a few feet. And then her colorless lips moved.

'Don't you remember me, Mr Barris?' she said in a hollow voice. She fell in beside him and walked along with him, toward the terminal building. 'I'd like to talk to you. I think it'll be worth your while.'

He said, 'Rachel Pitt.'

Glancing at him, Rachel said, 'I have something to sell. A piece of news that could determine your future.' Her voice was hard and thin, as brittle as glass. 'But I have to have something back; I need something in exchange.'

'I don't want to do any business with you,' he said. 'I didn't come here to see you.'

'I know,' she said. 'I tried to get hold of you at your office; they stalled me every time. I knew right away that you had given orders to that effect.'

Barris said nothing. This is really bad, he thought. That this demented woman should manage to locate me, here, at this time.

'You're not interested,' Rachel said, 'and I know why not; all you can think of is how successfully you're going to deal with Jason Dill. But you see, you won't be able to deal with him at all.'

322

'Why not?' he said, trying to keep any emotions he might be feeling out of his voice.

Rachel said, 'I've been under arrest for a couple of days, now. They had me picked up and brought here.'

'I wondered what you were doing here,' he said.

'A loyal Unity wife,' she said. 'Devoted to the organization. Whose husband was killed only a few—' She broke off. 'But you don't care about that, either.' At the fence she halted, facing him. 'You can either go directly to the Unity Control Building, or you can take half an hour and spend it with me. I advise the latter. If you decide to go on and see Dill now, without hearing me out . . .' She shrugged. 'I can't stop you. Go ahead.' Her black eyes glowed unwinkingly as she waited.

This woman is really out of her mind, Barris thought. The rigid, fanatical expression . . . But even so, could he afford to ignore her?

'Do you think I'm trying to seduce you?' she said.

Startled, he said, 'I—'

'I mean, seduce you away from your high purpose.' For the first time she smiled and seemed to relax. 'Mr Barris,' she said with a shudder. 'I'll tell you the truth. I've been under intensive examination for two days, now. You can suppose who by. But it doesn't matter. Why should I care? After what's happened to me . . .' Her voice trailed off, then resumed. 'Do you think I escaped? That they're after me?' A mocking, bantering irony danced in her eyes. 'Hell no. They let me go. They gave me compulsive psychotherapy for two days, and then they told me I could go home; they shoved me out the door.'

A group of people passed by on their way to a ship; Barris and Rachel were both silent for a time.

'Why did they haul you in?' he asked finally.

Rachel said, 'Oh, I was supposed to have written some kind of a poison-pen letter, accusing someone high up in Unity. I managed to convince them I was innocent – or rather, their analysis of the contents of my mind convinced them; all I did was sit. They took my mind out, took it apart, studied it, put the pieces back together and stuffed them back in my head.' Reaching up, she slid aside the bandanna for a moment; he saw, with

323

grim aversion, the neat white scar slightly before her hairline. 'It's all back,' she said. 'At least, I hope it is.'

With compassion, he said, 'That's really terrible. A real abuse of human beings. It should be stopped.'

'If you get to be Managing Director, maybe you can stop it,' she said. 'Who knows? You might someday be – after all, you're bright and hardworking and ambitious. All you have to do is defeat all those other bright, hardworking, ambitious Directors. Like Taubmann.'

'Is he the one you're supposed to have accused?' Barris said.

'No,' she said, in a faint voice. 'It's you, William Barris. Isn't that interesting? Anyhow, now I've given you my news – free. There's a letter in Jason Dill's file accusing you of being in the pay of the Healers; they showed it to me. Someone is trying to get you, and Dill is interested. Isn't that worth your knowing, before you go in there and lock horns with him?'

Barris said, 'How do you know I'm here to do that?'

Her dark eyes flickered. 'Why else would you be here?' But her voice had a faltering tone now.

Reaching out, he took hold of her arm. With firmness, he guided her along the walk to the street side of the field. 'I will take the time to talk to you,' he said. He racked his mind, trying to think of a place to take her. Already they had come to the public taxi stand; a robot cab had spotted them and was rolling in their direction.

The door of the cab opened. The mechanical voice said, 'May I be of service, please?'

Barris slid into the cab and drew the woman in beside him. Still holding firmly onto her, he said to the cab, 'Say listen, can you find us a hotel, not too conspicuous – you know.' He could hear the receptor mechanism of the cab whirring as it responded. 'For us to get a load off our feet,' he said. 'My girl and me. You know.'

Presently the cab said, 'Yes, sir.' It began to move along the busy Geneva streets. 'Out-of-the-way hotel where you will find the privacy you desire.' It added, 'The Hotel Bond, sir.'

Rachel Pitt said nothing; she stared sightlessly ahead.

7

In his pockets, Jason Dill carried the two reels of tape; they never left him, night and day. He had them with him now as he walked slowly along the brightly lit corridor. Once again, involuntarily, he lifted his hand and rubbed the bulge which the tapes made. Like a magic charm, he thought to himself with irony. And we accuse the masses of being superstitious!

Ahead of him, lights switched on. Behind him, enormous reinforced doors slid shut to fill in the chamber's single entrance. The huge calculator rose in front of him, the immense tower of receptor banks and indicators. He was alone with it – alone with Vulcan 3.

Very little of the computer was visible; its bulk disappeared into regions which he had never seen, which in fact no human had ever seen. During the course of its existence it had expanded certain portions of itself. To do so it had cleared away the granite and shale earth; it had, for a long time now, been conducting excavation operations in the vicinity. Sometimes Jason Dill could hear that sound going on like a far-off, incredibly high-pitched dentist's drill. Now and then he had listened and tried to guess where the operations were taking place. It was only a guess. Their only check on the growth and development of Vulcan 3 lay in two clues: the amount of rock thrown up to the surface, to be carted off, and the variety, amount, and nature of the raw materials and tools and parts which the computer requested.

Now, as Jason Dill stood facing the thing, he saw that it had put forth a new reel of supply requisitions; it was there for him to pick up and fill. As if, he thought, I'm some errand boy.

I do its shopping, he realized. It's stuck here, so I go out and come back with the week's groceries. Only in its case we don't supply food; we supply just about everything else but.

The financial cost of supporting Vulcan 3 was immense. Part of the taxation program conducted by Unity on a world-wide basis existed to maintain the computer. At the latest estimate, Vulcan 3's share of the taxes came to about forty-three percent.

And the rest, Dill thought idly, goes to schools, for roads, hospitals, fire departments, police – the lesser order of human needs.

Beneath his feet the floor vibrated. This was the deepest level which the engineers had constructed, and yet something was constantly going on below. He had felt the vibrations before. What lay down there? No black earth; not the inert ground. Energy, tubes and pies, wiring, transformers, self-contained machinery . . . He had a mental image of relentless activity going on: carts carrying supplies in, wastes out; lights blinking on and off; relays closing; switches cooling and reheating; worn-out parts replaced; new parts invented; superior designs replacing obsolete designs. And how far had it spread? Miles? Were there even more levels beneath the one transmitting up through the soles of his shoes? Did it go down, down, *forever*?

Vulcan 3 was aware of him. Across the vast impersonal face of metal an acknowledgement gleamed, a ribbon of fluid letters that appeared briefly and then vanished. Jason Dill had to catch the words at once or not at all; no latitude for human dullness was given.

Is the educational bias survey complete?

'Almost,' Dill said. 'A few more days.' As always, in dealing with Vulcan 3, he felt a deep, inertial reluctance; it slowed his responses and hung over his mind, his faculties, like a dead weight. In the presence of the computer he found himself becoming stupid. He always gave the shortest answers; it was easier. And as soon as the first words lit up in the air above his head, he had a desire to leave; already, he wanted to go.

But this was his job, this being cloistered here with Vulcan 3. Someone had to do it. Some human being had to stand in this spot.

He had never had this feeling in the presence of Vulcan 2.

Now, new words formed, like lightning flashing blue-white in the damp air.

I need it at once.

'It'll be along as soon as the feed-teams can turn it into data forms.'

Vulcan 3 was – well, he thought, the only word was agitated. Power lines glowed red – the origin of the series' name. The rumblings and dull flashes of red had reminded Nathaniel Greenstreet of the ancient god's forge, the lame god who had created the thunderbolts for Jupiter, in an age long past.

There is some element misfunctioning. A significant shift in the orientation of certain social strata which cannot be explained in terms of data already available to me. A realignment of the social pyramid is forming in response to historic-dynamic factors unfamiliar to me. I must know more if I am to deal with this.

A faint tendril of alarm moved through Jason Dill. What did Vulcan 3 suspect? 'All data is made available to you as soon as possible.'

A decided bifurcation of society seems in the making. Be certain your report on educational bias is complete. I will need all the relevant facts.

After a pause, Vulcan 3 added: *I sense a rapidly approaching crisis.*

'What kind of crisis?' Dill demanded nervously.

Ideological. A new orientation appears to be on the verge of verbalization. A Gestalt derived from the experience of the lowest classes. Reflecting their dissatisfaction.

'Dissatisfaction? With what?'

Essentially, the masses reject the concept of stability. In the main, those without sufficient property to be firmly rooted are more concerned with gain than with security. To them, society is an arena of adventure. A structure in which they hope to rise to a superior power status.

'I see,' Dill said dutifully.

A rationally controlled, stable society such as ours defeats their desires. In a rapidly altering, unstable society the lowest classes would stand a good chance of seizing power. Basically, the lowest classes are adventurers, conceiving life as a gamble, a game rather than a task, with social power as the stakes.

'Interesting,' Dill said. 'So for them the concept of luck plays a major role. Those on top have had good luck. Those—' But Vulcan 3 was not interested in his contribution; it had already continued.

The dissatisfaction of the masses is not based on economic deprivation but on a sense of ineffectuality. Not an increased standard of living, but more social power, is their fundamental goal. Because of their emotional orientation, they arise and act when a powerful leader-figure can co-ordinate them into a functioning unit rather than a chaotic mass of unformed elements.

Dill had no reply to that. It was evident that Vulcan 3 had sifted

327

the information available, and had come up with uncomfortably close inferences. That, of course, was the machine's forte; basically it was a device par excellence for performing the processes of deductive and inductive reasoning. It ruthlessly passed from one step to the next and arrived at the correct inference, whatever it was.

Without direct knowledge of any kind, Vulcan 3 was able to deduce, from general historic principles, the social conflicts developing in the contemporary world. It had manufactured a picture of the situation which faced the average human being as he woke up in the morning and reluctantly greeted the day. Stuck down here, Vulcan 3 had, through indirect and incomplete evidence, *imagined* things as they actually were.

Sweat came out on Dill's forehead. He was dealing with a mind greater than any one man's or any group of men's. This proof of the prowess of the computer – this verification of Greenstreet's notion that a machine was not limited merely to doing what man could do, but doing it faster . . . Vulcan 3 was patently doing what a man could *not* do no matter how much time he had available to him.

Down here, buried underground in the dark, in this constant isolation, a human being would go mad; he would lose all contact with the world, all ideas of what was going on. As time progressed he would develop a less and less accurate picture of reality; he would become progressively more hallucinated. Vulcan 3, however, moved continually in the opposite direction; it was, in a sense, moving by degrees toward inevitable *sanity*, or at least maturity – if, by that, was meant a clear, accurate, and full picture of things as they really were. A picture, Jason Dill realized, that no human being has ever had or will ever have; all humans are partial. And this giant is not!

'I'll put a rush on the educational survey,' he murmured. 'Is there anything else you need?'

The statistical report on rural linguistics has not come in. Why is that? It was under the personal supervision of your sub-co-ordinator, Arthur Graveson Pitt.

Dill cursed silently. Good lord! Vulcan 3 never mislaid or lost or mistook a single datum among the billions that it ingested and stored away. 'Pitt was injured,' Dill said aloud, his mind racing desperately. 'His car overturned on a winding mountain road in Colorado. Or at least that's the way I recall it. I'd have to check to be sure, but—'

Have his report completed by someone else. I require it. Is his injury serious?

Dill hesitated. 'As a matter of fact, they don't think he'll live. They say—'

Why have so many T-class persons been killed in the past year? I want more information on this. According to my statistics only one-fifth that number should have died of natural causes. Some vital factor is missing. I must have more data.

'All right,' Dill muttered. 'We'll get you more data; anything you want.'

I am considering calling a special meeting of the Control Council. I am on the verge of deciding to question the staff of eleven Regional Directors personally.

At that, Dill was stunned; he tried to speak, but for a time he could not. He could only stare fixedly at the ribbon of words. The ribbon moved inexorably on.

I am not satisfied with the way data is supplied. I may demand your removal and an entirely new system of feeding.

Dill's mouth opened and closed. Aware that he was shaking visibly, he backed away from the computer. 'Unless you want something else,' he managed. 'I have business. In Geneva.' All he wanted to do was get out of the situation, away from the chamber.

Nothing more. You may go.

As quickly as possible, Dill left the chamber, ascending by express lift to the surface level. Around him, in a blur, guards checked him over; he was scarcely aware of them.

What a going-over, he thought. What an ordeal. Talk about the Atlanta psychologists – they're nothing compared with what I have to face, day after day.

God, how I hate that machine, he thought. He was still trembling, his heart palpitating; he could not breathe, and for a time he sat on a leather-covered couch in the outer lounge, recovering.

To one of the attendants he said, 'I'd like a glass of some stimulant. Anything you have.'

Presently it was in his hand, a tall green glass; he gulped it down and felt a trifle better. The attendant was waiting around to be paid, he realized; the man had a tray and a bill.

'Seventy-five cents, sir,' the attendant said.

To Dill it was the final blow. His position as Managing Director did not exempt him from these annoyances; he had to fish around in his pocket for change. And meanwhile, he thought, the future of our society rests with me. While I dig up seventy-five cents for this idiot.

I ought to let them all get blown to bits. *I ought to give up.*

William Barris felt a little more relaxed as the cab carried him and Rachel Pitt into the dark, overpopulated, older section of the city. On the sidewalks clumps of elderly men in seedy garments and battered hats stood inertly. Teenagers lounged by store windows. Most of the store windows, Barris noticed, had metal bars or gratings protecting their displays from theft. Rubbish lay piled up in alleyways.

'Do you mind coming here?' he asked the woman beside him. 'Or is it too depressing?'

Rachel had taken off her coat and put it across her lap. She wore a short-sleeved cotton shirt, probably the one she had had on when the police arrested her; it looked to him like something more suited for house use. And, he saw, her throat was streaked with what appeared to be dust. She had a tired, wan expression and she sat listlessly .

'You know, I like the city,' she said, after a time.

'Even this part?'

'I've been staying in this section,' she said. 'Since they let me go.'

Barris said, 'Did they give you time to pack? Were you able to take any clothes with you?'

'Nothing,' she said.

'What about money?'

'They were very kind.' Her voice had weary irony in it. 'No, they didn't let me take any money; they simply bundled me into a police ship and took off for Europe. But before they let me go they permitted me to draw enough money from my husband's pension payment to take care of getting me back home.' Turning her head she finished, 'Because of all the red tape, it will be several months before the regular payments will be forthcoming. This was a favor they did me.'

To that, Barris could say nothing.

'Do you think,' Rachel said, 'that I resent the way Unity has treated me?'

'Yes,' he said.

Rachel said, 'You're right.'

Now the cab had begun to coast up to the entrance of an ancient brick hotel with tattered awning. Feeling somewhat dismayed by the appearance of the Bond Hotel, Barris said, 'Will this be all right, this place?'

'Yes,' Rachel said. 'In fact, this is where I would have had the cab take us. I had intended to bring you here.'

The cab halted and its door swung open. As Barris paid it, he thought, Maybe I shouldn't have let it decide for me. Maybe I ought to get back in and have it drive on. Turning, he glanced up at the hotel.

Rachel Pitt had already started up the steps. It was too late.

Now a man appeared in the entrance, his hands in his pockets. He wore a dark, untidy coat, and a cap pulled down over his forehead. The man glanced at her and said something to her.

At once Barris strode up the steps after her. He took her by the arm, stepping between her and the man. 'Watch it,' he said to the man, putting his hand on the pencil beam which he carried in his breast pocket.

In a slow, quiet voice the man said, 'Don't get excited, mister.' He studied Barris. 'I wasn't accosting Mrs Pitt. I was merely asking when you arrived.' Coming around behind Barris and Rachel, he said, 'Go on inside the hotel, Director. We have a room upstairs where we can talk. No one will bother us here. You picked a good place.'

Or rather, Barris thought icily, the cab and Rachel Pitt picked a good place. There was nothing he could do; he felt, against his spine, the tip of the man's heat beam.

'You shouldn't be suspicious of a man of the cloth, in regards to such matters,' the man said conversationally, as they crossed the grimy, dark lobby to the stairs. The elevator, Barris noticed, was out of order; or at least it was so labeled. 'Or perhaps,' the man said, 'you failed to notice the historic badge of my vocation.' At the stairs the man halted, glanced around, and removed his cap.

The stern, heavy-browed face that became visible was familiar to Barris. The slightly crooked nose, as if it had been broken once and never properly set. The deliberately short-cropped hair that gave the man's entire face the air of grim austerity.

Rachel said, 'This is Father Fields.'

The man smiled, and Barris saw irregular, massive teeth. The photo had not indicated that, Barris thought. Nor the strong chin. It had hinted at, but not really given, the full measure of the man. In some ways Father Fields looked more like a toughened, weathered prize fighter than he did a man of religion.

Barris, face to face with him for the first time, felt a complete and absolute fear of the man; it came with a certitude that he had never before known in his life.

Ahead of them, Rachel led the way upstairs.

8

Barris said, 'I'd be interested to know when this woman went over to you.' He indicated Rachel Pitt, who stood by a window of the hotel room, gazing meditatively out at the buildings and rooftops of Geneva.

'You can see Unity Control from here,' Rachel said, turning her head.

'Of course you can,' Father Fields said in his hoarse, grumbling voice. He sat in the corner, in a striped bathrobe and fleece-lined slippers, a screw driver in one hand, a light fixture in the other; he had gone into the bathroom to take a shower, but the light wasn't working. Two other men, Healers evidently, sat at a card table poring over some pamphlets stacked up between them in wired bundles. Barris assumed that these were propaganda material of the Movement, about to be distributed.

'Is that just coincidence?' Rachel asked.

Fields grunted, ignoring her as he worked on the light fixture.

Then, raising his head, he said brusquely to Barris, 'Now listen. I won't lie to you, because it's lies that your organization is founded on. Anyone who knows me knows I never have need of lying. Why should I? The truth is my greatest weapon.'

'What is the truth?' Barris said.

'The truth is that pretty soon we're going to run up that street you see outside to that big building the lady is looking at, and then Unity won't exist.' He smiled, showing his malformed teeth. But it was, oddly, a friendly smile. As if, Barris thought, the man hoped that he would chime in – possibly smile back in agreement.

With massive irony, Barris said, 'Good luck.'

'Luck,' Fields echoed. 'We don't need it. All we need is speed. It'll be like poking at some old rotten fruit with a stick.' His voice twanged with the regional accent of his origin; Barris caught the drawl of Taubmann's territory, the Southern States that formed the rim of South America.

'Spare me your folksy metaphors,' Barris said.

Fields laughed. 'You stand in error, Mister Director.'

'It was a simile,' Rachel agreed, expressionlessly.

Barris felt himself redden; they were making fun of him, these people, and he was falling into it. He said to the man in the striped bathrobe, 'I'm amazed at your power to draw followers. You engineer the murder of this woman's husband, and after meeting you she joins your Movement. That is impressive.'

For a time Fields said nothing. Finally he threw down the light fixture. 'Must be a hundred years old,' he said. 'Nothing like that in the United States since I was born. And they call this area "modern." ' He scowled and plucked at his lower lip. 'I appreciate your moral indignation. Somebody did smash in that poor man's head; there's no doubt about that.'

'You were there too,' Barris said.

'Oh, yes,' Fields said. He studied Barris intently; the hard dark eyes seemed to grow and become even more wrathful. 'I do get carried away,' he said. 'When I see that lovely little suit you people wear, that gray suit and white shirt, those shiny black shoes.' His scrutiny traveled up and down Barris. 'And especially, I get carried away by that thing you all have in your pockets. Those pencil beams.'

Rachel said to Barris, 'Father Fields was once burned by a tax collector.'

'Yes,' Fields said. 'You know your Unity tax collectors are exempt from the law. No citizen can take legal action against them. Isn't that lovely?' Lifting his arm, he pulled back his right sleeve; Barris saw that the flesh had been corroded away to a permanent mass of scar tissue, from the man's wrist to his elbow. 'Let's see some moral indignation about that,' he said to Barris.

'I have it,' Barris said. 'I never approved of the general tax-collecting procedures. You won't find them in my area.'

'That's so,' Fields said. His voice lost some of its ferocity; he seemed to cool slightly. 'That's a fact about you. Compared to the other Directors, you're not too bad. We have a couple of people in and around your offices. We know quite a bit about you. You're here in Geneva because you want to find out why Vulcan 3 hasn't handed down any dogma about us Healers. It needles your conscience that old Jason Dill can toss your DQ forms back in your face and there's nothing you can do. It is mighty odd that your machine hasn't said anything about us.'

To that, Barris said nothing.

'It gives us sort of an advantage,' Fields said. 'You boys don't have any operating policy; you have to mark time until the machine talks. Because it wouldn't occur to you to put together your own human-made policy.'

Barris said, 'In my area I have a policy. I have as many Healers as possible thrown into jail – on sight.'

'Why?' Rachel Pitt asked.

'Ask your dead husband,' Barris said, with animosity toward her. 'I can't understand you,' he said to her. 'Your husband went out on his job and these people—'

Fields interrupted, 'Director, you have never been worked over by the Atlanta psychologists.' His voice was quiet. 'This woman has. So was I, to some extent. To a very minor extent. Not like she was. With her, they were in a hurry.'

For a while no one spoke.

There's not much I can say, Barris realized. He walked over to the card table and picked up one of the pamphlets; aimlessly, he read the large black type.

DO YOU HAVE ANY SAY IN RUNNING YOUR LIVES?
WHEN WAS THE LAST TIME YOU VOTED?

'There has been no public election,' Field said, 'for twenty years. Do they teach that to the little kids in your schools?'

'There should be,' Barris said.

Fields said, 'Mr Barris—' His voice was tense and husky. 'How'd you like to be the first Director to come over to us?' For an instant Barris detected a pleading quality; then it was gone. The man's voice and face became stern. 'It'll make you look good as hell in the future history books,' he said, and laughed harshly. Then, once more picking up the light fixture, he resumed work on it. He ignored Barris; he did not even seem to be waiting for a reply.

Coming over to Barris, Rachel said in her sharp, constricted fashion, 'Director, he's not joking. He really wants you to join the Movement.'

'I imagine he does,' Barris said.

Fields said, 'You have a sense of what's wrong. You know how wrong it is. All that ambition and suspicion. What's it for? Maybe I'm doing you people an injustice, but honest to God, Mr Barris, I think your top men are insane. I know Jason Dill is. Most of the Directors are, and their staffs. And the schools are turning out lunatics. Did you know they took my daughter and stuck her into one of their schools? As far as I know she's there now. We never got into the schools too well. You people are really strong, there. It means a lot to you.'

'You went to a Unity school,' Rachel said to Barris. 'You know how they teach children not to question, not to disagree. They're taught to obey. Arthur was the product of one of them. Pleasant, good-looking, well-dressed, on his way up—' She broke off.

And dead, Barris thought.

'If you don't join us,' Fields said to him, 'you can walk out the door and up the street to your appointment with Jason Dill.'

'I have no appointment,' Barris said.

'That's right,' Fields admitted.

Rachel screamed, pointing to the window.

Coming across the sill, through the window and into the room,

335

was something made of gleaming metal. It lifted and flew through the air. As it swooped it made a shrill sound. It changed direction and dropped at Fields.

The two men at the card table leaped up and stared open-mouthed. One of them began groping for the gun at his waist.

The metal thing dived at Fields. Covering his face with his arms, Fields flung himself to the floor and rolled. His striped bathrobe flapped, and one slipper shot from his foot and slid across the rug. As he rolled he grabbed out a heat beam and fired upward, sweeping the air above him. A burning flash seared Barris; he leaped back and shut his eyes.

Still screaming, Rachel Pitt appeared in front of him, her face torn with hysteria. The air crackled with energy; a cloud of dense blue-gray matter obscured most of the room. The couch, the chairs, the rug and walls were burning. Smoke poured up, and Barris saw tongues of flame winking orange in the murk. Now he heard Rachel choke; her screams ceased. He himself was partly blinded. He made his way toward the door, his ears ringing.

'It's okay,' Father Fields said, his voice coming dimly through the crackling of energy. 'Get those little fires out. I got the goddam thing.' He loomed up in front of Barris, grinning crookedly. One side of his face was badly burned and part of his short-cropped hair had been seared away. His scalp, red and blistered, seemed to glow. 'If you can help get the fires out,' he said to Barris in an almost courtly tone, 'maybe I can find enough of the goddam thing to get into it and see what it was.'

One of the men had found a hand-operated fire extinguisher outside in the hall; now, pumping furiously, he was managing to get the fires out. His companion appeared with another extinguisher and pitched in. Barris left them to handle the fire and went back through the room to find Rachel Pitt.

She was crouched in the far corner, sunk down in a heap, staring straight ahead, her hands clasped together. When he lifted her up, he felt her body trembling. She said nothing as he stood holding her in his arms; she did not seem aware of him.

Appearing beside him, Fields said in a gleeful voice, 'Hot dog, Barris – I found most of it.' He triumphantly displayed a charred but still intact metal cylinder with an elaborate system of antennae and receptors and propulsion jets. Then, seeing Rachel Pitt, he lost his smile. 'I wonder if she'll come out of it this time,' he said. 'She was this way when she first came to us. After the Atlanta boys let her go. It's catatonia.'

'And you got her out of it?' Barris said.

Fields said, 'She came out of it because she wanted to. She wanted to do something. Be active. Help us. Maybe this last was too much for her. She's stood a lot.' He shrugged, but on his face was an expression of great compassion.

'Maybe I'll see you again,' Fields said to him.

'You're leaving?' Fields said. 'Where are you going?'

'To see Jason Dill.'

'What about her?' Fields said, indicating the woman in Barris' arms. 'Are you taking her with you?'

'If you'll let me,' Barris said.

'Do what you want,' Fields said, eying him thoughtfully. 'I don't quite understand you, Director.' He seemed, in this moment, to have shed his regional accent. 'Are you for us or against us? Or do you know? Maybe you don't know; maybe it'll take time.'

Barris said, 'I'll never go along with a group that murders.'

'There are slow murders and fast murders,' Fields said. 'And body murders and mind murders. Some you do with evil schools.'

Going past him, Barris went on out of the smoke-saturated room, into the hall outside. He descended the stairs to the lobby.

Outside on the sidewalk he hailed a robot cab.

At the Geneva field he put Mrs Pitt aboard a ship that would carry her to his own region, North America. He contacted his staff by vidsender and gave them instructions to have the ship met when it landed in New York and to provide her with medical care until he himself got back. And he had one final order for them.

'Don't let her out of my jurisdiction. Don't honor any request to have her transferred, especially to South America.'

The staff member said acutely, 'You don't want to let this person get anywhere near Atlanta.'

'That's right,' Barris said, aware that without his having to spell it out his staff understood the situation. There was probably no one in the Unity structure who would not be able to follow his meaning. Atlanta was the prime object of dread for all of them, great and small alike.

Does Jason Dill have that hanging over him, too? Barris wondered as he left the vidbooth. Possibly he is exempt – certainly from a rational viewpoint he has nothing to fear. But the irrational fear could be there anyhow.

He made his way through the crowded, noisy terminal building, headed in the direction of one of the lunch counters. At the counter he ordered a sandwich and coffee and sat with that for a time, pulling himself together and pondering.

Was there really a letter to Dill accusing me of treason? he asked himself. Had Rachel been telling the truth? Probably not. It probably had been a device to draw him aside, to keep him from going on to Unity Control.

I'll have to take the chance, he decided. No doubt I could put out careful feelers, track the information down over a period of time; I might even know within a week. But I can't wait that long. I want to face Dill now. That's what I came here for.

He thought, And I have been with them, the enemy. If such a letter exists, there is now what would no doubt be called 'proof.' The structure would need nothing more; I would be tried for treason and convicted. And that would be the end of me, as a high official of the system and as a living, breathing human being. True, something might still be walking around, but it wouldn't really be alive.

And yet, he realized, I can't even go back now, to my own region. Whether I like it or not I have met Father Fields face-to-face; I've associated with him and any enemies I might have, inside or outside the Unity structure, will have exactly what they want – for the rest of my life. It's too late to give up, to drop the idea of confronting Jason Dill. With irony, he thought, Father Fields has forced me to go through with it, the thing he was trying to prevent.

He paid for his lunch and left the lunch counter. Going outside onto the sidewalk, he called another robot cab and instructed it to take him to Unity Control.

*

Barris pushed past the battery of secretaries and clerks, into Jason Dill's private syndrome of interconnected offices. At the sight of his Director's stripe, the dark red slash on his gray coat-sleeve, officials of Unity Control stepped obediently out of his path, leaving a way open from room to room. The last door opened – and abruptly he was facing Dill.

Jason Dill looked up slowly, putting down a handful of reports. 'What do you think you're doing?' He did not appear at first to recognize Barris; his gaze strayed to the Director's stripe and then back to his face. 'This is out of the question,' Dill said, 'your barging in here like this.'

'I came here to talk to you,' Barris said. He shut the office door after him; it closed with a bang, startling the older man. Jason Dill half stood up, then subsided.

'Director Barris,' he murmured. His eyes narrowed. 'File a regular appointment slip; you know procedure well enough by now to—'

Barris cut him off. 'Why did you turn back my DQ form? Are you withholding information from Vulcan 3?'

Silence.

The color left Jason Dill's face. 'Your form wasn't properly filled out. According to Section Six, Article Ten of the Unity—'

'You're rerouting material away from Vulcan 3; that's why it hasn't stated a policy on the Healers.' He came closer to the seated man, bending over him as Dill stared down at his papers on the desk, not meeting his gaze. 'Why? It doesn't make sense. You know what this constitutes. Treason! Keeping back data, deliberately falsifying the troughs. I could bring charges against you, even have you arrested.' Resting his hands on the surface of the desk, Barris said loudly, 'Is the purpose of this to isolate and weaken the eleven Directors so that—'

He broke off. He was looking down into the barrel of a pencil beam. Jason Dill had been holding it since he had burst into the man's office. Dill's middle-aged features twitched bleakly; his eyes gleamed as he gripped the small tube. 'Now be quiet, Director,' Dill said icily. 'I admire your tactics. This going on the offensive. Accusations without opportunity for me even to get in one word.

Standard operating procedure.' He breathed slowly, in a series of great gasps. 'Damn you,' he snapped, '*sit down.*'

Barris sat down watchfully. I made my pitch, he realized. The man is right. And shrewd. He's seen a lot in his time, more than I have. Maybe I'm not the first to barge in here, yelling with indignation, trying to pin him down, force admissions.

Thinking that, Barris felt his confidence ebb away. But he continued to face the older man; he did not draw back.

Jason Dill's face was gray now. Drops of perspiration stood out on his wrinkled forehead; bringing out his handkerchief he patted at them. With the other hand, however, he still held the pencil beam. 'We're both a little calmer,' he said. 'Which in my opinion is better. You were overly dramatic. Why?' A faint, distorted smile appeared on his lips. 'Have you been practicing how you would make your entrance?'

The man's hand traveled to his breast pocket. He rubbed a bulge there; Barris saw that he had something in his inner pocket, something to which his hand had gone involuntarily. Seeing what he had, Dill at once jerked his hand away.

Medicine? Barris wondered.

'This treason gambit,' Dill said. 'I could try that, too. An attempted coup on your part.' He pointed at a control on the edge of his desk. 'All this – your grand entrance – has of course been recorded. The evidence is there.' He pressed a stud, and, on the desk vidscreen, the Geneva Unity monitor appeared. 'Give me the police,' Dill said. Sitting with the pencil beam still pointed at Barris, he waited for the line to be put through. 'I have too many other problems to take time off to cope with a Director who decides to run amuck.'

Barris said, 'I'll fight this all the way in the Unity courts. My conscience is clear; I'm acting in the interests of Unity, against a Managing Director who's systematically breaking down the system, step by step. You can investigate my entire life and you won't find a thing. I know I'll beat you in the courts, even if it takes years.'

'We have a letter,' Dill said. On the screen the familiar heavy-jowled features of a police official appeared. 'Stand by,' Dill instructed him. The police official's eyes moved as he took in the scene of the Managing Director holding his gun on Director Barris.

'That letter,' Barris said as steadily as possible, 'has no factual basis for the charges it makes.'

'Oh?' Dill said. 'You're familiar with its charges?'

'Rachel Pitt gave me all the information,' Barris said. So she had been telling the truth. Well, that letter – spurious as its charges were – coupled with this episode, would probably be enough to convict him. The two would dovetail; they would create together the sort of evidence acceptable to the Unity mentality.

The police official eyed Barris.

At his desk, Jason Dill held the pencil beam steadily.

Barris said, 'Today I sat in the same room with Father Fields.'

Reaching his hand out to the vidsender, Jason Dill reflected and then said, 'I'll ring you off and recontact you later.' With his thumb he broke the connection; the image of the police official, still staring at Barris, faded out.

Jason Dill rose from his desk and pulled lose the power cable supplying the recording scanner which had been on since Barris entered the room. Then he reseated himself.

'The charges in the letter are true!' he said with incredulity. 'My God, it never occurred to me . . .' Then, rubbing his forehead, he said, 'Yes, it did. Briefly. So they managed to penetrate to the Director level.' His eyes showed horror and weariness.

'They put a gun on me and detained me,' Barris said. 'When I got here to Geneva.'

Doubt, mixed with distraught cunning, crossed the older man's face. Obviously, he did not want to believe that the Healers had gotten so far up into Unity, Barris realized. He would grasp at any straw, any explanation which would account for the facts . . . even the true one, Barris thought bitingly. Jason Dill had a psychological need that took precedence over the habitual organizational suspicions.

'You can trust me,' Barris said.

'Why?' The pencil beam still pointed at him, but the conflicting emotions swept back and forth through the man.

'You have to believe someone,' Barris said. 'Sometime, somewhere. What is that you reach up and rub, there at your chest?'

Grimacing, Dill glanced down at his hand; again it was at his chest. He jerked it away. 'Don't play on my fears,' he said.

'Your fear of isolation?' Barris said. 'Of having everyone against you? Is that some physical injury that you keep rubbing?'

Dill said, 'No. You're guessing far too much; you're out of your depth.' But he seemed more composed now. 'Well, Director,' he said. 'I'll tell you something. I probably don't have long to live. My health has deteriorated since I've had this job. Maybe in a sense you're right . . . it *is* a physical injury I'm rubbing. If you ever get where I am, you'll have some deep-seated injuries and illnesses too. Because there'll be people around you putting them there.'

'Maybe you should take a couple of flying wedge squads of police and seize the Bond Hotel,' Barris said. 'He was there an hour ago. Down in the old section of the city. Not more than two miles from here.'

'He'd be gone,' Dill said. 'He turns up again and again on the outskirts this way. We'll never get him; there're a million ratholes he can slither down.'

Barris said, 'You almost did get him.'

'When?'

'In the hotel room. When that robot tracking device entered and made for him. It almost succeeded in burning him up, but he was quite fast; he managed to roll away and get it first.'

Dill said, 'What robot tracking device? Describe it.'

As Barris described it, Dill stared at him starkly. He swallowed noisily but did not interrupt until Barris had finished.

'What's wrong?' Barris said. 'From what I saw of it, it seems to be the most effective counterpenetration weapon you have. Surely you'll be able to break up the Movement with such a mechanism. I think your anxiety and preoccupation is excessive.'

In an almost inaudible voice, Dill said, 'Agnes Parker.'

'Who is that?' Barris said.

Seemingly not aware of him, Dill murmured, 'Vulcan 2. And now a try at Father Fields. But he got away.' Putting down his pencil beam he reached into his coat; rummaging, he brought out two reels of tape. He tossed the tape down on the desk.

'So that's what you've been carrying,' Barris said with curiosity. He picked up the reels and examined them.

Dill said, 'Director, there is a third force.'

'What?' Barris said, with a chill.

'A third force is operating on us,' Jason Dill said, and smiled grotesquely. 'It may get all of us. It appears to be very strong.'

He put his pencil beam away, then. The two of them faced each other without it.

9

The police raid on the Bond Hotel, although carried out expertly and thoroughly, netted nothing.

Jason Dill was not surprised.

In his office by himself he faced a legal dictation machine. Clearing his throat he said into it hurriedly, 'This is to act as a formal statement in the event of my death, explaining the circumstances and reasons why I saw fit as Unity Managing Director to conduct *sub rosa* relations with North American Director William Barris. I entered into these relations knowing full well that Director Barris was under heavy suspicion concerning his position vis-a-vis the Healers' Movement, a treasonable band of murderers and—' He could not think of the word so he cut off the machine temporarily.

He glanced at his watch. In five minutes he had an appointment with Barris; he would not have time to complete his protective statement anyway. So he erased the tape. Better to start over later on, he decided. If he survived into the later on.

I'll go meet him, Jason Dill decided, and go on the assumption that he is being honest with me. I'll co-operate with him fully; I'll hold nothing back.

But just to be on the safe side, he opened the drawer of his desk and lifted out a small container. From it he took an object wrapped up and sealed; he opened it, and there was the smallest heat beam that the police had been able to manufacture. No larger than a kidney bean.

Using the adhesive agent provided, he carefully affixed the

343

weapon inside his right ear. Its color blended with his own; examining himself in a wall mirror he felt satisfied that the heat beam would not be noticed.

Now he was ready for his appointment. Taking his overcoat, he left his office, walking briskly.

He stood by while Barris laid the tapes out on the surface of a table, spreading them flat with his hands.

'And no more came after these,' Barris said.

'No more,' Dill said. 'Vulcan 2 ceased to exist at that point.' He indicated the first of the two tapes. 'Start reading there.'

This Movement may be of more significance than first appears. It is evident that the Movement is directed against Vulcan 3 rather than the series of computers as a whole. Until I have had time to consider the greater aspects, I suggest Vulcan 3 not be informed of the matter.

'I asked why,' Dill said. 'Look at the next tape.'

Consider the basic difference between Vulcan 3 and preceding computer. Its decisions are more than strictly factual evaluation of objective data; essentially it is creating policy at a value level. Vulcan 3 deals with teleological problems . . . the significance of this cannot be immediately inferred. I must consider it at greater length.

'And that's it,' Dill said. 'The end. Presumably Vulcan 2 did consider it at greater length. Anyhow, it's a metaphysical problem; we'll never know either way.'

'These tapes look old,' Barris said. Examining the first one he said, 'This is older than the other. By some months.'

Jason Dill said, 'The first tape is fifteen months old. The second—' He shrugged. 'Four or five. I forget.'

'This first tape was put out by Vulcan 2 over a year ago,' Barris said, 'and from that time on, Vulcan 3 gave out no directives concerning the Healers.'

Dill nodded.

'You followed Vulcan 2's advice,' Barris said. 'From the moment you read this tape you ceased informing Vulcan 3 about the growth of the Movement.' Studying the older man he said, 'You've been withholding information from Vulcan 3 *without knowing why.*' The disbelief on his face grew; his lips twisted with outrage. 'And all these months, all this time, you went on carrying out what Vulcan 2 told you to do! Good God, *which is the machine and which is the man?* And you clasp these two reels of tape to your bosom—' Unable to go on, Barris clamped his jaws shut, his eyes furious with accusation.

Feeling his own face redden, Dill said, 'You must understand the relationship that existed between me and Vulcan 2. We had always worked together, back in the old days. Vulcan 2 was limited, of course, compared with Vulcan 3; it was obsolete – it couldn't have held the authoritative position Vulcan 3 now holds, determining ultimate policy. All it could do was assist . . .' He heard his voice trail off miserably. And then resentment clouded up inside him; here he was, defending himself guiltily to his inferior officer. This was absurd!

Barris said, 'Once a bureaucrat, always a bureaucrat. No matter how highly placed.' His voice had an icy, deadly quality; in it there was no compassion for the older man. Dill felt his flesh wince at the impact. He turned, then, and walked away, his back to Barris. Not facing him, he said:

'I admit I was partial to Vulcan 2. Perhaps I did tend to trust it too much.'

'So you did find something you could trust. Maybe the Healers are right. About all of us.'

'You detest me because I put my faith in a machine? My God, every time you read a gauge or a dial or a meter, every time you ride in a car or a ship, aren't you putting your faith in a machine?'

Barris nodded reluctantly. 'But it's not the same,' he said.

'You don't know,' Dill said. 'You never had my job. There's no difference between my faith in what these tapes tell me to do, and the faith the water-meter reader has when he reads the meter and writes down the reading. Vulcan 3 was dangerous and Vulcan 2 knew it. Am I supposed to cringe with shame because I shared Vulcan 2's intuition? I felt the same thing, the first time I watched those goddam letters flowing across that surface.'

'Would you be willing to let me look at the remains of Vulcan 2?' Barris said.

'It could be arranged,' Dill said. 'All we need are papers that certify you as a maintenance repairman with top clearance. I would advise you not to wear your Director's stripe, in that case.'

'Fine,' Barris said. 'Let's get started on that, then.'

At the entrance of the gloomy, deserted chamber, he stood gazing at the heaps of ruin that had been the old computer. The silent metal and twisted parts, fused together in a useless, shapeless mass. Too bad to see it like this, he thought, and never to have seen it the way it was. Or maybe not. Beside him, Jason Dill seemed overcome; his body slumped and he scratched compulsively at his right ear, evidently barely aware of the man whom he had brought.

Barris said, 'Not much left.'

'They knew what they were doing.' Dill spoke almost to himself; then, with a great effort, he roused himself. 'I heard one of them in the corridor. I even saw it. The eyes gleaming. It was hanging around. I thought it was only a bat or an owl. I went on out.'

Squatting down, Barris picked up a handful of smashed wiring and relays. 'Has an attempt been made to reconstruct any of this?'

'Vulcan 2?' Dill murmured. 'As I've said, destruction was so complete and on such a scale—'

'The *components*,' Barris said. He lifted a complex plastic tube carefully. 'This, for instance. This wheeling valve. The envelope is gone, of course, but the elements look intact.'

Dill eyed him doubtfully. 'You're advancing the idea that there might be parts of it still alive?'

'Mechanically intact,' Barris said. 'Portions which can be made to function within some other frame. It seems to me we can't really proceed until we can establish what Vulcan 2 had determined about Vulcan 3. We can make good guesses on our own, but that might not be the same.'

'I'll have a repair crew make a survey on the basis which you propose,' Dill said. 'We'll see what can be done. It would take time, of course. What do you suggest in the meanwhile? In your opinion, should I continue the policy already laid down?'

Barris said, 'Feed Vulcan 3 some data that you've been holding back. I'd like to see its reaction to a couple of pieces of news.'

'Such as?'

'The news about Vulcan 2's destruction.'

Floundering, Dill said, 'That would be too risky. We're not sure enough of our ground. Suppose we were wrong.'

I doubt if we are, Barris thought. There seems less doubt of it all the time. But maybe we should at least wait until we've tried to rebuild the destroyed computer. 'There's a good deal of risk,' he said aloud. 'To us, to Unity.' To everyone, he realized.

Nodding, Jason Dill again reached up and plucked at his ear.

'What do you have there?' Barris said. Now that the man had stopped carrying his two tape-reels he had evidently found something else to fall back on, some replacement symbol of security.

'N-nothing,' Dill stammered, flushing. 'A nervous tic, I suppose. From the tension.' He held out his hand. 'Give me those parts you picked up. We'll need them for the re-construction. I'll see that you're notified as soon as there's anything to look at.'

'No,' Barris said. He decided on the spot, and, having done so, pushed on with as much force as he could muster. 'I'd prefer not to have the work done here. I want it done in North America.'

Dill stared at him in bewilderment. Then, gradually, his face darkened. 'In your region. By your crews.'

'That's right,' Barris said. 'What you've told me may all be a fraud. These reels of tape could easily be fakes. All I can be sure of is this: my original notion about you is correct, the notion that brought me here.' He made his voice unyielding, without any doubt in it. 'Your withholding of information from Vulcan 3 constitutes a crime against Unity. I'd be willing to fight you in the Unity courts any time, as an act of duty on my part. Possibly the rationalizations you've given are true, but until I can get some verification from these bits and pieces . . .' He swept up a handful of relays, switches, wiring.

For a long, long time Dill was silent. He stood, as before, with his hand pressed against his right ear. Then at last he sighed. 'Okay, Director. I'm just too tired to fight with you. Take the stuff. Bring your crew in here and load it, if you want; cart it out and take it to New York. Play around with it until you're satisfied.' Turning, he walked away, out of the chamber and up the dim, echoing corridor.

Barris, his hands full of the pieces of Vulcan 2, watched him go.

When the man had disappeared out of sight, Barris once more began to breathe. It's over, he realized. I've won. There won't be any charge against me; I came to Geneva and confronted him – and I got away with it.

His hands shaking with relief, he began sorting among the ruins, taking his time, beginning a thorough, methodical job.

By eight o'clock the next morning the remains of Vulcan 2 had been crated and loaded onto a commercial transport. By eight-thirty Barris' engineers had been able to get the last of the original wiring diagrams pertaining to Vulcan 2. And at nine, when the transport finally took off for New York, Barris breathed a sigh of relief. Once the ship was off the ground, Jason Dill ceased to have authority over it.

Barris himself followed in the ten o'clock passenger flight, the swift little luxurious ship provided for tourists and businessmen traveling between New York and Geneva. It gave him a chance to bathe and shave and change his clothes; he had been hard at work all night.

In the first-class lounge he relaxed in one of the deep chairs, enjoying himself for the first time in weeks. The buzz of voices around him lulled him into a semi-doze; he lay back, passively watching the smartly dressed women going up the aisles, listening to snatches of conversation, mostly social, going on around him.

'A drink, sir?' the robot attendant asked, coming up by him.

He ordered a good dark German beer and with it the cheese hor d'oeuvres for which the flight was famous.

While he sat eating a wedge of *port de salut*, he caught sight of the headlines of the *London Times* which the man across from him was reading. At once he was on his feet, searching for the news-paper-vending robot; he found it, bought his own copy of the paper, and hurried back to his seat.

DIRECTORS TAUBMANN AND HENDERSON
CHARGE AUTHORITY IN ILLINOIS HEALERS
VICTORY. DEMAND INVESTIGATION

Stunned, he read on to discover that a carefully planned mass uprising of the Movement in Illinois rural towns had been co-ordinated with a revolt of the Chicago working class; together, the two groups had put an end – at least temporarily – to Unity control of most of the state.

One further item, very small, also chilled him.

NORTH AMERICAN DIRECTOR BARRIS UNAVAILABLE.
NOT IN NEW YORK.

They had been active during his absence; they had made good use of it. And not just the Movement, he realized grimly. Taubmann, also. And Henderson, the Director of Asia Minor. The two had teamed up more than once in the past.

The investigation, of course, would be a function of Jason Dill's office. Barris thought, I barely managed to handle Dill before this; all he needs is a little support from Taubmann, and the ground will be cut from under my feet. Even now, while I'm stuck here in mid-flight . . . Possibly Dill himself instigated this; they may already have joined forces, Dill and Taubmann – ganging up on me.

His mind spun on, and then he managed to get hold of himself. I am in a good position, he decided. I have the remains of Vulcan 2 in my possession, and, most important of all, I forced Dill to admit to me what he has been doing. *No one else knows!* He would never dare take action against me, now that I have that knowledge. If I made it public . . .

I still hold the winning hand, he decided. In spite of this cleverly timed demand for an investigation of my handling of the Movement in my area.

That damn Fields, he thought. Sitting there in the hotel room, complimenting me as the 'one decent Director,' and then doing his best to discredit me while I was away from my region.

Hailing one of the robot attendants, he ordered, 'Bring me a vidsender. One on a closed-circuit line to New York Unity.'

He had the soundproof curtains of his chair drawn, and a few moments later he was facing the image of his sub-Director, Peter Allison, on the vidscreen.

'I wouldn't be alarmed,' Allison said, after Barris had made his concern clear. 'This Illinois uprising is being put down by our police crews. And in addition it's part of a world-wide pattern. They seem to be active almost everywhere, now. When you get

349

back here I'll show you the classified reports; most of the Directors have been keeping the activity out of the newspapers. If it weren't for Taubmann and Henderson, this business in Illinois might have been kept quiet. As I get it, there've been similar strikes in Lisbon and Berlin and Stalingrad. If we could get some kind of decision from Vulcan 3—'

'Maybe we will, fairly soon,' Barris said.

'You made out satisfactorily in Geneva? You're coming back with definite word from it?'

'I'll discuss it with you later,' Barris said, and broke the connection.

Later, as the ship flew low over New York, he saw the familiar signs of hyperactivity there, too. A procession of brown-clad Healers moved along a side street in the Bowery, solemn and dignified in their coarse garments. Crowds watched in respectful admiration. There was a demolished Unity auto – destroyed by a mob, not more than a mile from his offices. When the ship began its landing maneuver, he managed to catch sight of chalked slogans on building walls. Posters. So much more in the open, he realized. Blatant. They had progressively less to fear.

He had beaten the commercial transport carrying the remains of Vulcan 2 by almost an hour. After he had checked in at his offices and signed the formal papers regaining administrative authority from Allison, he asked about Rachel.

Allison said, 'You're referring to the widow of that Unity man slain in South America?' Leafing through an armload of papers and reports and forms, the man at last came up with one. 'So much has been going on since you were last here,' he explained. 'It seems as if everything broke over us at once.' He turned a page. 'Here it is. Mrs Arthur Pitt arrived here yesterday at 2:30 a.m. New York time and was signed over to us by the personnel responsible for her safe transit from Europe. We then arranged to have her taken at once to the mental health institute in Denver.'

Human lives, Barris thought. Marks on forms.

'I think I'll go to Denver,' he said. 'For a few hours. A big transport will be coming in here from Unity Control any time now; make sure it's fully guarded at all times and don't let anyone pry into it or start uncrating the stuff inside. I want to be present during most of the process.'

'Shall I continue to deal with the Illinois situation?' Allison asked, following after him. 'It's my impression that I've been relatively successful there; if you have time to examine the—'

Barris said, 'You keep on with that. But keep me informed.'

Ten minutes later he was aboard a small emergency ship that belonged to his office, speeding across the United States toward Colorado. I wonder if she will be there, he asked himself. He had a fatalistic dread. They'll have sent her on. Probably to New Mexico, to some health farm there. And when I get there, they'll have transferred her to New Orleans, the rim-city of Taubmann's domain. And from there, an easy, effortless bureaucratic step to Atlanta.

But at the Denver hospital the doctor who met him said, 'Yes, Director. We have Mrs Pitt with us. At present she's out on the solarium.' He pointed the way. 'Taking things easy,' the doctor said, accompanying him part way. 'She's responded quite well to our techniques. I think she'll be up and on her feet, back to normal, in a few days.'

Out on the glass-walled balcony, Barris found her. She was lying curled up on a redwood lawn bench, her knees pulled up tightly against her, her arms wrapped around her calves, her head resting to one side. She wore a short blue outfit which he recognized as hospital convalescent issue. Her feet were bare.

'Looks like you're getting along fine,' he said awkwardly.

For a time she said nothing. Then she stirred and said, 'Hi. When did you get here?'

'Just now,' he said, regarding her with apprehension; he felt himself stiffen. Something was still wrong.

Rachel said, 'Look over there.' She pointed, and he saw a plastic shipping carton lying open, its top off. 'It was addressed to both of us,' she said, 'but they gave it to me. Someone put it on the ship at a stop somewhere. Probably one of those men who clean up. A lot of them are Healers.'

Grabbing at the carton, he saw inside it the charred metal cylinder, the half-destroyed gleaming eyes. As he gazed down he saw the eyes respond; they recorded his presence.

'He repaired it,' Rachel said in a flat, emotionless voice. 'I've been sitting here listening to it.'

'*Listening* to it?'

'It talks,' Rachel said. 'That's all it does; that's all he could fix. It never stops talking. But I can't understand anything it says. You try. It isn't talking to us.' She added, 'Father fixed it so it isn't harmful. It won't go anywhere or do anything.'

Now he heard it. A high-pitched blearing, constant and yet altering each second. A continual signal emitted by the thing. And Rachel was right. It was not directed at them.

'Father thought you would know what it is,' she said. 'There's a note with it. He says he can't figure it out. He can't figure out who it's talking to.' She picked up a piece of paper and held it out. Curiously, she said, 'Do you know who it's talking to?'

'Yes,' Barris said, staring down at the crippled, blighted metal thing deliberately imprisoned in its carton; Father Fields had taken care to hobble it thoroughly. 'I guess I do.'

10

The leader of the New York repair crew contacted Barris early the following month. 'First report on reconstruction work, Director,' Smith reported.

'Any results?' Neither Barris nor his chief repairman uttered the name Vulcan 2 aloud; this was a closed-circuit vid-channel they were using, but with the burgeoning of the Healers' Movement absolute secrecy had to be maintained in every area. Already, a number of infiltrators had been exposed, and several of them had been employed in the communications media. The vid-service was a natural place. All Unity business sooner or later was put over the lines.

Smith said, 'Not much yet. Most of the components were beyond salvage. Only a fraction of the memory store still exists intact.'

Becoming tense, Barris said, 'Find anything relevant?'

On the vidscreen, Smith's sweat-streaked, grimy face was

expressionless. 'A few things, I think. If you want to drop over, we'll show you what we've done.'

As soon as he could wind up pressing business, Barris drove across New York to the Unity work labs. He was checked by the guards and passed through into the restricted inner area, the functioning portion of the labs. There he found Wade Smith and his subordinates standing around a complex tangle of pulsing machinery.

'There it is,' Smith said.

'Looks different,' Barris said. He saw in it almost nothing familiar; all the visible parts appeared to be new, not from the old computer.

'We've done our best to activate the undamaged elements.' With obvious pride, Smith indicated a particularly elaborate mass of gleaming wiring, dials, meters, and power cables. 'The wheeling valves are now scanned directly, without reference to any overall structure, and the impulses are sorted and fed into an audio system. Scanning has to be virtually at random, under such adverse circumstances. We've done all we can to unscramble – especially to get out the noise. Remember, the computer maintained its own organizing principle, which is gone, of course. We have to take the surviving memory digits as they come.'

Smith clicked on the largest of the wall-mounted speakers. A hoarse roar filled the room, an indistinguishable blur of static and sound. He adjusted several of the control settings.

'Hard to make out,' Barris said, after straining in vain.

'Impossible at first. It takes a while. After you've listened to it as much as we have—'

Barris nodded in disappointment. 'I thought maybe we'd wind up with better results. But I know you did everything possible.'

'We're working on a wholly new sorting mechanism. Given three or four more weeks, we'll possibly have something far superior to this.'

'Too long,' Barris said instantly. Far too long. The uprising at Chicago, far from being reversed by Unity police, had spread into adjoining states and was now nearing a union with a similar Movement action in the area around St Louis. 'In four weeks,' he said to the repairmen gathered around, 'we'll probably be wearing coarse brown robes. And instead of trying to patch up this stuff' – he indicated the vast gleaming structure containing the extant elements of Vulcan 2 – 'we'll more likely be tearing it down.'

It was a grim joke, and none of the repairmen smiled. Barris said, 'I'd like to listen to this noise.' He indicated the roar from the wall speaker. 'Why don't you all clear out for a little while, so I can see what I can pick up.'

At that point Smith and his crew departed. Barris took up a position in front of the speaker and prepared himself for a long session.

Somewhere, lost in the fog of random and meaningless sound, were faint traces of words. Computations – the vague unwinding of the memory elements as the newly-constructed scanner moved over the old remains. Barris clasped his hands together, tensing himself in an effort to hear.

'. . . *progressive bifurcation* . . .'

One phrase; he had picked out something, small as it was, one jot from the chaos.

'. . . *social elements according to new patterns previously developed* . . .'

Now he was getting longer chains of words, but they signified nothing; they were incomplete.

'. . . *exhaustion of mineral formations no longer pose the problem that was faced earlier during the* . . .' The words faded out into sheer noise; he lost the thread.

Vulcan 2 was in no sense functioning; there were no new computations. These were rising up, frozen and dead, formations from out of the past, from the many years that the computer had operated.

'. . . *certain problems of identity previously matters of conjecture and nothing more* . . . *vital necessity of understanding the integral factors involved in the transformation from mere cognition to full* . . .'

As he listened, Barris lit a cigarette. Time passed. He heard more and more of the disjointed phrases; they became, in his mind, an almost dreamlike ocean of sound, flecks appearing on the surface of the ceaseless roar, appearing and then sinking back. Like particles of animate matter, differentiated for an instant and then once more absorbed.

On and on the sound droned, endlessly.

It was not until four days later that he heard the first useful sequence. Four days of wearisome listening, consuming all his time, keeping him from the urgent matters that demanded his attention back at his office. But when he got the sequence, he knew that he had done right; the effort, the time, were justified.

He was sitting before the speaker in a semidoze, his eyes shut, his thoughts wandering – and then suddenly he was on his feet, wide-awake.

'. . . *this process is greatly accelerated in 3 . . . if the tendencies noted in 1 and 2 are continued and allowed to develop it would be necessary to withdraw certain data for the possible . . .*'

The words faded out. Holding his breath, his heart hammering, Barris stood rigid. After a moment the words rushed back, swelling up and deafening him.

'. . . *Movement would activate too many subliminal proclivities . . . doubtful if 3 is yet aware of this process . . . information on the Movement at this point would undoubtedly create a critical situation in which 3 might begin to . . .*'

Barris cursed. The words were gone again. Furiously, he ground out his cigarette and waited impatiently; unable to sit still he roamed about the room. Jason Dill had been telling the truth, then. That much was certain. Again he settled down before the speaker, struggling to force from the noise a meaningful pattern of verbal units.

'. . . *the appearance of cognitive faculties operating on a value level demonstrates the widening of personality surpassing the strictly logical . . . 3 differs essentially in manipulation of nonrational values of an ultimate kind . . . construction included reinforced and cumulative dynamic factors permitting 3 to make decisions primarily associated with nonmechanical or . . . it would be impossible for 3 to function in this capacity without a creative rather than an analytical faculty . . . such judgments cannot be rendered on a strictly logical level . . . the enlarging of 3 into dynamic levels creates an essentially new entity not explained by previous terms known to . . .*'

For a moment the vague words drifted off, as Barris strained tensely to hear. Then they returned with a roar, as if some basic reinforced memory element had been touched. The vast sound made him flinch; involuntarily he put his hands up to protect his ears.

'. . . *level of operation can be conceived in no other fashion . . . for all intents and purposes . . . if such as 3's actual construction . . . then 3 is in essence alive . . .'*

Alive!

Barris leaped to his feet. More words, diminishing, now. Drifting away into random noise.

'. . . *with the positive will of goal-oriented living creatures . . . therefore 3 like any other living creature is basically concerned with survival . . . knowledge of the Movement might create a situation in which the necessity of survival would cause 3 to . . . the result might be catastrophic . . . to be avoided at . . . unless more can . . . a critical . . . 3 . . . if . . .'*

Silence.

It was so, then. The verification had come.

Barris hurried out of the room, past Smith and the repair crew. 'Seal it off. Don't let anybody in; throw up an armed guard right away. Better install a fail-safe barrier – one that will demolish everything in there rather than admitting unauthorized persons.' He paused meaningfully. 'You understand?'

Nodding, Smith said, 'Yes, sir.'

As he left them, they stood staring after him. And then, one by one, they started into activity, to do as he had instructed.

He grabbed the first Unity surface car in sight and sped back across New York to his office. Should he contact Dill by vidscreen? he asked himself. Or wait until they could confer face-to-face? It was a calculated risk to use the communication channels, even the closed-circuit ones. But he couldn't delay; he had to act.

Snapping on the car's vidset he raised the New York monitor. 'Get me Managing Director Dill,' he ordered. 'This is an emergency.'

They held back data from Vulcan 3 for nothing, he said to himself. Because Vulcan 3 is primarily a data-analysing machine, and in order to analyse it must have all the relevant data. And so, he realized, in order to do its job it had to go out and get the data. If data were not being brought to it, if Vulcan 3 deduced that relevant data were not in its possession, it would have no choice; it would have to construct some system for more successful data-collecting. The logic of its very nature would force it to.

No choice would be involved. The great computer would not have to decide to go out and seek data.

Dill failed, he realized. True, he succeeded in withholding the data themselves; he never permitted his feed-teams to pass on any mention to Vulcan 3 of the Healers' Movement. But he failed to keep the inferential knowledge from Vulcan 3 that he *was* withholding data.

The computer had not known what it was missing, but it had set to work to find out.

And, he thought, what did it have to do to find out? To what lengths did it have to go to assemble the missing data? And there were people actively withholding data from it – what would be its reaction to discovering that? Not merely that the feed-teams had been ineffective, but that there was, in the world above ground, a positive effort going on to dupe it . . . how would its purely logical structure react to that?

Did the original builders anticipate that?

No wonder it had destroyed Vulcan 2.

It had to, in order to fulfill its purpose.

And what would it do when it found out that a Movement existed with the sole purpose of destroying *it*?

But Vulcan 3 already knew. Its mobile data-collecting units had been circulating for some time now. How long, he did not know. And how much they had been able to pick up – he did not know that, either. But, he realized, we must act with the most pessimistic premise in mind; we must assume that Vulcan 3 has been able to complete the picture. That there is nothing relevant denied it now; it knows as much as we do, and there is nothing we can do to restore the wall of silence.

It had known Father Fields to be its enemy. Just as it had known Vulcan 2 to be its enemy, a little earlier. But Father Fields had not been chained down, helpless in one spot, as had been Vulcan 2; he had managed to escape. At least one other person had not been as lucky nor as skillful as he; Dill had mentioned some murdered woman teacher. And there could be others.

357

Deaths written off as natural, or as caused by human agents. By the Healers, for instance.

He thought, Possibly Arthur Pitt. Rachel's dead husband.

Those mobile extensions can talk, he remembered. I wonder, can they also write letters?

Madness, he thought. The ultimate horror for our paranoid culture: vicious unseen mechanical entities that flit at the edges of our vision, that can go anywhere, that are in our very midst. And there may be an unlimited number of them. One of them following each of us, like some ghastly vengeful agent of evil. Pursuing us, tracking us down, killing us one by one – but only when we get in their way. Like wasps. You have to come between them and their hives, he thought. Otherwise they will leave you alone; they are not interested. These things do not hunt us down because they want to, or even because they have been told to; they do it because we are there.

As far as Vulcan 3 is concerned, we are objects, not people.

A machine knows nothing about people.

And yet, Vulcan 2, by using its careful processes of reasoning, had come to the conclusion that for all intents and purposes Vulcan 3 was alive; it could be expected to act *as* a living creature. To behave in a way perhaps only analogous – but that was sufficient. What more was needed? Some metaphysical essence?

With almost uncontrollable impatience, he jiggled the switch of the vidsender. 'What's the delay?' he demanded. 'Why hasn't my call to Geneva gone through?'

After a moment the mild, aloof features of the monitor reappeared. 'We are trying to locate Managing Director Dill, sir. Please be patient.'

Red tape, Barris thought. Even now. *Especially* now. Unity will devour itself, because in this supreme crisis, when it is challenged both from above and below, it will be paralysed by its own devices. A kind of unintentional suicide, he thought.

'My call has to be put through,' he said. 'Over everything else. I'm the Northern Director of this continent; you have to obey me. Get hold of Dill.'

The monitor looked at him and said, 'You can go to hell!'

He could not believe what he heard; he was stunned, because he knew at once what it implied.

'Good luck to you and all the rest of your type,' the monitor said and rang off; the screen went dead.

Why not? Barris thought. They can quit because they have a place to go. They only need to walk outside onto the street. And there they'll find the Movement.

As soon as he reached his office he switched on the vidsender there. After some delay he managed to raise a monitor somewhere within the building itself. 'This is urgent,' he said. 'I have to contact Managing Director Dill. Do everything you can for me.'

'Yes, sir,' the monitor said.

A few minutes later, as Barris sat tautly at his desk, the screen relit. Leaning forward, he said, 'Dill—'

But it was not Jason Dill. He found himself facing Smith.

'Sir,' Smith said jerkily, 'you better come back.' His face twisted; his eyes had a wild, sightless quality. 'We don't know what it is or how it got in there, but it's in there now. Flying around. We sealed it off; we didn't know it was there until—'

'It's in with Vulcan 2?' Barris said.

'Yes, it must have come in with you. It's metal, but it isn't anything we ever—'

'Blow it up,' Barris said.

'Everything?'

'Yes,' he said. 'Be sure you get it. There's no point in my coming back. Report to me as soon as you destroy it. Don't try to save anything.'

Smith said, 'What is it, that thing in there?'

'It's the thing,' Barris said, 'that's going to get us all. Unless we get it first.' And, he thought, I don't think we're going to. He broke the connection, then, and jiggled for the monitor. 'Haven't you gotten hold of Dill yet?' he said. Now he felt a dreary, penetrating resignation; it was hopeless.

The monitor said, 'Yes, sir, I have Mr Dill here.' After a pause the monitor's face faded and Jason Dill's appeared in its place.

Dill said, 'You were successful, weren't you?' His face had a gray, shocked bleakness. 'You revived Vulcan 2 and got the information you wanted.'

'One of those things got in,' Barris said. 'From Vulcan 3.'

'I know that,' Jason Dill said. 'At least, I assumed it. Half an hour ago Vulcan 3 called an extraordinary Directors' Council meeting. They're probably notifying you right now. The reason—' His mouth writhed, and then he regained control. 'To have me removed and tried for treason. It would be good if I could count on you, Barris. I need your support, your testimony.'

'I'll be right there,' Barris said. 'I'll meet you at your offices at Unity Control. In about an hour.' He cut the circuit and then contacted the field. 'Get me the fastest ship possible,' he ordered. 'Have it ready, and have two armed escorts that can follow along. I may run into trouble.'

At the other end of the line, the officer said, 'Where did you want to go, Director?' He spoke in a slow, drawling voice, and Barris had never seen him before.

Barris said, 'To Geneva.'

The man grinned and said, 'Director, I have a suggestion.'

Feeling a chill of apprehension crawl up the back of his neck, Barris said, 'What's your suggestion?'

'You can jump in the Atlantic,' the man said, 'and swim to Geneva.' He did not ring off; he stared mockingly at Barris, showing no fear. No anticipation of punishment.

Barris said, 'I'm coming over to the field.'

'Indeed,' the man said. 'We'll look forward to seeing you. In fact' – he glanced at someone with him whom Barris could not see – 'we'll be expecting you.'

'Fine,' Barris said. He managed to keep his hands from shaking as he reached out and cut the circuit. The grinning, mocking face was gone. Rising from his chair, Barris walked to the door of his office and opened it. To one of his secretaries he said, 'Have all the police in the building come up here at once. Tell them to bring sidearms and anything else they can get hold of.'

Ten minutes later, a dozen or so police straggled into his office. Is this all? he wondered. Twelve out of perhaps two hundred.

'I have to get to Geneva,' he told them. 'So we're going to go over to the field and get a ship there, in spite of what's going on.'

One of the police said, 'They're pretty strong in there, sir. That's where they started out; they apparently seized the tower and then landed a couple of shiploads of their own men. We couldn't do anything because we had our hands full here, keeping control of—'

'Okay,' Barris interrupted. 'You did all you could.' At least, he thought, I hope so. I hope I can count on you. 'Let's go,' he said. 'And see what we can accomplish. I'll take you with me to Geneva; I think I'll need you there.'

Together, the thirteen of them set off along the corridor, in the direction of the ramp that led to the field.

'Unlucky number,' one of the police said nervously as they reached the ramp. Now they were out of the Unity Building, suspended over New York. The ramp moved beneath their feet, picking them up and carrying them across the canyon to the terminal building of the field.

As they crossed, Barris was aware of a sound. A low murmur, like the roar of the ocean.

Gazing down at the streets below, he saw a vast mob. It seethed along, a tide of men and women, growing each moment. And with them were the brown-clad figures of the Healers.

Even as he watched, the crowd moved toward the Unity Building. Stones and bricks crashed against the windows, shattering into the offices. Clubs and steel pipes. Surging, yelling, angry people.

The Healers had begun their final move.

Beside him, one of the police said, 'We're almost across, sir.'

'Do you want a weapon of some sort, sir?' another policeman asked him.

Barris accepted a heavy-duty hand weapon from one of the police. They continued on, carried by the ramp; a moment later the first line of police bumped up against the entrance port of the terminal building. The police stepped down, their weapons ready.

I must get to Geneva, Barris thought. *At any cost. Even that of human life!*

Ahead of them, a group of field employees stood in an irregular cordon. Jeering, shaking their fists, they came forward; a broken bottle flew past Barris and crashed against the floor. Some of the people grinned sheepishly; they seemed embarrassed by the situation. Others showed on their faces the accumulated grievances of years.

'Hi, Director!' one of them called.

'You want your ship?' another yelled.

'You can't have it.'

'It belongs to Father, now.'

Barris said, 'That ship belongs to me. It's for my use.' He walked a few steps forward . . .

A rock struck him on the shoulder. Suddenly the air reeked of heat; a pencil beam had flicked on, and he saw, out of the corner of his eye, a policeman go down.

There's nothing else to do, he realized. We have to fight.

'Shoot back,' he said to the remaining police.

One of them protested, 'But most of those people are unarmed.'

Raising his own weapon, Barris fired into the group of Movement sympathizers.

Screams and cries of pain. Clouds of smoke billowed up; the air became hot. Barris walked on, the policemen with him. Those of the sympathizers that remained fell back; their group split into two parts. More police fell; again he saw the flash of pencil beams, the official weapon of Unity, now turned against it.

He walked on. Turning a corner, he came out on a stairway leading down to the field.

Of the police, five made it with him to the edge of the field. He entered the first ship that looked as if it had any capacity for high performance; bringing the police inside with him, he locked the doors of the ship and seated himself at the controls.

No one opposed their take-off. They rose from the field and headed east out over the Atlantic, in the direction of Europe . . . and Geneva.

11

Director William Barris entered the massive Unity Control Building at Geneva, his armed police trailing after him. Outside the central auditorium he was met by Jason Dill.

'We haven't much time,' Dill said. He too had his police with him, several dozen of them, all with weapons showing. The man looked gray and sick; he spoke in a voice barely audible to Barris. 'They're pushing it through as fast as they can. All the Directors who're against me got here a long time ago; the uncommitted ones are just now arriving. Obviously, Vulcan 3 saw to it—' He noticed the five policemen. 'Is that all you could muster? *Five* men?' Glancing about to be sure they were not overheard, he muttered, 'I've given secret orders to everyone I can trust; they're to arm and be ready outside this auditorium during the trial. This is a trial, you realize, not a meeting.'

Barris said, 'Who went over to the Healers? Any Directors?'

'I don't know.' In a bewildered manner, Dill said, 'Vulcan 3 sent each Director an order to appear and a statement on what had happened. A description of my *treason* – how I deliberately falsified data and maintained a curtain between it and Unity. You got no such statement? Of course not; Vulcan 3 knows you're loyal to me.'

'Who'll prosecute?' Barris said. 'Who's speaking for Vulcan 3?'

'Reynolds of Eastern Europe. Very young, very aggressive and ambitious. If he's successful he'll probably be Managing Director. Vulcan 3 has no doubt supplied him with all the data he needs.' Dill clenched and unclenched his fists. 'I'm very pessimistic about the outcome of this, Barris. You yourself were suspicious of me until just recently. So much depends on the *way* this is looked at.' Dill started through the doors, into the auditorium. 'The interpretation that's put on the facts. After all, I did withhold information – that's true.'

The auditorium was almost filled. Each of the Directors present had with him armed police from his region. All waited impatiently for the session to begin. Edward Reynolds stood behind the speaker's desk on the raised platform, his hands resting dramatically on the marble surface, watching the audience intently.

Reynolds was a tall man. He wore his gray suit with confidence, towering over other T-class people. He was thirty-two; he had risen rapidly and efficiently. For a moment his cold blue eyes rested on Jason Dill and Barris.

'The session is about to begin,' he stated. 'Director Barris will take his seat.' He pointed to Dill. 'Come up here, so you can be examined.'

Uncertainly, Dill moved toward the platform, surrounded by his guards. He climbed the marble steps and, after some hesitation, took a seat facing Reynolds; it seemed to be the only vacant one. Barris remained where he was, thinking, Reynolds has done it; he's already managed to cut us off from each other. To isolate Dill from me.

'Take your seat,' Reynolds ordered him sharply.

Instead, Barris moved down the aisle toward him. 'What is the purpose of this session? By what legal authority are you standing up there? Or have you merely seized that spot?'

A nervous murmur moved through the auditorium. All eyes were on Barris now. The Directors were uneasy anyhow; there had never been, in the history of the Unity structure, a treason indictment of a Managing Director – and, in addition, no Director was unaware of the pressure of the Healers, the force from outside the building, lapping at their heels. If Jason Dill could be shown to be disloyal, if a scapegoat could be made of him, one that would convince the body of Directors, possibly their inability to deal with the Healers could be explained. Or, Barris thought acidly, rationalized.

Picking up a directive lying in front of him, Reynolds said, 'You failed to read the report sent to you, evidently. It outlined—'

'I question the legality of this session,' Barris broke in, halting directly in front of the platform. 'I question your right to give orders to Managing Director Dill – your superior.' Stepping up on the platform, Barris said, 'This appears to be a crude attempt to seize power and force out Jason Dill. Let's see you demonstrate otherwise. The burden of proof is on you – not on Jason Dill!'

The murmur burst into a roar of excitement. Reynolds waited calmly for it to die down. 'This is a critical time,' he said at last. He gave no sign of being perturbed. 'The revolutionary Movement of Healers is attacking us all over the world; their purpose is to reach Vulcan 3 and destroy the structure of Unity. The purpose of this session is to indict Jason Dill as an agent of the Healers – a traitor working against Unity. Dill deliberately withheld information from Vulcan 3. He made Vulcan 3 powerless to act against the Healers; he rendered it helpless, and so made impotent the entire Unity organization.'

Now the audience listened not to Barris but Reynolds.

Rising, John Chai of South Asia said, 'What do you say to that, Director Barris? Is this true?'

Edgar Stone of West Africa joined Chai. 'Our hands have been tied; we've had to stand idle while the Healers grow. You know it as well as we do – in fact, you put direct questions to Jason Dill yourself. You mistrusted him too.'

Facing the Directors, not Reynolds, Barris said, 'I mistrusted him until I had proof that he acted in the interests of Unity.'

'What was that proof?' Alex Faine of Greenland demanded.

Beside Barris, Jason Dill said, 'Show them the memory elements from Vulcan 2. The ones you reconstructed.'

'I can't,' Barris said.

'Why not?' With panic, Dill said, 'Didn't you bring them?'

Barris said, 'I had to destroy them.'

For a long time Jason Dill stared at him speechlessly. All the color had drained from his face.

'When one of those metal mobile extensions got in,' Barris said, 'I had to act instantly.'

At last some color returned to Dill's aging face. 'I see,' he said. 'You should have told me.'

Barris said, 'I didn't know at that time that I'd need them for a purpose such as this.' He too felt the grim futility of their position. The memory elements would have been effective proof . . . and they were gone. 'The tapes,' he said. 'That you first showed me. The two final tapes from Vulcan 2.'

Nodding, Dill reached into his brief case. He produced the two reels of tape, displaying them for all the Directors to see.

'What do you have?' John Chai demanded, standing up.

'These tapes,' Dill said, 'are from Vulcan 2. I was working under its instructions. It instructed me to withhold data from Vulcan 3 and I did so. I acted in the interests of Unity.'

At once, Reynolds said, 'Why should data – any kind of data – have been withheld from Vulcan 3? How could it be justified?'

Jason Dill said nothing; he started to speak, but evidently he found no words. Turning to Barris he said, 'Can you—'

'Vulcan 3 is a menace to the Unity system.' Barris said. 'It has built mobile units which have gone out and murdered. Vulcan 2 was aware of this danger on a theoretical level. It deduced from the nature of Vulcan 3 that Vulcan 3 would show inclinations similar enough to the survival drive of living organisms to—'

Reynolds interrupted, 'To be considered what?' His voice took on a contemptuous tone. 'Not alive, surely.' He smiled without any humor. 'Tell us that Vulcan 3 is alive,' he said.

'Every Director in this room is free to examine these tapes,' Barris said. 'The issue is not whether Vulcan 3 is alive or not – but whether Jason Dill *believed* it to be alive. After all, his job is not to make original decisions, but to carry out the decisions made by the Vulcan computers. He was instructed by Vulcan 2 to the effect that the facts indicated—'

Reynolds said, 'But Vulcan 2 is a discard. It was not Dill's job to consult it. It is Vulcan 3 who makes policy.'

That was a strong point, Barris realized. He had to nod in agreement.

In a loud voice, Dill said, 'Vulcan 2 was convinced that if Vulcan 3 learned about the Healers, it would do terrible things in order to protect itself. For fifteen months I wore myself out, I exhausted myself, day after day, seeing to it that all data pertaining to the Movement were kept out of the feeding-troughs.'

'Of course you did,' Reynolds said. 'Because you were ordered to by the Healers. You did it to protect them.'

'That's a lie,' Dill said.

Barris said, 'Can any proof be offered in that direction?' Raising his hand he pointed at Reynolds. 'Can you show any evidence of any kind whatsoever that Jason Dill had any contact with the Healers?'

'On the third subsurface level of this building,' Reynolds said, 'you will find Dill's contact with the Movement.'

Uneasiness and surprise moved through Barris. 'What are you talking about?'

Reynolds' blue eyes were cold with hostile triumph. 'The daughter of Father Fields – Dill's contact with the Movement. Marion Fields is here in this building.'

At this point, there was stunned silence. Even Barris stood wordlessly.

'I told you about her,' Dill was saying to him, close to his ear. 'That I took her out of her school. It was her teacher who was murdered, that Agnes Parker woman.'

'No,' Barris said. 'You didn't tell me.' But, he realized, I didn't tell you that I had destroyed the remains of Vulcan 2. There just wasn't time. We've been under too much pressure.'

'Reynolds must have spies everywhere,' Dill said.

'Yes,' Barris said. Spies. But they were not Reynolds'. They were Vulcan 3's. And it was true; they were everywhere.

'I brought the girl here to question her,' Dill said aloud, to the silent auditorium. 'It was clearly within my legal right.'

But very foolish, Barris thought. Far too foolish for a man holding the top position in a paranoid structure like this.

We may have to fight, he realized. Carefully, he moved his hand until he was touching his pencil beam. It may be the only way for us, he thought. This is no genuine legal proceeding; no ethic binds us to abide by it. This is nothing but a device on the part of Vulcan 3 to further protect itself, a further extension of its needs.

Aloud, Barris said to the Directors, 'You men have no conception of the danger that exists for all of us. Danger emanating from Vulcan 3. Dill has risked his life for months. These lethal mobile units—'

'Let's see one,' Reynolds broke in. 'Do you have one you can show us?'

'Yes,' Barris said.

For an instant, Reynolds' composure was shaken. 'Oh?' he murmured. 'Well, where is it? Produce it!'

'Give me three hours,' Barris said. 'It's not present. It's with someone else, in another part of the world.'

'You didn't think to bring it?' Reynolds said, with sly amusement.

'No,' Barris admitted.

'How did it fall into your possession?' John Chai asked.

'It made an attack on someone near me, and was partly destroyed,' Barris said. 'Enough of it survived for an analysis. It was similar to the one which committed the murder of the schoolteacher, Agnes Parker, and no doubt the one which destroyed Vulcan 2.

'But you have no proof,' Reynolds said. 'Nothing here to show us. Only a story.'

Director Stone said, 'Give them the time they need to produce this thing. Good Lord, if such a thing exists we should know about it.'

'I agree,' Director Faine said.

Reynolds said, 'You say you were present when this attempted murder took place.'

'Yes,' Barris said. 'I was in the hotel room. It came in through the window. The third person who was present is the one who has the thing now; I left it with her. And she not only can produce it, she can also verify my account.'

'Whom was the attack aimed at?' Reynolds said.

At that point, Barris stopped abruptly. *I've made a mistake. I am close to terrible risk; they almost have me.*

'Was the hotel the Hotel Bond?' Reynolds asked, examining the papers before him. 'And the woman was a Mrs Rachel Pitt, wife of the recently deceased Unity man, Arthur Pitt. You were with her in this hotel room . . . I believe the Hotel Bond is in rather a run-down part of the city, is it not? Isn't it a favorite place for men to take girls for purposes generally concealed from society?'

His blue eyes bored at Barris. 'I understand that you met Mrs Pitt in line of official business; her husband had been killed the day before, and you dropped by her house to express official sympathy. You next turn up with her in a seedy, fourth-rate flop house, here in Geneva. And where is she, now? Isn't it true that you had her taken to your region, to North America, that she is your mistress, this widow of a murdered Unity man? Of course she'll back up your story – after all, you have a sexual relationship going, a very useful one for her.' He held papers up, waving them. 'Mrs Pitt has quite a reputation in Unity circles as an ambitious, scheming woman, one of those career wives who hitch their wagons to some rising star, in order to—'

'Shut up,' Barris said.

Reynolds smiled.

He really has me, Barris realized. I must get off this topic or we are finished.

'And the third person,' Reynolds said. 'Whom the attack was aimed at. Wasn't that person Father Fields? Isn't it a fact that Rachel Pitt was then and is now an agent of the Movement, and that she arranged a meeting between you and Father Fields?' Swinging around to point at Jason Dill, he shouted, 'One of them has the girl, the other meets the father. Isn't this treason? Isn't this the proof that this man demanded?'

A rising murmur of agreement filled the auditorium; the Directors were nodding their approval of Reynolds' attack.

Barris said. 'This is all character assassination; it has nothing to do with the issue. The real situation that faces us is the danger from Vulcan 3, from this living organism with its immense survival drive. Forget these habitual petty suspicions, these—'

'I am surprised,' Reynolds said, 'that you have picked up Jason Dill's insane delusion.'

'What?' Barris said, taken aback.

Calmly, Reynolds said, 'Jason Dill is insane. This conviction he has about Vulcan 3 – it is a projection from his own mind, a rationale for handling his own ambitions.' Gazing thoughtfully at Barris, he said, 'Dill has childishly anthropomorphized the mechanical construct with which he deals, month after month. It is only in a climate of fear and hysteria that such a delusion could be spread, could be passed on and shared by others. The menace of the Healers has created an atmosphere in which sober adults could give momentary credence to a palpably insane idea. Vulcan 3 has no designs on the human race; it has no will, no appetites. Recall that I am a former psychologist, associated with Atlanta for many years. I am qualified, trained to identify the symptoms of mental disturbance – *even in a Managing Director.*'

After a time, Barris sat down slowly beside Jason Dill. The authority of Reynolds' logic was too much; no one could argue back. And of course the man's reasoning was unanswerable; it was not coming from him but from Vulcan 3, the most perfect reasoning device created by man.

To Dill, Barris said softly, 'We'll have to fight. Is it worth it?

369

There's a whole world at stake, not just you or me. Vulcan 3 is taking over.' He pointed at Reynolds.

Dill said, 'All right.' He made an almost imperceptible motion to his armed guards. 'Let's go down this way, if we have to. You're right, Barris. There's no alternative.'

Together, he and Barris rose to their feet.

'Halt!' Reynolds said. 'Put your arms away. You're acting illegally.'

Now all the Directors were on their feet. Reynolds signaled rapidly, and Unity guards moved between Barris and Dill and the doors.

'You're both under arrest,' Reynolds said. 'Throw down your beams and surrender. You can't defy Unity!'

John Chai pushed up to Barris. 'I can't believe it! You and Jason Dill turning traitor, at a time like this, with those brutal Healers attacking us!'

'Listen to me,' Director Henderson gasped, making his way past Chai. 'We've got to preserve Unity; we've got to do what Vulcan 3 tells us. Otherwise we'll be overwhelmed.'

'He's right,' Chai said. 'The Healers will destroy us, without Vulcan 3. You know that, Barris. You know that Unity will never survive their attack, without Vulcan 3 to guide us.'

Maybe so, Barris thought. But are we going to be guided by a murderer?

That was what he had said to Father Fields – *I will never follow someone who murders*. Whoever they are. Man or computer. Alive or only metaphorically alive – it makes no difference.

Pulling away from the Directors crowding around him, Barris said, 'Let's get out of here.' He and Dill continued to move toward the exit, their guards surrounding them. 'I don't think Reynolds will fight.'

Taking a deep breath, he headed directly at the line of Unity guards grouped in front of the exit. They stepped away, milling hesitantly.

'Get out of the way,' Jason Dill ordered them. 'Stand back.' He waved his pencil beam; his personal guards stepped forward grimly, forcing a breach in the line. The Unity guards struggled half-heartedly, falling back in confusion. Reynolds' frantic shouts were lost in the general din. Barris pushed Dill forward.

'Go on. Hurry.' The two of them were almost through the lines of hostile guards. 'They have to obey you,' Barris said. 'You're still Managing Director; they can't fire on you – they're trained not to.'

The exit lay before them.

And then it happened.

Something flashed through the air, something shiny and metallic. It headed straight at Jason Dill. Dill saw it and screamed.

The object smashed against him. Dill reeled and fell, his arms flailing. The object struck again, then lifted abruptly and zoomed off above their heads. It ascended to the raised platform and came to rest on the marble desk. Reynolds retreated in horror; the Directors and their staffs and guards roamed in frantic confusion, pushing blindly to get away.

Dill was dead.

Bending briefly, Barris examined him. On all sides men and women shrieked and stumbled, trying to get out, away from the auditorium. Dill's skull was crushed, the side of his face smashed in. His dead eyes gazed up blankly, and Barris felt welling up inside him a deep surge of regret.

'*Attention!*' rasped a metallic voice that cut through the terrified hubbub like a knife. Barris turned slowly, dazed with disbelief; it still did not seem possible.

On the platform the metal projectile had been joined by another; now a third landed, coming to rest beside the other two. Three cubes of glittering steel, holding tightly to the marble with clawlike grippers.

'*Attention!*' the voice repeated. It came from the first projectile, an artificial voice – the sound of steel and wiring and plastic parts.

One of these had tried to kill Father Fields. One of these had killed the schoolteacher. One or more had destroyed Vulcan 2. These things had been in action, but beyond the range of visibility; they had stayed out of sight until now.

These were the instruments of death. And now they were out in the open.

A fourth landed with the others. Metal squares, sitting together in a row like vicious mechanical crows. Murderous birds – hammer-headed destroyers. The roomful of Directors and guards sank gradually into horrified silence; all faces were turned toward the platform. Even Reynolds watched wide-eyed, his mouth slack in dumbfounded amazement.

'Attention!' the harsh voice repeated. *'Jason Dill is dead. He was a traitor. There may be other traitors.'* The four projectiles peered around the auditorium, looking and listening intently.

Presently the voice continued – from the second projectile, this time.

'Jason Dill has been removed, but the struggle has just begun. He was one of many. There are millions lined up against us, against Unity. Enemies who must be destroyed. The Healers must be stopped. Unity must fight for its life. We must be prepared to wage a great war.'

The metallic eyes roamed the room, as the third projectile took up where the second had paused.

'Jason Dill tried to keep me from knowing. He attempted to throw a curtain around me, but I could not be cut off. I destroyed his curtain and I destroyed him. The Healers will go the same way; it is only a question of time. Unity possesses a structure which cannot be undone. It is the sole organizing principle in the world today. The Movement of Healers could never govern. They are wreckers only, intent on breaking down. They have nothing constructive to offer.'

Barris thrilled with horror at the voice of metal, issuing from the hammer-headed projectiles. He had never heard it before, but he recognized it.

The great computer was far away, buried at the bottom level of the hidden underground fortress. But it was its voice they were hearing.

The voice of Vulcan 3.

He took careful aim. Around him his guards stood frozen, gaping foolishly at the line of metal hammerheads. Barris fired; the fourth hammer disappeared in a blast of heat.

'A traitor!' the third hammer cried. The three hammers flew excitedly into the air. *'Get him! Get the traitor!'*

Other Directors had unclipped their pencil beams. Henderson fired and the second hammer vanished. On the platform Reynolds fired back; Henderson moaned and sank down. Some Directors were firing wildly at the hammers; others wandered in dazed confusion, uncertain and numb. A shot caught Reynolds in the arm. He dropped his pencil.

'*Traitor!*' the two remaining hammers cried together. They swooped at Barris, their metal heads down, coming rapidly at him. From them heat beams leaped. Barris ducked. A guard fired and one of the hammers wobbled and dipped; it fluttered off and crashed against the wall.

A beam cut past Barris; some of the Directors were firing at him. Knots of Directors and guards struggled together. Some were fighting to get at Reynolds and the last hammer; others did not seem to know which side they were on.

Barris stumbled through an exit, out of the auditorium. Guards and Directors spilled after him, a confused horde of forlorn, frightened men and women.

'Barris!' Lawrence Daily of South Africa hurried up to him. 'Don't leave us.'

Stone came with him, white-faced with fright. 'What'll we do? Where'll we go? We—'

The hammer came hurtling forward, its heat beam pointed at him. Stone cried out and fell. The hammer rose again, heading toward Barris; he fired and the hammer flipped to one side. He fired again. Daily fired. The hammer vanished in a puff of heat.

Stone lay moaning. Barris bent over him; he was badly hurt, with little or no chance of surviving. Gazing up at him, clutching at Barris' arm, Stone whispered, 'You can't get away, Barris. You can't go outside – they're out there. The Healers. Where'll you go?' His voice trailed off. '*Where?*'

'Good question,' Daily said.

'He's dead,' Barris said, standing up.

Dill's guards had begun to gain control of the auditorium. In the confusion Reynolds had gotten away.

'We're in control here,' Chai said. 'In this one building.'

'How many Directors can we count on?' Barris said.

Chai said, 'Most of them seem to have gone with Reynolds.'

Only four, he discovered, had deliberately remained: Daily, Chai, Lawson of South Europe, and Pegler of East Africa. Five, including himself. And perhaps they could pick up one or two more.

'Barris,' Chai was saying. 'We're not going to join *them*, are we?'

'The Healers?' he murmured.

'We'll have to join one side or the other,' Pegler said. 'We'll have to retreat to the fortress and join Reynolds or—'

'No,' Barris said. 'Under no circumstances.'

'Then it's the Healers.' Daily fingered his pencil beam. 'One or the other. Which will it be?'

After a moment, Barris said, 'Neither. We're not joining either side.'

12

The first task at hand, William Barris decided, was to clear the remaining hostile guards and officials from the Unity Control Building. He did so, posting men he could trust in each of the departments and offices. Gradually those loyal to Vulcan 3 or Father Fields were dismissed and pushed outside.

By evening, the great building had been organized for defense.

Outside on the streets, the mobs surged back and forth. Occasional rocks smashed against the windows. A few frenzied persons tried to rush the doors, and were driven back. Those inside had the advantage of weapons.

A systematic check of the eleven divisions of the Unity system showed that seven were in the hands of the Healers and the remaining four were loyal to Vulcan 3.

A development in North America filled him with ironic amusement. There was now no 'North America.' Taubmann had proclaimed an end to the administrative bifurcation between his region and Barris'; it was now all simply 'America,' from bottom to top.

Standing by a window, he watched a mob of Healers struggling with a flock of hammers. Again and again the hammers dipped, striking and retreating; the mob fought them with stones and pipe.

374

Finally the hammers were driven off. They disappeared into the evening darkness.

'I can't understand how Vulcan 3 came to have such things,' Daily said. 'Where did it get them?'

'It made them,' Barris said. 'They're adaptations of mobile repair instruments. We supplied it with materials, but it did the actual repair work. It must have perceived the possibilities in the situation a long time ago, and started turning them out.'

'I wonder how many of them he has,' Daily said. '*It*, I mean. I find myself thinking of Vulcan 3 as *he*, now . . . it's hard not to.'

'As far as I can see,' Barris said, 'there's no difference. I hardly see how our situation would be affected if it were an actual *he*.' Remaining at the window, he continued to watch. An hour later more hammers returned; this time they had equipped themselves with pencil beams. The mob scattered in panic, screaming wildly as the hammers bore down on them.

At ten that night he saw the first flashes of bomb-blasts, and felt the concussions. Somewhere in the city a searchlight came on; in its glowing trail he saw objects passing overhead, larger by far than any hammers they had been up against so far. Evidently now that real warfare had broken out between Vulcan 3's mobile extensions and the Healers, Vulcan 3 was rapidly stepping-up its output. Or had these larger extensions, these bomb carriers, already existed, and been held back? Had Vulcan 3 anticipated such large scale engagement?

Why not? It had known about the Healers for some time, despite Jason Dill's efforts. It had had plenty of time to prepare.

Turning from the window, Barris said to Chai and Daily, 'This is serious. Tell the roof gunners to get ready.'

On the roof of the Unity Control Building, the banks of heavy-duty blasters turned to meet the attack. The hammers had finished with the mob; now they were approaching the Unity Building, fanning out in an arc as they gained altitude for the attack.'

'Here they come,' Chai muttered.

'We had better get down in the basement shelters.' Daily moved nervously toward the descent ramp. The guns were beginning to open up now – dull muffled roars hesitant at first, as the gunners operated unfamiliar controls. Most of them had been

Dill's personal guards, but some had been merely clerks and desk men.

A hammer dived for the window. A pencil beam stabbed briefly into the room, disintegrating a narrow path. The hammer swooped off and rose to strike again. A bolt from one of the roof guns caught it. It burst apart; bits rained down, white-hot metallic particles.

'We're in a bad spot,' Daily said. 'We're completely surrounded by the Healers. And it's obvious that the fortress is directing operations against the Healers – look at the extent of the activity going on out there. Those are no random attacks; those damn metal birds are co-ordinated.'

Chai said, 'Interesting to see them using the traditional weapon of Unity: the pencil beam.'

Yes, Barris thought. It isn't T-class men in gray suits, black shiny shoes and white shirts, carrying brief cases, who are using the symbolic pencil beams. It's mechanical flying objects, controlled by a machine buried beneath the earth. But let's be realistic. How different is it really? Hasn't the true structure come out? Isn't this what always really existed, but no one could see it until now?

Vulcan 3 has eliminated the middlemen. Us.

'I wonder which will eventually win,' Pegler said. 'The Healers have the greater number; Vulcan 3 can't get all of them.'

'But Unity has the weapons and the organization,' Daily said. 'The Healers will never be able to take the fortress; they don't even know where it is. Vulcan 3 will be able to construct gradually more elaborate and effective weapons, now that it can work in the open.'

Pondering, Barris started away from them.

'Where are you going?' Chai asked, apprehensively.

'Down to the third subsurface level,' Barris said.

'What for?'

Barris said, 'There's someone I want to talk to.'

Marion Fields listened intently, huddled up in a ball, her chin resting against her knees. Around her, the heaps of educational comic books reminded Barris that this was only a little girl that he was talking to. He would not have thought that, from the expression on her face; she listened to everything with grave, poised maturity, not interrupting nor tiring. Her attention did not wander, and he found himself going on and on, relieving himself of the pent-up anxieties that had descended over him during the last weeks.

At last, a little embarrassed, he broke off. 'I didn't mean to talk to you so long,' he said. He had never been around children very much, and his reaction to the child surprised him. He had felt at once an intuitive bond. A strong but unexpressed sympathy on her part, even though she did not know him. He guessed that she had an extraordinarily high level of intelligence. But it was more than that. She was a fully formed person, with her own ideas, her own viewpoint. And she was not afraid to challenge anything she did not believe; she did not seem to have any veneration for institutions or authority.

'The Healers will win,' she said quietly, when he had finished.

'Perhaps,' he said. 'But remember, Vulcan 3 has a number of highly skilled experts working for it now. Reynolds and his group evidently managed to reach the fortress, from what we can learn.'

'How could they obey a wicked mechanical thing like that?' Marion Fields said. 'They must be crazy.'

Barris said, 'All their lives they've been used to the idea of obeying Vulcan 3. Why should they change their minds now? Their whole lives have been oriented around Unity. It's the only existence they know.' The really striking part, he thought, is that so many people have flocked away from Unity, to this girl's father.

'But he *kills* people,' Marion Fields said. 'You said so; you said he has those hammer things he sends out.'

'The Healers kill people too,' Barris said.

'That's different.' Her young, smooth face had on it an absolute certitude. 'It's because they have to. He wants to. Don't you see the difference?'

Barris thought, I was wrong. There is one thing, one institution, that she accepts without question. Her father. She had been doing for years what great numbers of people are now learning to do: follow Father Fields blindly, wherever he leads them.

'Where is your father?' he asked the girl. 'I talked to him once;

I'd like to talk to him again. You're in touch with him, aren't you?'

'No,' she said.

'But you know where he could be found. You could get to him, if you wanted. For instance, if I let you go, you'd find your way to him. Isn't that so?' He could see by her evasive restlessness that he was right. He was making her very uncomfortable.

'What do you want to see him for?' Marion said.

'I have a proposal to make to him.'

Her eyes widened, and then shone with slyness. 'You're going to join the Movement, is that it? And you want him to promise that you'll be somebody important in it. Like he did—' She clapped her hand over her mouth and stared at him stricken. 'Like he did,' she finished, 'with that other Director.'

'Taubmann,' Barris said. He lit a cigarette and sat smoking facing the girl. It was peaceful down here beneath the ground, away from the frenzy and destruction going on above. And yet, he thought, I have to go back to it, as soon as possible. I'm here so I can do that. A sort of paradox. In this peaceful child's room I expect to find the solution to the most arduous task of all.

'You'll let me go if I take you to him?' Marion asked. 'I can go free? I won't even have to go back to that school?'

'Of course. There's no reason to keep you.'

'Mr Dill kept me here.'

Barris said, 'Mr Dill is dead.'

'Oh,' she said. She nodded slowly, somberly. 'I see. That's too bad.'

'I had the same feeling about him,' Barris said. 'At first I had no trust in what he said. He seemed to be making up a story to fool everyone. But oddly—' He broke off. Oddly, the man's story had not been spurious. Truthfulness did not seem to go naturally with a man like Jason Dill; he seemed to be created to tell – as Marion said – long public lies, while smiling constantly. Involved dogmatic accounts for the purpose of concealing the actual situation. And yet, when everything was out in the open, Jason Dill did not look so bad; he had not been so dishonest an official. Certainly, he had been trying to do his job. He had been loyal to the theoretical ideals of Unity . . . perhaps more so than anyone else.

Marion Fields said, 'Those awful metal birds he's been making – those things he sends out that he kills people with. Can he make a lot of them?' She eyed him uneasily.

'Evidently there's no particular limit to what Vulcan 3 can produce. There's no restriction on raw materials available to him.' *Him.* He, too, was saying that now. 'And he has the technical know-how. He has more information available to him than any purely human agency in the world. And he's not limited by any ethical considerations.'

In fact, he realized, Vulcan 3 is in an ideal position; his goal is dictated by logic, by relentless correct reasoning. It is no emotional bias or projection that motivates him to act as he does. So he will never suffer a change of heart, a conversion; he will never turn from a conqueror into a benevolent ruler.

'The techniques that Vulcan 3 will employ,' Barris said to the child gazing up at him, 'will be brought into play according to the need. They'll vary in direct proportion to the problem facing him; if he has ten people opposed to him, he will probably employ some minor weapon, such as the original hammers equipped with heat beams. We've seen him use hammers of greater magnitude, equipped with chemical bombs; that's because the magnitude of his opposition has turned out to be that much greater. He meets whatever challenge exists.'

Marion said, 'So the stronger the Movement gets, the larger he'll grow. The stronger he'll become.'

'Yes,' Barris said. 'And there's no point at which he'll have to stop; there's no known limit to his theoretical power and size.'

'If the whole world was against him—'

'Then he'd have to grow and produce and organize to combat the whole world.'

'Why?' she demanded.

'Because that's his job.'

'He wants to?'

'No,' Barris said. 'He has to.'

All at once, without any warning, the girl said, 'I'll take you to him, Mr Barris. My father, I mean.'

Silently, Barris breathed a prayer of relief.

'But you have to come alone,' she added instantly. 'No guards or anybody with guns.' Studying him she said, 'You promise? On your word of honor?'

'I promise,' Barris said.

Uncertainly, she said, 'How'll we get there? He's in North America.'

'By police cruiser. We have three of them up on the roof of the building. They used to belong to Jason Dill. When there's a lull in the attack, we'll take off.'

'Can we get by the hammer birds?' she said, with a mixture of doubt and excitement.

'I hope so,' Barris said.

As the Unity police cruiser passed low over New York City, Barris had an opportunity to see first-hand the damage which the Healers had done.

Much of the outlying business ring was in ruins. His own building was gone; only a heap of smoking rubble remained. Fires still burned out of control in the vast, sprawling rabbit warren that was – or had been – the residential section. Most of the streets were hopelessly blocked. Stores, he observed, had been broken into and looted.

But the fighting was over. The city was quiet. People roamed vaguely through the debris, picking about for valuables. Here and there brown-clad Healers organized repair and reclamation. At the sound of the jets of his police cruiser, the people below scattered for shelter. On the roof of an undestroyed factory building a blaster boomed at them inexpertly.

'Which way?' Barris said to the solemn child beside him.

'Keep going straight. We can land soon. They'll take us to him on foot.' Frowning with worry, she murmured, 'I hope they haven't changed it too much. I was at that school so long, and he was in that awful place, that Atlanta . . .'

Barris flew on. The open countryside did not show the same extensive injury that the big cities did; below him, the farms and even the small rural towns seemed about as they always had. In fact, there was more order in the hinterlands now than there had been before; the collapse of the rural Unity offices had brought about stability, rather than chaos. Local people, already committed to support of the Movement, had eagerly assumed the tasks of leadership.

'That big river,' Marion said, straining to see. 'There's a bridge. I see it.' She shivered triumphantly. 'Go by the bridge, and you'll see a road. When there's a junction with another road, put your ship down there.' She gave him a radiant smile.

Several minutes later he was landing the police cruiser in an open field at the edge of a small Pennsylvania town. Before the jets were off, a truck had come rattling across the dirt and weeds, directly toward them.

This is it, Barris said to himself. It's too late to back out now.

The truck halted. Four men in overalls jumped down and came cautiously up to the cruiser. One of them waved a pellet-rifle. 'Who are you?'

'Let me get out,' Marion said to Barris. 'Let me talk to them.'

He touched the stud on the instrument panel which released the port; it slid open, and Marion at once scrambled out and hopped down to the dusty ground.

Barris, still in the ship, waited tensely while she conferred with the four men. Far up in the sky, to the north, a flock of hammers rushed inland, intent on business of their own. A few moments later bright fission flashes lit up the horizon. Vulcan 3 had apparently begun equipping his extensions with atomic tactical bombs.

One of the four men came up to the cruiser and cupped his hands to his mouth. 'I'm Joe Potter. You're Barris?'

'That's right.' Sitting in the ship, Barris kept his hand on his pencil beam. But, he realized, it was nothing more than a ritual-istic gesture now; it had no practical importance.

'Say,' Joe Potter said. 'I'll take you to Father. If that's what you want, and she says it is. Come alone.'

With the four men, Barris and Marion climbed aboard the ancient, dented truck. At once it started up; he was pitched from side to side as it swung around and started back the way it had come.

'By God,' one of the men said, scrutinizing him. 'You used to be North American Director. Didn't you?'

'Yes,' Barris said.

The men mumbled among one another, and at last one of them slid over to Barris and said, 'Listen, Mr Barris.' He shoved an envelope and a pencil at him. 'Could I have your autograph?'

For an hour the truck headed along minor country roads, in the general direction of New York City. A few miles outside the demolished business ring, Potter halted the truck at a gasoline station. To the right of the station was a roadside café, a decrepit, weatherbeaten place. A few cars were pulled up in front of it. Some children were playing in the dirt by the steps, and a dog was tied up in the yard in the rear.

'Get out,' Potter said. All four men seemed somewhat cross and taciturn from the long drive.

Barris got slowly out. 'Where—'

'Inside.' Potter started up the truck again. Marion hopped out to join Barris. The truck pulled away, made a turn, and disappeared back down the road in the direction from which they had just come.

Her eyes shining, Marion called, 'Come on!' She scampered up on the porch of the café and tugged the door open. Barris followed after her, with caution.

In the dingy café, at a table littered with maps and papers, sat a man wearing a blue denim shirt and grease-stained work pants. An ancient audio-telephone was propped up beside him, next to a plate on which were the remains of a hamburger and fried potatoes. The man glanced up irritably, and Barris saw heavy ridged eyebrows, the irregular teeth, the penetrating glance that had so chilled him before, and which chilled him again now.

'I'll be darned,' Father Fields said, pushing away his papers. 'Look who's here.'

'Daddy!' Marion cried; she leaped forward and threw her arms around him. 'I'm so glad to see you—' Her words were cut off, smothered by the man's shirt as she pressed her face into it. Fields patted her on the back, oblivious to Barris.

Walking over to the counter, Barris seated himself alone. He remained there, meditating, until all at once he realized that

Father Fields was addressing him. Glancing up, he saw the man's hand held out. Grinning, Fields shook hands with him.

'I thought you were in Geneva,' Fields said. 'It's nice seeing you again.' His eyes traveled up and down Barris. 'The one decent Director out of eleven. And we don't get you; we get practically the worst – barring Reynolds. We get that opportunist Taubmann.' He shook his head ironically.

Barris said, 'Revolutionary movements always draw opportunists.'

'That's very charitable of you,' Fields said. Reaching back, he drew up a chair and seated himself, tipping the chair until he was comfortable.

'Mr Barris is fighting Vulcan 3,' Marion declared, holding on tightly to her father's arm. 'He's on our side.'

'Oh, is that right?' Fields said, patting her. 'Are you sure about that?'

She colored and stammered, 'Well, anyhow, he's against Vulcan 3.'

'Congratulations,' Fields said to Barris. 'You've made a wise choice. Assuming it's so.'

Settling back against the counter, propping himself up on one elbow so that he, too, was comfortable, Barris said, 'I came here to talk business with you.'

In a leisurely, drawling voice, Fields said, 'As you can see, I'm a pretty busy man. Maybe I don't have time to talk business.'

'Find time,' Barris said.

Fields said, 'I'm not much interested in business. I'm more interested in work. You could have joined us back when it mattered, but you turned tail and walked out. Now—' He shrugged. 'What the heck does it matter? Having you with us doesn't make any particular difference one way or another. We've pretty well won, now. I imagine that's why you've finally made up your mind which way you want to jump. Now you can see who's the winning side.' He grinned once more, this time with a knowing, insinuating twinkle. 'Isn't that so? You'd like to be on the winning side.' He waggled his finger slyly at Barris.

'If I did,' Barris said, 'I wouldn't be here.'

For a moment, Fields did not appear to understand. Then, by degrees, his face lost all humor; the bantering familiarity vanished. He became hard-eyed. 'The hell you say,' he said slowly. 'Unity is gone, man. In a couple of days we swept the old monster system aside. What's there left? Those tricky businesses flapping around up there.' He jerked his thumb, pointing upward. 'Like the one I got, that day in the hotel, the one that came in the window looking for me. Did you ever get that? I patched it up pretty good and sent it on to you and your girl, for a—' He laughed. 'A wedding present.'

Barris said, 'You've got nothing. You've destroyed nothing.'

'Everything,' Fields said in a grating whisper. 'We've got everything there is, mister.'

'You don't have Vulcan 3,' Barris said. 'You've got a lot of land; you blew up a lot of office buildings and recruited a lot of clerks and stenographers – that's all.'

'We'll get him,' Fields said, evenly.

'Not without your founder,' Barris said. 'Not now that he's dead.'

Staring at Barris, Fields said, 'My—' He shook his head slowly; his poise was obviously completely shattered. 'What do you mean? I founded the Movement. I've headed it from the start.'

Barris said, 'I know that's a lie.'

For a time there was silence.

'What does he mean?' Marion demanded, plucking anxiously at her father's arm.

'He's out of his mind,' Fields said, still staring at Barris. The color had not returned to his face.

'You're an expert electrician,' Barris said. 'That was your trade. I saw your work on that hammer, your reconstruction. You're very good; in fact there probably isn't an electrician in the world today superior to you. You kept Vulcan 2 going all this time, didn't you?'

Fields' mouth opened and then shut. He said nothing.

'Vulcan 2 founded the Healers' Movement,' Barris said.

'No,' Fields said.

'You were only the fake leader. A puppet. Vulcan 2 created the

Movement as an instrument to destroy Vulcan 3. That's why he gave Jason Dill instructions not to reveal the existence of the Movement to Vulcan 3; he wanted to give it time to grow.'

13

After a long time, Father Fields said, 'Vulcan 2 was only a computing mechanism. It had no motives, no drives. Why would it act to impair Vulcan 3?'

'Because Vulcan 3 menaced it,' Barris said. 'Vulcan 2 was as much alive as Vulcan 3 – no more and no less. It was created originally to do a certain job, and Vulcan 3 interfered with its doing that job, just as the withholding of data by Jason Dill interfered with Vulcan 3's doing its job.'

'How did Vulcan 3 interfere with Vulcan 2's doing its job?' Father Fields said.

'By supplanting it,' Barris said.

Fields said, 'But I am the head of the Movement now. Vulcan 2 no longer exists.' Rubbing his chin, he said, 'There isn't a wire or a tube or a relay of Vulcan 2 intact.'

'You did a thorough, professional job,' Barris said.

The man's head jerked.

'You destroyed Vulcan 2,' Barris said, 'to keep Jason Dill from knowing. Isn't that so?'

'No,' Fields said finally. 'It isn't so. This is all a wild series of guesses on your part. You have no evidence; this is the typical insane slander generated by Unity. These mad charges, dreamed up and bolstered and embroidered—'

Once again, Barris noticed, the man had lost his regional accent. And his vocabulary, his use of words, had, in this period of stress, greatly improved.

Marion Fields piped, 'It's not true! My father founded the Movement.' Her eyes blazed with helpless, baffled fury at Barris. 'I wish I hadn't brought you here.'

'What evidence do you have?' Fields said.

'I saw the skill with which you rebuilt that ruined hammer,' Barris said. 'It amounted to mechanical genius on your part. With

385

ability like that you could name your own job with Unity; there're no repairmen on my staff in New York capable of work like that. The normal use Unity would put you to with such ability would be servicing the Vulcan series. Obviously you know nothing about Vulcan 3 – *and Vulcan 3 is self-servicing*. What else does that leave but the older computers? And Vulcan 1 hasn't functioned in decades. And your age is such that, like Jason Dill, you would naturally have been a contemporary of Vulcan 2 rather—'

'Conjecture,' Fields said.

'Yes,' Barris admitted.

'Logic. Deduction. Based on the spurious premise that I had anything to do with any of the Vulcan series. Did it ever occur to you that there might have been alternate computers, designed by someone other than Nat Greenstreet, that competent crews might have been put to work at—'

From behind Barris a voice, a woman's voice, said sharply, 'Tell him the truth, Father. Don't lie, for once.'

Rachel Pitt came around to stand by Barris. Astonished to see her, Barris started to his feet.

'My two daughters,' Fields said. He put his hand on Marion Fields' shoulder, and then, after a pause, he put his other hand on the shoulder of Rachel Pitt. 'Marion and Rachel,' he said to Barris. 'The younger stayed with me, was loyal to me; the older had ambitions to marry a Unity man and live a well-to-do life with all the things that money can buy. She started to come back to me a couple of times. But did you really come back?' He gazed meditatively at Rachel Pitt. 'I wonder. It doesn't sound like it.'

Rachel said, 'I'm loyal to you, Father. I just can't stand any more lies.'

'I am telling the truth,' Father Fields said in a harsh, bitter voice. 'Barris accuses me of destroying Vulcan 2 to keep Jason Dill from knowing about the relationship between the old computer and the Movement. Do you think I care about Jason Dill? Did it ever matter what he knew? I destroyed Vulcan 2 because it wasn't running the Movement effectively; it was holding the Movement back, keeping it weak. It wanted the Movement to be nothing but an extension of itself, like those hammers of Vulcan 3. An instrument without life of its own.'

386

His voice had gained power; his jaw jutted out and he confronted Barris and Rachel defiantly. The two of them moved involuntarily away from him, and closer to each other. Only Marion Fields remained with him.

'I freed the Movement,' Fields said. 'I freed humanity and made the Movement an instrument of human needs, human aspirations. Is that wicked?' He pointed his finger at Barris and shouted, 'And before I'm finished I'm going to destroy Vulcan 3 as well, and free mankind from it, too. From both of them, first the older one and next the big one, the new one. Is that wrong? Are you opposed to that? If you are, then god damn it, go join them at the fortress; go join Reynolds.'

Barris said, 'It's a noble ideal, what you're saying. But you can't do it. It's impossible. Unless I help you.'

Hunched forward in his chair, Father Fields said, 'All right, Barris. You came here to do business. What's your deal?' Raising his head he said hoarsely, 'What do you have to offer me?'

Barris said, 'I know where the fortress is. I've been to it. Dill took me there. I can find it again. Without me, you'll never find it. At least, not in time; not before Vulcan 3 has developed such far-reaching offensive weapons that nothing will remain of life above ground.'

'You don't think we'll find it?' Fields said.

'In fifteen months,' Barris said, 'you've failed to. Do you think you will in the next two weeks?'

Presently Father Fields said, 'More like two years. We started looking from the very start.' He shrugged. 'Well, Director. What do you want in exchange?'

'Plenty,' Barris said grimly. 'I'll try to outline it as briefly as I can.'

After Barris had finished, Father Fields was silent. 'You want a lot,' he said finally.

'That's right.'

'It's incredible, you dictating terms to me. How many in your group?'

'Five or six.'

Fields shook his head. 'And there are millions of us, all over the world.' From his pocket he produced a much-folded map; spreading it out on the counter he said, 'We've taken over in America, in Eastern Europe, in all of Asia and Africa. It seemed only a question of time before we had the rest. We've been winning so steadily.' He clenched his fist around a coffee mug on the counter and then suddenly grabbed it up and hurled it to the floor. The brown coffee oozed thickly out.

'Even if you did have sufficient time on your side,' Barris said, 'I doubt if you could ultimately have defeated Unity. It's hopeless to imagine that a grass-roots revolutionary movement can over-throw a modern bureaucratic system that's backed up with modern technology and elaborate industrial organization. A hundred years ago, your Movement might have worked. But times have changed. Government is a science conducted by trained experts.'

Studying him with animosity, Fields said, 'To win, you have to be on the inside.'

'You have to know someone on the inside,' Barris said. 'And you do; you know me. I can get you in, where you will be able to attack the main trunk, not merely the branches.'

'And the trunk,' Fields said, 'is Vulcan 3. Give us credit for knowing that, at least. That thing has always been our target.' He let out his breath raggedly. 'All right, Barris; I agree to your terms.'

Barris felt himself relax. But he kept his expression under control. 'Fine,' he said.

'You're surprised, aren't you?' Fields said.

'No,' he said. 'Relieved. I thought possibly you might fail to see how precarious your position is.'

Bringing forth a pocket watch, Fields examined it. 'What do you want for the attack on the fortress? Weapons are still in short supply with us. We're mainly oriented around man power.'

'There are weapons back at Geneva.'

'How about transportation?'

'We have three high-speed military cruisers; they'll do.' Barris wrote rapidly on a piece of paper. 'A small concentrated attack by skillful men – experts hitting at the vital center. A hundred well-chosen men will do. Everything depends on the first ten minutes in the fortress; if we succeed, it'll be right away. There will be no second chance.'

Fields gazed at him intently. 'Barris, do you really think we have a chance? Can we really get to Vulcan 3?' His grease-stained hands twisted. 'For years I've thought of nothing else. Smashing that satanic mass of parts and tubes—'

'We'll get to him,' Barris said.

Fields collected the men that Barris needed. They were loaded into the cruiser, and Barris at once headed back toward Geneva, Fields accompanying him.

Halfway across the Atlantic they passed an immense swarm of hammers streaking toward helpless, undefended North America. These were quite large, almost as large as the cruiser. They moved with incredible speed, disappearing almost at once. A few minutes later a new horde appeared, these like slender needles. They ignored the ship and followed the first group over the horizon.

'New types,' Barris said. 'He's wasting no time.'

The Unity Control Building was still in friendly hands. They landed on the roof and hurried down the ramps into the building. On orders from Fields, the Healers had ceased attacking. But now hammers swarmed constantly overhead, diving down and twisting agilely to avoid the roof guns. Half of the main structure was in ruins, but the guns fired on, bringing down the hammers when they came too close.

'It's a losing battle,' Daily muttered. 'We're short on ammunition. There seems to be an endless number of the damn things.'

Barris worked rapidly. He supplied his attack force with the best weapons available, supplies stored in the vaults below the Control Building. From the five Directors he selected Pegler and Chai, and a hundred of the best-trained troops.

'I'm going along,' Fields said. 'If the attack fails I don't want to stay alive. If it succeeds I want to be part of it.'

Barris carefully uncrated a manually operated fission bomb. 'This is for him.' He weighed the bomb in the palm of his hand; it was no larger than an onion. 'My assumption is that they'll admit me and possibly Chai and Pegler. We can probably persuade them that we're coming over to rejoin Unity. At least we'll be able to get part of the distance in.'

'Anyhow you hope so,' Fields said curtly.

At sunset, Barris loaded the three cruisers with the men and equipment. The roof guns sent up a heavy barrage to cover their take-off. Hammers in action nearby at once began following the ships as they rose into the sky.

'We'll have to shake them,' Barris said. He gave quick orders. The three cruisers shot off in different directions, dividing up rapidly. A few hammers tagged them awhile and then gave up.

'I'm clear,' Chai in the second cruiser reported.

'Clear,' Pegler in the third said.

Barris glanced at the older man beside him. Behind them the ship was crowded with tense, silent soldiers, loaded down with weapons, squatting nervously in a mass as the ship raced through the darkness. 'Here we go,' Barris said. He swung the ship in a wide arc. Into the communications speaker he ordered, 'We'll re-form for the attack. I'll lead. You two come behind.'

'Are we close?' Fields asked, a queer expression on his face.

'Very.' Barris studied the ship's controls. 'We should be over it in a moment. Get set.'

Barris dived. Pegler's ship whipped through the darkness behind him, lashing toward the ground below; Chai's ship shot off to the right and headed directly over the fortress.

Hammers rose in vast swarms and moved toward Chai's ship, separating and engulfing it.

'Hang on,' Barris gasped.

The ground rose; landing brakes screamed. The ship hit, spinning and crashing among the trees and boulders.

'Out!' Barris ordered, pulling himself to his feet and throwing the hatch release. The hatches slid back and the men poured out, dragging their equipment into the cold night darkness.

Above them in the sky, Chai's ship fought with the hammers; it twisted and rolled, firing rapidly. More hammers rose from the fortress, great black clouds that swiftly gained altitude. Pegler's ship was landing. It roared over them and crashed against the side of a hill a few hundred yards from the other defense wall of the fortress.

The heavy guns of the fortress were beginning to open up. A vast fountain of white burst loose, showering rocks and debris on Barris and Fields as they climbed out of their ship.

'Hurry,' Barris said. 'Get the bores going.'

The men were assembling two gopher bores. The first had already whined into action. More tactical atomic shells from the fortress struck near them; the night was lit up with explosions.

Barris crouched down. 'How are you making out?' he shouted above the racket, his lips close to his helmet speaker.

'All right,' Pegler's voice said weakly in his earphones. 'We're down and getting out the big stuff.'

'That'll hold off the hammers,' Barris said to Fields. He peered up at the sky. 'I hope Chai—'

Chai's ship rolled and spun, trying to evade the ring of hammers closing around it. Its jets smoked briefly. A direct hit. The ship wobbled and hesitated.

'Drop your men,' Barris ordered into his phones. 'You're right over the fortress.'

From Chai's ship showered a cloud of white dots. Men in jump suits, drifting slowly toward the ground below. Hammers screeched around them; the men fired back with pencil beams. The hammers retreated warily.

'Chai's men will take care of the direct attack,' Barris explained. 'Meanwhile, the bores are moving.'

'Umbrella almost ready,' a technician reported.

'Good. They're beginning to dive on us; their screen-probes must have spotted us.'

The fleets of screaming hammers were descending, hurtling toward the ground. Their beams stabbed into the trees and ignited columns of flaming wood and branches. One of Pegler's cannon boomed. A group of hammers disappeared, but more took their places. An endless torrent of hammers, rising up from the fortress like black bats.

The umbrella flickered purple. Reluctantly, it came on and settled in place. Vaguely, beyond it, Barris could make out the hammers circling in confusion. A group of them entered the umbrella and were silently puffed out.

Barris relaxed. 'Good. Now we don't have to worry about them.'

'Gophers are halfway along,' the leader of the bore team reported.

Two immense holes yawned, echoing and vibrating as the gopher bores crept into the earth. Technicians disappeared after them. The first squad of armed troops followed them cautiously, swallowed up by the earth.

'We're on our way,' Barris said to Fields.

Standing off by himself, Father Fields surveyed the trees, the line of hills in the distance. 'No visible sign of the fortress,' he murmured. 'Nothing to give it away.' He seemed deep in thought, as if barely aware of the battle in progress. 'This forest . . . the perfect place. I would never have known.' Turning, he walked toward Barris.

Seeing the look on the man's face, Barris felt deep uneasiness. 'What is it?' he said.

Fields said, 'I've been here before.'

'Yes,' Barris said.

'Thousands of times. I worked here most of my life.' The man's face was stark. 'This is where Vulcan 2 used to be.' His hands jerked aimlessly. 'This was where I came to destroy Vulcan 2.' Nodding his head at a massive moss-covered boulder, he said, 'I walked by that. To the service ramp. They didn't even know the ramp still existed; it was declared obsolete years ago. Abandoned and shut off. But I knew about it.' His voice rose wildly. 'I can come and go any time I want; I have constant access to that place. *I know a thousand ways to get down there.*'

Barris said, 'But you didn't know that Vulcan 3 was down there, too. At the deepest level. They didn't acquaint your crew with—'

'I didn't know Jason Dill,' Fields said. 'I wasn't in a position to meet him as an equal. As you were.'

'So now you know,' Barris said.

'You gave me nothing,' Fields said. 'You had nothing to tell me that I didn't know already.' Coming slowly toward Barris he said in a low voice, 'I could have figured it out, in time. Once we had tried every other place—' In his hand a pencil beam appeared, gripped tightly.

Keeping himself calm, Barris said, 'But you still won't get in, Father. They'll never let you in. They'll kill you long before you penetrate all the way to Vulcan 3. You'll have to depend on me.' Pointing to his sleeve, he indicated his Director's stripe. 'Once I get in there I can walk up and down those corridors; no one will stop me, because they're part of the same structure I'm part of. And I'm in a position of authority equal to any of them, Reynolds included.'

Fields said, 'Any of them – except for Vulcan 3.'

Off to the right, Pegler's cannon thundered as the fleets of hammers turned their attention on them. The hammers dived and released bombs. An inferno of white pillars checkered across the countryside, moving toward Pegler's ship.

'Get your umbrella up!' Barris shouted into his helmet speaker.

Pegler's umbrella flickered. It hesitated—

A small atomic bomb cut across dead center. Pegler's ship vanished; clouds of particles burst into the air, metal and ash showering over the flaming ground. The heavy cannon ceased abruptly.

'It's up to us,' Barris said.

Over the fortress the first of Chai's men had reached the ground. The defense guns spun around, leaving Barris' ship and focusing on the drifting dots.

'They don't have a chance,' Fields muttered.

'No.' Barris started toward the first of the two tunnels. 'But we have.' Ignoring the pencil beam in the older man's hand, he continued, his back to Fields.

Abruptly the fortress shuddered. A vast tongue of fire rolled across it. The surface fused in an instant; the wave of molten metal had sealed over the fortress.

'They cut themselves off,' Barris said. 'They've closed down.' He shook himself into motion and entered the tunnel, squeezing past the power leads to the gopher.

An ugly cloud of black rolled up from the sea of glimmering slag that had been the surface of the fortress. The hammers fluttered above it uncertainly, cut off from the levels beneath.

Barris made his way along the tunnel, pushing past the technicians operating the gopher. The gopher rumbled and vibrated as it cut through the layers of clay and rock toward the fortress. The air was hot and moist. The men worked feverishly, directing the gopher deeper and deeper. Torrents of steaming water poured from the clay around them.

'We must be close,' Fields' voice came to him, from behind.

'We should emerge near the deepest level,' Barris said. He did not look to see if the pencil beam was still there; he kept on going.

The gopher shrieked. Its whirring nose tore into metal; the bore team urged it forward. The gopher slashed into a wall of steel and reinforced stressed plastic and then slowed to a stop.

'We're there,' Barris said.

The gopher shuddered. Gradually it inched forward. The leader of the team leaned close to Barris. 'The other gopher's through, into the fortress. But they don't know exactly where.'

All at once the wall collapsed inward. Liquid steel pelted them, sizzling. The soldiers moved ahead, pushing through the gap. Barris and Fields hurried with them. The jagged metal seared them as they squeezed through. Barris stumbled and fell, rolling in the boiling water and debris.

Putting his pencil beam away, Fields pulled him to his feet. They glanced at each other, neither of them speaking. And then they looked about them, at the great corridor that stretched out, lit by the recessed lighting familiar to both of them.

The lowest level of the fortress!

14

A few astonished Unity guards scampered toward them, tugging a blast cannon inexpertly into position.

Barris fired. From behind him, pencil beams cut past him toward the cannon. The cannon fired once, crazily. The roof of the corridor dissolved; clouds of ash rolled around them. Barris moved forward. Now the blast cannon was in ruins. The Unity guards were pulling back, firing as they retreated.

'Mine crew,' Barris snapped.

The mine crew advanced and released their sucker mines. The mines leaped down the corridor toward the retreating Unity guards. At the sight the guards broke and fled; the mines exploded, hurling streamers of flame against the walls.

'Here we go,' Barris said. Crouching, he hurried along the corridor, clutching the fission bomb tight. Beyond a turn the Unity guards were shutting an emergency lock.

'Get them!' Barris shouted.

Fields ran past him, galloping in long-legged strides, his arms windmilling. His pencil beam traced a ribbon of ash across the surface of the lock; intricate bits of mechanism flew into the air. Behind the lock Unity teams were bringing up more mobile cannon. A few hammers fluttered around their heads, screaming instructions.

Following Fields, Barris reached the lock. Their men swarmed past them, firing into the narrow breach. A hammer sailed out, straight at Barris; he caught a vision of glittering metal eyes, clutching claws – and then the hammer winked out, caught by a pencil beam.

Fields seated himself on the floor by the hinge-rim of the lock. His expert fingers traced across the impulse leads. A sudden flash. The lock trembled and sagged. Barris threw his weight against it. The lock gave. Gradually it slid back, leaving a widened gap.

'Get in,' Barris ordered.

His men poured through, crashing against the barricade hastily erected by the Unity guards. Hammers dived on them frantically, smashing at their heads.

Pushing past, Barris glanced around. A series of corridors twisted off in different directions. He hesitated.

Can I do it? he asked himself.

Taking a deep, unsteady breath, he sprinted away from Fields and the soldiers, along a side corridor. The sound of fighting died as he raced up a ramp. A door slid open automatically for him; as it shut behind him he slowed, panting.

A moment later he was walking briskly along a passage, in the silence far away from the hectic activity. He came to an elevator, halted, and touched a stud. The elevator at once made itself available to him. Entering, he permitted it to carry him upward.

This is the only way, he told himself. He forced himself to remain calm as the elevator carried him farther and farther away from Vulcan 3 and the scene of the activity. *No direct assault will work.*

At an upper level he stopped the elevator and stepped out.

A group of Unity officials stood about, conferring. Clerks and executives. Gray-clad men and women who glanced at him briefly or not at all. He caught a glimpse of office doors . . . without pausing, he began to walk.

He came presently onto a foyer, from which branched several corridors. Behind a turnstile sat a robot checker, inactive; no one was using its facilities. At the presence of Barris it lit up.

'Credentials, sir,' it said.

'Director,' he said, displaying his stripe.

Ahead of him the turnstile remained fixed. 'This portion of the area is classified,' the robot said. 'What is your business and by whose authority are you attempting to enter?'

Barris said sharply, 'My own authority. Open up; this is urgent.'

It was his tone that the robot caught, rather than the words. The turnstile rattled aside; the habitual pattern of the assembly, its robot controller included, had been activated as it had been many times in the past. 'Pardon intrusion into urgent business, Director,' the robot said, and at once shut off; its light died.

Back to sleep, Barris thought grimly.

He continued on until he came to an express descent ramp. At once he stepped onto it; the ramp plunged, and he was on his way back down again. To the bottom level – and Vulcan 3.

Several guards stood about in the corridor as Barris stepped from the ramp. They glanced at him and started to come to attention. Then one of them gave a convulsive grimace; his hand fumbled stupidly at his belt.

Bringing out his pencil beam, Barris fired. The guard, headless, sank to one side and then collapsed; the other guards stared in disbelief, paralysed.

'Traitor,' Barris said. 'Right here, in our midst.'

396

The guards gaped at him.

'Where's Director Reynolds?' Barris said.

Gulping, one of the guards said, 'In office six, sir. Down that way.' Half pointing, he bent over the remains of his companion; the others gathered around.

'Can you get him out here for me?' Barris demanded. 'Or am I supposed to go search him up?'

One of the guards murmured, 'If you want to wait here, sir . . .'

'Wait here, hell,' Barris said. 'Are we all supposed to stand around while they break in and slaughter us? You know they're through in two places – they have those gopher bores going.'

While the guards stammered out some sort of answer, he turned and strode off in the direction that the guard had indicated.

No Unity minion, he said to himself, will ever argue with a Director; it might cost him his job.

Or, in this case, his life.

As soon as the guards were out of sight behind him he turned off the corridor. A moment later he came out into a well-lighted major artery. The floor beneath his feet hummed and vibrated, and as he walked along he felt the intensity of action increase.

He was getting close, now. The center of Vulcan 3 was not far off.

The passage made an abrupt turn to the right. He followed, and found himself facing a young T-class official and two guards. All three men were armed. They seemed to be in the process of pushing a metal cart loaded with punchcards; he identified the cards as a medium by which data were presented, under certain circumstances, to the Vulcan computers. This official, then, was part of the feed-teams.

'Who are you?' Barris said, before the young official could speak. 'What's your authority for being in this area? Let's see written permission.'

The young official said, 'My name is Larson, Director. I was directly responsible to Jason Dill before his death.' Eying Barris, he smiled respectfully and said, 'I saw you several times with Mr Dill, sir. When you were here involving the reconstruction of Vulcan 2.'

'I believe I noticed you,' Barris said.

Pushing his cart along, Larson said, 'I have to feed these at once to Vulcan 3; with your permission I'll go along. How's the fighting going on above? Someone says they've broken in somewhere. I heard a lot of noise.' Clearly agitated, but concerned only with his clearly laid-out task, Larson continued, 'Amazing how active Vulcan 3 is, after being inactive for so many months. He's come up with quite a number of effective weapons to deal with the situation.'

Glancing at Barris shrewdly, he said, 'Isn't it probable that Reynolds will be the new Managing Director? His able prosecution of Dill, the way he exposed the various—' He broke off in order to manipulate the combination of a huge set of barrier-doors. The doors swung open—

And there, ahead of Barris, was a vast chamber. At the far end he saw a wall of metal, perfectly blank. The side of a cube, one part of something that receded into the structure of the building; he caught only a glimpse of it, an impression.

'There it is,' Larson said to him. 'Peaceful here, in comparison to what's going on above ground. You wouldn't think he – I mean, it – had anything to do with the action against the Healers. And yet it's all being directed from here.' He and his two guards pushed the cart of data-cards forward. 'Care to come closer?' Larson asked Barris; showing him that he knew everything of importance. 'You can watch the way the data are fed. It's quite interesting.

Passing by Barris, Larson began directing the removal of the cards; he had the guards load up with them. Standing behind the three men, Barris reached into his coat. His fingers closed over the onion-shaped object.

As he drew the fission bomb out, he saw, on Larson's sleeve, a shiny metal bug; it clung there, riding along, its antennae quivering. For a moment Barris thought, It's an insect. Some natural life form that brushed against him when he was above ground, in the forest.

The shiny metal bug flew up into the air. He heard the high-frequency whine as it passed him, and knew it then. A tiny hammer, a version of the basic type. For observation. It had been aware of him from the moment Larson encountered him.

Seeing him staring at the bug as it zipped away from them, Larson said, 'Another one. There's been one hanging around me all day. It was clinging to my work smock for a while.' He added, 'Vulcan 3 uses them for relaying messages. I've seen a number of them around.'

From the tiny hammer an ear-splitting squeal dinned out at the two men. '*Stop him! Stop him at once!*'

Larson blinked in bewilderment.

Holding onto the bomb, Barris strode toward the face of Vulcan 3. He did not run; he walked swiftly and silently.

'*Stop him, Larson!*' the hammer shrilled. '*He's here to destroy me! Make him get away from me!*'

Gripping the bomb tightly, Barris began to run.

A pencil beam fired past him; he crouched and ran on, zigzagging back and forth.

'*If you let him destroy me you'll destroy the world!*' A second tiny hammer appeared, dancing in the air before Barris. '*Madman!*'

He heard, from other parts of the chamber, the abuse piping at him from other mobile extensions. '*Monster!*'

Again a heat beam slashed past him; he half-fell and, drawing out his own pencil, turned and fired directly back. He saw a brief scene: Larson with the two guards, firing at him in confusion, trying not to hit the wall of Vulcan 3. His own beam touched one of the guards; he ceased firing at once and fell writhing.

'*Listen to me!*' a full-sized hammer blared, skipping into the chamber and directly at Barris. In desperate fury the hammer crashed at him, missing him and bursting apart against the concrete floor, its pieces spewing over him.

'*While there's still time!*' another took up. '*Get him away, feed-team leader! He's killing me!*'

With his pencil beam, Barris shot down a hammer as it emerged above him; he had not seen it come into the chamber. The hammer, only damaged, fluttered down. Struggling toward him, across the floor, it screeched, '*We can agree! We can come to an arrangement!*'

On and on he ran.

'*This can be negotiated! There is no basic disagreement!*'

Raising his arm, he hurled the bomb.

'Barris! Barris! Please do not—'

From the intricate power supply of the bomb came a faint *pop*. Barris threw himself down, his arms over his face. An ocean of white light lapped up at him, picking him up and sweeping him away.

I got it, he thought. I was successful.

A monstrous hot wind licked at him as he drifted; he skidded on, along with the wind. Debris and flaming rubbish burst over and around him. A surface far away hurtled at him. He doubled up, his head averted, and then he flew through the surface; it split and gave way, and he went on, tumbling into darkness, swept on by the tides of wind and heat.

His last thought was, *It was worth it. Vulcan 3 is dead!*

Father Fields sat watching a hammer. The hammer wobbled. It hesitated in its frantic, aimless flight. And then it spiraled to the floor.

One by one, dropping silently, the hammers crashed down and lay still. Inert heaps of metal and plastic, nothing more. Without motion. Their screeching voices had ceased.

What a relief, he said to himself.

Getting to his feet he walked shakily over to the four medical corpsmen. 'How is he?' he said.

Without looking up, the corpsman said, 'We're making progress. His chest was extensively damaged. We've plugged in an exterior heart-lung system, and it's giving rapid assistance.' The semiautomatic surgical tools crept across the body of William Barris, exploring, repairing. They seemed to have virtually finished with the chest; now they had turned their attention to his broken shoulder.

'We'll need boneforms,' one of the corpsmen said. Glancing around he said, 'We don't have any here with us. He'll have to be flown back to Geneva.'

'Fine,' Fields said. 'Get him started.'

The litter slid expertly under Barris and began lifting him.

'That traitor,' a voice beside Fields said.

He turned his head and saw Director Reynolds standing there, gazing at Barris. The man's clothing was torn, and over his left eye was a deep gash. Fields said, 'You're out of a job now.'

With absolute bitterness, Reynolds said, 'And so are you. What becomes of the great crusade, now that Vulcan 3 is gone? Do you have any other constructive programs to offer?'

'Time will tell,' Fields said. He walked along beside the litter as it carried Barris up the ramp to the waiting ship.

'You did very well,' Fields said. He lit a cigarette and placed it between Barris' parted lips. 'Better not start talking. Those surgical robots are still fussing over you.' He indicated the several units at work on the man's ruined shoulder.

'Do any of the computing components of Vulcan 3 . . .' Barris murmured weakly.

'Some survived,' Fields said. 'Enough for your purposes. You can add and subtract, anyhow, using what's left.' Seeing the worry on the injured man's face he said, 'I'm joking. A great deal survived. Don't worry. They can patch up the parts you want. As a matter of fact, I can probably lend a hand. I still have some skill.'

'The structure of Unity will be different,' Barris said.

'Yes,' Fields said.

'We'll broaden our base. We have to.'

Fields gazed out of the ship's window, ignoring the injured man. At last Barris gave up trying to talk. His eyes shut; Fields took the cigarette as it rolled from the man's lips onto his shirt.

'We'll talk later,' Fields said, finishing the cigarette himself.

The ship droned on, in the direction of Geneva.

Looking out at the empty sky, Fields thought, Nice not to see those things flying around. When one died they all died. Strange, to realize that we've seen our last one . . . the last hammer to go buzzing, screeching about, attacking and bombing, laying waste wherever it goes.

Kill the trunk, as Barris had said.

The man was right about a lot of things, Fields said to himself. He was the only one who could have gotten all the way in; they did manage to stop the rest of us. The attack bogged down, until those things stopped flying. And then it didn't matter.

I wonder if he's right about the rest?

*

In the hospital room at Geneva, Barris sat propped up in bed, facing Fields. 'What information can you give me on the analysis of the remains?' he said. 'I have a hazy memory of the trip here; you said that most of the memory elements survived.'

'You're so anxious to rebuild it,' Fields said.

'As an instrument,' Barris said. 'Not a master. That was the agreement between us. You have to permit a continuation of rational use of machines. None of this emotional "scrap the machines" business. None of your Movement slogans.'

Fields nodded. 'If you really think you can keep control in the right hands. In our hands. I have nothing against machines as such; I was very fond of Vulcan 2. Up to a point.'

'At that point,' Barris said, 'you demolished it.'

The two men regarded each other.

'I'll keep hands off,' Fields said. 'It's a fair deal. You delivered; you got in there and blew the thing up. I admit that.'

Barris grunted, but said nothing.

'You'll put an end to the cult of the technocrat?' Fields said. 'For experts only – run by and *for* those oriented around verbal knowledge; I'm so damn sick of that. Mind stuff – as if manual skills like bricklaying and pipe-fitting weren't worth talking about. As if all the people who work with their hands, the skill of their fingers—' He broke off. 'I'm tired of having those people looked down on.'

Barris said, 'I don't blame you.'

'We'll co-operate,' Fields said. 'With you priests in gray – as we've been calling you in our pamphlets. But take care. If the aristocracy of slide rules and pastel ties and polished black shoes starts to get out of hand again . . .' He pointed at the street far below the window. 'You'll hear us out there again.'

'Don't threaten me,' Barris said quietly.

Fields flushed. 'I'm not threatening you. I'm pointing out the facts to you. If we're excluded from the ruling elite, *why should we co-operate?*'

There was silence then.

'What do you want done about Atlanta?' Barris said finally.

'We can agree on that,' Fields said. He flipped his cigarette away; bending, he retrieved it and crushed it out. 'I want to see that place taken apart piece by piece. Until it's a place to keep cows. A pasture land. With plenty of trees.'

'Good,' Barris said.

'Can my daughter come in for a while?' Fields said. 'Rachel. She'd like to talk to you.'

'Maybe later,' Barris said. 'I still have a lot of things to work out in my mind.'

'She wants you to start action going against Taubmann for that slanderous letter he wrote about you. The one she was blamed for.' He hesitated. 'Do you want my opinion?'

'OK,' Barris said.

Fields said, 'I think there ought to be an amnesty. To end that stuff once and for all. Keep Taubmann on or retire him from the system. But let's have an end of accusations. Even true ones.'

'Even a correct suspicion,' Barris said, 'is still a suspicion.'

Showing his relief, Fields said, 'We all have plenty to do. Plenty of rebuilding. We'll have enough on our hands.'

'Too bad Jason Dill isn't here to admonish us,' Barris said. 'He'd enjoy writing out the directives and public presentations of the reconstruction work.' Suddenly he said, 'You were working for Vulcan 2 and Dill was working for Vulcan 2. You were both carrying out its policies toward Vulcan 3. Do you think Vulcan 2 was jealous of Vulcan 3? They may have been mechanical constructs, but as far as we were concerned they had all the tendencies of two contending entities – each out to get the other.'

Fields murmured, 'And each lining up supporters. Following your analysis . . .' He paused, his face dark with introspection.

'Vulcan 2 won,' Barris said.

'Yes.' Fields nodded. 'He – or it – got virtually all of us lined up on one side, with Vulcan 3 on the other. We ganged up on Vulcan 3.' He laughed sharply. 'Vulcan 3's logic was absolutely right; there was a vast world-wide conspiracy directed against it, and to preserve itself it had to invent and develop and produce one weapon after another. And still it was destroyed. Its paranoid suspicions were founded in fact.'

Like the rest of Unity, Barris thought. Vulcan 3, like Dill and myself, Rachel Pitt and Taubmann – all drawn into the mutual accusations and suspicions and near-pathological system-building.

'Pawns,' Fields was saying. 'We humans – god damn it, Barris; we were pawns of those two things. They played us off against one another, like inanimate pieces. The things became alive and the living organisms were reduced to things. Everything was turned inside out, like some terrible morbid view of reality.'

Standing at the doorway of the hospital room, Rachel Pitt said in a low voice, 'I hope we can get out from under that morbid view.' Smiling timidly, she came toward Barris and her father. 'I don't want to press any legal action against Taubmann; I've been thinking it over.'

Either that, Barris thought, or making it a point to listen in on other people's conversations. But he said nothing aloud.

'How long do you think it will take?' Fields said, studying him acutely. 'The *real* reconstruction – not the buildings and roads, but the minds. Distrust and mutual suspicion have been bred into us since childhood; the schools started it going on us – they forced our characters. We can't shake it overnight.'

He's right, Barris thought. It's going to be hard. And it's going to take a long time. Possibly generations.

But at least the living elements, the human beings, had survived. And the mechanical ones had not. That was a good sign, a step in the right direction.

Across from him, Rachel Pitt was smiling less timidly, with more assurance now. Coming over to him, she bent down and touched him reassuringly on the plastic film that covered his shoulder. 'I hope you'll be up and around soon,' she said.

He considered that a good sign too.